PRAISE FOR CHRISTOPHER REICH

Matterhorn

"Reich keeps his foot on the gas . . ."
—*Publishers Weekly*

"This would make a great movie, and fans of the Bond tales and special-ops action novels should add this to their reading lists."
—*Library Journal*

"Another winner from a consistently satisfying writer."
—*Booklist*

"An all-round great thriller in a brilliant and evocative setting. A must for action lovers and espionage junkies."
—*Deadly Pleasures Mystery Magazine*

Once a Thief

"A stylish, jet-propelled thriller full of intriguing characters and surprising twists. Simon Riske is a character I'll want to meet again."
—Jeff Abbott, *New York Times* bestselling author of *Blame*

"Reich paints his characters in broad strokes, much in the manner of Ian Fleming in the James Bond novels, giving us the big picture and letting us fill in the small details from our imaginations. In fact, comparison to the James Bond novels is apt in many ways: the dashing spy, the snappy dialogue, the glamorous locales (in this case, Corsica, the French Alps, and Switzerland, among others). An entertaining escapist adventure."
—*Booklist*

"*Once a Thief* is a good read and moves at a good clip. Reich's readers who are fans of his previous Simon Riske books will enjoy this one and will look forward to Riske's next adventure."

—*New York Journal of Books*

"The exotic locales and plot twists, not to mention enough action to keep you turning each page, make *Once a Thief* an enjoyable experience."

—*Bookreporter*

"Heart pounding . . . Reich combines great action with surprises readers won't see coming. One doesn't have to care much about cars or high finance to enjoy this cinematic thriller."

—*Publishers Weekly*

"Intricately plotted."

—*Kirkus Reviews*

The Prince of Risk

"*The Prince of Risk* is a terrific thriller, written by a guy who knows what he's doing. Check it out. I think you'll love it."
—Steve Berry, #1 bestselling author of *The Lost Order* and *The Patriot Threat*

"*The Prince of Risk* will knock your socks off. Christopher Reich seamlessly weaves the high-stakes world of hedge funds and international terrorism into a frightening, big-time thriller that pulls you into his world and rockets ahead like a runaway train. Reich knows how to deliver and does."

—Robert Crais, *New York Times* bestselling author

"At the moment I'm reading a great new financial thriller by Christopher Reich, *The Prince of Risk*. One thing Doug Preston and I love to do in our books is come up with scary but credible near-future scenarios—and crafting just such scenarios is a talent Reich has in spades."

—Lincoln Child, *New York Times* bestselling author

The Palace

"In Reich's entertaining third Simon Riske novel . . . Simon has less success with this operation than with the one in Amsterdam, and he's soon on the run. Appealing supporting characters ex-Mossad agent Danni Pine and top-notch financial reporter London Li come to his aid. An unexpected closing twist promises exciting developments to come. Clever, sophisticated Riske stands out in the crowded action-hero field."

—*Publishers Weekly*

"On a mission to free his friend, Riske winds up in a cat and mouse chase with a skilled assassin. Simon Riske novels feature nonstop action in vividly rendered international locales, and this third in the series delivers on both counts. Stylish escapism."

—*Booklist*

"Simon Riske returns for another high-octane ride . . . Riske is a likable character, a nice blending of quick wit, a misspent youth, and better impulses; he's not above picking a pocket or stealing a Ferrari, but he's on the side of the angels."

—*Kirkus Reviews*

Crown Jewel

"A stylish international thriller . . . Reich's solid tradecraft and nonstop action are humanized by the hint of a relationship of the heart."
—*Booklist*

"An entertaining sequel . . . Reich infuses his narrative with numerous plot threads that seem separate but end up satisfyingly intersecting for a suspenseful ending. Readers will want to see a lot more of Riske."
—*Publishers Weekly*

"Simon Riske returns for another car-studded adventure . . . Monaco, fast cars, rich women, bad Bosnians—what more is there?"
—*Kirkus Reviews*

The Take

"It's *To Catch a Thief* meets Jason Bourne."
—Jeff Abbott, *New York Times* bestselling author of *Blame*

"Make sure your seat belt is fastened and your tray table is up: This is one hard and fast battle royale. Tension, turmoil, and drama ooze from every page. There's not a wasted word in this high-octane game changer."
—Steve Berry, #1 bestselling author of *The Lost Order* and *The Patriot Threat*

"A fast, wild ride with no less than the balance of power in the Western world at stake."
—*Parade*

"*The Take* is a slick, elegant, and gripping spy thriller of the first order. With a brilliant heist, a twisting web of secrets and intrigue, and an adrenaline-fueled plot, Reich whisked me out of my world and into his from the explosive first pages. Simon Riske is my favorite kind of hero—flawed, dark, and utterly intriguing. Fabulous!"
—Lisa Unger, *New York Times* bestselling author of *The Red Hunter*

"A beautifully constructed heist is only the beginning of this spectacular thriller, which sets thief versus thief, spy versus spy, and even cop versus cop. *The Take* is dazzling fun that surprises to the last page, with a hero who deserves an encore."
—Joseph Finder, *New York Times* bestselling author of *The Switch* and *Judgment*

"There's plenty of action, interesting bits of tradecraft, and well-sketched locales in London, Paris, and Marseille. Best of all is Reich's succinct prose style."
—*Booklist*

"Likable, rascally, and suave, Riske is as distinctive as Reich's other series lead, Jonathan Ransom."
—*Publishers Weekly*

"Reich's stylish and action-packed thriller introduces an appealing new protagonist . . . Recommend to fans of Daniel Silva."
—*Library Journal*

"*The Take* is impossible to put down: nonstop action, a mysterious letter, and a fascinating, complicated, and sexy hero whose tool bag of wit and strength helps him fight his way through the dangerous back alleys of glittering European capitals. An engrossing thriller."
—Christina Kovac, author of *The Cutaway*

"An out-of-control joyride for those who like their heroes flawed, scarred, and on the edge. Reich has created an irresistible character that will leave readers both wincing and cheering with every page."
—Kyle Mills, #1 bestselling author of *Fade* and *Rising Phoenix*

THE
TOURISTS

ALSO BY CHRISTOPHER REICH

Mac Dekker Series

Matterhorn

Simon Riske Series

The Take
Crown Jewel
The Palace
Once a Thief

Dr. Jonathan Ransom Series

Rules of Deception
Rules of Vengeance
Rules of Betrayal

Stand-Alone Novels

The Devil's Banker
Invasion of Privacy

The First Billion

The Prince of Risk

The Runner

Numbered Account

The Patriots Club

THE TOURISTS

CHRISTOPHER REICH

This is a work of fiction. Names, characters, organizations, places, events, and incidents are either products of the author's imagination or are used fictitiously. Otherwise, any resemblance to actual persons, living or dead, is purely coincidental.

Text copyright © 2025 by Christopher Reich
All rights reserved.

No part of this book may be reproduced, or stored in a retrieval system, or transmitted in any form or by any means, electronic, mechanical, photocopying, recording, or otherwise, without express written permission of the publisher.

Published by Thomas & Mercer, Seattle

www.apub.com

Amazon, the Amazon logo, and Thomas & Mercer are trademarks of Amazon.com, Inc., or its affiliates.

EU product safety contact:
Amazon Media EU S. à r.l.
38, avenue John F. Kennedy, L-1855 Luxembourg
amazonpublishing-gpsr@amazon.com

ISBN-13: 9781662516580 (hardcover)
ISBN-13: 9781662516566 (paperback)
ISBN-13: 9781662516573 (digital)

Cover design by Jarrod Taylor
Cover image: © David Pairé / Arcangel Images; © Datingjungle / Unsplash

Printed in the United States of America
First edition

*To my wife, Laura, and my daughters,
Noelle and Katja*

PROLOGUE

February 2014
Golan Heights
Israeli-Syrian Border

The first bullet struck the truck's windshield. The second ricocheted off a boulder a few meters to their left.

"Who the hell is it?" shouted Benny as bursts of gunfire lit up the horizon.

Ava pushed him flat against the ground. "Does it matter who it is? Keep your head down."

"I'd like to know who's trying to kill me," said Benny.

"Them," said Ava, gesturing with her Uzi. "That's who. Them."

"Some help you are," said Benny.

They lay on the cold, hard earth of the easternmost Golan Heights, spitting distance from the Purple Line, the line of demarcation between Israel and Syria, fixed after Israel conquered the territory first in June 1967, and then again in October 1973. It was night, 3:00 a.m., frigid and windy, dense cloud obscuring the stars. The nearest village was Al Katzim, fifteen kilometers to the north.

"What do we do?" asked Jonny, official title Jonathan Oren, PhD, professor of nuclear physics, Cambridge University.

"We finish what we came here for," said Ava.

"Aren't you going to call in backup?"

"What do you have in mind?" asked Ava. "A couple of F-16s?"

"I wouldn't say no," said Jonny.

"Did you forget, Dr. Oren, that we are not here?" said Ava. "You can't send backup to a team that doesn't exist."

"If we don't exist, why are they firing at us?" asked Benny angrily.

"Because we're Jews and they're Arabs," said Ava. "That's what it usually comes down to."

It was a flippant answer, but she refused to countenance the alternative. That "they," the creeps blowing off their weapons four hundred meters across the border, knew why Ava, Benny, and Jonny were there and had come to take possession of what they'd been sent to collect.

Ava was Mossad via Shin Bet, trained in counterterrorism, and the leader of the small team. She was pushing forty, and at that moment, feeling every minute of it. A black knit beanie hid her hair. Camouflage face paint darkened her cheeks. Like all of them, she wore black utilities and boots.

Benny was with Unit 8200—army signals intelligence—just a kid, maybe twenty-five, a tech rock star. Benny was tasked with retrieving the transmitter. Jonny was the big dog, a physicist on temporary duty (very much against his wishes). It was Jonny's job to make sure they didn't blow themselves to kingdom come.

Ava pulled on her night vision glasses and scanned the horizon. She didn't like what she saw. Silhouettes of a half dozen vehicles—jeeps, Hi-Lux pickups, sedans—and too many men to count. She had no idea who they were. Syrian regulars, rebels, ISIS. It didn't really matter. There was a civil war going on. Each was as bad as the others.

"Get up," she said. "We have a job to do."

"But they're firing at us," said Benny.

"If any of them could shoot," said Ava, "we'd be dead already."

"Fire back," said Benny. "You're the one with the gun."

"With this?" said Ava, tapping the Uzi submachine gun at her side. "I'd have a better chance slinging a rock at them. Now shut up and dig."

Benny got to his knees and grabbed the shovel. It was a spading shovel—sharp at the nose, its blade forged from alloyed steel—but it barely dented the frozen ground. "Whose idea was it," he asked, breathing heavily, "to send us out here in the middle of February?"

"Keep at it," said Ava, patting his shoulder. "That's a good boy."

She slid over to the physicist. "Dr. Oren, you can't stay here. Take the transmitter to the truck. Get in the back seat and lay down. You'll be safer there."

"But Samson . . ."

"We'll take care of Samson."

Dr. Jonny Oren raised his head tentatively. Gunfire rang out, and he buried his face into the cold earth. "I'll never make it," he said, lying as flat as a shadow.

"We'll wait a minute," said Ava, soothingly. She couldn't be angry with him. He was a scientist, not a soldier.

"Yes, a minute," said Oren. "Maybe two."

Ava scooted over to the transmitter. It was a heavy rectangular object, painted olive drab, the size of an ammo box. Wires sprouted from one end, where it was to be connected to Samson. She waited for a lull in firing, then jumped to her feet. Using both hands, she picked up the transmitter and sprinted to the truck. She opened the rear door and slung the transmitter inside. At that instant, a volley of bullets struck the door, the racket making her ears ring.

Ava threw herself to the ground. She landed on her side, the wind knocked out of her. Maybe she wasn't the only one with night vision glasses. With her foot, she slammed the door shut. She lay still for a moment, too shaken to move. The fear passed. It took longer for her to catch her breath.

Flipping onto her stomach, she commando crawled back to her colleagues. "How's it coming?" she asked Benny.

"Almost there."

Ava inched closer and saw that he'd dug a considerable amount. The hole was as deep as her forearm. With a grunt, Benny thrust the shovel into the earth. It struck something hard and metallic.

"Hit it harder next time," said Ava. "Then it won't matter who's shooting at us."

"It can't go off without a code," said Jonny Oren. "For that, the transmitter needs to be attached."

"Good to know," said Ava. "I'll sleep better at night."

She reached her hand into the hole and brushed the dirt off a circular metallic plate. There was no digital readout, no buttons, no switches. It didn't look like much.

Samson.

The name said it all.

"Dig around the sides," she said to Benny. "I'll help you lift it."

Benny slid the shovel into the hole and excavated the soil on all sides of the circular device while Ava scooped out the dirt with both hands.

From across the plain came a crescendo of catcalls, exhortations, and ululations. Kalashnikovs fired lengthy volleys into the sky, the muzzle bursts sparkling like fireworks. Headlights lit up the desert. Motors revved. The Hi-Lux pickups. She knew their sound, and she knew that they carried thirty-caliber machine guns bolted to their flatbeds.

"*Hamatzav-Kara,*" she muttered. We're in deep shit.

Ava knew then that their presence—whoever *they* were—was no coincidence. They hadn't decided to gather at this exact spot at this exact time for the hell of it.

"FYI," she said to Benny. "The party's about to get started."

Benny rammed the shovel into the dirt as if it were a jackhammer. "That's as good as we're going to get."

Ava thrust her arm into the hole. Her fingers touched the device's rough canvas casing. "Got it," she said, wrapping her fingers around the handle.

Benny dropped the shovel and fell to the ground beside her. "Got it."

"Lift on three," said Ava. "One . . . two . . ."

The Tourists

Ava and Benny struggled to free the device from its decades-old tomb. It was not especially heavy, maybe fifteen pounds, but time and the elements had welded it to the earth. With a final heave, it came free.

It was tall and cylindrical, resembling a sturdy fire extinguisher and wrapped in an olive canvas sleeve with shoulder straps attached. Samson was not meant to be buried but to be carried by infantry into battle. It was more than powerful enough to bring a temple down on the Philistines' heads. Ten temples. A hundred, even.

The earth beneath their feet began to shake. The sound of approaching vehicles grew louder.

"Dr. Oren," called Ava. "We've got it. Let's go home."

"I can't," said Oren, his hands clawing at the dirt. "I can't."

"Move your ass," shouted Benny. "Unless you want it shot off. Do you hear that?"

Oren lifted his head an inch off the ground. He nodded.

"Now," said Ava kindly. "We have to go."

Oren clambered to his feet. He blinked madly, brushing the dirt and gravel off his uniform, taking stock of himself. "I'm better," he said. A pronouncement. "I'm not frightened anymore."

A bullet struck his forehead dead center. Blood and bone and brain sprayed from the rear of his skull. He dropped to the ground like a rag doll.

"Take Samson," said Ava. "I'll get Dr. Oren."

"He's dead," said Benny. "Leave him."

"We don't do that." Ava slung her Uzi behind her back. She handed the device to Benny. "Go," she said. "I'll be right there."

"And if you're not?" Benny turned and ran before she could answer.

Ava knelt and slid an arm under Oren's body. She hauled him to a sitting position, then lifted him by his hips and hoisted him over a shoulder. He was small, bone thin. Even so, she struggled beneath his weight.

Ahead, Benny reached the truck. He threw Samson into the rear seat and secured it inside its protective case. He gave Ava a thumbs-up, then jumped behind the wheel. He fired the engine. The truck's headlights illuminated.

"No," screamed Ava. "Off! Off!"

Before the words had left her mouth, machine gun fire raked the truck. A rain of bullets struck the hood, the engine block, the windshield. Tires burst. Glass shattered. The barrage intensified until the vehicle seemed to be dancing. A bullet punctured the gas tank. There was an explosion.

Ava looked over her shoulder. It was no good. They were too close. Any moment, she would be caught in their beams.

Still, she couldn't run away.

She laid Jonny Oren onto the ground and ran to the truck. Flames enveloped the chassis. She had a glimpse of Benny, or what was left of him. She darted into the fire and grabbed the door handle. The metal scorched her fingers. She yanked with all her might. The door was jammed.

There it was: Samson in its protective case. So close. She pulled harder. The smell of cauterized flesh stung her nose. Again, she pulled, but no.

A bullet grazed her ear, stunning her. She stumbled away from the car.

Still, she refused to run.

Ava dropped to a knee and pulled the Uzi to her shoulder. The first trucks came into sight. She could see the green-and-black banners whipping in the wind; the soldiers, scarves covering their faces, Kalashnikovs at the ready. There were fifty of them, maybe more. Too many.

Ava lowered the Uzi.

"God help us, everyone," she whispered.

She ran into the night.

PART I

CHAPTER 1

Restaurant Jules Verne
Paris, France

Mac Dekker didn't know a ring could be so heavy. A gold band. A two-carat diamond solitaire. A jewelry box. Together they couldn't weigh more than a few ounces. He shifted in his chair. So, why was it that he felt as if he were carrying a hand grenade in his pocket?

"What a view," he said, gazing out the window.

"Beautiful," said Ava Attal. "Like a painting. Who is it that does clouds so well?"

"Monet," said Mac. "No, Van Gogh. Or is it Cézanne? Turner?"

After a morning at the Musée d'Orsay, he considered himself an expert on impressionism. Well, almost.

From their table at the restaurant Jules Verne, located on the second floor of the Eiffel Tower, four hundred feet above the ground, they looked south down the grassy expanse of the Champ de Mars to the École Militaire, and farther still, Les Invalides. It was mid-October. The sky was a pale blue. Fat, billowy clouds drifted over the city. The river Seine cut a moss green swath across the cityscape. A picture-postcard day.

"Autumn in Paris," said Ava. "I could get used to this."

"I thought you liked the mountains," said Mac.

"I love the mountains. I love the Chalet Ponderosa. I love Zinal. It will always be our place."

Mac considered this. There was something decidedly past tense in her words. "Place" was not the same as "home." You visited a place, but you lived in a home. "'And' or 'but'?" he asked.

"Pardon me?"

"'And' or 'but'?" Mac repeated. "You said it will always be our place."

"*And,*" said Ava. "I will always love it there."

"Not so fast," said Mac. "Answer the question."

"I did."

Mac smiled, studying her expression. Ava Marie Attal was tall and athletic, somewhere in her forties, dark hair touching her shoulders, with bottle green eyes and a stern countenance. People often mistook her as humorless. A martinet, even. Then she smiled and laughed her loud, unapologetic laugh, and they knew they were mistaken. Not a martinet at all, nor humorless. Just a serious woman and, given her profession, justly so. Ava had spent her adult life in the service of her country, first as a security officer in Shin Bet, Israel's domestic intelligence agency, and then as a covert operative for Mossad, its spy service. Think FBI and CIA.

She wasn't beautiful. Her nose was long and narrow with a slight crook, her mouth too broad. Not beautiful but something else. Something better, at least to Mac. She was formidable. Smart, accomplished, and confident. He found her almost unbearably attractive.

"Go on," said Mac. "*But . . .*"

"*But,*" said Ava. "There's a whole wide world out there. Look, the Louvre. The Place de la Concorde. So much to see."

"In Paris?"

"The world," said Ava, taking his hand. "Oh, Mac. Poor you. You've been gone so long, you've forgotten."

Mackenzie "Mac" Dekker was nearly a decade her senior. He was tall enough; "six feet on a good day," he liked to say. He was lean and broad shouldered and restless. Even now, he found it hard not to tap his foot. He had blue eyes and a direct gaze—though not as direct as Ava's—hair as black and thick as ever, even if it was receding at the temples.

He was wearing a dove gray suit for the occasion. They'd purchased it the day before at Harrison, a stylish boutique off the Avenue Victor Hugo. A forty-two long off the rack and it fit like a glove. "The suit from *North by Northwest*," the salesman had informed him. "It looks even better on you." Doubtful, thought Mac, but he thanked him nonetheless. Sometime lies did wonders.

"Ten years, more or less," said Mac, gazing out the window. *The world.* It was a concept he would have to get used to again. He smiled, excited by the prospect. "What do kids say now? 'It's been a minute.'"

Nine years ago, he'd been forced into exile to save his life and the lives of his family. A longtime field operative with the Central Intelligence Agency, he'd been betrayed by his best friend and made to look like a Russian double agent. Unable to prove his innocence, he'd faked his death and escaped to the village of Zinal in the Swiss Alps. For nearly a decade, he'd lived below the radar, never once contacting his family, his friends, or the woman he loved. And then, just one year ago, his son, Will, was killed while climbing the Matterhorn, and everything changed.

The world.

Mac had spent his professional life traveling to all four corners of the globe. His most frequent stops had included Baghdad, Kabul, Aleppo, and other garden spots not usually found on Tripadvisor's "Top Ten Most Romantic Destinations." Sometimes he forgot who he was— or rather, who he'd once been.

A US Marine at the age of twenty. Honor graduate of sniper school. Force Recon, then onto MARSOC (Marines Special Operations Command). Deployments to Bosnia, Colombia, Afghanistan. After 9/11, a lateral move to the CIA. Better pay, longer hair, and he didn't have to polish his boots. Different title, same job description. He was still a scalp hunter—some said the best . . . though he wasn't sure the ability to infiltrate enemy lines and shoot a man dead at a thousand yards was something to be proud of. All told, more than two decades in and out of war zones.

"You're right," said Mac. "Time to change how I think. New perspective, right?"

"A new perspective," said Ava. "I like that. For both of us."

The waiter approached and handed each of them a sturdy bound menu. Inside the cover was a quote from Jules Verne, the French author after whom the restaurant was named. Mac read it to himself. No, he thought, it couldn't be. "Tell me you didn't set this up."

Ava narrowed her eyes. "What?"

"The menu," said Mac. "The quote. You told them to give me this one."

Ava smiled, mystified. "I don't understand."

"'Solitude and isolation are painful things and beyond human endurance,'" said Mac, reading the quote aloud. "Come on. How did they know?"

"It was fated," said Ava, with a wave to the heavens. "How could they have given you any other menu?"

Mac didn't buy it for a second. On the other hand, it seemed like more than a coincidence. Cue the spooky music. "What does yours say?"

"'We may brave human laws, but we cannot resist natural ones.'"

"Interesting," said Mac, wondering which human laws he might defy and which natural ones held him in check.

"Now let's do the hard part," said Ava. "What do you think? Tasting menu?"

Mac read the dishes silently. Lobster. Galette. Langoustine. It was a far cry from bread and sausage. "I'm in," he said. "But what's a galette?"

"We'll find out soon enough," said Ava. "After lunch I thought we could walk through the Jardin du Luxembourg, then maybe a light supper at Fouquet's."

"Sounds ambitious," said Mac.

The Tourists

"And you were thinking?"

"A nap."

Ava shook her head. Wrong answer. "You're not the only one who's been given a new lease on life." She set down the menu and raised her left arm. A year earlier, she'd undergone reconstructive surgery on her shoulder to repair damage done by a high-caliber bullet. "The doctors gave me the all clear. I'm as good as new."

"You didn't tell me."

"I wanted it to be a surprise."

Mac lifted a glass of champagne. "To a full recovery."

"L'Chaim," said Ava. "To life."

"L'Chaim." Mac signaled for the server and ordered for them both. "And some more champagne. Make it a bottle. We're celebrating. The Domaine du Roi."

Ava raised a brow, her lips signaling her approval. "I like a man who knows how to spend a little money."

"Is that right?" Mac felt something touching his leg, something warm and much too familiar.

Ava ran her toes along his calf. "On second thought," she said, almost purring. "Maybe a nap might be just the right thing."

"You . . . a nap?" said Mac. Then the light went on. "Oh, *a nap*."

Ava narrowed her eyes seductively. "I thought all those naked women in the museum might inspire you."

"All I have to do is look at you."

"You're shameless," said Ava.

"I'm in love," said Mac.

"How do you feel?" she asked.

Mac looked around him. It was finally setting in. "Like a free man."

CHAPTER 2

Zinal, Switzerland
One month earlier

Mac looked at the sky.

Dark clouds tumbled over the mountaintops and advanced across the valley, an ominous gray blanket slowly blocking out the sun. He felt a drop of rain. A storm was moving in.

"Slow down, Kat," he shouted. "Let Papa catch up."

He continued down the hill, doing his best to keep up with the little girl. They were off trail, and he had to be watchful for gopher holes and clumps of heather.

"Another one!" His granddaughter, Katya, ran ahead, calling out whenever she spotted an edelweiss. She was four years old, blond, and endlessly inquisitive.

"Good for you," said Mac, but all the while his eyes scanned the slopes. It was his sniper's gaze. Focused, suspicious, wary. He wasn't concerned about the storm. He gave it a quarter of an hour until it started coming down. There was something else.

They were being watched.

He hadn't seen anyone, not yet, but he knew all the same. The hairs on the back of his neck stood at attention, as if an electric current pulsed through the air. He'd had the feeling too many times to count. *Ignore at your peril.*

The Tourists

"Papa, here! Look!" The little girl stooped to pluck a flower. Mac marveled at how he'd come to love her so. Barely twelve months had passed since she'd come into his life. It hadn't been easy at first. Up at the crack of dawn. Constant supervision. Endless engagement. *"Oh really? Is that right? Good for you, sweetheart."* Now he couldn't imagine his life without her. He'd been a lousy father the first time around, absent for months at a time; absent in a different way when he'd been at home. Katya was his second chance.

Her mother had been Russian, an officer in the SVR, Russia's spy service. Like his son, Will, she had been betrayed by a mole inside the CIA. Like his son, she had died on the Matterhorn.

Katya ran to him, proudly displaying a fistful of flowers. Mac scooped her up into his arms and counted the edelweiss in her hand. "Four," he said. "One more than yesterday."

"Tomorrow I'll find five."

"I'm counting on it," said Mac, kissing her on the cheek and setting her down.

That was when he saw him. A short, portly man, more or less his age, navy jacket, new hiking boots, walking sticks. A day tourist like any other who came up on weekends. Except today was Wednesday, and they weren't anywhere near the marked trails. And besides, Mac recognized him.

They'd finally come for him.

"Hello, Mac. Long time, no see." The man threw off a casual salute. His name was Don Baker. Back in the day, he'd been Mac's boss. Deputy assistant director of special operations or something like that.

"Hello, Don." Mac waved and gave a look around. Two women had taken up positions behind him. Both were dressed in jeans and sweaters, worn boots; locals, to look at. Mac knew better.

"Don't just stand there like a stranger," growled Baker. "Get over here. I want a handshake and a hug."

Mac wasn't afraid. Baker hadn't ventured all this way to Switzerland to kill him. Not here. Not at three o'clock in the afternoon on a rainy

15

autumn day, a stone's throw from the town's main drag. This was about something else.

He took Katya's hand. Together they approached the visitor. Baker hadn't aged well. Heavy jowls. Bulbous nose. Rheumy eyes and bags heavy enough to anchor a carrier. The only thing that hadn't changed was his hair, an impressive reddish-brown thatch that better belonged on a college undergrad.

"You found me," said Mac. As ordered, he shook Baker's hand. The hug could wait.

"You didn't make it hard," said Baker. "Lit up a lot of screens."

"What took you so long?"

"We'll come to that." Baker leaned down to address the little girl. "Your name is Katya, right? I'm a friend of your grandfather. We used to work together."

"Did you take care of the cows too?" asked Katya.

"Cows?" Baker asked Mac, alarmed.

"I look after them during the summer," Mac explained. "Up on the alp." He gestured to the hillside behind them. "Swiss brown. About sixty of them. There's a dairy up there and . . . ah, forget it."

"Cows," said Baker, raising his brows. "So, you're what . . . a herder?"

"Something like that," said Mac.

Baker laughed spiritedly. "Well, I never. The great Mac Dekker, a cowherd." He put a hand on Mac's arm. "I'm sorry about Will. Damn good man."

"He was," said Mac.

"Not sure I could have done what he did."

"He did what he had to," said Mac. It was a question that kept him up at night. Where had his son gotten the strength to sacrifice his life? "How 'bout a drink?"

"About time you found your manners," said Baker, throwing an arm around Mac's shoulder. "And make it a double, goddamn it."

The Tourists

They sat in Mac's study. It was a cozy room with arolla pine walls, a leather sofa in one corner, and a fireplace. Mac found a bottle of scotch with an unpronounceable name that had gathered dust for years.

"I'll say this," Baker began, but not before taking a sip. "You came back with a bang. Not a peep for eight years, then 'Boom!' There was your face on every camera in Switzerland. Sierre, Zermatt, Zurich. A regular movie star."

"I didn't have a choice," said Mac.

"You look good on camera, by the way," said Baker. "Especially after you got rid of the beard."

Ah, the beard, Mac remembered. Part of his effort to look older. No one looked twice at a seventy-year-old with graying hair and bad posture. "I thought you'd come sooner."

"We considered it," said Baker. "But it was all over so quickly. What was it? A couple of days? And, by then Ilya was dead and we knew everything."

"You never knew about him? About Thorpe?"

Thorpe was Calvin Thorpe—formerly CIA station chief for Switzerland—since deceased.

"That he was a double?" Baker grimaced, a bad memory confronted. "There were suspicions. You had lots of friends, me included. It was hard to swallow the story he was peddling."

"But not too hard," said Mac.

"It came down to the money," said Baker. "No one believed the Russians would dump five million into an account just to nail one guy."

"That's why they did it," said Mac. "They knew you'd fall for it every time."

Baker nodded, a world-weary shrug his only apology. "Goddamn agency," he said. "It gets crazy on the seventh floor. Someone whispers 'mole' and the whole place starts seeing shadows. You know how it is."

"I was a field guy, Don."

"The best."

"Give it a rest," said Mac. "I'm too old for that."

"You and me both, buddy." Baker finished his drink in a swallow, then slammed the glass onto the coffee table. "I'm here to apologize and make good."

"That right?" Mac laughed cynically. "I don't blame you, Don. Like you said, it's how things work."

"I'm not kidding," said Baker. "I've come to bring you back to life. Officially."

Mac put down his glass. "How 'officially'?"

"Clear your name. Take the target off your back. That kind of 'officially.'"

"Bullshit," said Mac.

Baker placed his hand over his heart. "Hand to God."

Mac stared at Baker. Was this for real? The CIA did not admit it was wrong. "Tell me you're kidding, Don, and we can both laugh about it later."

Baker gazed at him earnestly. "No joke, buddy."

"I want it in writing," said Mac.

"Why spoil a good thing?" said Baker. "Some secrets best remain buried."

"I'm not dead, Don."

"I'm not talking about you," said Baker. "No one needs to know that the Agency had a Russian mole on its payroll for twenty years."

"He got my son killed."

"And he paid for it with his life," said Baker. "I'm sorry. I truly am. We all are." He leaned closer. Time to make his case. "Look, Mac, we've got a bunch of crazies in Congress looking for a reason to defund the intelligence community. Why poke the hornet's nest? I've been sent to say 'thank you' and—"

"Keep your mouth shut," said Mac.

"—and to inform you that your salary for the past nine years has been deposited into an account at the Valais Cantonal Bank. Tax free. You received a promotion too. Senior Executive Service."

The Tourists

Senior Executive Service pay was the holy grail of government workers and only offered to the longest-serving and highest-ranking officials. It was nothing like Wall Street, but no one went to work for the government to get rich.

"You're serious?" said Mac.

"As a heart attack, buddy. This is your lucky day." Baker slid an envelope across the table. Mac opened it and removed a deposit slip from the Cantonal Bank of Valais in the amount of $1.55 million. He glanced up at Baker, then back at the receipt. His first reaction was suspicion. It was too much money. There had to be a catch. Then he saw it. The account belonged to Robert Steinhardt, the identity he'd assumed all those years ago.

"Tell me the rest of it," said Mac.

"Are you kidding me?" said Baker. "We hand you a million and a half bucks, tell you you're a free man, target officially off your back, and you're not happy. Go on. Get out of here. Live as you please. Travel. Do some climbing. Milk some cows. Enjoy life."

"I'm waiting," said Mac.

Baker rose and poured himself another drink. "Rules are simple enough. Keep your head down. Don't talk about this—not a word. In fact, we'd prefer you didn't reach out to anyone from the old days."

"Want to clarify that?"

"No contact whatsoever," said Baker. "Mackenzie David Dekker is dead. Stay that way."

"And that's an order," said Mac.

"Want to give me back the check?"

Mac took a second look at the deposit slip, allowing himself a moment to absorb what that kind of money meant and weigh it against Baker's demands. The decision was easy enough. Mac had no plans to go spouting off his mouth. Discretion had always been part of the job. "Understood," he said.

"You need anything," said Baker, ". . . and I'm talking emergencies only . . . call me. I'll give you my direct number."

"And Jane?" Mac's daughter, Jane McCall, had followed him into the business. Currently, she was acting CIA station chief in Berlin.

"She's family," said Baker. "I imagine she's happy to have her father back in her life. We don't see any reason to keep you from reestablishing your relationship. But quietly, Mac. Church mice. And don't ask her to fix any parking tickets."

"Why would I?" said Mac.

"Who knows?" said Baker. "Things happen."

"Church mice," said Mac.

"Exactly." Baker stepped closer. "Just so you know," he continued, the cheeriness suddenly gone, "not everyone is on board with how your matter was resolved, not least the money. A few of the guys aren't so forgiving. They think you made them . . . *made us, the Agency* . . . look bad. 'Once convicted, always convicted,' the thinking goes. Be careful, buddy. You might not get a second reprieve."

"What are you trying to tell me, Don?"

"They won't miss a second time," said Baker. "Don't give them a reason."

Mac didn't take Baker's words as a threat. Like he'd said: *rules*. Cross the line and this is what will happen. Mac was a big boy. Fair was fair. "Thanks for the heads-up."

"So, we're good?" said Baker.

"Solid," said Mac.

"Well, hip hip hooray then," boomed Baker before slapping Mac on the back. "You can smile now, you rich SOB."

Mac smiled.

Baker finished his drink. "So, what the hell have you been up to for the last nine years besides humping cows?"

As usual it was Baker who had the last word. They'd talked the last nine years. The changes at the Agency. Who'd left, who'd died, who'd been promoted. All the gossip.

Mac gave Baker the inside scoop on what had gone down a year earlier. Everything he knew about Hercules, the Russian plot against the Kyiv water supply system. He wanted Baker to know the details. How close they'd come to disaster. How Mac's actions had prevented it. One day he might need a friend on the seventh floor.

"Sorry to miss Ava," said Baker, as they stood in the doorway of the Chalet Ponderosa. Night had fallen. The air was cold, sharp, tangy with woodsmoke.

"She's in St. Moritz," said Mac. "Physical therapy."

"How's that coming?"

"Pretty good," said Mac. "Shoulder surgery is tough. Amazing doctor. Gerhard Lutz. He's a wizard."

"Lutz? In St. Moritz?"

"Know him?"

Baker shook his head. "For a second, I thought it rang a bell. But no. Never heard the name."

Mac dismissed the comment, wondering why Baker was so defensive. "I'll give Ava your best."

Baker laid a meaty palm on Mac's shoulder. "A word?"

"Sure," said Mac.

"Be careful," said Baker.

"What do you mean?"

Baker pulled a face. An uncomfortable truth that needed airing. "You know . . . *the Israeli thing*."

"What about it?" asked Mac.

"I don't have to tell you," said Baker. "Israelis only fight for one side. Their own."

CHAPTER 3

Paris
Present day

Mac had decided to ask over dessert. The question remained: before or after? Maybe after dessert and before coffee was served.

"What do you want to do?" asked Ava. "It's been a month since Don visited. Surely, you've been thinking."

"I've been trying to decide if I'm happy," said Mac. "I spent nine years training myself to forget the world, to forget my old life, to be content doing what I had to do to keep my family and myself safe. It worked. I like it up there. I like being on the alp in the summer, working at the resort in winter. I like being away from the world."

"But all that's changed," said Ava. "You can go anywhere."

"*We can go*," said Mac.

Ava nodded, placing her hand on his. "We can go. We can live anywhere we choose."

"I'm still getting used to that concept. Somehow it was easier when I couldn't choose."

"I understand," said Ava. "But listen, Mac, darling, we can spend Christmas there, visit every summer."

Mac read the excitement in her eyes and knew that their time in the mountains had come to an end. The last twelve months had passed quickly. There was Ava's operation. Weeks spent in the hospital. Once home, she had dedicated herself to her recovery. Daily walks. Sessions with her physical therapist. Visits to St. Moritz for stem cell therapy.

Mac studied her. This woman he loved. Of course she was right. He couldn't expect her to live in a town of a thousand souls tucked away at the end of an alpine valley. He tried to picture her on the alp, caring for the cows, cleaning out the barn. He laughed at the thought. Not going to happen.

"What about you?" he asked. "Plans?"

She smiled. "Somehow it was easier when I couldn't choose."

"And now?"

"We'll see," said Ava, lightly, almost dismissively, but Mac read something behind her eyes. He knew the look. She was up to something. Whether that meant returning to Mossad or engaging in other, less opaque work on her country's behalf, he didn't know. He wasn't sure how he felt about either prospect.

Mac's hand brushed the box. He had a sudden and terrifying thought. What if marriage wasn't something she had in mind? They'd never really discussed the future. What if she said no?

Hell, he thought, taking a breath. Get it over with. It wasn't going to get any easier just thinking about it.

"Before we go any further," said Mac. "I need to ask you something."

"That sounds ominous," said Ava. "Should I be frightened?"

"I hope not," said Mac. "Then again . . ." He fished in his pocket for the box.

"You're not going to ask if you can get out of going to Versailles tomorrow?"

"No. You don't have to worry about that. I want to see Versailles."

"Good," said Ava. "Go ahead. I'm all ears."

Mac smiled. Suddenly, his throat felt tight, his mouth dry. "It's been a tough year," he began. "The operation. All the work to get better. Both of us taking care of a little girl. On top of that, wondering if and when they were going to come after us . . . well, me, at least. I think we managed pretty well."

"Very well," said Ava.

"What I mean to say is that I enjoy being with you."

"I enjoy being with you," said Ava.

"We make a good team," said Mac.

"We do."

"And we both agree we have to find a new place to live," he said.

"I'm glad we do," said Ava.

"What I want to say is that I love you very much."

"I love you too."

Mac's hand tightened on the box. "So, I wanted to ask you . . ."

Ava's phone rang. She looked at the screen. Her expression hardened. It was important. "Mac, I'm sorry. Can I?"

"Go ahead," he said. "But I may eat your dessert."

"Don't you dare." Ava stood and came around the table and kissed him. "Be right back." She walked from the dining room, placing the phone to her ear. *"Grüß Gott."*

Mac watched her disappear down the hall. He took out the jewelry box and set it on the table. There. He'd done it. When she returned and sat down, she'd see it. He'd give her a moment, then pop the question.

He drank some more champagne and stared out the window. What a city. It truly was breathtaking. Ava was right. They could go anywhere. Well, almost anywhere. DC was out. For that matter, so were the States. He couldn't risk running into someone he knew. Baker had been plenty clear. Mac was to keep his head down. He had enemies waiting to pounce. It was a fair bargain—one he'd agreed to when he accepted the US government's money. Who needed the States?

Ava was originally from France. Why not here? Provence was nice. Maybe Arles or Aix. He could use some more sun. The food was certainly good. It would be onion soup for lunch and duck à l'orange for dinner.

The server brought dessert. Raspberry sorbet and pears. He spied the jewelry box and rushed to refill their champagne. "With compliments of the house," he said.

"She hasn't said yes yet," said Mac. "Wish me luck."

"Bonne chance," said the server.

Mac checked his watch. Ava had been gone too long. Ten minutes . . . no, *twelve*, to be exact. He felt a stab between his shoulders. A tinge of unease. Ava wasn't a gabber; quite the opposite. She was a woman of few words, especially when it came to business. "Brusque" wouldn't be an inappropriate word to describe her. He wondered who she was speaking with. A native German speaker? *"Grüß Gott"* was the greeting commonly used in Bavaria and Austria.

Mac looked over his shoulder. The restaurant was emptying out. It was past 3:30 p.m. He noted that only one other table remained occupied. Another couple. Gray haired. Elegantly dressed. They held hands across the table, content to stare into each other's eyes. A picture of Mac and Ava in fifteen years?

Mac slid the jewelry box back into his pocket. He tapped his fingers on the table. There it was again. A distinct feeling that something was wrong. He picked up the champagne and put it back down. He didn't want any more alcohol in his system. *Not if . . .*

Mac stopped himself. He laughed. What in the world was he thinking? Ava was out of the game. She'd spent the last twelve months at his side. He couldn't remember her once mentioning "the Office," as she referred to Mossad. There was absolutely no reason to think anything was amiss.

And yet . . .

He glanced over his shoulder again, willing Ava to appear. The servers had gathered by the kitchen door. He caught their impatient glances. Please leave. You've had your meal. It's time to start preparing for the evening service.

Mac took out his phone and called Ava. The call went directly to voicemail after a single ring. Odd. That happened only if the phone was off. *Not odd. Troubling.* Again, he felt the stab between his shoulders.

Mac stood and signaled to the maître d'. "Excuse me, but have you seen the woman who was seated at my table? She took a call about fifteen minutes ago and hasn't returned."

"She is wearing a black dress, hair up, very attractive?"

Mac nodded, but he could have done without the last part. The French. "That's her."

"I'm sorry," said the maître d' with concern. "I have not seen her anywhere."

Mac looked this way and that. The main dining room was a large rectangular space, windows on three sides, tables spaced evenly. There was a second, smaller room also visible, looking north toward the Trocadéro. That room was empty. "Can you have someone check the ladies' room?"

"Right away." The maître d' dispatched a server to check. "I'm sure everything is fine," he continued unconvincingly. "Perhaps madame is taking photos. Such a lovely day."

"Perhaps," said Mac.

The server returned and reported that there was no one in the women's restroom.

"Is there anywhere else she could be?" asked Mac.

"There is only the kitchen, and a private dining room above us."

"Can you show me?"

"Of course." The maître d' walked down the hall and opened a paneled door. He was a small man and slight, dressed in an immaculate black suit, his thick gray hair teased like cotton candy. Mac followed him up a flight of stairs to a small dining room. Even with the lights out, it was immediately apparent that the room was empty.

"Let us check the kitchen," offered the maître d'.

Mac followed him down the stairs and through a pair of swinging doors into the restaurant's capacious kitchen. Bright lights. Stainless steel. A staff of twenty. The chefs appeared nonplussed as Mac circled the room.

"Perhaps she took the elevator to the ground?" suggested the maître d'.

"She wouldn't leave without telling me," said Mac, rather lamely. "But yes, let's check."

Mac followed the maître d' down the hallway to the dim alcove, where a private elevator delivered diners from the ground floor plaza. A liveried attendant stood by the doors. Mac addressed him in French, describing Ava and inquiring if she had recently left the restaurant. The response was an emphatic no.

Where could she be? Mac was no longer troubled; he was flat-out panicked.

He retraced his steps down the hall. Then he saw it. A glimmer of gold on the carpet. He bent to look more closely. An earring. He picked it up. *Ava's earring.* It was broken, the post missing, a smidge of blood visible.

"Did you find something?" asked the maître d'.

"An earring," said Mac. "It belongs to . . . to . . . her." He stood and studied the corridor. He spotted a camera high in one corner. There had to be others in the restaurant. "You have cameras. Can I see them?"

"Of course we have them, but—"

"But what?" asked Mac.

"This is a legal matter," said the maître d'. "We are not allowed to share this with . . . well, strangers."

"I'm asking a favor," said Mac.

The maître d' frowned. "I will have to contact the police. We must wait until they arrive."

The police. They'd want Mac's name. Passport. From there, who knew? The police were to be avoided at all costs.

"No," replied Mac. "That won't be necessary. Is there another way out?"

"An emergency exit to the exterior stairwell."

"Show me."

The maître d' retraced his steps to the opposite side of the dining room and threw open the emergency exit. An urgent bell pinged several times. There was no way someone could open it without drawing attention to themself. Mac passed through the door onto a steel grate, through which one could view the stairwell descending to the ground. Mac bent over the rail, searching. There was no one on the stairs.

He called her phone a second time. Again, the call went directly to voicemail. Ava's phone was still powered off. "It's me. I have your earring. What's going on? I'm worried."

"Are you certain you don't wish for me to call the police?" asked the maître d'.

Mac shook his head.

The maître d' opened his hands. "But where is she? Where can she have gone?"

Mac was unable to provide an answer.

Ava Attal had vanished.

CHAPTER 4

Hotel Bristol
Paris

The hotel lobby was calm and airy, a towering bouquet of flowers placed on a center table. Mac made a beeline for reception.

"Did I beat madame back?" he asked playfully, hardly slowing.

"Indeed, you did," snapped the hotelier, matching Mac's smile. "I have not seen her. You enjoyed your lunch?"

But by then Mac was already climbing the stairs. He knew better than to take the hotelier's words at face value. If Ava could disappear from a restaurant high up the Eiffel Tower, she could sneak into a large hotel without being seen.

Room 421 was at the end of the hall. He touched the key card to the lock and opened the door. He entered the suite boldly, marching into the salon, seeing at once that it was empty.

"Ava," he called, if only to make himself feel better, to permit himself one last moment of normalcy.

No one answered.

He continued into the bedroom. The maid had cleaned the room. Clothing was folded neatly on the dresser. Fresh bottles of mineral water sat on the nightstands. The air tingled with an invigorating lemon fragrance. He studied the maroon carpet. No footprints disturbed the perfect vacuum tracks.

He had, in fact, beaten madame back to the hotel.

Mac crossed to the bathroom, a palace of white marble, mirrors, gold fixtures, and a bathtub large enough for two. The night before, he and Ava had enjoyed a hot, luxuriating soak after a bout of vigorous lovemaking. Ava had been particularly forthright, he recalled, offering wordless but unmistakable direction. At one point, she'd straddled him, one hand on the wall for support, allowing herself to be unusually vocal.

"I hope I didn't wake anyone in the next room," she'd said afterward.

"The next room?" said Mac. "What about the next block?"

"Well, don't blame me," said Ava, eyes locked on his, then she had laughed and laid her head on his chest.

Mac returned to the bedroom. He went to the window and gazed down on the boulevard. A normal autumn afternoon in Paris. Light rain. Leaves falling from beech trees lining the sidewalk. Men and women hurrying home after a trying day at work. Yet there was nothing normal about it. Not for him.

At this moment, he was sure of only one thing. He'd entered the restaurant one person. He'd left another. His life as an unburdened civilian had proven miserably brief. He was no longer Robbie Steinhardt, Swiss citizen, if of dubious origin—a tourist enjoying a romantic getaway in the City of Light with the woman he loved and hoped to make his wife. He was Mac Dekker. The old Mac Dekker.

He dropped into a chair. Where, he asked himself, had Ava gone?

Off the bat, there were two possibilities. First, her disappearance was an act of retribution. A reckoning. A measure to punish Ava for something she'd done in the past—some perceived injustice that demanded a balancing of the scales. Put simply: payback.

Mac had only a vague knowledge of her professional history. More than he, she was bound by her occupation's code of silence. The majority of her work was graded top secret or higher. He knew, for example, that she'd lived and worked as a covert operative in Jordan for five years, teaching French at a secondary school. But never once had she shared details about her time in Amman. He didn't ask. She didn't tell. The fact that she'd made it back to Tel Aviv alive and in one piece led him to believe she was good at her job.

He also knew that she'd lived in Paris for several years, working as a cultural secretary out of the Israeli embassy. He did not believe her primary responsibility was arranging exhibits of traditional Israeli folk dancing or shepherding the odd musician on their tour of France. She was a trained spy. By definition, she cultivated sources, ran networks, and gathered information. And that's where it ended. Unlike Mac, she was never the sharp end of the spear. She was not a killer.

It was entirely reasonable, then, to suspect that someone from somewhere deep in her past, someone unable to live another day with their wronged soul had traveled to Paris seeking vengeance. Reasonable, but unlikely. Why here? Why now?

No, Mac decided, Ava's disappearance had nothing to do with her past.

The second possibility was more realistic. Ava's disappearance had to do with the present. She was involved in something. She was operational.

Mac ran over their long lunch in the restaurant Jules Verne. Surely she'd given some indication—dropped a hint, let slip a word or two—that something was amiss. But no, not for a moment had she appeared worried, preoccupied, or distracted. On the contrary. She'd been as blithe and free spirited as he could remember. As Ava had herself toasted, "L'Chaim." To life.

Otherwise, had Mac noticed anything out of place? It was a professional habit—a *déformation professionnelle*, the French called it—to take careful note of those around him. Upon their arrival at the restaurant, the dining room had been nearly full. He'd counted sixteen tables in all. In his mind's eye, he reviewed them all, moving from the left side of the dining room to the right. Tables of two and four persons. Mostly couples. Two families. Several businessmen. He'd caught snatches of a half dozen languages. French, of course. English, Dutch, Arabic, Chinese, and German. Primarily tourists, if he had to guess.

At the table to their right sat a husband and wife from the Gulf, both very much taken with one another—young, attractive, affluent. His and hers Rolex Daytonas, a diamond solitaire big enough to cut glass, and a crocodile Birkin bag that had caught Ava's eye. "Psst," she'd whispered. "That silly bag costs a hundred thousand euros. Can you imagine?"

To their left sat a pair of German businessmen who insisted on drinking beer throughout their meal and talking about their favorite football teams.

No, Mac concluded with certainty. He hadn't noticed anything indicating that he or Ava was in danger. No overt staring. No undue interest. No abruptly averted glances. It was a uniformly well-dressed, cosmopolitan clientele, all of them seemingly thrilled to pay €300 apiece for a fixed-course meal.

At least Mac could take consolation from one thing: His powers of observation were as sharp as ever. Maybe the Prevagen Ava mercilessly pushed on him actually worked.

One thing was certain. If Ava had been abducted—there, he had finally said the word—there was a reason. Events didn't happen in a vacuum. Newton's third law. For every action there is an equal and opposite reaction. Ava was involved in something, and it had not gone as planned.

If this was the case—and suddenly Mac believed it to the core—he had to admit something else.

Ava had lied to him. She had purposely kept her activities secret from him.

Once a spy, always a spy.

Somewhere, he knew, there was a clue.

CHAPTER 5

Hotel Bristol
Paris

A keen energy gripped Mac. Minutes ago, he had been acting out of fear, thinking defensively, maneuvering off his back foot. No longer. He was angry, a man affronted. A wronged man seeking redress.

He opened the armoire and removed her backpack, a black leather Tumi that she carried everywhere. He sat on the bed and opened it, then removed the contents item by item. Compact, lipstick, sunglasses, scarf. A rain jacket folded into a pouch. And there at the bottom, her Moleskine agenda.

He opened the journal and skimmed the pages. A few notes on each day. Lunch with so and so. Physical therapy at 1:00 p.m. And, more cryptically, abbreviations. *"D.S." "TNT." "Call Z.G."* Who was Z.G.? Who was TNT?

Just then, the door to the suite opened. Mac raised his head. Footsteps. A man speaking softly, his voice deep, gravelly. "Just got into their room. No, I don't see anyone. Just wait . . . I'll find it."

Mac set down the journal, moved to the doorway, and placed his back against the wall. He had no weapons. Next to him, on a side table, sat a decorative statuette. Napoleon on his rearing horse, his hand raised in victory. Mac picked it up and spun it in his hand to hold it like a billy club.

"Don't worry," said the man. "I'll take care of everything."

French with a Middle Eastern accent. Libyan, Egyptian, Lebanese.

Mac peeked around the door and caught a glimpse of a dark jacket, close-cropped hair. A tall man, broad shouldered, stood in the center of the sitting room, his back turned to him.

Mac drew a breath, raised the statuette, and charged through the door. "You!"

The man spun. Seeing Mac, he cried out and raised an arm to protect himself. "Please, no!"

Mac noted his uniform. Blue blazer, gray trousers, name tag. *"Pierre."* The fruit basket he was carrying fell to the floor.

Mac stopped in his tracks. He lowered the statuette. "I'm sorry," he said. "I thought you were . . ."

"Concierge service," said Pierre. He gestured at the fruit strewn across the carpet. "May I?"

Mac set the statuette on a table. "Yes, of course, go ahead."

Pierre kneeled to gather the fruit.

"I didn't order anything," said Mac.

"A delivery." Pierre placed the fruit basket on the table. "I'm sorry to disturb you."

"Wait." Mac dug a ten-euro note from his pocket. "Again, I'm sorry."

Pierre accepted the banknote. With haste, he left the room.

Mac went to the bar and poured himself a glass of water. He drew a breath, willing his heart to slow. He caught a glimpse of himself in the window. A wide-eyed, desperate man stared back.

Mac really was out of practice. His memory might still be sharp, but his instincts were shot to hell. He didn't want his legacy to include scaring a bellman to death, or worse, braining an innocent man with a statue of Napoleon Bonaparte.

He returned to the bedroom, moving with greater urgency. He checked Ava's nightstand. Cough drops. Tissue. Nothing else.

To the bathroom. He opened Ava's leather medicine bag. Antacid. Codeine. Xanax. The intelligence officer's holy trinity. Tucked into a pouch was a foil vacuum pack with twelve round, chalky white tablets; three were missing. Aspirin? Painkillers? Vitamins? The only marking on the packet was a minuscule twelve-digit alphanumeric code. Not an expiration date. Something else. He turned the packet toward the light. Only then could he see it. A large Hebrew letter stamped onto the pack. Resh. The letter "R." It meant nothing to him, which was odd in and of itself. Ava packed only what she needed. He popped out a tablet and dropped it into his pocket. To investigate further.

Mac returned to the bedroom and opened the closet, then zeroed in on Ava's stainless steel carry-on. He picked it up and slung it onto the bed. He thumbed the fasteners. The case was locked. He retrieved a nail file from his own medicine kit. He required less than a minute to pick both locks and open the carry-on. Tennis shoes, shorts, socks, tank top. Someone hadn't consulted the weather forecast. He shook the case. Nothing else was inside. So why lock it?

Mac ran his fingers along the inside of the suitcase, prodding the material. He completed the perimeter, then attacked the bottom. He felt nothing but the smooth, hard shell. He spun the case so that the top faced him. Immediately, his fingers touched something hard and angular. His fingers traced a rectangular form, maybe one inch in height. He guided his hand left to right. Again, he tripped over a blunt object concealed by the opaque plastic lining, this one rounded, the length of a ballpoint pen. A third object was concealed in the upper corner. There were several more.

Mac ran a fingernail along the edge of the lining, separating it from the case. He gave a tug. It came free, exposing the hidden objects. All were colored a drab green. All were held in place by clamps. He pulled each free. All were fabricated from high-density plastic. A total of five pieces.

Mac knew what he was looking at. He'd trained with long guns, rifles, high-caliber machine guns, but his expertise included weapons of a smaller caliber, handguns included. Here, lying harmlessly on the bedspread, were the components of a pistol: barrel, magazine, stock, and frame. And separately, a container holding six bullets.

Mac put it together in a minute. It looked like a nine-millimeter semiautomatic. There was no serial number, no brand engraved anywhere. The pistol had been manufactured by a 3D printer. Taken apart, it would escape detection at any airport, train station, or hub where luggage might be passed through an x-ray machine. The bullets, however, were not plastic. They were hollow points designed to mushroom on impact. Conclusion: Ava had purchased them once they'd arrived in Paris.

Mac slid the magazine into the stock. He racked the slide, surprised at how smoothly it chambered a round. Not quite his Sig Sauer, but impressive.

Mac weighed the pistol in his hand. Why had Ava brought a firearm to Paris on a three-day romantic getaway . . . a celebration of their new life as "official" civilians? Given recent events, the question answered itself. And again, he felt the barbed lance of betrayal.

He held the pistol at arm's length and aimed it out the window toward the Place de la Concorde and the Obelisk. Why then, if she suspected she might be in danger, hadn't she carried it with her to the restaurant?

Confused, he set the pistol down on the table next to the basket of fruit. He observed that there was a small ecru envelope tucked between an apple and an apricot. He plucked the envelope free. It was addressed to "Famille Steinhardt." He opened it and removed the card. Two words: "Get out." He turned it over. No name. What was that supposed to mean? "Get out." Was it meant for him? For Ava?

There was a knock at the door. Now what? "Who is it?"

He dropped the envelope and walked down the short hallway to the door. "Coming," he said, putting his eye to the peephole.

He heard a faint click. A millisecond later, the door opened violently, crushing his cheek, stunning him. A big man entered and shoved him against the wall, striking him on the side of the head with an open palm. Another man slipped in behind him, shutting the door and closing the security clasp.

Mac retreated, raising an arm in self-defense. A cosh slammed into his shoulder, paralyzing him, forcing him farther backward and into the living area. The man struck him again, this time on the shoulder. Mac fell to the floor. He observed that there were two men in the room, both dressed in dark suits, both bearded, Middle Eastern to look at. He knew immediately that whoever they were, they had come to kill him. It was because of Ava. She was only half the job. Mac was the other half.

If she knew something, Mac knew something.

The bigger man raised his hand high, maneuvering closer to strike Mac. He hesitated, and in that moment, Mac turned onto his side and swept his foot parallel to the floor. He landed the blow on the assailant's calf, knocking his legs from beneath him. With a cry, the man tumbled backward. His head struck the coffee table, upending it, sending the fruit basket and the pistol onto the floor.

Mac eyed the gun lying a few feet away, beneath an antique escritoire. It was out of reach. He rolled to his left and jumped to his feet as the second man—shorter, stocky, with hooded eyes—leaped at him. The shorter man held a knife in his hand: a push dagger, the stubby, razor-sharp blade protruding from between his knuckles. It was a slashing knife. A weapon to slit a throat, to gut a man, and only after to plunge it in for the kill.

Mac stepped backward, twisting as the man lunged. The blade narrowly missed his torso. Mac aimed a blow to the man's shoulder, propelling himself past him. The attacker stumbled, off balance. Mac spied the statuette of Napoleon. This time he would put it to good use. He snatched it up and backhanded it against the man's skull. The sound was dull and hollow, a baseball bat striking a pumpkin. The man's knees gave out. He crashed into a dresser and collapsed onto the carpet. He lay there shuddering, legs kicking, emitting a terrible gurgling noise. After a moment, he rolled onto his back, and Mac saw that he had stabbed himself through the bottom of his jaw and that the blade had impaled itself in his palate.

A gunshot went off, impossibly loud in the high-ceilinged salon. A vase to Mac's right shattered. Mac threw himself onto the carpet as the tall man straightened himself to his full height. He held Ava's pistol and stepped forward, arm outstretched, the barrel pointed at Mac's chest. Less than ten feet separated them.

The man pulled the trigger. Dry fire. The bullet had jammed. He racked the slide, forcing the bullet to return to the chamber, and fired again. *Click!* Again, the pistol jammed.

Mac yanked the blade from the second man's jaw and buried it into his chest; a wrench of his wrist to puncture the heart, then a violent motion to free it. Blood geysered from the mortal wound. Mac stood, adjusting his grip on the knife, right hand balled into a fist, the three-inch blade extending from between his middle and ring fingers. He advanced on the taller man, who racked and reracked the pistol, vainly trying to clear the jam.

"Who are you?" asked Mac, first in English, then Arabic.

The man stared at Mac with hate, not answering. He spun the pistol in his hand so that he held it by the barrel and could use it to club Mac. He shuffled to his left, toward the center of the salon. Mac mirrored him.

"Tell me what you're doing here! Did you take Ava?"

The man jumped at Mac, wildly swinging the pistol.

Mac dodged it easily, slashing the assailant's wrist as he circled to his left. The man glanced down as blood seeped from the rent in his jacket.

"Talk to me," said Mac. "Who do you work for? The Mukhābarāt? The Revolutionary Guard? Who?" Mac angled his head. "Don't tell me you're Mossad."

"*Alawham,*" he cursed. Vermin.

Definitely not Mossad.

The man bounded closer, holding the pistol at shoulder height. He jumped at Mac and swung the weapon. Mac stepped backward, slashing his outstretched arm. The man cried out, glancing at the new wound. Mac looked into the man's eyes. Both of them knew how this would end.

"Why did they take her?" asked Mac. "What is this about? Tell me who you are."

"Where is it?" said the man. "Give it to me, *habibi*."

"What are you looking for?"

"Give it to me, and I will tell you where she is. We trade."

"Yeah, a trade," said Mac. "First, you tell me where she is, and then I'll give it to you."

The man laughed tiredly. There would be no trade.

"I told him," said the Arab. "*Shafra al Shamun* is bullshit. I knew she didn't have it."

"Have what?" asked Mac. "*Shafra*" in Arabic meant "code" or "book."

A heavy fist pounded at the door. Heated voices. "Monsieur Steinhardt. Open up. Monsieur Steinhardt! S'il vous plaît!"

The hotel staff had heard the gunshot and tracked down its source.

"It's over," said Mac. "You aren't going anywhere. Tell me. Where's Ava?"

"Where do you think she is?" The man smiled bitterly and tossed the pistol at Mac's feet. "We have her."

"Where?"

"Did you really think you could stop us? Just the two of you alone?"

The door to the room opened, banging loudly against the security clasp. "Monsieur Steinhardt, are you all right?"

The Arab's eyes went to the French doors leading to the small balcony.

"No," said Mac.

"Inshallah," said the man beneath his breath, then darted across the salon and jumped the coffee table. Arms raised above his head, he crashed through the French doors. Wood splintered. Glass shattered. The man struck the wrought iron balustrade, flipped head over heels, and disappeared from view. Seconds later, his body struck the pavement four floors below with a mighty clap.

Mac ran to the balcony and peered down at the lifeless body.

"Mr. Steinhardt. Open the door."

Mac surveyed the room. What a mess. He picked up Ava's pistol and secured it in his waistband. He approached the man he'd killed. A check of his jacket yielded a wallet, a hotel key card, and a passport. Kingdom of Saudi Arabia.

Mac looked toward the door. It was too soon for police to have arrived. He imagined it was the hotel's general manager, the head of security, maybe someone from housekeeping. Either way, too many people. Too many questions. There was a dead man in the salon who had quite visibly been murdered. Another man lay on the street directly below the window. Also dead. Mac took stock of his own clothing. Blood stained his shirt and jacket sleeve. A check of his belly and chest to make sure it was not his own. All good.

He wiped off the knife and slid it into his jacket pocket. He foresaw the consequences. He would not be permitted to leave the premises. He would be made to stay. Everyone would be very polite. Mac would explain what had happened, leaving out the most important details, namely his true identity and former profession. Any minute, the police would arrive. First, the local gendarmerie, and thereafter, the Sûreté, the national police. Mac would be questioned. The suite would be searched. More police would arrive . . . then the DGSI, the French FBI. A gushing fire hose of local and federal law enforcement personnel would flood the premises. At some point, Ava's pistol would be discovered. And not just any pistol, a 3D-manufactured nine-millimeter that had been smuggled into the country.

From there, things would get worse. Arrest. A ride to the Préfecture de Police. Detention. Questions about his identity. Was he really Robbie Steinhardt? Was he a true Swiss? Any hopes of keeping under the radar would be scotched. So much for his agreement with the Agency. Don

Baker would not be pleased. Neither would Mac's detractors on the seventh floor.

Far worse than any of that, however, Mac would be prevented from searching for Ava.

Not going to happen.

Mac buttoned his jacket. There, on the carpet next to his shoe, lay the small envelope accompanying the fruit basket.

Two words.

"Get out."

Mac looked toward the window.

Get out.

Good advice.

CHAPTER 6

Orly Airfield
Paris

At Orly Airport, ten miles south of the Paris city center, beneath a bleak sky, a small, energetic crowd congregated on the apron of runway 3A. All eyes gazed intently and with bubbling excitement at a large aircraft descending majestically. The Airbus A330 touched down. A puff of smoke from the tires. The whine of the aircraft's reverse thrusters. A cheer went up from the assembly.

"Princess Anouschka has arrived," announced a tall, strikingly handsome man standing at the head of the crowd.

The man removed his sunglasses and turned to the assembly, waving while offering a dazzling smile for the many phones raised high and directed toward him. His name was Tariq bin Nayan bin Tariq al-Sabah. He was thirty-three years old, the second son of the emir of Qatar's first wife, and, as such, heir to a fortune valued at $500 billion. He had large, friendly brown eyes, fashionably trimmed hair, and a perfectly manicured goatee. His friends, family, and ten million fans on social media knew him better as TNT. No one loved the moniker better than Tariq himself. To underline the point, he wore a black baseball cap with the bold initials embroidered on its brim.

The jet taxied to the end of the runway and turned toward them. The familiar blue-and-gold livery of Qatar Airways came into view.

The Tourists

The aircraft continued toward a large hanger before coming to a halt. Only then did the customs officials open the gate and allow the crowd to rush onto the tarmac proper.

Tariq, however, never rushed. He strolled agreeably. He laughed easily. He chatted amiably. Today, however, the easygoing manner was a facade. Today, he did not feel joyous, buoyant, or relaxed. To the contrary. Today, TNT felt as tense as a coiled spring.

The weekend had arrived.

The weekend that would define the rest of his days.

"Today," he whispered to himself, "my next life begins."

To welcome the princess, he had chosen a Louis Vuitton tracksuit, vintage Air Jordans, and a Richard Mille wristwatch, which he'd purchased that morning in a boutique on the Avenue Matignon for €1.1 million.

TNT was an influencer. Each day he posted pictures of himself across social media, on Instagram, Twitter, and TikTok, among others, showcasing his luxurious lifestyle. There were pictures of him falconing in the desert, deep-sea fishing in the Pacific, shopping on Rodeo Drive, dining in Las Vegas, and dancing in St.-Tropez. Most frequently, however, he liked to post photographs of his fleet of high-performance automobiles: Ferraris, Porsches, Lamborghinis, and, of course, his Bugattis.

He took his responsibility as an influencer seriously. No one, he wanted all to agree, lived a better life than TNT.

A loader drove to the rear of the aircraft and positioned itself below the cargo door. After a moment, the platform began to rise. Handlers in fluorescent orange vests guided four uniform container loads out of the fuselage. TNT and his entourage gathered near as the platform reached the ground.

A compact blond woman dressed in jeans and a corduroy vest accompanied the first container as it was transferred to a truck.

"Good flight?" asked TNT.

"We had some turbulence over Italy," said the woman. She was British, in charge of Anouschka.

"And Anouschka? How did she handle it?"

"She didn't seem to mind," said the woman.

"She's a better flier than I am," said Tariq. "Then again, she's only five."

The shipping container was transferred to a truck and driven into the hangar, where it was rolled down a ramp onto the concrete floor. Handlers swung open the door. Princess Anouschka lolled her head over the gate, looking as majestic as ever.

"There you are," said Tariq, running a hand over the white blaze on her forehead. "I'm sorry about the bumpy ride. Nothing is going to stop you from winning again."

The horse's response was a loud, vigorous snort.

Anouschka was a five-year-old American Thoroughbred, the winner of the Breeders' Cup and five other grade-I races over the past two years. She'd come to Paris to race the autumn season at Longchamp, beginning with the Dauphin Stakes. Her owner was TNT's father, Sheikh Nayan bin Tariq al-Sabah, the richest man in the world.

TNT looked on as the horse was led to the customs desk, where her passport and health records were examined. Even horses had to pass immigration control.

A second Qatar Airways jet landed as the first was being unloaded. It was much smaller, an Airbus A330F, but also a cargo jet. Tariq's heart beat faster just looking at it. He led his retinue out of the hangar. As always, he was accompanied by his security detail. He never went anywhere alone and rarely with fewer than a half dozen people, all male.

He arrived as the first automobile was being unloaded. A Ferrari. The moment it touched ground, he knelt beside it and took a selfie. He did the same next to the Lamborghini and the Porsche. It didn't matter that he was only staying in Paris for the weekend or that he had no intention of driving them. It was his duty to show the world how

The Tourists

a prince from the Gulf traveled. He posted the pics to social media. #BienvenueAParis. #APrincesLife. #LetsRollPeople.

A final car left the fuselage and descended to the tarmac.

"Saving the best for last," he said to the loadmaster.

Tariq ran his hand over the hood of the black-sapphire Bugatti Chiron. It was a two-door sports car, curvy, low to the ground, with fat side vents, a sloping roof, and an aggressive grill. Something between the Batmobile and a Formula 1 racer. The car had an eight-liter, sixteen-cylinder engine yielding 1,480 horsepower. Zero to sixty in 2.4 seconds. Top speed: three hundred miles per hour. It was the fastest production car on planet earth. The price, if you were permitted to buy one: $4 million.

For once, Tariq did not take a photograph. Not today. Not this weekend.

It took a few minutes for the car to be properly unloaded. All the import paperwork had been handled in Doha. It was simply a matter of giving the French customs authorities their copy. He saw no one coming his way. As expected, they were too involved vetting the world-famous Thoroughbred to pay attention to a sports car. He congratulated himself on his astute planning. #brilliant.

"Sir, a moment."

Tariq looked over his shoulder. A customs inspector had come out of his office. An older man with gray hair, clipped mustache, and rigid posture, his uniform just so. One of those. He held a clipboard in one hand and a pen in the other. Evidently, he did not care for racehorses.

"I have the papers here, sir," said TNT, his smile more dazzling than ever.

"We'll need to weigh the vehicle," said the inspector.

"It was weighed in Doha. It's all right here."

The inspector examined the paperwork before handing it back. "Please drive it onto the scales. It will only take a minute."

"Must we?" said Tariq. "I'd love to get back to my horse. It was a difficult flight for her."

"I'm sorry to hear that."

"I knew you'd understand."

The inspector removed his glasses and cleaned them with a handkerchief. "The scales. Now."

Tariq climbed into the Bugatti. The hangar was busy, cargo vehicles entering and exiting, some driving quickly, others moving at a snail's pace. He kept the car in first gear, feathering the accelerator, holding the car in check. With care and precision, he drove it to the south side of the hangar, where the customs officials maintained their offices. He felt a bead of sweat pop on his forehead.

The inspector directed the vehicle onto an industrial scale set into the floor. He wore a name tag on his uniform. *LeClerc.* Of course it was.

"Four thousand five hundred forty-three pounds," said Inspector LeClerc, inking the number onto his forms.

"May I go now?" asked Tariq. "We're headed to the track. Longchamp. The big race is Sunday . . . in case you'd like to come. We have a lovely box."

The inspector perked up. "Champagne?"

"From our own estate," said Tariq. "Domaine du Roi. As much as you'd like. We'll make sure you have a case to take home."

LeClerc was unmoved. "I thought you Muslims didn't drink."

"We don't," said Tariq. "The estate was an investment."

"No thank you," said LeClerc. "I'll be in church Sunday."

"If you reconsider . . ."

"Too much," said Inspector LeClerc, reading from his clipboard.

"Pardon me?"

"Four thousand five hundred thirty pounds," said LeClerc. "Your vehicle weighs thirteen pounds more than when it was weighed in Doha."

"It must be an error," said Tariq. "Thirteen pounds. It's nothing."

"Are you attempting to smuggle narcotics into the country, Mr. Al-Sabah?"

"What?" The question felt like a slap in the face. "No. Of course not."

"Is your vehicle carrying cocaine, fentanyl, or methamphetamine?"

This was too much. The impudence. Tariq had never touched a drug in his life. "It is not," he stated.

It was difficult to keep his emotions in check. If they were in Qatar, he could have the man thrown in jail for such comments. But they weren't in Qatar, he reminded himself. They were in France. In this hangar, Inspector LeClerc was emir.

"Please drive the vehicle to the inspection bay."

Tariq got back into the car. His palms were clammy, his shirt damp, clinging to his back. He was sweating for real now.

LeClerc was already walking toward the bay.

Tariq stared at the man, despising him. He started the engine, gunning it, taking the RPMs to the redline. The roar of the engine was earsplitting, louder still inside the hangar. At the sudden deafening noise, LeClerc jumped out of his shoes. His glasses fell to the ground. He dropped his clipboard and clapped his hands to his ears.

It was then that Tariq knew that the weekend was fated for success and that the Prophet was smiling upon him.

As LeClerc bent to pick up his clipboard, a loader approached from the opposite direction. It was a low, wide vehicle traveling ten miles per hour, less even. Either LeClerc did not see it or the driver of the loader did not see LeClerc. The inspector stumbled as he tried to gather up the clipboard. He took a step into the oncoming vehicle's path. The loader swerved to miss him. Too late. The vehicle struck him dead on. LeClerc hit the ground and slid a short distance on the slick concrete. He lay still, either unconscious or dead.

TNT looked on, but only for a moment.

He eased the Bugatti into first gear and drove slowly—very slowly, indeed—out of the hangar.

CHAPTER 7

Hotel Bristol
Paris

Mac inched his way along one of the narrow ledges that lined each floor and ran horizontally across the facade of the hotel. Wrought iron balconies fronted each room. He shimmied from balcony to balcony until he reached a stout drainpipe. He gave it a tug. It held firm. He transferred his weight onto the pipe and carefully slid down, hand over hand. A young woman spotted him as he made it the last few feet and dropped onto the pavement. She eyed him warily and kept walking.

Mac looked to his right. A fan-shaped glass portico extended over the sidewalk at the hotel entrance. No sign of the doorman. Pedestrians continued to pass, none offering any indication that they'd witnessed his suspicious behavior. Dusk had camouflaged his escape.

Mac turned and walked in the opposite direction. A police car sped past, lights flashing, tires screaming as it halted. Mac refused to look behind him. He turned the corner and decided he needed a taxi. He spotted a green roof light and stepped into the street. The cabbie slowed, rolling down his window.

"Where to?"

"Gare du Nord," said Mac.

The cabbie shook his head, muttering something about going in the opposite direction. He drove off. Mac raised his hand, waiting for another. A second police car approached. Mac retreated to the sidewalk, lowering his head. He continued another block, then turned north, heading up the Rue Cambacérès.

It was nearly dark. Scratch the taxi. Mac ducked into the alcove of a modest apartment building. In quick succession, he powered off his phone and removed the SIM card. It was a homing beacon that recorded his every movement even when the phone was off. He placed the card between his rear molars, crushed it, and spat it out. No, not as good as the langoustines. He was, however, certain no one could track him any further.

Across the street was a branch of Crédit Agricole. He stopped at the ATM and withdrew his daily maximum of €3,000. He had an additional €600 in his wallet. Charge cards were heretofore verboten.

Two blocks further on was a C&A clothing store. He walked in wearing his new gray suit and walked out wearing baggy jeans, Vans, a Paris St.-Germain football jersey, and a baseball cap. Goodbye, Cary Grant. Hello, Kendrick Lamar. All he was missing was a braided gold chain.

He continued heading north and east. He avoided the main thoroughfares, keeping to side streets. He stopped at a corner kiosk and purchased three cheap cell phones—burners—that he could use once or twice, then throw away.

Ahead was a sign for the Métro. He descended a few stairs into the station before he spotted a camera. He pulled up abruptly. How could he be so careless? The Paris Métro, he knew from experience, was bristling with cameras. Cameras at entries. Cameras at turnstiles. Cameras on the platforms. In short, cameras covering every square inch of every station.

Any minute—perhaps even at this very moment—the police would be provided a copy of his passport photograph. It was simply a matter of feeding the image into their database and ordering their facial-recognition software to scrape every camera in the mass transit system—or any other linked network—to come up with a match. They'd find him in ten seconds. Fifteen max.

No, thought Mac, turning right around and running up the stairs, the Métro was out of the question.

Rain began to fall. He dug his hands into his pockets. He spotted a familiar restaurant; a café that he recalled made a decent espresso. He knew this part of town. He'd holed up at a few safe houses nearby—run-down studios or one-bedroom apartments—during an extended job in the city fifteen years ago. Operation Skylark. Mac shuddered at the name.

A French intelligence officer—a captain in the domestic security service—had been found to be passing top secret information to a Middle Eastern prince who maintained a residence in the city. The CIA informed the DGSE—its French counterpart—about the matter. Evidence was proffered. The French, however, refused to act.

Mac didn't know more than that. It wasn't his job to ask. It was his job to follow orders, to carry out instructions to the best of his ability. In this case, those orders required Mac to eliminate the French officer, Captain Guy de Villiers, and to do so in a manner that taught the Saudis and the French a lesson.

In other words, make it ugly. Make it visible. Make it embarrassing.

Mac slowed, recalling the operation. Bad memories. They'd chosen the wrong man for assassination. It was the Saudi who'd been stealing secrets from the Frenchman and passing them on. All this Mac had learned while surveilling them. But no one was going to green-light killing a Saudi—not a member of the ruling family. Mac protested and was overruled. And so, he did his job. He followed his instructions.

It had been a while since he'd dwelled on Skylark or his role in it. Until then, he'd considered himself an instrument of national policy. One of the few chosen to defend his country against all enemies. The sharp end of the stick. It sounded homespun, corny even, but it wasn't naive. Not by a long shot. Mac had enough experience in the dark corners of the world, the murky passageways where the truest intentions of states were laid bare, to know that the world needed him.

Skylark had changed that.

Skylark forced Mac to look in the mirror. It removed the mantle of respectability that cloaked his actions. It disallowed the immunity his country, and his unvarnished belief in it, had granted him and his conscience. After all was said and done, he was a killer. A taker of lives. An executioner. No flag's colors could change that.

CHAPTER 8

27 Avenue Montaigne
Paris

TNT's home in Paris was a grand six-story townhome on the Avenue Montaigne. Built in 1911 and designed, like most buildings in the Golden Triangle—the area bordered by the Champs-Élysées, Avenue George V, and Avenue Montaigne—in the Haussmannian style, it was constructed of *pierre de taille*, or cut stone, with dormer windows, terraces on higher floors, and a mansard roof, the second slope laid at a forty-five-degree angle to reflect sunlight onto the streets below. Marlene Dietrich had lived down the street. St. Laurent's first studio was across the street. One day, TNT wanted the world to say that Prince Tariq al-Sabah had lived here.

He guided the Bugatti through the carriageway and into the inner courtyard. He climbed out and threw the keys to his valet. "Keep it close," he said. "No one gets near it."

"Wash and wax?"

"No," snapped Tariq. "Just watch it."

Security men flanked the rear entrance. One held the door as Tariq entered. "Welcome back, Excellency."

He found his father lounging on the couch in the media room watching television. It was nearly six, which meant his day had not officially begun. He wore boxer shorts and a baggy T-shirt from the last

Rolling Stones tour. His hair fell to his shoulders and was a ratty mess. His stomach, Tariq remarked, was regal.

"Who's screwing who, Papa?" he asked, kissing his father on the cheek.

"Promise me you'll never marry a woman from the OC," said his father, His Excellency Sheikh Nayan bin Tariq al-Sabah, the emir of Qatar.

Tariq studied the screen. A group of blond women argued with one another in a fancy kitchen. "Orange County?" he said. "What happened to New York?"

"They're too tough even for me," said his father.

Tariq laughed dutifully. If it ever got out that the emir of Qatar was addicted to reality television, they would have to abdicate the throne. "Can I get you anything?"

"A beer would be nice. Nonalcoholic."

"Right away." It was their joke. Tariq fetched a Heineken from the fridge. Alcohol content 5 percent.

"And Princess Anouschka?" asked the emir.

"She's fine. Ready to race Sunday."

"Let's hope so," said the emir. "The Dauphin Stakes is the biggest race of the season. We will go together."

"With pleasure."

"My son, the movie star."

"Not movies, Father. Social media."

The emir sat up, his dark, disapproving eyes taking note of his son's attire. "This is how you go out? With a baseball cap?"

"It wasn't an official occasion," said Tariq.

"You're a government minister. Every occasion is official."

"I'm confused," said Tariq. "We wish to modernize our country, yet I am to dress like my ancestors."

"Do you not respect them?"

"It is not a question of respect," said Tariq, "but of presenting a modern image. We are not Bedouin."

"You mean a 'Western' image," said the emir.

Tariq smiled. It was always like this. One step forward, two steps back. The last thing the world needed was another swarthy Arab in a *thobe* and keffiyeh. Alas, it was not an argument he could win.

"May I inquire, how are things proceeding?" he asked, politely. He was referring to a conference being held at that very moment at the Élysée Palace under the utmost secrecy, involving Saudi Arabia, the United Arab Emirates, Qatar, and Israel.

"Talking and talking," said the emir. "That's all the Israelis know how to do."

"And the others?" asked Tariq.

His father struggled to his feet. He was not a tall man, but even here, in his boxer shorts and T-shirt, his hair looking as if he'd just stuck a finger in the electric socket, he exuded dignity and bearing. "Also talking and talking," he said. "I don't know who is worse, the Saudis, the Emiratis, or the Israelis. Sooner or later, it appears, we will have an agreement."

"An agreement? Inshallah," said Tariq, "you will bring peace to the region once and for all."

"Inshallah," said his father. "But it is your brother Jabr's doing."

"We are all proud of him," said Tariq.

"There is to be a ceremony," said the emir. "Sunday, it seems. You will attend, of course. And dressed properly. But shh! No one is to know."

"Of course." Tariq patted his father's shoulder while nodding obediently. "Not a whisper to anyone."

"Your brother took your suggestion to offer the French president our champagne as a gesture of goodwill between our countries."

"And?"

"The French president agreed."

"A wise man," said Tariq.

Last year, the family had purchased the Domaine du Roi, one of the oldest and most exclusive producers of champagne in France. The sale had caused a sensation; one of France's crown jewels in the hands of a Middle Eastern kingdom.

"I'll drive out in the morning and get it myself," said Tariq.

"The '68, if they have it," said the emir. "But don't say I told you. Your brother wishes to make the announcement himself. The agreement is to be his victory."

"You have my word," said Tariq.

The emir touched his son's cheeks. "One day you will serve him."

"Who?"

"Your brother Jabr," said the emir. "When he assumes the throne. He will need your counsel, especially on smaller matters."

TNT fought to keep his tone pleasant. The taste of his bile was insufferable. It would be a cold day in Doha when he served as a minister in his brother's government. "Until then, Father, my devotion is to you."

"And to your fancy cars!"

Tariq laughed. "This is true. May I ask where the ceremony will take place?"

"There is only one palace in Paris fit for four rulers," said the emir.

Tariq raised his eyebrows in appreciation. He knew better than to say the name aloud. "I'm proud of you, Father. I know this wasn't easy for you."

"Times change," said the emir, then he took a long swig of beer and burped loudly. "We must change with them. Jabr has convinced me of that."

Tariq kissed his father on both cheeks and bowed his head, then took his leave.

Yes, he agreed, running up the stairs to his suite. Times change. But Tariq did not want to change with them. Not at all. It was his job to stop them from changing.

He had until Sunday.

God willing.

CHAPTER 9

Goutte d'Or
Paris

Mac Dekker had left Paris. He had left France. He had left the European continent altogether.

Walking along the Rue Custine on this chill, drizzly evening, he was in the heart of French West Africa. Senegal, Côte d'Ivoire, Benin. Take your pick. The farther away, the better.

Mac passed a boutique selling dashikis, an open-air market offering fried okra, and a street vendor hawking loose cigarettes. Music poured from storefronts. Fela Kuti, Sunny Adé, others Mac didn't recognize.

The neighborhood of the Goutte d'Or was situated in the eighteenth arrondissement, three miles from the Hotel Bristol, a little east of Montmartre and a stone's throw from Porte de la Chapelle. It was home to many sub-Saharan immigrants who had come to France from the countries it had once colonized. It was, in his estimation, the last place the police would search for a wealthy Swiss tourist wanted for murder.

The restaurant was named La Goulue—not African exactly, but it would do. He took a table in the back and ordered a Gazelle lager, chicken tagine and dirty rice, and a bowl of plantain chips. Waiting for his food, he set up a burner phone. He dialed a number in Germany—Berlin area code. The call went directly to voicemail. A woman asked him to leave a name and number. Her voice was about as welcoming as Ava's. Then again, they were in the same business.

"Hey, Jaycee, it's me," said Mac, as coolly as he could manage. "Call me on this number. No hurry. Everything's copacetic."

The beer arrived. Mac gulped half of it down, hand cupped around the cold bottle. The phone rang. He had it to his ear in a flash. "Hey."

"Give me ten," said his daughter, Jane McCall, acting chief of station, Berlin, for the Central Intelligence Agency. "This a good number?"

"For a little bit," said Mac.

"Jesus."

The call ended.

Mac finished his beer and ordered another. His food arrived. He ate quickly, not knowing where and when he'd have time for another meal. He drained his second beer. The phone rang the moment he set down the bottle.

"Jaycee."

"Dad," said his daughter, Jane McCall. "'Copacetic,' really?"

It was their code word. "Copacetic," not meaning "all in order, nothing's the matter," but the opposite: "Everything is beyond f-ed up." The worst of all possible situations.

"They've got Ava," said Mac.

"What? Who?" asked Jane.

"I don't know for sure. Maybe the Saudis. Maybe someone else."

"Jesus, Dad. I thought this was supposed to be a romantic getaway."

"I thought so too."

"Did you pop the—" said Jane, then: "Dad, I'm sorry. I wasn't thinking. Please. Okay, go ahead. I'm listening."

It hit Mac at once. The tight throat. The warmth in his chest. The welling of his eyes. Everything had happened so quickly, so unexpectedly, so violently, he hadn't had a moment to process it. Ava was missing. His Ava. The woman he loved more than any other. His everything. In his world—*in their world*—"missing" meant one thing. "Give me a second," he said.

"You're scaring me."

"Honey, I'm scared too."

"I'm here, Dad. It's going to be okay. We'll get her back. Just calm down."

Mac wiped at his eyes. "That is not what you're supposed to say."

Jane laughed. "I think I was the one who taught you that."

"Yes, you were."

"Man up, Dekker," said Jane, with authority. "It's not going to get any easier just looking at it."

"That's my line," said Mac, laughing despite himself. He noticed a few diners eyeing him—the old guy with tears streaming down his face. He lowered his head.

"Will loved it," said Jane. "It was his line too."

The mention of his son, Will, bucked up Mac's spirits. His son, who had sacrificed his life to expose a terrorist plot to kill thousands. A hero.

"Here's what went down," said Mac, gathering himself. He needed ten minutes to narrate the afternoon's events. Ava's abduction from the restaurant, his futile search for her and the earring he found on the carpet, the Saudis breaking into his room with the intent of killing him, and his subsequent escape.

"You have their names?"

"Just one," said Mac, consulting the passport. "Abdul Al-Hassan. Born 1988 in Buraydah."

"Buraydah," said Jane. "Really?"

"That's what it says. Why?"

"That's where they all came from," said Jane. "I mean originally, like in 1850."

"Who?"

"The Al Saud, the family that's ruled the Kingdom of Saudi Arabia for the past hundred years or so."

"These guys weren't royalty," said Mac. "I can tell you that much."

"Doesn't matter. If that's his tribal home, he's one of them. Old Wahhabi."

It was not what Mac wanted to hear. Old Wahhabi meant extremism, and extremism was never good. "And you know this how?"

"I spent two years in Riyadh," said Jane. "During your sabbatical."

"Ha ha," said Mac. "Very funny."

"I'll check him out," said Jane.

"Carefully," said Mac. "Remember what Don Baker told me. I'm not allowed to ask you to fix any parking tickets."

"I can manage. So, what now? Who are the police looking for? Robbie Steinhardt or Mac Dekker?"

"Steinhardt."

"Will your identity hold up?"

"It should. No reason to do a deep dive unless they catch me."

"It's going to come up on our radar," said Jane. "Two dead Saudis in a Paris hotel room. Front-page news on every analyst's screen."

"I'll worry about that later," said Mac. "Right now, I need a bolt-hole."

"I figured," said Jane. "Tout de suite, I presume."

"Ten minutes ago," said Mac.

"Where are you now?"

"At a Senegalese restaurant in the eighteenth."

"You must stick out like a sore thumb," said Jane.

"Actually, I feel safer here than on the street."

"I need some time," said Jane. "Can't leave any tracks that might piss off your old buddies in Langley."

"Hurry," said Mac.

"And you have no idea what this is all about?"

"None," said Mac, then: "Maybe one thing. The guy said something about a code of Shamun. *Shafra al Shamun.* My Arabic's lousy. I didn't quite get it."

"'Shamun' is 'Samson,'" said Jane. "Like from the Bible. Samson and Delilah."

"'Code of Samson,'" said Mac. "What does that mean? I probably misheard."

"Let me think about it," said Jane. "Maybe it will ring a bell. Can you sit tight for an hour?"

"Think so," said Mac.

"Dad, I need to ask. You have something planned, don't you?"

"An idea," said Mac. "Something went down in that restaurant. Ava didn't just vanish. Someone took her. It's gotta be on their cameras."

"You're going back?"

"Wouldn't you?"

"No, Dad, I wouldn't," said Jane. "But I'd send some guy like you. Be careful."

"Just check on the Saudis," said Mac. "And, Jane, let me know if you have a show running in Paris."

"We always have a show running in Paris."

"You know what I mean," said Mac. "It could be with our brethren in Tel Aviv."

"Mossad? Why do you ask?"

"Come on, Jane. You know Ava. This didn't happen out of the blue."

"I guess it didn't."

"But, Jane, softly."

"Church mice," said Jane.

"Church mice," said Mac. "That's it for now. Gotta run."

"Dad," she said, before he could hang up.

"Yeah, Jaycee."

"I love you."

"Love you too."

CHAPTER 10

Langley, Virginia, United States

"It was my understanding that you advised Mac Dekker to keep his head down," said Eliza Porter Elkins.

"I did," said Don Baker.

It was 4:00 p.m. on the East Coast of the United States. Baker sat in a chair across the desk from the CIA's newly appointed associate deputy director of operations. Rain pounded the windows of the seventh-floor office, hard enough to obscure the view of the Northern Virginia countryside. Baker resented being here. He was not responsible for Mac Dekker. Not then and not now. It was a case of guilt by association.

Elkins licked her finger and turned a page in the dossier open on her desk. "Two Saudi diplomats killed at the Hotel Bristol," she said. "One defenestrated, the other stabbed to death." She glanced up, amused. "I didn't know people still used that word."

"Ma'am?"

"'Defenestrated.' It means 'thrown from a window.'"

"I figured," said Baker. "*Fenestra* is Latin for 'window.'"

"Very good, Mr. Baker," said Elkins, graciously. "I'm impressed."

"Benefits of a Catholic school education," said Baker. "I have the scars to prove it. And 'Don,' please."

"Very good, Don. Sorry about those scars."

Elkins smiled. She was a pretty lady, very pretty and very much a lady. He guessed she was sixty, though given her looks that was hard to believe. She was tall and blond and curvaceous, if that was a word you were allowed to use anymore. She was dressed in a dark skirt and a blazer with a cream-colored V-neck blouse that dove a little low for government standards. Not that anyone would ever say anything. Not to Eliza Porter Elkins. Not to a woman whose grandfather helped found not only the OSS but also the Agency itself. Not to a woman whose father was, at age eighty-five, the sitting senior senator from West Virginia. Not to a woman whose family owned exactly 51 percent of the land of that same state, including most of its coal mines.

The woman was impressive in her own right. Annapolis honor graduate. Helicopter pilot. She'd come to the Agency after running Consular Affairs at the State Department and before that serving as deputy director of the DIA, the Defense Intelligence Agency. Three weeks ago, she'd stepped into her new office on the seventh floor of the CIA headquarters.

"Robert Steinhardt . . . that's what he goes by?" she asked. "I'm sorry, I'm only just getting up to speed on all this."

"For the past nine years or so," said Baker. It was his first one-on-one interaction with his new boss, and he was eager to oblige. "I told him he should keep it."

"Keep the name," said Elkins. "And lay low."

"Exactly."

"He took the money, correct?" said Elkins, perusing the dossier. "A million and a half."

"We pretty much ruined his life," said Baker. "We had a bounty on his head for nine years, and that's after we failed to take him out in Beirut."

"Excuse me," she said. "'Failed to take him out?' That's not official diplomatic language."

"Red-flagged him," said Baker.

The blue eyes narrowed. A toss of the head. Her long, manicured fingers played with the gold chains around her neck. He was a sucker for fire-engine red nail polish.

"We, uh, tried to kill him," said Baker. "We missed."

"Thank you, Don. I appreciate the clarification." She closed the dossier and gave him her full attention. "Some say we shouldn't have rescinded the order."

"He was innocent," said Baker. "True blue. We know that now."

"You're sure? You, Don?"

"I am."

"Good," said Elkins, happy to be on solid ground. "I can rely on that."

"You can."

Elkins rose from her desk and walked to a sideboard. An array of crystal decanters stood filled with various amber-colored spirits. She consulted her watch. "Four p.m.," she said. "Are we allowed? I'm feeling a little naughty. Bourbon all right?" She picked up one of the decanters and he noticed it was only a quarter full. "Say when."

"That's fine," said Baker when she'd poured two fingers.

Elkins emptied the rest into her own glass. She handed him his, then sat down on the visitors' couch. She had lovely legs. "How long do you think it will hold up?" she asked. "The whole Swiss-identity thing."

"It's lasted this long," said Baker. "They'd have to catch him first. After that I don't know."

"Is the passport real?"

"Real enough."

"From our shop, or did he work a deal with the Swiss?" asked Elkins. She shook her head and said wistfully: "He can be quite persuasive."

"You know him?" asked Baker. News to him.

"I've heard," said Elkins, fast as a whip.

"I guess he handled it himself," said Baker. "He has his own contacts."

"'He' being Mac Dekker?"

"That's correct," said Baker.

Elkins sipped and nodded. "Just wanted to make sure that the Robert Steinhardt who the entire Paris police department is looking for in connection with the murder of two Saudi nationals is, in fact, Mackenzie David Dekker. Mac for short."

"It's him," said Baker. "It's our Mac."

"Your Mac," said Elkins. "I only just got here." She finished her drink. "Have you talked to him lately?"

"You mean after I visited him in Switzerland? No."

"You're sure," said Elkins, looking at him from beneath her brow. Gone was the polite, self-effacing banter. This was business now. "We can find out."

"I'm sure," said Baker, holding his ground.

"I'd like you to tell me, then, Don, as Mac's oldest friend—his champion, I'm made to believe—exactly what you believe is going on?"

"I can't say offhand. But if Mac killed anyone, he had a reason. I'd say he was provoked."

"Provoked? Out of the blue . . . just like that. In his hotel room." She pulled a face. She wasn't having it. "Remind me, do the Saudis have anything against the Swiss we don't know about?"

Baker shook his head. "Not that I'm aware of."

"Me neither," said Elkins. "Here's the rub: When a coin drops with Saudi Arabia on one side, guess who I see on the other?"

"Israel," said Baker.

"Ten points, Don. Israel. Our staunchest ally in the Middle East; some say the fifty-first state. You see, if the report is correct, it says that Mr. Dekker was at the hotel with a woman."

"Ava Attal."

"Ava Marie Attal. Full colonel. Mossad. Before that, Shin Bet. Tell me about her."

"That's all I know," said Baker. "She was at the Farm a while back for a refresher course. I met her once, maybe twice. That's it."

"What does she look like? Attractive?"

"Depends on your type."

"Is she yours?"

"She's taller than me," said Baker.

Elkins gave him a look. Everyone was taller than Don Baker.

"Dark hair," he continued. "Tall. Athletic. Smart. Motivated. She was banged up pretty badly last year. Mac told me she was concentrating on getting better."

Elkins put her elbows on the table, fingers steepled. "Question: Was she working with Dekker when all that trouble transpired ten years ago? When one of your operatives double-crossed him . . . *double-crossed us* . . . and went over to the Russians?"

Baker nodded.

"And she helped him foil an attack in Ukraine last year?"

"She was instrumental in uncovering the SVR plot against Kyiv, yes."

"So, they're thick as thieves," said Elkins.

"They love each other," said Baker. "If that's what you're driving at. They've been living together at his place in the Alps for a year. They're bringing up his granddaughter as their own. She's four."

Elkins was no longer listening. She sat, staring out the window, looking as if she were far, far away.

"Ms. Elkins?" said Baker.

"A child," she muttered beneath her breath. "At that age?"

"Eliza? Ma'am?"

Finally, she looked back at Baker. The color had drained from her face. "Blanched" was the word. "Blanched" from *blanchir*. French. To whiten. Something else Baker had picked up in high school. She looked ten years older.

"I've got to be honest, Don," she said. "I'm worried. Two Saudis dead at a Paris hotel. Mac Dekker on the run. Ava Attal unaccounted for. And you believe it was all just some accident. A coincidence, perhaps."

"I didn't say that," Baker protested. "But I know Mac. He said he was out of the game. I believe him."

"I guess he forgot to tell the Saudis," said Elkins. "Or were they after her . . . *Attal*?"

Baker said he didn't know. Elkins asked if he'd reached out to Dekker. He replied that he'd tried the only number he had and that it hadn't gone through. She didn't appear to like his answer.

"Is it your opinion," she asked, "that we should just sit on our hands and wait to see how things play out?"

"I say wait a little longer," answered Baker. "He may contact us. Tell us what's up."

"Would you?"

Baker shook his head reluctantly. "Give me some time," he said. "We have plenty of resources in Paris. Let me make some calls."

"Time is one thing we haven't got," said Elkins. "Not this weekend."

"Oh? What's going down in Paris?" asked Baker, sitting up straighter. Western Europe was his territory. He didn't appreciate being kept in the dark. "Nothing has come across my desk."

"For once someone can keep a secret," said Elkins.

"Eliza, do we have a play running in Paris?"

"*We* don't have anything running there," said Elkins.

"Who does? The Saudis?"

"Look who's the clever boots." The color had come back to her face, and with it, her convivial manner. "Don Baker. Winner of the Latin prize, scars and all. Whatever 'it' is—and I'm neither confirming nor denying—we need to make sure that neither Mac Dekker nor Ava Attal come within a country mile of it. Ironclad. Understand?"

"You're not thinking . . . ?"

"What? Oh, that?" Elkins laughed, eyes saying he was crazy. "That kind of thing went out with Colby and Webster, the old gunslingers. No, I have something else in mind. Pack your bags, Don. You and I are both of us going to Paris. We're going to track down Mac Dekker and find out for ourselves just what the hell is going on."

"Tonight?" asked Baker.

"We'll swing by your place and pick you up," said Elkins. "How does an hour sound?"

"I'll be ready." Baker smiled compliantly, but beneath the smile lay a hard-earned mantle of distrust. "One thing, Eliza."

"What is it?"

"Remember . . . he's still Mac Dekker."

"Is that a threat, Don?" said Elkins.

"It's whatever you want it to be," said Baker.

CHAPTER 11

Goutte d'Or
Paris

Mac Dekker had one phone call yet to make. A call he couldn't miss.

"Is this my little sweetheart?"

"Hello, Papa," said Katya Dekker, his four-year-old granddaughter. "It snowed today."

"Did it?"

"The backyard looks like a giant duvet."

"A duvet? My, that must be something."

"Fritz loves it. He didn't want to come inside, even for his dinner."

Fritz was their Bernese mountain dog. They'd brought him into the family soon after Katya arrived, hoping that he would help her cope with her parents' deaths.

"How is Martin?" asked Mac.

"He made me *fir-fir* for breakfast."

"What's that?"

"It's the porridge he ate when he was little. It has goat's milk."

Martin was a young man with whom he'd worked the past two summers on the alp. He was an Eritrean refugee who'd come to Switzerland as a boy. He'd earned a university degree in agriculture and taken a job managing a dairy high on the hills above Zinal. Good people. Mac had asked if Katya might stay with his family while he and Ava visited Paris.

"Did you like it?" he asked.

"I prefer an omelet."

"That's very grown up of you," said Mac.

"Why aren't you FaceTiming?" asked Katya.

"My phone isn't working right now."

"Where's Ava?"

"She's in the other room," said Mac.

"Papa, are you sure she can't hear us?" asked Katya, whispering.

"Positive, angel. What is it?"

"Did you ask her yet?"

"Ask her?"

"Yes. You know," said Katya. "If she wants to be my mommy?"

"How do you know about that?"

"You told Martin that it was a special trip," Katya continued, and he could imagine her holding the phone with both hands close to her face. "You said that you had something important to ask."

"Did I?"

"I saw the ring," she continued breathlessly. "You were keeping it in the bathroom next to the floss. I'm not stupid, you know?"

"On the contrary," said Mac. "Right now, we have to keep this our secret. When I ask, you'll be the first to find out."

"She promised to bring me back a doll," said Katya. "Mommies only bring back those for their daughters."

"How do you know that?" asked Mac.

"Because that's what my mommy always brought me when she'd been away."

Mac smiled, if only to hold back his emotions. "Katya, I have to go now."

"Are you off for a lovely dinner?"

"Yes," said Mac, in awe as usual over her vivid and far-too-mature imagination. "And we will raise a toast to you."

"Don't worry," said Katya. "I know she'll say yes."

"Are you sure?"

"Ava doesn't have another daughter," said Katya. "She needs me."

CHAPTER 12

Langley, Virginia

"Yes, Don, I do know Mac Dekker."

Eliza Porter Elkins opened a fresh bottle of Maker's Mark and poured it into the decanter. She was drinking too much these days, but she needed someone to talk to, and she was her own best friend. No one else was as witty, perceptive, or honest. She refilled her glass, then stood at the window and peered out at the rolling countryside. The leaves were turning. Another month and the trees would be bare.

Eliza buzzed her assistant. "Hold all calls."

She flicked a switch on her table lamp, activating sound baffles that threw off white noise, making it impossible for any unfriendly parties to listen in. She took a cell phone from the bottom drawer of her desk. It was a stealth special, modified for just this kind of thing. Untraceable. No number. No GPS. The equivalent of digital scrambled eggs.

She hit speed dial and was connected to a nameless office in the bowels of the NCTC, the National Counterterrorism Center, down the road in McLean. She identified herself, then asked to speak with their European substation, located (conveniently) in Paris, France.

"One moment, please, while we connect you."

"Thank you," said Eliza, before enjoying a long, slow sip of bourbon.

In her mind's eye, she wasn't gazing out upon a bleak, rainy autumn landscape. She was staring up at the noonday sun near Baghdad, thinking she'd never seen a light so harsh and unforgiving. March 2006. She was forty, recently retired from the US Navy, a lieutenant commander with seventeen years in as a helicopter pilot. Her bird was a Sikorsky Sea King, and later the MH-60 Sierra, combat search and rescue. It was her first trip overseas out of uniform. She was eager to do a good job. No, not just a good job; an exemplary job.

Eliza had come to the Middle East previously as a member of the Iraq Survey Group, or ISG. The ISG's mandate was to search Iraq top to bottom for proof that Saddam Hussein was indeed manufacturing weapons of mass destruction. For years now, the country had heard rumors of chemical weapons and yellowcake and secret laboratories where the Iraqi strongman was expending millions of dollars to build nuclear weapons that might be used against the West. Not just rumors. There was hard intelligence. Irrefutable fact. A casus belli.

But two years after the invasion, nothing had been found. Perhaps a few rockets tipped with mustard gas left over from the Iran–Iraq War, twenty years earlier. Maybe a few tins of sarin poison gas, just enough to foul a small village's water supply. But that was all. No centrifuges. No enriched uranium. No sophisticated laboratories. Nada.

A report had been written—"The Duelfer Report," it was called—and presented to Congress. Depending on which side of the aisle one sat, the report was viewed either as a humiliating admission of failure on the part of the teams searching the country or evidence of gross misrepresentation on the part of the administration. In the end, however, pretty much everyone agreed. The government had flat-out lied to the American people.

Eliza had traveled six thousand miles across the globe to rewrite that narrative. Her trip was a last-ditch effort to repair the president's reputation; a personal mission on his behalf, made at the request of Eliza's father, Senator Davis Porter Elkins, ranking member of Congress and chairman of the Armed Services Committee.

"What is this place?" asked Eliza, staring up a tall, ugly concrete wall topped with concertina wire.

"Abu Ghraib," said her official escort and bodyguard, Mackenzie "Call me Mac" Dekker, a retired marine major, now with the Central Intelligence Agency.

"I thought it was bigger," she said.

"Big enough, I guess," said Dekker.

By then, everyone knew about Abu Ghraib and the serial mistreatment of Iraqi prisoners of war. Even so, the place was worse than she expected. The smell, the confines, the creepy feeling of paranoia once inside the complex. It was as if the evil of Saddam's regime had seeped into the prison walls and possessed everyone who set foot inside.

Eliza and Dekker were shown to an interrogation room. The man she had flown six thousand miles to see was seventy, frail after a month in prison, his skin grayer than the few strands of his hair that remained. Officially, he was Dr. Mahmoud Shah, by his own account a professor of physics at Baghdad University. Back in DC, the senator and his minions called him "the Savior."

"It is a container for radioactive materials," said Dr. Shah fervently, recognizing Eliza for what she was. His last chance. "From Hussein's most advanced government laboratory."

The so-called container sat on the table between them. It resembled a cocktail shaker, stainless steel with a bulky cap, maybe twenty-five inches tall, and more than anything else, amateurish.

"What do you think?" she asked Dekker, who'd shepherded teams from the ISG a year earlier.

"Who found this?" said Dekker. He was tall and broad, tan as a saddle and as weathered. Those blue eyes, the dark, close-cropped hair, the way he sat, owning the table. He wore a gray short-sleeved shirt over his Kevlar vest, and dark trousers and mesh desert boots. He had a pistol strapped to a web belt, and he wore it low on his thigh like a gunslinger.

"He tried to sell it to an undersecretary at the embassy," said Eliza.

"For real?" said Dekker. "This?"

Eliza nodded, not meeting his gaze. It was imperative to maintain a professional distance. It was imperative not to acknowledge the slipshod contraption on the desk. It was imperative not to betray a hint of desperation. It was imperative that "the savior" be believed.

"Why was he arrested?" asked Dekker.

"Suspicion of involvement in a government program to manufacture weapons of mass destruction."

"He's your smoking gun," said Dekker, not quite loudly enough for public consumption.

"Excuse me," said Eliza, angered by his impudence. Dekker was her escort, a newly minted field grade, barely more than a flunky. She was Eliza Porter Elkins, emissary of the president of the United States.

"I don't believe that this came from a government lab," said Dekker.

"We have no way of knowing where it came from," said Eliza. "It might have been an early prototype."

"So there might be more where this came from," suggested Dekker.

"That would not be an unreasonable conclusion," said Eliza.

Dekker laughed derisively. "I call bullshit," he said.

"What do you mean?" she demanded.

"On this," said Dekker. "Whatever it is." He reached out and tapped the metal container with his fingernail. "I used to take apart engines with my dad. He had a sixty-eight Camaro SS. Red with a white racing stripe down the hood. Three hundred fifty cubic inches. V8. This feels like it's made from the carburetor. And this from a radiator . . . or something like that. Go ahead. See for yourself."

"We have to take every possibility seriously," said Eliza.

"What happens to him?" asked Dekker, nodding at the old Iraqi.

"What do you mean?"

"If you decide the device is real," said Mac. "Which it isn't."

"Not up to me," said Eliza. "And we haven't made an official determination."

"You're not going to send him to GITMO, are you? He's a con man. He wanted a little money. Isn't that right?"

Shah shook his head violently and let loose a loud, passionate screed in Arabic.

At which point, Mac picked up the "suspected radioactive container sourced from one of Saddam Hussein's most advanced engineering laboratories" and pulled it apart.

"Stop," said Eliza, rising from her chair. "That's government property."

"It's not lead," said Dekker, looking inside the cylindrical metal flask. "The first thing you need if you want to transport radioactive material is lead. And not just a quarter inch thick. If anyone put five grams of uranium-235 inside this, it would burn its way through in ten minutes."

"I didn't know you possessed expertise in nuclear physics," said Eliza.

"I've helped you guys before," said Mac. "You didn't find anything then; you're not going to find it now."

They left the prison thirty minutes later, Eliza with the promise to return the next day to complete her interrogation. Eliza most certainly would not bring Dekker back with her. There were plenty of other Agency employees capable of driving with her to the prison and, once there, of keeping their mouths shut.

But the story didn't end there.

On the drive back to the Green Zone, Eliza asked that they pass through Sadr City, the Baghdad suburb ruled by the Mahdi Army, the Shia sect led by a duplicitous cleric, Muqtada al-Sadr.

"Not a good idea," said Dekker, speaking to her from the front seat of their armored Chevrolet Suburban. "We're not welcome."

"I'm told the city has been pacified," said Eliza. "The senator would appreciate an on-the-ground report."

"A sitrep?"

"Precisely."

"Suit yourself." Dekker told the driver to take them through Sadr City. Ten minutes later, they left the highway and entered Baghdad proper.

"Sadr wants to rule the country," Dekker said. "He doesn't respect the Americans. He doesn't listen to the Sunnis. The only people he pretends to like are the Iranians, and secretly he hates them too."

Sadr City was an occupied ruin, buildings gutted from shellfire, roads pulverized, the whole place a wasteland.

The Tourists

"This is their Wisconsin and M," he went on, pointing out various landmarks. A restaurant, a café, a ruined movie theater.

"What can we do to win them over?" Eliza asked.

"Leave," said Dekker.

It was at that moment that the IED exploded. The lead vehicle was destroyed, blown high into the sky. A direct hit. Eliza's vehicle ground to a halt. Debris and fire rained down. There were two vehicles behind them, and she had a clear memory of them reversing at speed and rounding a corner out of view and her thinking, "Oh my God. We're dead."

Eliza's vehicle couldn't reverse. Its engine was damaged, and the driver couldn't get it started, no matter how much he swore. She stared out the window, too dazed to be frightened. A dozen figures lurked in doorways and on rooftops, firing at them. Striking the armored vehicle, the bullets sounded like a xylophone played by a drunk musician.

"Stay put," said Dekker.

Like that he was out the door, M4 assault rifle at his shoulder. Aim and fire. Aim and fire. She watched as he shot the men dead one after another, never flinching as bullets struck the vehicle behind him, the ground at his feet, and seemingly passed through his hair. It was over in a minute. Either the bad guys were all dead or they'd run away. By the time Mac opened the door to sound the all clear, a Bell Jet Ranger was hovering above them, blasting at the surrounding rooftops.

"I didn't know it was so loud," Eliza said to him at dinner that evening. "My ears are still ringing."

They were sitting at a squalid hole-in-the-wall inside the Green Zone, one everyone called "the Baghdad Country Club." There was a stereo powered by someone's iPod. A few tables. Fake shrubbery. And too many mercenaries to count—"private contractors" was their formal title—most of them three sheets to the wind.

Eliza had no recollection of what they ate. Nor could she recall what they talked about, except that it wasn't about Dr. Shah or the eight-hundred-pound gorilla in the room. It was all a haze. She was married and, she admitted, unhappily so. He was divorced, disillusioned with the war and subsequent occupation. Two wayward souls. A war zone. A scrape with death. A bottle of arrack, the local firewater. He was, she decided, the bravest man she'd ever met. Nature took its course.

Later, she wondered if she'd given herself to him out of desire, or if it was something else, something less genuine, a kind of payment or inducement. You can have me, but at a price. And the price was Dr. Shah and his slipshod contraption. The laughable container of radioactive materials. Keep your mouth shut.

Either way, it hadn't worked. A week later Mac Dekker had betrayed her. Eliza Porter Elkins never forgot it.

"NCTC Paris," said a bland male voice.

"Intervention," said Eliza.

"One moment."

"Intervention," said a new robotic voice, not American, but hard to place. Spanish? Italian? Greek?

"We have a liability outstanding," said Eliza. "Name: Mackenzie David Dekker. American citizen. Retired company asset. A.k.a. Robert Steinhardt. Swiss national. Last seen in Paris today at four p.m. at or near the Hotel Bristol."

She set forth the details of the assignment, including Dekker's description as well as the instructions on apprehension and captivity. She ended with two words: "red flag."

There was a pause. Static on the line. Someone was being patched in. A supervisor.

"This is Intervention, level two," came a new voice, older, seasoned. "Please confirm formal issuance of a red flag on Mackenzie David Dekker."

Eliza hesitated. Past was past. Present was present. And now here she was with Mac Dekker's life in her hands.

Karma.

"Please confirm," the older voice repeated. "Ma'am? Ma'am? Are you there?"

CHAPTER 13

27 Avenue Montaigne
Paris

Dahlia was waiting for him in the drawing room on the sixth floor.

"A sight for sore eyes," said Tariq.

"As pretty as a princess?"

"Far prettier," he said, taking her into his arms. "And not so hairy. Shall I call you Princess Dahlia?"

"Hmm, Princess Dahlia," she said. "I like the sound of that."

"Tell me, princess, do you prefer hay or oats with your champagne?"

"Caviar. The real stuff. Beluga from the Caspian Sea."

"You have royal tastes," said Tariq.

"Then I've come to the right place," said Dahlia.

Tariq kissed her. She smelled of vanilla and sandalwood. Maybe one day she would be a princess, indeed.

Her name was Dahlia Shugar. She was twenty-eight, tall and blond, the dyed variety, with olive skin, hazel eyes, and a womanly figure. They'd met at the Bvlgari boutique in Beverly Hills earlier that summer. She wasn't a shop girl. She was the store manager. He'd bought a ruby ring, a diamond Serpenti necklace, and a forty-carat diamond tiara. The bill was something over $4 million. She had not been impressed. His request for a date was politely refused. He returned an hour later with a mocha latte and a red rose. Only then did she agree to have dinner with him. Never once did she ask for whom he'd bought the jewelry.

They'd spent the night in his suite at the Beverly Wilshire Hotel. When she slipped from his bed at dawn, he asked himself if he was in love. To his amazement, he decided he wasn't sure. He certainly couldn't say no. For Tariq, that was close enough.

And so, he ordered his people to look into her. Nothing serious. A body frisk, so to speak. They reported that Dahlia had graduated from UCLA with honors, that she'd lived at her present address for three years, that she held $38,560 in her bank account, and that her parents were, as she'd stated, from Italy and Lebanon, the father Catholic, the mother Maronite, both deceased. She wasn't Muslim; then again, she wasn't a Jew.

A woman who told the truth. Refreshing.

"Come sit with me." Tariq picked up the crocodile Birkin bag from the couch and placed it on the table.

"I'm not sure I should," said Dahlia, eyeing him suspiciously.

"The prince commands it." He patted the couch, and Dahlia sat next to him. He kissed her neck. "Look, I have a picture to show you. From lunch."

"I don't want to see the langoustines," said Dahlia. "I hate food pics."

"It's of us," said TNT, handing her his phone. "Two hundred thousand likes on TikTok already."

Dahlia studied the selfie of the two of them smiling at their table at the restaurant earlier that afternoon. "Very nice," she said.

"Is that all?" he asked.

"You look handsome," said Dahlia.

"Check the background," said Tariq, pointing to a dark-haired woman seated at a table for two, next to the window, a man across from her with his back to the camera. "It's her. She didn't even know it."

Dahlia regarded the woman. "Yes, I see."

He kissed her again, placing a hand on her thigh, squeezing her firm flesh. "How do you feel? Is everything all right?"

"Fine."

"Certain?" he asked.

"A bit shaken, to be honest," said Dahlia. "I've never done anything like that."

"It's to be expected." He slipped his finger beneath her undergarment and touched soft, moist skin.

"Please," she said, arching her back. "Stop."

"And you are still committed?" he asked.

"Of course," she whispered. "More than ever."

"I know you are," said Tariq, feeling himself stir.

"Please," said Dahlia. "Someone may come. Stop."

"Are you sure?" he whispered, kissing her, biting her lip.

"Yes . . . no."

He slid a finger inside her. "Which one?"

Dahlia moaned, her body trembling. She placed a hand on him. "Damn you."

"Get on the floor," he said.

"Here?"

"On the floor."

"But the door is open—"

"Do as I say."

"Yes, Tariq." Dahlia slid off the couch and lay down on the carpet. Tariq pulled down her skirt and her undergarments. "Yes, my prince."

"Yes, my prince," she said, with respect, staring him in the eye.

Tariq unbuckled his belt and lowered his pants to his ankles. He looked upon her. She had not groomed, as he'd requested. The sight enflamed him. With care, he entered her. She pulled his face to hers and kissed him.

When they had finished, he lay by her side, panting. He turned his head and looked in her eyes. She smiled at him wickedly, and he felt himself stir again.

"You are a bad, bad man," she said.

Tariq smiled, content with himself. "You don't know the half of it."

"May I ask you something?"

"Of course, my darling. Anything."

"Who is she?"

Tariq put a finger to her lips. "The enemy, my sweet. The enemy."

CHAPTER 14

St.-Germain-des-Prés
Paris

A church bell tolled midnight as Mac arrived at 55 Rue du Bac.

The bolt-hole was a one-bedroom flat on a broad, leafy street in St.-Germain-des-Prés, in the heart of the Left Bank. Entry was governed by an alphanumeric keypad. The flat was dark and spare, very neat, the air stinging with ammonia-based cleaner, more a holding cell than any kind of comfortable abode. There was a bed and chairs and utilitarian tables. Lots of stainless steel and square edges. No decoration whatsoever. No plants. No pictures. Men and women didn't live here; not men and women with real lives and real families and real friends. Operatives did. Operatives did not have any of those. Operatives were on government time and government dollars.

One foot inside the door and Mac felt part of himself slip away. The human part. The part that loved camping and climbing and playing hide-and-seek with his granddaughter. The part that liked listening to Clapton on a rainy Sunday and grilling steaks on a sunny afternoon. The part that liked lying beside Ava in the middle of the night, feeling the warmth of her close to him and listening to her breathe.

He closed and locked the door behind him, and that was that. Mac Dekker was back in the game.

Once a spy, always a spy.

Maybe he wasn't so different from Ava after all.

A quick check of the accommodations.

First, the kitchen. The refrigerator was stocked with energy drinks and protein bars and packaged meats: roast beef, ham, salami.

Next, the bathroom: toothbrushes wrapped in plastic, combs, Q-tips. The medicine cabinet was filled to bursting. One look brought a grim smile to Mac's face. Percocet, oxycodone, Dexedrine—the latter better known as "go pills." It was a pharmacy with all the good stuff. Ambien, and if that wasn't enough, propofol, surgical-grade anesthetic. Z-Paks, eyewash, laxatives (opioids clogged you up harder than a cement truck). Gauze, a needle, surgical thread, and, last but not least, a box of Band-Aids . . . the small size. Who said the Agency didn't have a sense of humor?

Mac closed the cabinet and took a few steps into the bedroom. He dropped onto the bed, bouncing a little as he ran a hand over the coarse woolen blanket. The top sheet was stiff as cardboard. The pillow was small and hard. Oliver Twist, he thought, would feel right at home.

Mac was bone tired, but sleep was not an option. He stood and stripped off his clothes, then stepped into the shower. He gave himself a minute of lukewarm and three minutes of cold thereafter. Cold, colder, coldest.

He dried himself vigorously, then wrapped the towel around his waist and returned to the medicine cabinet. He shook two go pills into his palm and dry swallowed them. He put two more onto the sink and added a half dozen oxycodones alongside them. Battle supplies. He didn't know if or when he'd be back, and he didn't want pain or fear or fatigue to hamper his efforts. To be honest, he didn't mind the buzz he got from mixing the two. Sometimes feeling like Superman wasn't a bad thing.

Mac went into the kitchen and sat down at the table. He'd told Jane he had a plan, and the first part of that plan involved finding out exactly what had happened inside the restaurant this afternoon. He put a phone on the table and searched for webcams of the Eiffel Tower. The list was endless. Several sites featured cameras mounted on the edifice itself, all offering varied views of the Parisian cityscape: the brightly lit Sacré-Cœur, Les Invalides. Most showed the Eiffel Tower itself, but from a great distance.

Finally, he found a view that proved helpful. The webcam was situated across the river from the monument near the Place du Trocadéro and offered a live view of the lower half of the monument, as if someone had zoomed in and left it there.

Mac took a screenshot and, using the edit tools of his photo app, zoomed in until he had a clear, if pixilated, view of the esplanade beneath the tower. He could see that barriers had been erected around its perimeter. At this hour, the monument was officially closed to visitors. Even so, he made out a group of police officers—he couldn't count how many.

The restaurant, he recalled, had limited hours. Lunch was served from noon to 1:30 p.m. and dinner from seven to nine. It didn't seem like a long time for an establishment to be open, until one considered that diners needed two to three hours to consume a meal, longer if celebrating an occasion. The kitchen, he guessed, would need at least an hour after the last guest departed to clean up. Establishments like the Jules Verne did not leave dirty plates in the sink until morning.

It was twelve thirty.

Still time.

Mac called the restaurant. As expected, the call went to a message stating that the establishment was closed and asking him to leave a message. He hung up. It was his experience that restaurants, like most institutions, had several phone numbers, often with consecutive suffixes. Instead of -87 78, he dialed -87 79. The phone rang and rang. Mac swore under his breath. So much for experience.

"Allo?"

Mac jumped at the voice. "Restaurant Jules Verne?"

"Kitchen. What do you want?"

"This is the Hôtel de Crillon," said Mac, choosing another of the city's gilded hostelries. "A guest is convinced she lost a diamond bracelet while dining with you this evening. Can you check for me?"

"Call back tomorrow. If they found something, they will let you know."

"Our guest is very important," said Mac. "Between you and me, she's quite difficult. You know the type. I promised I would come to your premises and check myself."

"Listen, I'm a *dishwasher*, understand? I can't help you. The bosses went home ten minutes ago."

"I just need to look in the dining room," said Mac. "It will be a quick check. Five minutes. She believes it fell beneath the table. She was sitting in the center of the room."

"Did you hear me? I'm a dishwasher. The boss has the keys to the safe."

Mac expected as much. "Five hundred euros if you help me out."

"Five hundred?"

"I'll be there in twenty minutes," said Mac. "Come downstairs and make sure you tell the cops."

"If I'm there, I'm there."

The call ended before Mac could get another word in. *If he's there, he's there.* Just how much were they paying dishwashers these days?

CHAPTER 15

Eiffel Tower
Paris
Operation Sentinel

In 2017, following a series of terrorist attacks across the country, the French military deployed ten thousand soldiers working in concert with local police forces to protect France's most notable locations: museums, monuments, transport hubs, and places of interest. So-called hard targets. None was harder than the Eiffel Tower.

At 1:05 a.m., a considerable security presence patrolled the esplanade. A team of four soldiers—camouflage uniforms, berets, machine guns strapped to their chests—manned the barricades. There was no way around them.

"Evening," called Mac as he approached. "How are things?"

One of the soldiers, a tall, formidable dark-skinned woman, answered. "What do you want?"

"I need to go to the restaurant," said Mac, pointing at the Jules Verne four hundred feet above them, a few lights sparkling from its windows. He'd exchanged the soccer gear for his suit, wrinkled as it might be (the sleeve damp from his efforts to remove the bloodstains), and a pale blue shirt he'd found in a closet. He decided that he just didn't look like a Paris St.-Germain fan. "A guest lost her bracelet. I was told someone would be down to escort me inside."

The soldiers formed a casual circle around Mac. "I don't see anyone," said the soldier.

"I'll wait," said Mac.

"The area is closed. Come back tomorrow."

"Five minutes," said Mac. "Let me call to make sure he's coming down."

The soldier was firm and not so polite. "Tomorrow. Good night."

Still Mac didn't leave. He noticed another group of uniforms moving across the plaza toward them. Not soldiers, but gendarmes. Paris police. The soldiers might not be on the lookout for a six-foot-tall dark-haired man in connection with the murder of two men at the Hotel Bristol, but the police were.

Mac looked past the soldiers, toward the entry to the restaurant's private elevator. He saw no one.

"Is there a problem?" asked the soldier.

"No," said Mac. "Good night, then. I'll be back tomorrow."

He turned to leave.

"You're American?" It was another of the soldiers. A young man with a crew cut, stocky, his sleeves rolled up to show off his muscular arms.

"I am," said Mac. Evidently, his French wasn't as good as he'd thought.

"San Antonio," said the young soldier. "I lived there for a year during high school."

"The Alamo," said Mac, desperate to make conversation, hoping that the dishwasher might change his mind and show up.

"You are a Texan?"

"Me? No. I'm from Virginia, actually. Near Washington, DC."

"Okay, Mr. America," interjected the female soldier, with a withering look to her colleague. "Time to go. That means now."

Mac raised his hands. A defeated smile showed that he got the message. The police were twenty meters away and closing. One was talking animatedly into his chest mic, staring at him. Either way, it was time to scram.

The Tourists

"Good night, then." Mac turned and strode purposefully toward the taxi stand, empty at this hour. He threw a last look over his shoulder. There was no way he could get past the security patrol. Even if he did, then what? Climb the Eiffel Tower? Not a chance.

"Monsieur, I'm here!"

Mac spun. A thin man in a white smock, jeans, and clogs stood at the barricades next to the soldiers.

"You still want to look for the bracelet?" he called.

"I do," said Mac, rushing back to the barricades. "If it's all right with everyone."

"Go ahead," said the female soldier, after giving the dishwasher a good looking over. "I'm not in charge of the restaurant." She moved the barricade so that Mac could pass. He thanked her and accompanied the dishwasher to the elevator. Instead of climbing the short flight of stairs to the gallery, however, the dishwasher continued around the tented entry to a pair of steel doors standing open in the ground.

"There's another way in?" said Mac.

"You can't deliver food through the front door," said the dishwasher. "That's for guests."

Mac regarded the raised steel doors. Of course there was another way in. He'd known it all along.

Someone had been lying.

The dishwasher turned and extended his palm. "S'il vous plaît."

"Five hundred," said Mac, handing him the banknote.

The dishwasher stared at the bill, frowning. "Price went up. Throw in another hundred."

Mac remembered the policeman looking at him, perhaps too closely. Now was not the time to negotiate. He peeled off a €100 note.

"We good?"

CHAPTER 16

Restaurant Jules Verne
Paris

A single light shone on the grill in the kitchen. All the same, Mac could only marvel at its cleanliness. Every brass pot and pan gleaming; every surface polished to a sheen. The floor damp from a recent mopping.

"You're the last one here?" asked Mac, as the dishwasher led the way through the swinging doors into the dining room.

"Someone has to be."

Mac took a long look around, listening as well as observing. The room, bathed in shadow, appeared cavernous. The tables were set for tomorrow's lunch service. He advanced a step. He did not see, hear, or sense another presence.

"Take a look." The dishwasher's name, Francis, was embroidered on his smock. "They clean up after every service. I didn't hear anything about a diamond bracelet."

But Mac wasn't interested in looking for a bracelet, real or otherwise. "You have the keys?"

A look of confusion clouded Francis's face. "Keys?"

"To lock up," said Mac. "You are the last one here."

"Of course."

"And to the other offices? I need to look at the security cameras."

"But the bracelet . . ."

"No bracelet," said Mac. "I need to see the monitors. I was here earlier with a woman. She disappeared while we were eating lunch. I think someone took her against her will. Where do they keep the monitors? It's the law. Every public establishment is required to have cameras. Where are they?"

"I don't know," said Francis.

"Sure you do. In the boss's office?"

"Who are you? What do you really want?"

"I told you," said Mac, holding out an open palm. "The woman I was with vanished. I need to find out what happened. Give me the keys. S'il vous plaît."

Francis took a step back. He glanced over his shoulder.

"Don't," said Mac. "You won't make it."

But Francis was young and fit and strong, and Mac was, well, practically an old man. So Francis made his move. He spun and dashed back into the kitchen. Mac was on him in three steps. He threw him against the serving counter. Francis tumbled to the floor. Mac dropped onto his back, a knee pinioned against his spine. "Just give me the keys."

Mac didn't see the elbow coming. It glanced off his cheek, stunning him. He threw a hand to his face as Francis rolled to one side. Mac toppled onto the floor. Francis jumped to his feet, aiming a kick at Mac.

"Go screw yourself!" shouted the younger man.

Mac threw out his hand to knock the leg away. With his other hand, he grabbed Francis's ankle. Francis brought his free leg down on the back of Mac's neck. The blow was ineffectual. Mac released his ankle, rolled to one side and stood. Francis dashed around the counter. He looked wildly around the kitchen, searching, searching. His eyes locked onto something. He leaned across the counter and freed a copper pot from the rack.

"You don't want to do that," said Mac.

"Get out," said Francis, brandishing the pot as if it were a saber. "Leave . . . whoever you are."

"I can't do that," said Mac as he lunged toward Francis. As expected, Francis lashed out with the pot. Mac dodged it and slugged the kid in the jaw. Francis was stronger than he looked. He took the blow like a pro and swung the pot at Mac a second time. Mac ducked and felt the pot graze the top of his head. Coming out of a crouch, he threw a jab. His fist landed just below the man's eye. Francis stepped back, teetering. His gaze clouded. Mac caught him as his knees buckled and he lost consciousness.

Mac found the key ring in his front pocket, along with the €600. He took the keys and left the money, then returned to the freight elevator and locked the door. He didn't have time to keep an eye on Francis, and he didn't want the dishwasher causing any more problems.

With haste, he returned to the dining room and advanced down the hall leading to the guest elevator. Two unmarked doors flanked the entry. The last key he tried opened the door to his left. It was a storeroom for cleaning supplies: vacuums, towels, brooms.

He had better luck with the other office. The second key he chose opened the door. It was an executive's office, with a large desk and fancy chair and photographs on the wall of a man and his family.

He found the monitors inside a closet in an adjoining room. Six screens. A keyboard to control recording and playback. Nothing he hadn't seen before. The system was currently asleep, probably to save storage space. A relief. He didn't have to worry about being caught on camera.

Mac powered up the system, then set the time to the previous day at 1:00 p.m., approximately when he and Ava arrived. A check of the monitors showed the positioning of the cameras. There were cameras in the elevator, the entry hall, and the dining room, as well as in the kitchen. All the views Mac needed. He pressed Play, and the restaurant Jules Verne came to life.

At precisely 1:12 p.m., Mac viewed himself and Ava enter the elevator on the ground floor. Color picture. High def. At 1:15, they were shown to their table. Fast forward two hours and eight courses to 3:19. Still in the main dining room. He watched the lovey-dovey wealthy Arab couple seated at the table next to them pay their bill, then leave. A minute later, Ava took the phone call, the one she had answered with *"Grüß Gott."*

Mac's eyes shifted to another monitor as Ava entered the hallway, phone to her ear. After a few seconds, she ended the call and slid the phone into her pocket. But instead of returning to the table, she remained where she was, casually peering in both directions. It was evident that she was expecting someone.

Mac checked the time stamp. Two minutes had elapsed since Ava had left the table.

Ten seconds later, Ava turned abruptly. A man approached from the direction of the elevator. Tall, trim, elegantly attired, with thick, immaculately combed hair. Mac recognized him instantly. The handsome young Arab who had been seated beside them. The man he had just observed paying his bill.

To Mac's astonishment, Ava greeted him in the familiar European manner. Three kisses to the cheek. A handshake. The Arab spoke to Ava with urgency, punctuated by dramatic hand gestures. He motioned for Ava to come closer. He had something sensitive to impart. Of course he did. Why else were they surreptitiously meeting while Mac sat in the dining room barely fifty feet away?

Ava leaned her head closer. And as she did, another figure approached Ava from behind. It was a woman, the man's wife or girlfriend, the one with the impossibly expensive handbag. Ava turned, sensing her presence . . . but too late. The woman plunged a syringe into Ava's neck. Ava wheeled and took hold of the woman's wrist, struggling to free the syringe from her neck. She was the woman's physical superior, and for a moment, it appeared as if Ava would strike the smaller woman. Even from the elevated angle, Mac could read the rage in Ava's face. Then, in the snap of a finger, Ava folded at the knees. Her chin fell to her chest. The Arab man threw his shoulder under her arm. The woman aided him. Together, they half walked, half dragged Ava to the elevator.

Looking on the entire time was the maître d', the unctuous Frenchman who had personally conducted Mac on a tour of the restaurant and, with impressive sincerity, assured him that no one had seen madame. Liar! The maître d' exchanged words with the man and woman—the kidnappers—and shepherded all three onto the elevator.

Mac shifted between monitors as the maître d' returned to the restaurant, flattening his tie and checking his hair, but otherwise unperturbed, and Ava descended to the ground, the hostage of the Arab couple.

That was that.

There was no time to be stunned, no time to process everything he'd seen. Mac rewound the recording and searched for the clearest view of the Arab. He froze the image and snapped a photo with his phone. He repeated the process for the woman. No need for the maître d'. He planned on seeing him face to face soon enough.

Mac left the room as he had found it and returned to the kitchen. Francis was still out. Mac slapped him gently on the face, then not so gently.

"Francis, look at me. There. What is the name of your boss? Not the chef, but the maître d'."

"Gerard," said Francis, groggily.

"Last name?"

Francis hesitated, and Mac took hold of his shoulders and gave him a shake. "Rosenfeld," said Francis. "Gerard Rosenfeld."

"Rosenfeld . . . you're sure?"

"Of course."

Mac considered this. Rosenfeld was more likely than not a Jewish name. If Gerard Rosenfeld was Jewish, why was he conspiring with a man Mac assumed to be Middle Eastern, and therefore Muslim, to kidnap an Israeli woman with deep ties to Mossad, Israeli's foreign intelligence service?

"Where does he live?" asked Mac.

"Le Marais," said Francis, sitting up and probing the lump on his forehead. "You know, the Pletzl. The Jewish quarter. Rue des Rosiers. Why?"

The Pletzl . . . Yiddish for "the small place." Mac knew the area. "Do you have the address?"

"No."

"What about his phone number?"

Francis consulted his phone and read it out as Mac typed it into his contacts.

Suddenly, Mac realized, his world had become far more complicated.

"I'm leaving now," said Mac. "I want you to listen to me. Don't tell anyone I was here. Don't go to the police. Don't mention this to your boss. If someone asks about the bump on your head, make something up. Say you tripped and hit your head on the counter. Or you got drunk and had a fight. Just don't tell anyone that I was here. This isn't for my sake. It's for yours. You don't want to have anything to do with me. I can't say anything more, but please, *please*, Francis, believe me. Are we good?"

Francis nodded, more alert now.

"You never saw me," Mac said once more for good measure. "This never happened." He stood. "Oh, I'll need your phone. I can't take the chance you'll do something stupid."

Francis pulled a face and handed Mac his phone.

"Passcode?"

"Really?" said Francis.

"'Fraid so."

Francis told him the six-digit code.

"Remember what I told you," said Mac. "I wasn't here."

CHAPTER 17

27 Avenue Montaigne
Paris

"Excellency. A pleasure to see you again."

"Save it, Paul," said TNT. "It's me. Not my father."

"You're looking well," said Paul Sassoon. "My son relies on you for his fashion advice. You're costing me quite a lot of money."

"I'm paying you quite a lot of money," said Tariq. "But I'm happy that your son has such good taste."

"God forbid he wants one of your cars."

"If all goes according to plan," said Tariq, "one day very soon you will be able to give him one."

Paul Sassoon was the family banker. Half Swiss, half Qatari. Fifty years old. Elegant. Monied. It was after midnight, and he looked like he'd just stepped out of a board meeting. Not a hair out of place, his tie just so, his three-piece suit absent a wrinkle.

Tariq plopped down on a sofa and kicked his feet onto a low table. No suit for him. A flowing white *thobe* (to please his father) and vintage Adidas Robert Haillets straight out of the box, circa 1978, the year they started being known as "Stan Smiths." He snapped a selfie of his shoes and posted it.

"Sorry, Paul," he said, putting away the phone. "Have to keep the public happy." He cracked a bottle of Pellegrino. "So then, what do the jackals want now?"

The Tourists

A new day. Tariq's preferred time for business. When others were asleep. When eyes were closed. They sat together in the study on the fourth floor. Bookshelves filled with leather-bound classics lined the walls, floor to ceiling. Dumas, Hugo, Proust. All first editions. There was a German globe dating from the seventeenth century and a Rembrandt self-portrait and a Tiffany lamp from the old New York Public Library.

"Lean times," said Paul Sassoon. "Funding is drying up."

"They lost a war," said Tariq. "No one wants a repeat performance."

"Their view is that with additional funding, a different outcome was possible."

Tariq's laugh was a cry of outrage. It was always the same. More money was the answer. When the intifada failed, it was for lack of money. When Hezbollah's rockets missed their targets . . . lack of money. When October 7 brought down the wrath of God . . . lack of money.

In every instance, Tariq and his family had stepped up. Fifty million. One hundred. Two hundred. And for what? Tunnels. He was not paying them to build a subway system. He was paying them to kill Jews.

The problem, Tariq reasoned, was scale. Hamas, Hezbollah, ISIS . . . none of them thought big enough. All suffered from the same limited perspective, the same lack of vision. It was up to Tariq to show them.

He rolled up his sleeves, and as he did most nights, when executing his responsibilities, he reflected on how he had arrived here, especially on the most recent part. It had been a pleasant childhood. School in Doha, Amman, then in England. Eton, of course. Then college in the States. California. The Golden State. He was an adequate student, not an outstanding one.

Tariq was one of twenty children; he had one older brother, two younger sisters, and too many half brothers and sisters to count. The cousins numbered in the hundreds. A veritable menagerie of Al-Sabahs. In such an environment, it had been ingrained in him not to stand out. To go along. To be one of many . . . and to please keep his voice down while he was at it. He came to see that it was not just as an Al-Sabah but as a Qatari that he'd been taught not to seek an identity.

Everyone knew the Saudis. They had a brand. Saudis were too often seen as loud and brash and vulgar and threw their money around for everyone to admire. There was the story about a Saudi royal taking over the tenth floor of the Dorchester hotel, one of London's finest, and making a fire in the hall to roast a lamb. A sheikh straight out of the desert. This was an Arab, one step removed from a barbarian; a far cry from the media-savvy, progressive scion who ruled the country today—Prince Mohammed bin Salman, known as "MBS"—yet only sixty years separated the two men.

The Emiratis came to prominence in the nineties, a country of seven tiny states ruled by the Maktoum family. Smart, forceful, elegant, and disciplined. Abu Dhabi had oil. Dubai didn't. But Dubai did have warm weather, an attractive geographic location, a liberal tax code, and, not to be forgotten, alcohol, all under the guidance of a farseeing leader. Behold the miracle on the Gulf.

But what was Qatar's identity? It was a small thumb sticking into the Persian Gulf, blessed with abundant natural gas, plenty of sand, three million natives all on the national dole, and the soccer World Cup, already forgotten. Qatar had no reputation, good or bad.

Growing up, Tariq decided that anonymity didn't suit him. Maybe it was because he'd spent too much time in the West. Maybe it was just how he was made. Either way, he liked attention. He found his way to social media naturally. First Myspace, then Facebook, and on to Instagram, TikTok, Telegram, Twitter (or X), and all their varied cousins. It was the type of celebrity that suited him best. Attention without the messy part, that being human interaction. For that he had family and more family and more after that.

So, when exactly did two million likes stop being enough to satisfy his hungry, attention-seeking soul? When did his desire—no, *his addiction*—for likes morph into something sharper and more fiery, something called "ambition"? Tariq could give you the date. It was the night two years before, when he'd taken over responsibility for the funding of extranational organizations. He called them "freedom fighters." Others called them more pejorative names.

This, then, was power. People kowtowed to him, both as Tariq, or TNT, and as the secret representative of the Qatari government. And not just random handles in the Twittersphere. These were important people. Government ministers, heads of state, ranking executives. Movers. Shakers. The Davos crowd. Their attentions gratified him in a way his vain, meretricious interactions on social media never could.

It was Paul Sassoon who fueled his ambitions, rightly recognizing his God-given talents. Tariq was smart, and by that he meant smarter than his brother, Jabr. His sisters didn't count, and thank goodness for that. He was handsome. He was charismatic. More than that, he was Western. He passed for one of them. No hook nose, no hooded eyes. No one could call him a caricature. He was, in Sassoon's words, the "new face of Qatar."

TNT was also a dreamer, a fantasist, and maybe a fabulist too. He saw palaces where others saw windmills. But Don Quixote was poor, and Tariq al-Sabah was fabulously wealthy, a member of the richest family on planet earth. So maybe he didn't have to be a dreamer or a fantasist, and maybe the stories he told himself weren't so far fetched. Maybe he was a brilliant, transformational leader on the cusp of helping his beloved country realize its destiny as a guiding light for the Arab world.

And so to the business at hand.

"What are they asking for now?" he asked, settling back on the sofa.

Sassoon consulted his tablet. "Fifty for Hamas."

"Since when did they become reasonable?" Tariq's surprise was genuine.

"They're desperate," said Sassoon. "Out of munitions and matériel."

"All the money will go to the Iranians," said Tariq. "I don't like it."

"My understanding is that Russia is the primary supplier."

Russia through Belarus through the Chechens, that bastard Kadyrov always taking his piece. Baksheesh. Tariq hated it.

"And Hezbollah?" he asked. Despite the annihilation of their entire command, the Shia militia maintained a considerable fighting force on Israel's northern border and in the occupied territories.

"Two hundred," said Sassoon. "Rockets are expensive."

"They need more than rockets," said Tariq. He was growing bored. He could feel the seconds ticking. His mind went to the Bugatti. For the first time, he wondered if LeClerc, the upright inspector, had been wise to the plot. Had Tariq seen something in his eyes? A knowing glint? It didn't matter. LeClerc was in the hospital with a cranial hematoma. Fool that he was, Tariq had sent flowers and a get-well card.

"Give Hamas their fifty," said Tariq. "But only a hundred for Hezbollah. And nothing for ISIS."

Paul Sassoon frowned.

"Forget it," said Tariq, throwing up his hands. "You win. Give Hezbollah what they want. They can have two hundred. Take the money from our accounts in Luxembourg. Buy a tanker. LNGs are going for cheap these days. Inflate the purchase price. Siphon the money into their accounts in Egypt and Sudan. Christ, I hate these sanctions."

A smile. Sassoon noted all the information on his tablet. "And ISIS, really nothing?"

"Not a penny," said Tariq. "Do I look like an easy mark?"

Sassoon smiled. He was smart enough not to answer. "And our lovely friend from Tel Aviv?"

"Upstairs sleeping."

"Be careful," said Sassoon. "She is too smart to believe she can change your mind."

"You don't know her," said Tariq. "That one has a strong will."

"Remember where she comes from," said Sassoon. "Dispose of her as quickly as possible."

"That has been my plan all along," said Tariq. "I need to speak with her first."

"Whatever she says, don't believe it."

"I'm an Arab," said Tariq. "I don't believe anyone."

"Well said."

"Sunday," said Tariq, as he left the room. "A palace fit for four kings."

"We shall be ready, emir," said Sassoon, bowing his head.

CHAPTER 18

Montmartre, eighteenth arrondissement
Paris

The rain began to fall at two in the morning.

Cyrille de Montcalm sat at her kitchen table, on the third floor of a sixteenth-century *maison* on the Rue St.-Rustique, window open to free the smoke from her cigarette, listening to the ebb and flow of police communication across the Parisian cityscape.

A transmitter squawked. A cop radioed in about a drunk who'd driven his car through a hedge in Passy. Tow truck needed. No backup required.

Not her man.

Cyrille adjusted the volume on the transmitter. Police communication in Paris was conducted over the Mototrbo system, encrypted end to end. Each of the city's twenty arrondissements, or districts, was assigned its own frequency, with all calls relayed simultaneously to the Prefecture of Police.

Another squelch. Burglary in Clichy. Suspect took a necklace and a cat. Yes, she'd heard correctly. A cat.

Cyrille was forty last month, five feet two inches tall in her stockings, and slight as a dancer for the Ballet Nationale. Dancing, however, wasn't her thing. As a child, she'd studied judo. Her father was an instructor. She grew up wearing a *judogi* more than her favorite jeans. She was a black belt at twelve and a national champion at sixteen. A year later, she came out. Her father wanted none of it. No "queers" in the Montcalm family. She left, joined the army, and loved it, deploying to Africa on several occasions as part of a small counterterrorism force.

Then came the incident that derailed her career. Cyrille was pretty enough. Dark hair, blue eyes, nice ass. A few guys in her company wouldn't take no for an answer. Same old story. Cyrille didn't know what she was missing. It got nasty. She killed one of them. Crushed larynx and fractured spine. A standard Ippon throw. Her father would have been proud. Unfortunately, the dead man was an officer. There was no trial, just immediate separation from the service and forfeit of all benefits. Who said life was fair?

Cyrille had been a cop for twelve years, first with the Paris gendarmerie, and now the DGSI, the General Directorate for Internal Security. The job was great; the salary wasn't, so she did a little moonlighting. Five years now, she'd been a hitter. It didn't matter who hired her; she didn't ask, and they wouldn't have told her if she had. All anyone cared about was that Cyrille de Montcalm got the job done. Quickly, cleanly, and without any blowback. If she liked her work a little too much, she kept that part to herself. As far as she was concerned, it was all about the money. Cyrille had a wife and two kids, the younger one a boy with special needs, which was the polite way of saying he would require care his entire life. An extra €20,000 now and then made a big difference.

The American would be number twenty-one. *Lucky twenty-one.*

Her target could be anywhere, she thought, gazing out the window at the sea of lights. If she were the one wanted for murder, she would distance herself from the crime as quickly as possible. His name was Mackenzie "Mac" Dekker, a.k.a. Robert Steinhardt, and he was wanted in connection with two murders—diplomats, no less. Patagonia wouldn't be far enough. But they assured her he would be in Paris, so Paris it was.

The Tourists

Cyrille took a drag from her cigarette—Disque Bleu, no filter—and replaced it in the ashtray. She had no business smoking. She was a mother. She knew better. She had no business doing a lot of things. That was her excuse. She figured she'd be dead long before the cigarettes killed her.

A call from St.-Denis. A murder. The cop sounded shaken. Cyrille leaned closer. *Maybe* . . . Victim: Female. Eighteen years old. Suspect in custody. Her boyfriend.

Cyrille relaxed.

She needed six multiband transmitters to keep up. For now, it was the only means of locating Mac Dekker. A long shot to be sure. In the morning, she'd make herself pretty and stop by the hotel to sniff around. She'd been given his cell number, but it was dead. Dekker was in the business, too, or had been. He knew better.

She had a picture of him, but it was fifteen years old. Hopelessly out of date. She studied the photograph anyway. Not bad looking, but too American for her taste. The thick hair, the square jaw, the broad shoulders. She could imagine him planting a flag on a foreign shore.

Her brief stated that Mackenzie "Mac" Dekker was ex-CIA, a retired field operative, last seen at the Hotel Bristol. He was visiting Paris in the company of Ava Attal, former Mossad, his girlfriend/partner. Her location was also unknown.

Quite the couple, thought Cyrille. Sadly, there was no picture of the woman. She sounded like her type.

A last line stated that every precaution was to be taken when approaching the subject. The warning—if it was one—pissed her off. Cyrille de Montcalm always took every precaution.

She stood and stretched her legs. If Dekker was staying in the city, it was for a reason. It wasn't Cyrille's business to know why. Still, she was a cop and she was smart, so she wondered. Why risk your freedom, and possibly your life, hanging around a foreign city when you know the entire police department—and maybe someone just like her—is after you?

A squawk from the seventh arrondissement captured her attention. A cop at the Eiffel Tower radioed in about a worker assaulted by a tourist, possibly American, at the restaurant Jules Verne. The victim's name was Francis Matthieu. Matthieu stated that a tall man, aged fifty or older, pretended to have lost a bracelet there earlier that day but once inside demanded to see the security cameras. Something about his wife being missing, said the cop. Details unclear. A fight ensued. The foreigner got away. The watch commander advised the victim to file a report online.

Cyrille double-checked her brief. Foreigner? Check. Jules Verne? Check. Looking for wife? Check.

There it was.

Cyrille radioed in. She stated her name and rank and informed the police on scene that the suspect was a person of interest.

"Hold Matthieu for me," she said. "I'll be there in twenty minutes."

Cyrille took a last look at the brief. Once more she read the words, *Red Flag*.

She pulled on her jacket, making sure to take her pistol, knife, and stun gun. She kept the heavier stuff in the trunk of her car. She peeked into the bedroom. Her wife lay with their daughter, sound asleep. She blew them a kiss and left the apartment.

"Red flag" meant neutralize. Do not attempt to capture. Do not attempt to question.

Kill.

CHAPTER 19

Seventh arrondissement
Paris

Mac had his answer. Gerard Rosenfeld lived at 34 Rue des Rosiers, in the heart of the Marais.

Huddled in the doorway of an all-night pharmacy, a kilometer from the Eiffel Tower, Mac had needed seventy-four seconds to find the address. The internet was awash with sites offering to dole out biographical information for a price. It was simply a matter of entering a name, address, or phone number and paying a nominal fee. Mac had a name and a phone number. The fee was €4.95. He paid with a credit card. Anyone tracking his purchases would note the charge and the company name, but get no further. It was a digital site without a brick-and-mortar location. No mention of the information he was seeking would appear on a tertiary search.

Riskier was the five-kilometer walk across the center of Paris. It was 2:00 a.m. It was raining. A lone man walking the streets invited attention.

Mac shivered, a spasm of cold running the length of his spine. He turned up the collar of his jacket as he studied the route to Rosenfeld's home. He was concerned about stretches where he'd have to cross the Esplanade des Invalides and, later, traverse the intersection near the Pont Royal. Either would leave him exposed for at least two hundred meters—two football fields—give or take. A passing police car would take note of the lone pedestrian and would give him a look. He didn't relish the idea of trying to outrun them on foot.

A taxi was, similarly, out of the question. He hadn't killed two ordinary civilians. He'd murdered two diplomats . . . Saudi diplomats . . . in a country that placed a premium on good relations with the kingdom. He had no doubt that pressure was being exerted from the highest levels of the Élysée Palace to find the fugitive cold-blooded killer, Robert "Robbie" Steinhardt. He must assume his description had been circulated to every taxi company and every transport hub across the city, if not the entire country.

So now what?

A car approached from his left. Yellow halogen headlights of a police cruiser. A slow, deliberate speed. Mac turned away and buried his head in the dishwasher's phone. The car passed by. He raised his eyes. A Volkswagen with Belgian plates. False alarm.

He looked back at the phone and saw it. A black icon with white lettering.

Uber.

It was the first time he'd thought of the company since taking refuge in Zinal over nine years earlier. Ride-sharing was not an option in a remote mountain hamlet of four hundred souls. It was, however, his best option in a metropolis of two million.

He opened the app. When prompted for a destination, he did not enter Rosenfeld's address, but an address a block away. Last, he confirmed his current location. Three minutes later, a late-model Audi sedan pulled to the curb. He slid into the rear seat. The driver pulled away without a word or a look in his direction. A dashboard-mounted phone displayed the route toward Rosenfeld's apartment. For the moment, he was safe.

Mac put away Matthieu's phone and opened the burner he'd used to take pictures of the man and woman who'd abducted Ava from the restaurant. The photos were grainier than he'd hoped, nothing like the color high-def images he'd viewed in the restaurant. Still, there was a chance he'd get a match. Who the hell were these people?

He typed in the web address for Clearview AI, a commercially available facial-recognition software. All he had to do was upload the photos. The firm's software would compare the person in each to over fifty billion images it had scraped from public data-collection sites: social media, news outlets, law enforcement mug shots. Again and again, he tried to upload the photos, but the 5G connection was spotty. He gave up. It didn't matter. He was going to the source. He'd beat the information out of Gerard Rosenfeld if he had to.

He arrived a few minutes later. He waited for the Audi to pull away, then reversed his direction. He passed a deli, a boutique, a religious bookstore. Mezuzahs decorated many of the doorways. This was Le Pletzl, meaning "little place," the center of Jewish life in Paris. It was here, forty-odd years ago, that terrorists had attacked a delicatessen, Jo Goldenberg, in plain daylight, lobbing grenades into the restaurant and spraying the diners with machine gun fire. Six people were killed and many more wounded. Mac knew this because Ava had been involved in tracking down one of the suspects, a soldier working for the infamous Abu Nidal. Ava found him at a seaside rest home in Alexandria, Egypt. He was an old man by that time. Justice, however, did not dim with age. A drone carrying a half-kilo brick of plastic explosive did the rest.

Mac arrived at the doorway to number 34. The vestibule was unlocked. A directory inside listed the residents, a doorbell next to each name. *G. Rosenfeld. 3B.* Mac was in the right place. He checked his surroundings and spotted a camera high in one corner. There was a mirror on the wall. He looked a little waterlogged, but respectable, more or less.

Back to the directory.

A Mr. S. Katz lived in 1A. Mac pressed the bell. Thirty seconds passed. No response. 1B, Mrs. L. Kinsky. Again, no answer. 2B, Mr. A. Cohen. Mac rang the bell twice for good measure.

A gruff voice burst from the speaker. "Who is it?"

"It's me. Gerard Rosenfeld," said Mac. "I'm sorry. I forgot my key at the restaurant."

"Jerk," said Mr. A. Cohen.

So, thought Mac, they know each other.

The buzzer sounded. Mac opened the glass door to the lobby. He took the stairs to the third floor. There were two apartments, one to each side of the landing. No names or apartment numbers were posted to indicate which belonged to Rosenfeld. *When in doubt, go to the right.*

Mac banged on the door. "Police," he said, with authority. He held his open passport at eye level. It was two-thirty. He was betting that, woken from sleep and taken by surprise, Rosenfeld would be too groggy to focus.

The door opened a notch. Hooded, dark eyes peered out. A halo of silver hair. It was him.

"Hello again," said Mac.

Rosenfeld slammed the door on Mac's shoe. Mac was bigger, stronger, and ready to knock heads. He shoved the door open. Rosenfeld crashed onto the floor. Mac entered and closed the door behind them. "Remember me?"

Rosenfeld nodded.

"Of course you do," said Mac.

Rosenfeld's wife peeked her head out of the bedroom. "Gerard . . . is everything all right?"

"Stay there," commanded Mac, advancing on her. Before she could retreat, he grabbed her by the shoulders and led her into the hall. She was petite and frail, coarse red hair tumbling to the shoulders of her flannel nightgown. "I need to speak to your husband. It shouldn't be long." Mac looked around and led her to a guest bathroom. "Lock the door. Don't come out until I say."

The woman looked at her husband, eyes wide.

"Please, Laura," said Rosenfeld. "Do as he says."

The woman cursed, entering the bathroom. It was Hebrew, but Mac understood a few words. Something about this being his brother's fault. She slammed the bathroom door, and Mac heard the key turn the lock.

"Get up," said Mac, giving Rosenfeld a kick. All he could see was a reel of Ava being drugged and forced into the elevator. Rosenfeld was a party to the crime, an accessory at the least. Mac believed more.

Rosenfeld clambered to his feet. He was smaller than Mac remembered, a slight man with curly gray hair, fifty years old, give or take. In his dark pajamas—head bowed, shoulders hunched—he looked like a bullied schoolboy.

"Pour yourself a drink," said Mac.

"No thank you."

"I could use a coffee."

"You're not going to kill me?" said Rosenfeld.

"Depends on the coffee."

The kitchen was modern and airy. Rosenfeld made an espresso from an expensive machine. Mac drank the coffee at once, getting the jolt he needed.

They returned to the living room. It was a large, open room, with casual sofas and armchairs and throw pillows everywhere. Oil paintings of sunny landscapes decorated the walls. Photographs crowded an antique wooden dresser. The Wailing Wall, the dome on the Mount, a group of Hasidim at prayer.

"Sit."

Rosenfeld took a place on the couch.

Mac sat down next to him. With care, he slipped the pistol from his waistband and set it on the coffee table. Rosenfeld saw it and shuddered. Mac leaned close to the man and slapped him across the face. Just once. Very hard.

"Who is he?" asked Mac. "Who took Ava?"

Rosenfeld threw a hand to his cheek. "I thought you weren't going to—"

"Kill you?" said Mac. "That's up to you."

Rosenfeld looked at Mac. His mouth tightened, and he crossed his arms. Mac raised his hand dramatically, ready to deliver another blow. "Who took her? Tell me his name."

CHAPTER 20

Eiffel Tower
Paris

Cyrille de Montcalm made the drive from Montmartre to the Eiffel Tower in twelve minutes, a quarter of the time she'd need at any other hour. Two policemen waited at the barriers, with them a very impatient Francis Matthieu. Cyrille badged the cops and bantered with them for a minute, then told them to get the hell out of there. "Don't you have any *poules* to roust in the Bois?"

Smiles all around. A wave to wish them good night as they piled back into their vehicles.

"So," said Cyrille, directing the full force of her personality onto Matthieu. "How'd you get that shiner?"

The nice, chatty Cyrille had taken a break. This was the real Cyrille: pushy, pissed off, and about one misunderstood comment from blowing up. Matthieu was no longer the victim. In her eyes, he was the assailant and to be treated accordingly.

"He hit me," said Matthieu. "That's why I called you guys."

"You look like you can take care of yourself. Who was this guy . . . Conor McGregor?"

"I already explained. He was a foreigner, maybe American. He talked to some of the security earlier. They saw him too."

"Well, I didn't," said Cyrille. "Explain it again."

"He was six feet tall. An older guy, I don't know. But fast. I didn't see it coming."

"He just hauled out and hit you? Like that?"

"Do I have to go over this again?" Matthieu complained. "I just want to go home. Come on."

"Are you kidding me?" said Cyrille. "I get out of bed and come all the way down here to help you out, and you're copping an attitude."

"I didn't mean it that way."

"Then how did you mean it?" asked Cyrille, getting up in his face. "I ask a question; I want an answer."

"I'm sorry," said Matthieu. "It's late. Like I said, he told me he was with some hotel and that one of his guests had lost a bracelet."

"And you just let him in? I would have told him to bug off and come by in the morning."

"Not exactly."

"What does that mean?" demanded Cyrille.

Matthieu studied his shoes. "I . . . uh . . ."

"You put the squeeze on him," said Cyrille. "How much? Stop acting so guilty. Come on. Spill."

"Five hundred," said Matthieu.

"Nice," said Cyrille, with mock appreciation. "You should have been a businessman, not a dishwasher. So he pays you five hundred, you let him in, and what happens?"

"There wasn't a bracelet," said Matthieu. "It was BS. He wanted to see the security cameras. He said he'd been at the restaurant earlier with his wife or something and she was kidnapped."

"Kidnapped?" asked Cyrille. "From the Jules Verne. Are you messing with me?"

"That's what he said. I know it's impossible, but whatever. He wanted the see the security tapes."

"He was there earlier?" asked Cyrille.

"For lunch."

"Did you check the reservation book? The man's name is right there."

"It's locked up," said Matthieu. "I don't have the passcode."

Cyrille shook her head in disbelief. She wasn't mad at Matthieu. She was perplexed. Dekker hadn't tried to conceal his identity, not really, and he'd left Matthieu alive to tell everyone about it.

"I told him he couldn't see the cameras," said Matthieu. "That's when he hit me."

"Just belted you."

"He wanted the keys, and I wouldn't give them to him. I tried to get away. I got an elbow in."

"An elbow?"

"I almost got him with a casserole," said Matthieu.

"A what?"

"A pan."

Cyrille stared at Matthieu with a kind of wonder. How lucky was this guy to be alive? "Is that all he wanted? Just to look at the cameras?"

Matthieu nodded. "For his wife, I guess."

"Did he see her?"

"I don't know. I was kind of out of it. But afterwards, he asked me lots of questions about Monsieur Rosenfeld, our maître d'."

"Like what?"

"Where he lives. His phone number. I'm guessing that's where he went. To Rosenfeld's. Maybe you should call him."

"You tell that to the cops?"

"No, but I just figured he seemed kind of desperate. That's what I would do." Matthieu shifted on his feet. "That's when he stole my iPhone."

"He has your phone right now?"

Matthieu nodded. "He stole it."

"What's your number?" Cyrille entered the digits into her own phone. "Did you give him Rosenfeld's info?"

"Only his mobile number," said Matthieu. "I don't know exactly where he lives. Somewhere in the Marais, I think. Rue des Rosiers."

"You remember it? Rosenfeld's number?"

The Tourists

"No."

"So, what do you want out of this?" asked Cyrille.

"I want you to arrest this guy. I want my phone back. It was expensive."

"Did he take the five hundred euros too?"

"No."

Cyrille stepped away to light a cigarette. Something didn't add up. She looked at Matthieu. Young and dumb. She offered him a smoke. He took it and touched her hand as she lit it for him. And now he's flirting with a cop. What a *crapaud*.

"Know what that prick told me?" said Matthieu. "He said I shouldn't tell anyone about him. That if anyone asked about my face, I should just say I had an accident. He begged me. He said it was to protect me . . . not him."

Cyrille ground out her cigarette with the toe of her boot. "As if."

"Right?"

"Hey, it's late," she said, amicably. "Why don't I give you a ride home?"

"You don't mind?"

Cyrille touched his sleeve, gave him a look. "Not at all. Where you at?"

"Not far," said Matthieu. "Rue de Grenelle."

Cyrille walked him to the car. "Wait a sec. I have to unlock it from inside." She paused before climbing behind the wheel, doing a one-eighty of the area. Quiet as the grave. She grabbed a towel from the back seat and spread it across the passenger footwell. Leaning over, she unlocked the door.

Matthieu folded himself into the car. He struggled getting the safety belt over his shoulder.

"Do me a favor," said Cyrille. "I dropped my lighter down there earlier. By your feet. Take a look, will you?"

Matthieu bent forward, craning his neck. "I don't see it."

Cyrille placed the muzzle of her pistol against his skull and pulled the trigger.

Poor kid. He should have taken Dekker's advice.

CHAPTER 21

Rue des Rosiers
Paris

"TNT," said Rosenfeld. "It was TNT. Everyone knows him."

"I don't," said Mac. "Tell me."

"Tariq bin Nayan bin Tariq al-Sabah. He's famous."

"Al-Sabah? From Qatar?" Mac had spent years in the Middle East. The Al-Sabahs were the ruling family of Qatar, the very small, very conservative, very oil-rich state on the western edge of the Persian Gulf.

"The emir's second son," said Rosenfeld. "He's one of the new group. You know, 'influencers.' He posts pictures of himself on social media for his followers to view."

"I don't do social media," said Mac.

"They come to the restaurant every day," explained Rosenfeld. "They take pictures of the food—every course, every glass of wine and champagne. They pose."

"Who?"

"Influencers."

Again, that term. Mac knew it vaguely and took it to mean people who didn't do anything for a living but share pictures of themselves in the hope you find them more interesting than your own life. "But why would I want to see what someone else has for dinner?"

The Tourists

"Because your life is boring and theirs is not," Rosenfeld explained. "It's glamorous. It's sophisticated. It's better than yours."

"What does that have to do with Al-Sabah? TNT?" said Mac.

"The prince comes to the restaurant two or three times a year," said Rosenfeld. "He posts pictures of the view, his meal, his friends, his clothes. Millions of people see them. It's good for business."

"Is kidnapping your guests good for business?" demanded Mac.

"He asked me for a favor," said Rosenfeld. "He said he was playing a prank. Something amusing for his followers."

"A prank?" Mac wasn't buying it. Not for a second. "To abduct someone against their will? That's a crime. You can go to prison."

"He said it was all right. I shouldn't worry. He promised me."

"And you believed him?"

Rosenfeld nodded emphatically, as if any normal person would believe the prince.

"I saw the tape," said Mac. "You were there. You watched the woman put a syringe into Ava's neck. You saw her struggle. You helped them bundle her into the kitchen elevator. It was no prank. There was nothing amusing about it. Then you lied to me. Again and again, you lied to me."

"He told me I must," said Rosenfeld, near tears.

"TNT?"

"Yes."

"And you said, 'Of course.' It would be your pleasure."

Rosenfeld swallowed hard, avoiding Mac's glare.

"Why?"

Rosenfeld dug his chin into his neck, eyes closed.

"How much did he pay you?" asked Mac.

"Nothing."

"You're lying," said Mac. "How much?"

"Nothing," spat Rosenfeld, lifting his face to Mac.

"Then why?"

Rosenfeld looked away.

Mac picked up the pistol off the table and held it on his thigh. "I'm waiting. If not for money, then why?"

"Please," said Rosenfeld. It was a squeak.

Mac lifted the pistol and pressed the barrel against Rosenfeld's ribs. The man whimpered.

"No, stop!" It was Rosenfeld's wife, Laura. She ran from the bathroom. "Tell him, Gerard. Tell him who made you do it."

"Quiet," said Rosenfeld. "Not another word."

"It wasn't the prince. It was Gerard's brother," said Laura Rosenfeld, weeping. "He's a fanatic."

Rosenfeld rose suddenly and struck his wife across the face. She fell to the floor, blood darkening her teeth. "It was his brother," she repeated, through her tears. "Yehudi. In Jerusalem. He's a fanatic. They all are."

"Quiet, I told you," shouted Rosenfeld. "You'll ruin everything."

"He put him up to it," she continued. "Yehudi and his boss. They're all crazy. Tell him, Gerard."

Mac grabbed Rosenfeld and yanked him back onto the couch. "What is she talking about? Why are you helping TNT?"

"I don't know," said Rosenfeld. "I do as I'm told."

"Do you know who she is? Ava?"

Rosenfeld nodded. "Mossad."

"Did your brother tell you that?"

Again, Rosenfeld nodded.

"So why did you help Al-Sabah kidnap her?"

"I was told to," said Rosenfeld. "That was enough."

Mac put a hand on the man's shoulder and pressed the gun against his heart. "Tell me," he said calmly. "What do they want? Why is your brother helping the prince?"

Rosenfeld shook his head.

"Where is Ava?"

"I don't know. I swear."

"Where?"

"Stop," wailed his wife, Laura, struggling to get to her feet. "Don't kill him. I called the police. They'll find you. Don't kill him!"

It was then that Mac saw the phone in her hand. He ran to the window. He didn't see any police cars. He couldn't hear a siren. There was one last thing he needed to know.

"When?" asked Mac. "When did he tell you all this . . . When did your brother tell you to help TNT?"

Rosenfeld closed his eyes. He shook his head, mumbling.

"I asked you, 'When?'" Suddenly it was very important that Mac knew. "When did TNT tell you that he was planning on kidnapping Ava from the restaurant?"

"A week ago," said Rosenfeld.

Mac reeled at the news. The trip to Paris had been a last-minute decision. Ava had booked the table five days ago.

CHAPTER 22

Rue des Rosiers
Paris

Cyrille guided her Renault along the Rue des Rosiers, the window rolled down to better view the addresses. The Marais had changed dramatically in the past few years. When she was growing up, it had been a kind of ghetto, a place where Jews lived and few others visited. A dour, backward neighborhood populated by men in black coats and funny hats, a part of Paris stuck in the nineteenth century. Today it was as fashionable as the Left Bank. Department stores. Boutiques. Everything shiny and polished. *Très chic.* She was not sure that was a good thing.

At the corner of the Rue des Écouffes, she braked to a halt. She gazed at the four-story limestone building. Number 34. Her eyes moved to the top floor, where lights burned from a picture window. Either the occupant, Gerard Rosenfeld, was a very early riser, or he was receiving an unexpected visitor.

Cyrille turned left and parked two blocks farther along, in front of a synagogue. She killed the engine and threw her workbag onto the passenger seat. Matthieu was long gone. A quick stop in the Bois de Boulogne. A dark hollow. A deep pond. It would be a week before anyone found him.

A look over her shoulder to check for unwanted attention. The street was deserted. She unzipped the bag and removed an automatic pistol.

The Tourists

She attached a folding stock and a noise suppressor, then inserted the magazine—an abbreviated five-round clip—and chambered a round. She drove her thumb hard on the safety. She exited the car in a rapid, rehearsed motion, deftly sliding the pistol beneath her overcoat. She slipped on a beret for good measure. With the beret, you didn't know: man or woman.

She approached the corner with caution, like a tourist arriving at a hallowed site. The lights still shone from the top floor. No need for a confrontation. Sooner or later, the visitor would depart. Cyrille crossed the street and found shelter in the doorway of a coiffeur—the Salon Vogue—and retreated until she was concealed by shadow. From her vantage point, she had an unobstructed line of sight to the building's lobby and vestibule—both unlit—like her, bathed in darkness.

All she could do now was wait.

Cyrille hated waiting. Her thoughts went to dark places, invariably landing on the night that had changed everything. The Sahara. Outside of Timbuktu. Yes, darling, there was such a place, and it was as bleak and desolate as anyone could imagine.

Slow duty at Camp Barkhane. A peacekeeping force sent to protect the city's residents from the Islamic State of the Sahel, the local chapter of Terror Inc. The Islamic State was on vacation, or so Cyrille and her fellow soldiers had joked, as they passed around bottle after bottle of the local Malian tipple. One hundred forty proof and guaranteed to turn the mildest man into a howling wolf. And Cyrille's mates were not mild, not one of them. A few bottles and they turned their eyes on Cyrille. Pretty, brunette Cyrille, one of three women in the company, and the only one on duty that terrible night. First they joked, then they pawed, then they threatened. Every minute, she grew less human in their eyes. At 7:00 p.m., she'd been Sergeant Montcalm, the rock of the company. By 10:00, she was a "queer" who needed to be taught a lesson. By 11:00, she was an animal put there to fulfill their needs.

It was the lieutenant who egged them on. He was the one who pinned her arms behind her back and ordered the others to strip off her clothes. He wanted proof she was really a woman. She remembered the loud voices, the sweaty faces, the rough hands. The screen went black the moment one of them stuck his hand down her pants. It had come back into focus much later. By then, the lieutenant was dead and two of the men lay writhing on the barracks floor with broken limbs.

Cyrille hated waiting.

To calm herself, she drew a breath and repeated a mantra her sergeant had taught her on her first drop into Mali. *Res firma*. Resfeerma. Latin, roughly translated: "Stay hard." Sound advice.

A light appeared in the building's lobby. The door to the elevator opened. Mac Dekker stepped out and crossed to the vestibule. Cyrille slid the pistol from her coat and rested the stock against her shoulder. She inclined her head, sighting on Dekker's chest, then thumbed the safety off and laid her finger against the trigger. *Doucement*. Softly.

Dekker walked to the vestibule door but did not leave the building. He stood where he was, studying his phone . . . or more likely, Matthieu's phone. Cyrille could take the shot now, but she didn't want to break the glass and call attention to herself. Let Dekker come outside. No one would hear the muffled shot. Dekker would fall to the ground. Cyrille would dash across the street, deliver the coup de grâce, and be gone seconds later.

Up the street, a car turned the corner, tires screeching, and accelerated madly. A Simca, its old four-cylinder engine growling, music blasting from open windows. Cyrille ducked back into the shadows as the car passed.

Seconds later, she retook her position. To her chagrin, the vestibule was empty. Cyrille panicked. How? Where? Then she spotted Dekker, several doors down, cloaked in shadow beneath the awning of a café. Now, when Cyrille needed traffic—*just one car, please Lord*—there was none. The street was empty, the neighborhood so still she could hear a footfall. She studied Dekker. Take every precaution, her handler had advised.

And then?

There was no way Cyrille could approach Dekker without being seen. But what choice did she have? Her target stood one hundred feet away. She couldn't risk a shot at this distance. She was no sharpshooter. Shoot and miss, and she'd lose the element of surprise. If Dekker went to ground, there was no telling when Cyrille would get a second chance.

The Tourists

Cyrille raised the weapon to her shoulder. She shut her right eye. Her vision wasn't as good as it once was. Dekker appeared blurry and unsteady. She detached the stock, folded it, and stuffed it into her coat. She would take Dekker close up. It was what she did best.

Cyrille poked her head from the doorway and watched as Dekker stepped from the protection of the awning and onto the curb and looked in both directions. He was expecting someone.

It was now or never.

Cyrille left the doorway and walked up the street, head down, pistol concealed in her pocket. She sensed Dekker looking her way, but she didn't dare meet his gaze. She could see him out of the corner of her eye. A few steps and she would make her charge across the street, firing as she ran. There was no chance he could escape. Imagining the act, Cyrille enjoyed a burst of confidence.

And then the confidence evaporated.

Two blocks to the north, a police car rounded the corner, blue lights flashing, driving at speed. Another police car followed it, and another.

Cyrille ducked into a recessed doorway, throwing herself against a wall, shoulders as flat as she could pin them. The cars sped by, passing Dekker first, then her, and braking to a halt in front of Rosenfeld's building. Officers piled out of the cars. There was a great deal of commotion. Slamming doors, opening trunks, grabbing heavy firearms, shouting orders, throwing on helmets.

She looked for Dekker. There was no sign of him beneath the awning. No movement at all. Of course he'd vanished. He'd made a run for it like any sane man.

But no. Cyrille caught a glimmer of light. On, then off. Dekker's phone. Like her, he'd ducked into the shadows. What was he waiting for? A ride—what else? Had to be.

She freed the pistol from her jacket. Her plan could still work. The police were fifty feet away, across the street and to her right. Only a few remained near their vehicles; the rest were storming Rosenfeld's building. Dekker was hiding a hundred feet from them, maybe fifty feet from her position.

Cyrille took a knee and aimed at Dekker, elbow resting on her thigh, both hands supporting the weapon. It was a clean shot, the target immobile.

Then Dekker was moving, leaving the safety of the recessed doorway, stepping onto the sidewalk, hand raised. Cyrille followed him in her sights. A car approached and pulled to the curb. Dekker rushed toward it, reaching out an arm to open the rear door. Rideshare? An accomplice? It didn't matter.

Cyrille pulled the trigger three times in rapid succession. Three times the pistol spat fire, the shots masked by the police's continued ruckus.

She looked on as Dekker opened the door and threw himself into the back seat. Had she hit him? Impossible to know.

For a few seconds, the car didn't move.

Cyrille left the doorway and approached the automobile. The car's brake lights flashed. It accelerated. And then it was gone.

Mac Dekker knew what it was like to be shot at. He knew the hiss of the air, the curious sizzle felt on his skin, the momentary disruption in hearing that occurred when a bullet zipped past.

He threw himself into the back seat. "Go," he shouted.

The driver looked over his shoulder. "Good morning," he said. "Everything all right?"

Three shots. Someone had fired three rounds at him. Mac looked into the driver's eyes. He was a kindly man, a welcoming smile for his passenger at 4:00 a.m. No, he could not tell him.

"I'm fine," Mac answered. "Just in a hurry."

Still the driver hesitated. Mac ventured a look out the rear window. He caught a movement in a doorway across the street. A bent, urgent figure. Short, thin, emerging from the shadows, wearing a beret and a heavy topcoat, hands thrust into its pockets. A hitter.

Finally, the driver returned his attention to the road and slowly pulled away from the curb.

CHAPTER 23

Paris–Le Bourget Airport

The Gulfstream G550 business jet carrying Eliza Porter Elkins and Don Baker touched down at Paris–Le Bourget Airport at one minute after nine o'clock in the morning. Ground fog hugged the runway. For a moment the aircraft skidded on the damp tarmac. Baker squeezed his eyes shut, hands clawing the armrests.

Elkins saw his wan, shaken face. "It's okay, Don," she said, reaching across the aisle to touch his arm. "We made it."

Baker forced a smile. "Never gets easier."

The jet taxied to a hangar far away from the main terminal. A black Mercedes sedan waited inside.

Elkins threw her travel bag over her shoulder and deftly negotiated the steep, narrow stairs, making a beeline to the sedan. Baker carted his carry-on bag off the plane, nearly tripping and falling before he made it to the ground.

It had been a quick flight. Six hours instead of the usual seven. The onboard flight map had indicated an average altitude of 41,000 feet, well above normal. The airspeed of 630 miles per hour was likewise above normal. The CIA was as cost conscious as any commercial airline. Someone had given the pilot the order to floor it.

Fields, a tall, cadaverous man from the embassy, stood by the car. Saturday morning and he was dressed in a black suit, sunglasses covering his eyes.

"Give me the news," said Elkins.

"We have a sighting," said Fields. "A private contractor tracked him to an apartment in the fourth arrondissement. The Marais."

"Isn't that the Jewish neighborhood?" asked Elkins.

"It is," said Fields.

Elkins gave Baker a look. Another nail in Mac's coffin. "What else do we know?"

"Dekker was spotted leaving the address of Gerard Rosenfeld, the maître d' of the restaurant Jules Verne, at four a.m. The contractor learned that Dekker was looking for his wife, who had somehow vanished from the restaurant the day before. He forced his way back into the restaurant to view the security tapes."

"What did he see?"

"Unknown," said Fields. "But whatever it was led him to Rosenfeld."

"Is Rosenfeld an agent too?"

"Just a restauranteur, as far as we know."

"Excuse me," said Baker, addressing Fields. "But aren't our own people looking for Dekker?"

"They are," said Fields, "but we've called in some assistance from local sources."

"I know what a private contractor is," said Baker. "A hitter." He turned to Elkins. "Eliza, you said we were coming to find Mac and talk to him. Did you red-flag him?"

"Watch your tone," said Elkins, drawing him aside. "Things are more complicated than they appear. It's a question of risk mitigation."

"Mac doesn't need mitigating," said Baker.

"We are in no position to take anything for granted. You yourself informed Dekker that were he to involve himself in any overtly political activities, he'd risk the ire of the agency, did you not?"

"Yes, but—"

"And how would you classify his actions over the past twenty-four hours? Killing two diplomats, running from the police, and now forcing his way into a restaurant to look at security tapes. Who knows what he was doing inside that apartment at four a.m. talking to this man, Rosenfeld."

"I agree that it might appear suspicious," said Baker.

"Mac Dekker is an agent running in the field," said Elkins. "He broke his promise to us. He knows what he's bringing down on himself."

Baker took a breath. "Look, Eliza, the contractor said Mac was looking for Ava. It doesn't sound like they're working together."

"We can't assume that."

"Mac's not stupid," said Baker. "He wouldn't hang around if it wasn't for something vital. He knows what he's risking."

"Stop apologizing for Mac Dekker," said Elkins. "That ship has sailed. Yes, I red-flagged him. Believe me, it's the last thing I wanted to do."

As she brushed past him, Baker placed a firm hand on her shoulder, arresting her progress. "It's time you told me exactly what we're doing in Paris."

"Mr. Baker, if you please."

Baker lowered his hand.

Elkins snapped her head toward Fields. "Take us to the embassy. Now."

CHAPTER 24

St.-Germain-des-Prés
Paris

"Dad, you have to leave."

Mac pressed the phone to his ear. "Jaycee, that you?"

"Who else has the number?"

"I'm sorry," said Mac, a little hazy. "Hold on a sec. I must have dozed off."

He sat up and threw his feet onto the floor. He checked his watch. It was nine o'clock. He'd slept two hours. He looked around the flat, remembering where he was, his flight from Gerard Rosenfeld's apartment, one step ahead of the police.

"Jaycee, I'm here," he said, rousing himself. "Listen, I need your help."

"Dad, stop," said Jane. "You need to leave the safe flat immediately. Hear me? Get the hell out."

"Leave?" said Mac. "I haven't had my coffee yet."

"I'm not joking," Jane continued. "The DDO is flying to Paris. She might already be there. She's canvassing all the safe houses in Paris to see if any are in use."

"But no one knows I'm here," said Mac. "Right?"

"No one knows you—Mac Dekker—are there. But safe houses are equipped with security systems that let station chiefs know when they're in use. If anyone checks, they'll find a record of someone entering the premises. For all I know, there are cameras there too."

"Who is she?" asked Mac. "The new DDO. Anyone I'd know?"

"She came over from State," said Jane. "Consular Affairs."

Consular Affairs. There was a shady outfit. A bunch of glorified scalp hunters. "She's coming to Paris to look for me?" asked Mac.

"No one is saying as much, but yeah."

"How do you know? Friends tipping you off?"

"I just know," said Jane. "I've got ten years on the job. Give me some credit."

"Thanks for the heads-up," said Mac. "Last thing I want to do is get you into trouble."

"I'll only get in hot water if they find you there," said Jane.

Mac stood, grabbing the pistol off the night table and tucking it into his waistband. He could be dressed and gone in ninety seconds. "I'm up and moving," he said. "Can we talk later?"

"I'm not finished," said Jane. "Word is that you've been red-flagged."

The news hit Mac like a sock in the gut. "Red flag" was agency lingo for a termination notice. A contract issued for an individual's murder. He'd been red-flagged once before. He'd escaped, but at the cost of his name and nine years' exile. "Shoot first, ask questions later," he said. "That's extreme. Who the hell is the new DDO, anyway?"

"Eliza Porter Elkins. She likes to use all three names."

Mac thought he was hearing things. "Eliza Porter Elkins? For real?"

"Yeah. What about her?"

"Nothing, sweetheart," said Mac. "The name rings a bell, that's all. Think she's someone I escorted in Baghdad back in the day. Congressional delegation."

"Her father's a senator," said Jane. "He's the longest-serving member of Congress. She's got some juice."

"Yeah," said Mac, unexpectedly coming face to face with another of his past sins. "I know who he is . . . they are, um, whatever."

He remembered Eliza Porter Elkins vividly. To him, she was and always would be "Lizzie." It was a crazy time. The surge going full force, thousands of new troops pouring into the country. Missions carried out 24/7. Kill, kill, kill. IEDs on every street. So many of his brothers cut down. In a word, "hell."

And then there she was. A blond beauty asking smart questions. What happened, happened. He didn't regret it. But she'd seen things a different way. A way Mac had no business seeing things when he was counting his life in days, maybe hours. But try explaining that to a woman like her. A woman who got what she wanted. A woman with some juice, even then.

"What's going on down there?" asked Jane. "You've got a lot of very important people very scared."

"I found out who abducted Ava," said Mac. "Prince Tariq bin Nayan bin Tariq al-Sabah."

"TNT?" Jane's surprise was evident. "He's a dilettante, a showboat."

"You know him?" asked Mac.

"Not in any professional sense," said Jane. "I've seen some of the pictures he posts. He's like the Kardashians on steroids. He's the world's biggest car nut. His father made him Minister of the Interior last year to get him to spend more time at home. So far, it hasn't worked."

"An influencer," said Mac. "Whatever that is."

"What does he want with Ava?" asked Jane.

"They know each other," said Mac, replaying the scene from the security camera. "When they met, he gave her a kiss on the cheek. They talked for a second, then things went south. Looked heated. Out of nowhere, a woman jabbed a syringe into her neck. Some kind of drug. Ava was down in five seconds. She never saw it coming."

"That doesn't sound like Ava," said Jane.

No, Mac had to admit to himself. It didn't. Ava saw everything coming.

"All this happened in the restaurant?" said Jane. "I don't get it."

"He had help," said Mac and explained how Gerard Rosenfeld had aided and abetted TNT to steal Ava out of the nearly empty restaurant.

"I'm afraid to ask how you know all this," said Jane.

"Don't," said Mac.

Before conking out, he'd done a search on TNT. It took ten minutes of scouring his social media pages to get a picture of his opulent lifestyle. Clothes, watches, and like Jane said: cars, cars, cars.

Journalists shed a more informative light on him. Boarding school in England. College in the States. A bachelor's degree from USC. No dorms for him. He took over the top floor of the Four Seasons Beverly Wilshire hotel. A scandal about a gift of a Rolex to a professor. Questions about how much coursework he'd in fact completed.

That wasn't all Mac had discovered. The Al-Sabah royal family maintained an official website showcasing biographies of all its members—a total of some 653 men, women, and children. TNT wasn't quite the dilettante Jane claimed. There was another side to him that he seemed to want to keep hidden—a subject about which he didn't post pictures on social media. TNT had completed officer training at the Royal Military Academy Sandhurst in England and, afterward, graduated from the rigorous three-month US Army Ranger course. A Rolex would not buy you a Ranger tab; that you had to earn. Mac knew this from experience. The course was brutal, bordering on life-endangering. In ninety days, he had lost thirty-seven pounds, dislocated his shoulder, and, for one grueling three-hour stretch, gone blind from dehydration. His Ranger tab counted among his proudest possessions.

TNT was also a sharpshooter who'd competed for his country at the Olympic Games. He was not just the good-looking, jet-setting billionaire he wanted the world to believe. There was steel beneath the polished veneer. And more. Ambition.

Which man, Mac wondered, was the real TNT?

"You asked me if we had something running in Paris," said Jane. "We don't, at least nothing anyone is talking about. I haven't had time to check with Mossad, not that they'd tell me. But those guys who came after you in the hotel yesterday . . . the one whose name you gave me is a member of the Royal Guard, the Saudi king's bodyguards. Wherever the king goes, they go with him. If they're in Paris, so is the king. His name also came up as being a member of the Tiger Squad. One of their trained assassins. He was there in Istanbul when they cut up Khashoggi."

Jamal Khashoggi, the Saudi American dual-national journalist lured into the Saudi consulate in Istanbul, where he was strangled to death before his body was chopped into pieces and placed into trash bags for discreet removal. His murder was payback for a few scathing articles about the Saudi royal family.

"That explains the knife," said Mac.

"What? Dad! Those men came to kill you?"

Well, thought Mac, they certainly weren't the ones who sent the fruit basket. "I don't get it," he said. "First TNT, then the Saudis. But, listen, Jaycee, there's an Israeli involved, too, and he's not one of the good guys. Yehudi Rosenfeld."

"A relation of the other one?" asked Jane. "From the restaurant."

"His brother," said Mac. "Know him? He's a member of the Knesset, part of the Kach Party. They're way to the right. Anti-Arab, pro-settler, as extreme as an Israeli politician can get. Apparently, he co-opted his brother to help TNT."

"Why would Ava be working with TNT, the Qataris, or the Saudis, for that matter?" asked Jane. "And what are the Qataris doing palling around with the Jewish National Front? They hate each other."

"My question exactly," said Mac, as he finished dressing and headed for the door. "Now you have something to occupy yourself with. Find out, will you? I'm out of here. I'll call you in an hour."

"No, Dad. You can't," said Jane. "Too many people are watching me. Don't contact me. I can't talk to you again."

"Jane, I need your help."

"This isn't just about you anymore. *I've done all I can.* Please, get out of the city. Promise me."

"Not yet," said Mac.

"Ava can take care of herself," said Jane, with mounting frustration. "People want you dead. Think of Katya. She can't lose both of you."

"She's not going to," said Mac.

"If you stay, they'll find you," said Jane.

"Maybe. Maybe not."

"Get over yourself, dammit," said Jane. "Be a father first, for once. Ava didn't want you involved in this."

"I know what I'm doing," said Mac, knowing, of course, that he didn't.

"You can't save everyone."

"Just wait—"

"You disappeared once," said Jane. "Do it again."

"Jane . . ."

"Just do it. Get out. Hear me? Get out."

The line went dead. Mac stared at the phone.

Get out. It's what the card addressed to the "Famille Steinhardt" had said.

Mac removed the SIM card and flushed it down the toilet. He checked his pistol—round in the chamber, safety on. Did he have time to take a leak? No, he decided. That would have to wait. Jane had put herself in jeopardy to find him the bolt-hole and to warn him. He had to do as she instructed. *Get the hell out.*

Mac left the flat. He paused inside the foyer to peer through the windows on either side of the door. It was a sunny morning. Pedestrians thronged the sidewalk. He scanned the street for double-parked cars, vans, anything that might signal unwanted attention.

Eliza Porter Elkins was in Paris. Had she come alone? Was Don Baker with her? Who had tipped Jaycee off? A red flag. Again? All these thoughts raced through Mac's brain as he tried to figure out the best course of action.

"Screw it," he muttered, shouldering the door and hitting the street. It was too much for a simple field guy. He didn't do plotting and conniving and scheming. If they were there, they were there.

He headed east on the Boulevard St.-Germain, past the Brasserie Lipp and, across the street, the Café Deux Magots. The tables out front were taken. No sign of Hemingway, Fitzgerald, or Eliza Porter Elkins. Against every rule, he looked over his shoulder. If they were coming, he wanted to see them. *But no* . . . for now, he didn't see anyone stalking him. No stealthy assets with murder in their eyes. No little old ladies with poison-tipped umbrellas. No tall, buxom blonds looking to call in an airstrike on him.

He laughed at himself. You never saw 'em coming. Just like they never saw Mac coming.

He'd forgotten how lousy it felt to be on the run in enemy territory.

Mac turned the corner and entered the first shop he came to. It was a confiserie selling chocolates and pastries. The smell was heavenly. He browsed the displays while keeping watch out the window for a tail.

Jane was right. Sooner or later, they'd find him. They always did. A red flag. What were they so scared of? Strangely, the news fired him up. He was on the right path. Whatever Ava was involved in, whatever trouble she'd gotten into, it was important enough for a deputy director of the CIA to drop everything and fly to Paris.

He only wished Ava had confided in him. He was no longer angry with her. He loved her, and love, at its root, meant trust. Like it or not, he had to trust Ava's decision not to bring him into her affairs. But that was then . . . *that was before she'd been abducted.* He had no choice but to help her. There it was.

Sorry, Jaycee, your dad is never going to disappear again.

"Good morning." The salesgirl smiled at Mac from behind the display. "May I help you?"

Mac jumped, as if shaken from a reverie. Yes, he did need help. He couldn't do this alone. He'd never locate Ava if he had to constantly check over his shoulder.

"Harry Crooks," he blurted. Where in the world had the name come from?

"Excuse me?"

"Crooks . . . oh, uh, never mind," said Mac, once again present. "Nothing for me. I've gotta run."

Mac fled the store, talking to himself. "Harry Crooks. I wonder if the tough bastard's still alive."

CHAPTER 25

Boulevard du Montparnasse
Paris

TNT honked the horn.

Two lean, dark-eyed men hustled out a steel door. Both were dressed in black mechanics' jumpsuits with the name "Exotic European Motorcars" sewn on the breast. One unlocked the padlock securing the retracting door and with an effort rolled it skyward. The other waved TNT inside, walking backward into the repair bay.

TNT drove the Bugatti into the shop. Bright hexagonal LED lights hung from the ceiling. There were additional bays on either side. Both were empty. As soon as TNT entered, the door was lowered. TNT waited until it slammed shut, then climbed from the car.

The mechanics were Slavs. Ben and Goran from Serbia. Both had raced cars professionally years earlier. Ben had won a few Formula 3 races. Goran had made it as a backup driver on the McLaren team for a few years. Afterward, they'd worked on the Formula 1 circuit, part of one team or another. It was a hard life, on the road eight months a year, with hell to pay unless you podiumed. They quit and settled in Paris. With their connections, they built a business selling and servicing exotic motorcars, which meant the priciest vehicles manufactured by the world's most exclusive automobile companies. Ferrari, Lamborghini, and Bugatti, among others. It was exacting work, and that was before dealing with the clients. Labor costs started at €500 an hour and went up from there. The old saying held true: "If you have to ask the price, it's too expensive."

TNT greeted both men with a handshake and a hug.

"What . . . no picture?" said Goran. He was around fifty—crew cut, thin as a rail, always chewing gum. "Where's the camera?"

"Not today," said TNT. "No camera."

It was his practice to bring in the car every three months for a full service. This morning, however, he had come for a different reason. The reason he could not allow Customs Inspector LeClerc to take too close a look at the car.

"Something's wrong with the air filter," said TNT, after turning down a coffee, a cigarette, and a stick of gum, in that order.

"What you got?" asked Goran. "Too much sand?"

"You hanging around the stables again?" said Ben. "I tell you, not good for car. Dust, hay, horse shit." He was as small as a jockey, hunched, a constant smirk twisting his face. Ben was a horse racing enthusiast and, as such, always on the lookout for tips. "You here for big race? See you on TV yesterday. Nice horse."

"Something like that," said TNT. "Actually, I brought a little something from home. Something I didn't want the boys in customs to find, and no, it isn't drugs."

"Not for horses," said Ben, disappointed.

"A present," said TNT.

"In the air filter," said Goran, matter-of-factly.

"Air intake, actually," said TNT. "Bolted. It's fragile."

"No problem, boss," said Ben. "You let me know if that horse of yours going to win tomorrow."

TNT patted the slight man on the shoulder. "I guarantee it," he said, to the bemusement of both mechanics, who high-fived one another, already counting their winnings.

"You sit in waiting room, boss," said Goran. "Be done fast."

"I'll stay," said Tariq.

"You nervous, eh?" said Goran. "Think we're going to break your present."

"Important present," said TNT.

"You the boss." Goran climbed into the Bugatti and drove it forward a few feet. Ben locked down the tires to make sure the vehicle wouldn't budge.

The Bugatti Chiron was a mid-engine automobile. Its V-16 quad-turbo engine weighed one thousand pounds alone and was situated behind the passenger compartment on an elevated transverse mount. Ben removed the transparent plexiglass bonnet and handed it to Goran. The air intakes were shaped like hollow gourds and sat on top of the engine, one to either side. Each was thirty inches in length, forged from stainless steel, and painted glossy black.

"Where the present?" asked Goran, plugging in a variable-speed impact wrench and revving it.

"Left air intake," said TNT.

Goran removed the bolts that attached it to the chassis. He handed the wrench to Ben, then freed the intake valve from its clamps. "Heavy," he said.

"Thirteen pounds," said TNT.

"Lot of jewels," said Goran.

"You a thief?" asked Ben aggressively, which was what they took for humor.

Goran carried the intake to a trestle table. Bending at the waist, he peered inside. He barked instructions to Ben, who handed him a Phillips screwdriver. A minute later, Goran withdrew a slim, rectangular item wrapped in black Plasticine. The "present" was seventeen inches long, three inches wide, and four inches deep, more or less the size and shape of an ingot of gold. "I allowed to ask what is?"

"No," said TNT.

Goran tossed it halfway across the bay to Ben. "Fragile, eh? What you think?"

Ben shook the package, then put it to his ear. "Candy," he said.

"You're right," said TNT. "Candy."

The Slavs laughed.

"You promise your horse gonna win?" said Ben, clutching the package to his chest.

"Promise," said TNT.

"Here you go." Ben tossed the package to TNT. It was a lousy throw, too short and too low. TNT jumped forward and fell to a knee, getting his hands under it a moment before it hit the floor.

"What are you waiting for?" he said, standing up, smiling uneasily. "Put the car back together."

He entered the men's private office and shut the door. After setting the package on the table, he took a seat and leaned back, exhaling, staring at the ceiling.

When did it all begin? This scheme of his. This vision. This bold adventure.

A dinner in Doha. A seasonable night in February, always the nicest month of the year. Dinner at the restaurant Nobu in the Four Seasons Hotel. A table overlooking the water on the shore of the Persian Gulf. A view up the coastline to the business district. One skyscraper more modern, more daring than the next. A sight to make a Qatari heart proud.

It was his turn to dine the delegation from Hamas. *Hamas* was the acronym for the Islamic Resistance Movement, which was, more specifically, the Palestinian nationalist Sunni political party that had governed the Gaza Strip since 2006.

It was Hamas that, on October 7, 2023, sent its soldiers rampaging across the Israeli border to kill and capture as many Jews as possible. The action was viewed as a reprisal by those who ordered it and an act of war by those who had been attacked. The Israelis took their time to fashion a response. When it came, it was more thunderous than even the most pessimistic minds had foreseen. First there was artillery, then the campaign from the air, then the invasion.

The Tourists

The interesting thing about Gaza was that it belonged to no one. Not to Egypt, which bordered it to the south. Not to Israel, which surrounded it to the east and north. It was not even its own sovereign state. It was just a strip of land twenty-five miles long and four or five miles wide. One hundred forty square miles in total area and home to two million Palestinians no one wanted.

Nearly as soon as the conflict began, all concerned parties sent representatives to Doha—spies, government officials, business leaders, whatever—though even now Tariq wasn't sure why. No one seemed to want an end to the killing, at least at first. Israel was hell bent on massacring every last fighter in Gaza, Hamas or not. And Hamas was happy to let them try, hoping that as many civilians as possible were killed along the way. Hamas might lose the military campaign, but would be damned if it lost the public relations campaign. Besides, Tariq mused, a few thousand more martyrs sent to heaven meant a few thousand fewer mouths to feed on earth. No one said Hamas wasn't practical.

Doha was like a watering hole in Africa, where at dawn and dusk all the animals—predators and prey—could congregate without fear of being eaten or attacked. Hamas was camped at the St. Regis. Hezbollah at the Four Seasons. The Emiratis had taken over the Ritz-Carlton, and the Saudis were at the Mandarin Oriental. Israel, whose delegation paradoxically was the smallest, housed its people in hostels and guesthouses. Even if no one was ready to negotiate, they could at least exchange a few words over coffee.

Back to the Nobu. It had been a contentious day. TNT had no recollection of what had been agreed or refused by whom. The men he was dining with were in a particularly irascible state, which if one knew anything about Hamas—for which the go-to solution to any problem was to blow it up—was saying something.

"We must kill them. Kill them all." No need to reveal the man's name. TNT would call him Abdul. "I know how," said Abdul, in a fury.

"We have one of theirs. A bomb. We can use it. Boom. All gone. The Knesset. King Saul Boulevard. Take your pick."

"That would end things," said Tariq, agreeably, though he was wary of any further escalation. He knew better, however, than to talk logic; not with someone with hate oozing from his every pore. "What do you have in mind?"

"They call it 'Samson,'" said Abdul.

"Like the strong man," said Tariq, still wondering who "they" were. "A bomb. And you have it?"

Abdul nodded. "It is hidden. We are waiting for the right moment."

"Samson," said Tariq. Was this just a rant? Some unhinged revenge fantasy? It was the faraway look of steadfast determination that convinced Tariq that his new friend, Abdul, was telling the truth. He did have something. But what?

"Tell me more," said Tariq.

Abdul blinked and shuddered as if coming to his senses. He placed his hand on Tariq's arm and fixed him with a stare. "You can be trusted?"

"I am an Al-Sabah," said Tariq.

After a moment's contemplation, Abdul drew him aside. Over several cups of Turkish coffee—and yes, to be honest, some Turkish raki as well—he told him the story of how an Israeli nuclear weapon had been captured about ten years earlier. An ISIS militia had overrun a team of Israeli soldiers sent to remove a secret arsenal of battlefield nuclear weapons on the Golan Heights. The weapon—they learned from sources later that it was called "Samson"—was taken to a rebel base in Aleppo, but no one there knew exactly what they had gotten their hands on. The device was too sophisticated, far beyond their ken. Frankly, it scared them. As usual, ISIS needed money. A decision was made to sell it.

Here, TNT interrupted Abdul. "You say it is a 'battlefield nuclear weapon.' What does that mean?"

"One kiloton, so we believe," said Abdul. "Very small. Three inches wide. Seventeen inches long."

"I don't believe it," said Tariq. "How can it be?"

Abdul said that he, too, was surprised to learn a weapon such as this—a nuke—could be so small. "The problem is not the fissile material, the uranium or plutonium, my friend. It is the explosives needed to detonate the material. In 1945, the first bomb was the size of a car. By 1955—when the first battlefield nukes were manufactured—it could fit into a backpack. By 1970, it could fit in a suitcase. Always smaller. That was fifty years ago. A half century. Think of all the advancements since. Between you and me, I would not be surprised if today a bomb can be made the size of a deck of playing cards."

The device had traveled to Damascus, Abdul continued, where it was shown to members of the Syrian Ministry of Defense. A nephew of al-Assad, an engineer—everyone was a doctor in that family—paid $100,000 for it. And there in Damascus Samson stayed for years. The Syrians knew exactly what they had, but they couldn't do anything with it either. They had no nuclear program. The engineer summoned a team of Pakistani nuclear physicists, formerly part of AQ Khan's team. It was they who discovered that the device required two six-digit codes to be detonated. The first deactivated the safety. The second detonated the device. However, neither they nor anyone in the Syrian government possessed the technology or know-how to solve the problem. They were friendly with only one country that did: the Islamic Republic of Iran.

But Iran didn't want Samson either. The only nukes it was interested in measured in the hundreds of kilotons or more. Samson was a toy. One kiloton. A tactical nuke. It could make a big hole in the ground and foul up the air for a few months, but that was all. It was more trouble than it was worth.

Years went by. Rumors about Samson's existence circulated.

Until Hamas decided it wanted it . . . even if it could not be detonated. Hamas viewed it as an investment—something to be bargained with, sold, or God willing, used in the future. Ironically, it purchased it with money given by the Israeli government for the day-to-day management of Gaza. One hundred million dollars gone from the budget. But that was Hamas all over again. Money earmarked for the betterment of its people—for schools, for hospitals, for infrastructure, for food—was put to other use. War. Conflict. Confrontation. For without the prospect of one day bringing Allah's will to fruition and causing the removal of the Jewish people from land promised them—the Palestinians—by the Prophet Muhammad, peace be unto him, who were they?

Personally, TNT was agnostic on the question of Israeli statehood. He was a realist. The chances of the Palestinians in Gaza, the West Bank, Lebanon, or anywhere else pushing Israel into the sea were nil. Less than nil, really, as it was the Palestinians themselves who were threatened with annihilation and seemed to be doing everything within their means to bring it upon themselves. TNT wasn't against Israel so much as for Qatar, and for TNT. He was a mercenary fighting for the worthiest cause he knew: the greater good and elevation of Tariq bin Nayan bin Tariq al-Sabah.

And so it was that there, on the veranda of the restaurant Nobu, listening to the sea lap against the shore wall, while digesting a feast of the finest fresh fish known to man, he proposed to purchase Samson.

The price, said Abdul, was $500 million.

Tariq said yes.

It was not a rash decision. He did not buy it on a whim like he might buy a sports car or a jet or a motor yacht. The family might be worth $500 billion, but Tariq couldn't just write a check for a half a billion without an explanation. He knew better than to tell his father, or any of the financial masterminds who oversaw the fortune, why he needed the money. Instead, he couched the request as a plea for their Arab brothers. Hamas needed $500 million. The money was to be a down payment on rebuilding its subterranean tunnel system, the vaunted "Gaza underground," and thus the first step back on the road to defeating Israel. Did not Qatar want the same thing?

That was eight months ago.

The Tourists

Keeping an eye on the mechanics, Tariq consulted his contact list and placed a call.

"You have it?" asked an accented Israeli voice.

"In my hands," said TNT. "Do you have the codes?"

"In my head," said Yehudi Rosenfeld.

"I hope your memory is good."

"Impeccable," said Rosenfeld.

"Have they set a time?" asked TNT.

"Tomorrow. Ten a.m.," said Rosenfeld. "I'll give you the codes as soon as Samson is in place."

"It would be better to have them before," said Tariq.

"For you, maybe," said Rosenfeld. "You would be just as happy to blow all of us up. My master and I prefer to return home in one piece. We will have a country to govern, after all."

"My poor brother," said Tariq. "Jabr thinks you're his friend."

"Never," said Rosenfeld. "At least you're smart enough to know that."

CHAPTER 26

Passy, sixteenth arrondissement
Paris

"Hello, Harry."

"You're dead," said Harry Crooks.

"Nine years now," said Mac.

"Took you out in Beirut. Car bomb."

"A taxi bomb," said Mac. "But who's checking."

"Shake my hand," said Crooks. "I have to know this is for real."

"Hell, I'll give you a kiss if you want."

Crooks reached out and took Mac's hand. "You bloody bugger. It is you."

His friend had aged considerably. His hair was gone, his pate shaved as smooth as a billiard ball. He'd grown a beard, far more white than black. He had the same sparkly, inquisitive eyes; eyes that speared you, made you pay attention. But now they lurked behind a pair of owlish, horn-rimmed glasses.

Still, he looked as fit as ever. The same old Harry. Broad, powerful shoulders tapered to an athlete's waist. Biceps as big as softballs pressed through his tight black sweater. What was he? Sixty-five? Seventy? Not too far, Mac realized, in front of him.

They'd met at the tail end of the Iraq War. Crooks was a big shot at GCHQ—Government Communications Headquarters—the United

Kingdom's signals intelligence–gathering organization, the rough equivalent of America's NSA. He'd come to Baghdad to help set up a cutting-edge IED detection system that relied on intercepting phone signals. Mac had come to kill the people making the IEDs. The team's motto was "You track 'em, we whack 'em."

It wasn't until *Skylark*, however, that they'd really gotten to know each other.

"Nice to see you, too, by the way," said Mac. "Ummm . . . you mind if I come in?"

Crooks angled his wheelchair to block his entrance. "This isn't a social visit, is it? Hate small talk."

"No, Harry, it isn't."

"By all means, then," he said, rolling back and away, a smile brightening his features. "Come in. Mac Dekker. As I live and breathe."

Mac shut the door and followed Crooks down the hall and into a spacious living area. There was a leather couch and a recliner, bookshelves filled to overflowing. A Ghanaian flag hung in one corner, next to the Union Jack. Mac remembered something about Crooks's family immigrating to England when he was a teenager. In all these years, he'd never lost the accent.

The room's center of activity was a large L-shaped desk, filling up the far corner. Several laptops sat open alongside other electronic gadgetry, lots of loose papers, books.

"Still at it?" asked Mac, gesturing to the electronics scattered across the desk.

"You know me."

"The original gearhead."

A grenade had put Harry Crooks into a chair forty-odd years ago. Crooks was SAS, a sergeant, part of a team charged with taking an airfield during the Falklands War. He never talked about it, and Mac remembered whispers of his receiving the Victoria Cross, Britain's equivalent of the Medal of Honor.

"It's addictive, isn't it?" said Crooks. "Listening in. Snooping."

"Eavesdropping?" said Mac.

"I prefer 'investigating,'" said Crooks. "I spent thirty years trying to discover what the enemy didn't want me to. Not something you can just turn off. The desire to know."

Mac wasn't sure he had an answer. He'd spent the last chunk of his life trying to do the opposite. Not to snoop, not to listen in. It would have been too much otherwise.

"I won't ask how you found me," said Crooks.

"Christmas card," said Mac. "I remembered the address. Rue St.-Niklaus. I thought it was a funny name. It stuck with me."

"Bullshit."

"I looked you up," said Mac. "You're in the phone book."

Crooks pulled off his glasses and cleaned them on his sweater. "So, then, you going to tell me? Car bomb, taxi bomb . . . no bomb at all?"

"Long story," said Mac.

"I'm retired," said Crooks. "Take your time."

"After," said Mac gravely. It was not a subject he felt like going into. "If that's all right."

"It's like that, then," said Crooks, with sympathy. A man who knew pain and recognized it in others.

"And your wife?" asked Mac. "Still hitched?"

"Five years gone. Cancer."

"I'm sorry."

They shared a moment of silence. Time marched on. They were still alive when others weren't. Maybe when they had no right to be.

"How do you like your tea?" asked Crooks.

"Milk. Two sugars."

"Coming right up," said Crooks. "Make yourself at home."

He returned a few minutes later, a tray on his lap. He set the cups and kettle on a worn maple table.

"So it's you?" he asked, pouring the tea.

"Pardon?"

The Tourists

"Steinhardt . . . wanted for murder. Hotel Bristol. The two Saudis. That what this is about? Don't look surprised. You're burning up the wires. What do you think I do to keep busy? Picked it up yesterday evening on the police band. Caucasian male, six feet tall, dark hair, senior citizen, armed and dangerous."

"Senior citizen?" said Mac. "They really said that?"

"Well? Aren't you?" said Crooks.

"Almost," said Mac. "I guess."

"One of the policemen said the suspect escaped by climbing out of the window. Reminded me of someone I knew way back when."

"Was that here?" asked Mac, trying to recollect.

"Louveciennes," said Crooks.

Louveciennes was a commune on the western outskirts of the city, home to the Château Louis XIV. It wasn't a real château, at least not in the historic sense. It was a re-creation of a château that might have belonged to King Louis XIV, the Sun King, but built by the king of Saudi Arabia. At some point during *Skylark* Mac had climbed out of one of the château's windows.

"Forgot about that."

"I didn't," said Crooks. "You saved my life."

"Don't exaggerate."

"You saved all of our lives." Crooks lifted his cup high. "Cheers, then, mate. To resurrection."

Mac lifted his cup. "Live to fight another day."

They drank their tea. Crooks regarded Mac and smiled. "I'm sorry," he said. "I can tell you're in a bad way. It's just . . . just—"

"Harry, you don't know the half of it. I'm in the shit."

"I'm sorry to hear that," said Crooks. "Truly I am. It's just that I know good and well this is going to end badly, but by God, I don't give a damn. I'm with Mac Dekker, and we're going to open up a bloody big can of worms. I can't wait."

143

CHAPTER 27

US embassy
Paris

It was Eliza Porter Elkins's first visit to Paris. She'd traveled to England, Spain, and throughout Scandinavia. Somehow her European itineraries, both personal and professional, had never included France.

The drive into the city was unimpressive. The sky was gray and overcast. The buildings grayer, damp, drab, and all too similar. The sidewalks carpeted with fallen leaves. Well, she thought, gazing out the window, maybe she really hadn't missed that much.

Then the car crossed a bridge. Her first glance of the Seine. Pea green, roiling, crowding its banks. The buildings fell away. As if by command, the traffic disappeared. Alone, they sped across the Place de la Concorde, broad and sweeping, tires rattling over cobblestones. There was the Obelisk, Napoleon's hard-won trophy from his Egyptian campaign. How old was it? A thousand years? Two thousand? To her left, the Champs-Élysées, eight lanes flanked by poplars, climbing over a mile to the Arc de Triomphe. Her heart soared. For a few moments, her anxieties vanished. She was mistaken. She had missed that much.

France.

America's oldest diplomatic mission, founded in 1778 by Benjamin Franklin. France, without whose help a fledgling republic would never have won its independence. In a sense, then, America's oldest friend.

The Tourists

And so, the reason why Elkins had jumped onto a plane at the last minute, driven by her sworn duty and a secret fear. She could not allow an American—a former agent, to wit, and declared dead these past nine years—to interfere with the most important diplomatic conference of the new millennium. Not on her watch.

The US embassy to France was located in an elegant four-story building called the Chancery, facing the Champs-Élysées gardens. They parked in back, where a tall fence and a wall guaranteed their anonymity. Fields led them past the marine guards and into the building. An elevator whisked them to the third floor.

"Record time," said Sam McGee, showing them into his office. "Welcome in."

"Hope you didn't have to cancel your tennis match," said Elkins pointedly, remarking on his casual attire. Khakis, polo shirt, and a crew neck sweater.

McGee was tall and strapping, ten years in Special Activities, the paramilitary branch of the Agency, and not one to take shit from anyone, including his superiors. "No indoor courts, I'm afraid," he said. "With the leg I prefer pickleball."

"The leg?"

McGee hiked up his trousers, revealing a titanium prosthesis. "It's a little easier for me—and for people your age, I understand."

"Touché, Mr. McGee," said Elkins. "We should get along just fine."

"Doubtful, but let's give it a shot."

The office was spacious and well appointed, with furniture more suited to a country home than a government office. She made a note to ask her father, the senator, if she might borrow some of the furniture from the house in Potomac to redecorate her own office. She might work for the government. It didn't mean she had to work *like* them.

"You didn't mention the leg," she said, buttonholing Don Baker as they sat down.

"You didn't ask," he replied, sotto voce. "IED. Fallujah. Mac Dekker was with him."

"What happened to him?" she asked.

"Broken leg, knee, jaw," said Baker. "He was laid up six months. You can ask him about his tennis game when we find him."

Elkins gave him a look—*Watch it!*—and sat down in a comfortable armchair. Sam McGee sat opposite her. He was rather handsome, trim beard, high forehead, intelligent eyes. He asked how the flight was and if she wanted coffee. She said, "fine," and "yes, with three sugars and cream."

"Anything more on Dekker's whereabouts?" she inquired, now that they were on the safe side of small talk.

"Last seen around four a.m. in the Marais," said McGee.

"Nothing from the police?"

"We're keeping Mac's identity under wraps," said McGee. "They think they're looking for Robert Steinhardt, Swiss national. Unless you wish to instruct us to do otherwise?"

"Not at the moment," said Elkins. She smiled. "Don just informed me you worked together, you and Mac."

"Did a few hops downrange," said McGee. "That would be 2005 or 2006. Post surge. Yeah, we had our share of adventures. He went back to Bagram after that, then Syria." He caught himself. "Oh, you don't care about the past. You're wondering if I might have seen him lately."

"Well?" said Elkins, with an edge. *Took you long enough.*

McGee colored. "Excuse me, ma'am," he said, "but until ten o'clock last night, local time, I believed that Mac Dekker was dead. Out of the blue we receive a flash transmission that Mac is, in fact, Robert Steinhardt, Swiss citizen, wanted by the police here in Paris for the murder of two Saudi diplomats and that his capture is a level-one priority. An hour after that you issued a red flag for Mackenzie Dekker. Don, here, was good enough to fill me in on some of the particulars. Given the timing, I understand your concern. But I hope you'll excuse me if I say that my head is still spinning."

"Fair enough," said Elkins. "But it had better stop spinning now. Mac Dekker is alive and well, and God knows what he's up to. But he's here in Paris, and his consort, Ava Attal, who I'm not pleased to inform you is a decorated officer of Mossad—is also in Paris. On this weekend. Now if you'd be so kind, Mr. McGee, please tell me if you've seen him."

"No," said McGee.

"Good," said Elkins. "Happy to have that out of the way. Let's move on. Do we have any further communication from the contractor? I'd like to read the full transcript."

The identity of contractors was kept secret for purposes of compartmentalization and plausible denial. One department vetted them. Another hired them. The head of station or equivalent in rank monitored their activity.

"Did the contractor speak with this man, Gerald Rosenfeld?" she asked, studying the hard copy.

"Not that we know," said McGee. "The contractor broke off pursuit after the police arrived at Rosenfeld's residence."

"You have an address?" she asked. "Might be worth a visit."

"As a rule, we avoid getting involved in local law enforcement matters," said McGee.

"This is hardly local," said Elkins. "Any other time, I'd concur. But as you know . . ." She let the words die off as she glanced in Baker's direction.

"I've known Don a minute," said McGee. "I think it's safe to read him in."

"Hold on," said Elkins. "First tell me if you did that check on the safe houses."

"Three are in use," said McGee. "Two have been occupied for several weeks. One was reserved last night."

"By whom?"

"Rita Campbell. Field officer."

"One of yours?"

"She's out of Berlin," said McGee.

"You're kidding!" said Baker.

"What is it?" said Elkins.

"Jane McCall's in Berlin."

"Who's Jane McCall?" asked Elkins.

"His daughter," said Baker. "Jane Dekker McCall. He calls her Jaycee."

"I don't give a crap what he calls her," said Elkins. "Get her on the line."

McGee contacted his assistant and asked him to find Jane McCall. He came back momentarily and reported that she was away on business and that he had left a message for her to call back immediately.

Elkins didn't like the answer, but for the moment there was nothing to be done. "Do we have eyes on the site?" she asked.

"Of course," said McGee.

"What are you waiting for?" demanded Elkins. "He might be there right now."

Ten minutes later, Elkins stood next to Baker and McGee in the subterranean ops center. They were staring at a multiplex of screens broadcasting a live feed from every camera inside the safe house at 55 Rue du Bac.

"Doesn't look like anyone's there presently," said McGee.

"What about earlier?" said Elkins. "If his daughter reserved it, you can be damned well sure he showed up."

"The security system shows that someone entered the premises at 12:02 last night," said McGee. "They left at 12:56, returned at 5:15 this morning, and left an hour ago."

"That's him," said Elkins.

McGee instructed the tech to rewind the images to just before midnight.

At 12:02, a figure entered the apartment. He closed the door, then turned on the lights. Hello, Mac Dekker.

There was a dome camera in every room, and Elkins followed him into the kitchen, the bathroom, and the bedroom. The cameras were color and high-def, and though she didn't want to watch, she couldn't help herself. Damn him. The bastard was in better shape than he was twenty years ago.

"What are you waiting for?" asked McGee, giving her a look. "See if he uses a washcloth?"

"I want to see what he does before he goes out again," said Elkins, eyes on the screen.

"I'll bet you do," said McGee.

Elkins chose to ignore the gibe. Several minutes later, her diligence was rewarded. Mac sat at the kitchen table, a flip phone or "burner" in hand. "Sound?" she asked.

"Negative," said McGee.

"Wi-Fi?"

"Sure."

"See if he logged on and, if so, if we can track his browsing."

A moment later, a tech said that no one had logged on to the Wi-Fi network in question.

"Do better than that," said Elkins.

"We can geo-source the phone he's using," said the tech. "Need to plug in our best GPS coordinates for the address. Run all the numbers we find against location-history data gathered by all our captive search engines. Give me a minute."

Eliza had a sudden memory of the last time she'd seen Dekker. A week after their tryst, if that was the right word. A chance encounter, Dekker leaving the ambassador's residence in the Green Zone as she was entering. She blinked and felt as if she were there once again.

"Mac." His name escaped her mouth before she could stop it.

"Thought you were long gone," he said, pulling up, putting his hands on his hips to take a good look at her.

"Tonight," said Eliza. "What happened to you? One day you're there, the next gone."

"New assignment," said Mac. "HVT in Fallujah."

"HVT?"

"High-value target," said Mac. "Eight of spades. We use a deck of cards to keep track of 'em. Sorry I didn't get to hang around." He gave her a look. "I know you missed me."

"It wasn't like that," said Eliza. "You have more important things to do than babysit an inspector."

"So they told me."

"And?" she asked. "Did you get him?"

"Sooner or later," said Mac, "we always get 'em. And you—how'd everything turn out . . . you know, with Dr. Shah and his magic container?"

"We're still evaluating," said Eliza. "We want to bring in a few experts to validate his claims. Take a closer look at his work."

"You're not serious?"

"But I am," said Eliza. "*We are.* Me. My father. The Armed Services Committee. The American people deserve to know that we came here for a valid reason."

"Or an invalid one," said Mac. "I think what they deserve most is the truth."

The truth. A malleable commodity, in Eliza's worldview. One thing was certain: she needed Dekker on her side. "Come back," she said, taking his hand, swinging it gently.

"Back? Where?"

"The States. DC. I'd like to see you again."

"My job's here," said Mac.

"Your job can be anywhere," she said playfully, as if he were a sales rep for a software company, not a trained and blooded paramilitary officer. "Last I looked, the CIA has one or two small buildings in Langley."

Mac laughed, but not in the way she wanted.

"I'm serious," she said.

"Miss Elkins, I have some bad news," he said, fixing her with that gaze. "We're not leaving this place anytime soon."

"You can do good work in DC too."

"Me . . . a suit and tie? A commute?"

"Work for my father," said Eliza. "The senator. He could use a decorated veteran."

"Use one for what?" asked Mac.

"Legislative aide. Foreign policy adviser. Pick a title."

"And I don't even have to apply for the job."

"Of course you don't," said Eliza, with alacrity. "I'll tell Daddy. Done deal."

"No kidding," said Mac. "Just tell Daddy."

Eliza nodded, proud of herself and her august family in equal measure. "You do know he's the most powerful man on the Hill."

Just then, a crowd of men and women streamed out of the front entrance. Their newly purchased desert–war zone attire screamed "congressional delegation."

"Dekker," shouted a short, trim man in a khaki suit, his hand raised to be seen. Eliza recognized him on the spot. Senator Todd Lindhurst, ranking Dem on the Armed Services Committee. Not Daddy's favorite. "Good talking to you," said Lindhurst, straining to be heard. "I'll make sure to pass along what you told me. Appreciate the honesty." Lindhurst saw Eliza, and his tone cooled noticeably. "Miss Elkins, good day."

Like that, they were gone.

Eliza grasped Mac's arm. "You had a meeting with Lindhurst?"

"I was debriefing the ambassador, and he happened to be in the room."

"Oh, bullshit," said Eliza.

"They wanted a sitrep of our situation on the ground."

"Just on the ground?"

Mac nodded, crossing his arms over his chest.

"Did anyone ask about Dr. Shah?"

"It may have come up," said Mac.

"And you told him?"

"You know, Lizzie," said Mac. "Look around. We're not any good at this. Regime change. Empire building. You should have thought of the consequences before you got us into this mess." He made a show of checking his wristwatch, a beat-up Casio G-Shock. "Listen, I got to run. Have a safe flight home."

"You bastard," she said.

He came closer and kissed her on the cheek. "Back at ya," he whispered.

A week later, *The New York Times* and *The Washington Post* ran stories about the "Neocon's Last Gasp" and "another failed attempt to find the smoking gun."

A week after that, Eliza was let go, but not before being reprimanded before her father's own committee—and on C-SPAN, for all the world to see. It was the first and only time she'd lost a job.

It was not something she forgot.

"Mr. McGee," said Elkins, once again in the present. "When did you lose your leg?"

"Pardon me?"

"In Iraq. The accident with Mac Dekker."

"April 6, 2006," said McGee.

"I'm sorry for you," she replied.

"Shit happens," said McGee.

April 6, 2006. A week after she left Iraq. She'd been so angry, so caught up in her own hurt feelings, that she'd never wondered if something might have happened to him. *A broken leg, knee, and jaw. Laid up six months.* All this time she hadn't known.

"55 Rue du Bac is a five-story building," said the tech. "There are twenty-six handsets either in the building or within a ten-meter radius. That's as good as we can get without tapping into NSA."

That, Elkins knew, was never going to happen. Not without lots of paperwork. The director would have a conniption.

"Forget it," she said. "We'll never find him that way." She turned to Baker. "New idea. If Mac is so keen on finding Ava Attal, maybe we should be too. You said Rosenfeld works at a restaurant. He must speak English. Call and see if he's there. I want to know what he told Mac Dekker."

CHAPTER 28

Passy, sixteenth arrondissement
Paris

"I need phone numbers," said Harry Crooks.

The tea kettle was empty. Mac had finished recounting the events of the last twenty-four hours. He rose from his chair and made a tour of the living room.

"You can track a mobile signal?" he asked. "From here?"

"No," said Crooks. "Only the telecoms can track the exact location of a mobile handset in real time . . . or the people you and I used to work for. But I can track where a mobile handset has been."

"Without hacking a telecom?"

"You don't hack a telecom," said Crooks. "Every bad actor in the world tries to hack a telecom 24/7/365. It's the holy grail, isn't it? Once in a while some punk in Romania manages to siphon off a few million government identification numbers, credit cards, birthdays, but it stops there. Telecoms have moats and firewalls and more moats. Ring after ring of security to stop people like me. The information we want—you and I, here, this morning—we have to get from the inside."

"A Trojan horse," suggested Mac.

"Just a Trojan, actually," said Crooks. "Someone who likes earning a little extra cash. Someone who can help us cross the moat and jump the firewalls. For now, we're not interested in who Ava called or who called her. We're interested in where she went after your Qatari friends kidnapped her."

"No telecoms," said Mac.

"Something better," said Crooks.

"I'm listening."

"Every cell phone is like a permanent homing beacon. The handset is constantly pinging cell towers, sending GPS signals to satellites, as well as Bluetooth queries to other devices. You might as well be wearing an animal tracking collar around your throat. That traffic app on your phone is tracking your phone's location every second of every day. I can't find Ava at this precise moment, but I can find out where she was yesterday at three p.m. when the abduction occurred."

"But you said you can't get into a telecom."

"Don't need to. I can access a dozen companies that make it their business to know the location of every man, woman, and child every second of the day."

"Google?"

"Let's not name names," said Crooks. "But them or someone like them. Let's call it a search engine. A company that sells your location data to other interested parties."

"Like a traffic app?"

"Traffic, advertisers, marketers. They all want to know where you are 24/7. Money makes the world go round."

"And privacy?"

"Privacy doesn't stand a chance."

"What are you waiting for?"

"Bloody hell," said Crooks. "I can't just snap my fingers. Watch some TV. Better yet, take a walk in the garden. Give me thirty minutes."

Mac stood and stretched. He opened the French doors and wandered into the backyard. Rows of vegetables were planted to the left. A vine of tomatoes, green beans, radishes. There was a trellis and a stone bench and a gurgling fountain. Mac sat, looking up at the blue sky, thinking of Jane and her warning, and ruing her decision to follow him into the intelligence business. And now another chance to make right. A granddaughter that he must raise as his own.

A whistle brought his attention back to the present. He jumped to his feet and rushed inside. "Any luck?"

"Luck has nothing to do with it," said Crooks. "Draw up a chair. Come close so you can see the screen."

Mac dropped into a chair and scooted it close to Crooks. On the large curved monitor was a street map centered on the Eiffel Tower. A fat, red dotted line formed a rectangle around the monument, four square blocks in area. Inside the rectangle were numerous slim, white, baton-shaped icons each labeled with a phone number and, beneath the number, a handset ID.

"Behold the geo-fence," said Crooks, pointing to the map. "It's an arbitrary digital boundary I constructed that allows me to capture every mobile handset inside its perimeter."

"But there are hundreds of phones there," said Mac, eyeing the mishmash of batons stacked atop one another.

"Of course there are. You're looking at everyone visiting the monument. The fence isn't three-dimensional. I can't specify altitude. No worries . . . watch."

Crooks punched in Mac's and Ava's cell numbers. Two icons located dead center in the Eiffel Tower lit up blue. Crooks tapped some more keys, and all the other batons vanished. "At 3:06 p.m. both of you were seated in the restaurant. Ava took the call at 3:20, right?"

"Give or take," said Mac.

Crooks advanced the time signature to 3:20. Ava's icon didn't move. "Don't worry," he said. "GPS is only accurate to around fifteen feet. You said she stepped into the corridor and it was there that she was drugged. Too small a distance to register. We want to know where she goes after."

Crooks advanced the time signature in fifteen-second increments. Mac leaned closer, his heart thumping, as he watched Ava's icon jump to the right, then jump again. By 3:24, she had left the restaurant.

By 3:28, she was standing at the south side of the monument, at the Avenue Gustave Eiffel.

"Now let's see who's with her." Crooks tapped a few keys. The screen came alive with hundreds of batons. He zoomed in on Ava. Two batons were stacked atop hers.

"Two other people are with her," said Mac, pointing.

"Let's see where they go." Crooks double-clicked on each number, turning the icons red. For thirty seconds, Ava and the two unidentified parties remained standing on the Avenue Gustave Eiffel. And then, two new batons appeared at the right of the screen and sped jerkily along the street, stopping directly beside them.

"The getaway car," said Mac.

"Quick learner."

Another fifteen seconds passed. Mac imagined Ava being bundled into the back seat of a car, the kidnappers piling in after her. And then, all five icons—Ava's blue baton, her kidnappers' red batons, the drivers' white batons—advanced rapidly down the street. The moment the five icons breached the digital fence, they disappeared.

"Outside the perimeter," said Crooks.

"Go back," said Mac. "I want to make sure those two were inside the restaurant."

Crooks reset the time signature to 3:10. The two red icons appeared on the screen practically atop Mac and Ava, inside the restaurant. When Ava left, they went with her.

"I saw them on the security camera footage." Mac took out his phone and showed Crooks the photographs he'd taken of the kidnappers from the restaurant's security monitors.

"Is that the prince?" asked Crooks.

"That's him," said Mac. "Both of them were seated at a table beside us. They were watching us the entire time."

"Right there? Brazen of them."

"She thought it was a safe meet," said Mac.

"How do you know?" asked Crooks.

The Tourists

"She left her gun at the hotel," said Mac.

"I wouldn't have done," said Crooks.

Mac looked at his old friend. He'd had the same thought. You never went to a meet empty handed. Ava knew better.

"Still no idea why?" said Crooks. "I mean, the whole thing. What the woman was doing here? All these characters. Shady prince, Saudi hit men, some crazy politician in Jerusalem. She's Mossad all those years. Something's going down. Something big."

Mac shook his head. He'd come to the same conclusion. Something big was going down. But no matter how he tried, he couldn't find a thread to tie them all together. What did it matter anyway? His only concern was to find Ava and get her out of trouble. One step at a time.

"Can we follow the phone numbers?" he asked. "I want to see where they took her."

"Where did you say he lived . . . the shady prince?"

"Avenue Montaigne." Mac had come across an article from *Gulf Architectural Digest* showcasing the prince's opulent residence. It was nice, Mac thought, if you liked lots of gold and marble and the odd masterpiece here and there.

Crooks drew a new perimeter on the city map. This time the area was much larger, encompassing the Golden Triangle and the streets surrounding it. He entered Ava's number, as well as her kidnappers', and set the time signature at 3:35. "Let's take a look."

He pressed Play. The icons popped up on the screen at the nearest corner of the triangle. "Got 'em," said Mac, thumping Crooks on the shoulder.

The kidnappers were not immune to Paris traffic. Their vehicle required fifteen minutes to navigate the Quai d'Orsay and cross the Pont des Invalides. All three icons came to a halt before turning onto the Avenue Montaigne.

"Give me an address," said Mac.

Crooks zoomed in and the street addresses popped up. "27 to 29. Right next door to the Hôtel Plaza Athénée. Sweet digs."

"He's a prince, Harry. What do you expect?"

Crooks kept the program running. At 4:25, Ava's icon vanished. "Finally turned it off," said Crooks.

"We know where she is," said Mac.

"We know where her phone was yesterday afternoon at 4:25," said Crooks.

"That the best you can do?"

"Legally."

"Screw legally," said Mac. "I'm asking, Harry. Come on. Do me a solid."

Crooks studied Mac. He smiled softly, shaking his head. "Okay, then. But just once."

He placed a call. "I need a favor. Check if this number pinged any towers near 27 to 29 Avenue Montaigne during the last eighteen hours. Call me back."

Crooks hung up. "You know this is illegal," he said. "I could go to jail. The French authorities are touchy about privacy."

"Tell them I put a gun to your head."

"You wouldn't."

Mac slid the pistol from his waistband and set it on the table. "Up to you."

The phone rang. Crooks answered. He shot Mac a glance, then jotted down a number.

"Success?" asked Mac.

"Her phone popped up this morning, dialed one number, then powered off. The duration was six seconds. The call didn't go through. Maybe you know the number. Country code 41."

"That's Switzerland," said Mac.

"Province code 27."

"Valais," said Mac. "A canton."

"8878 9877." Crooks read off the numbers slowly. "Know it?"

Mac nodded. "It's my number. I destroyed the SIM card yesterday in case someone like you was looking for me."

The Tourists

"Wise move."

"What time did you say the call was placed again?"

"Six sixteen this morning."

"It's her," said Mac. "She's alive."

"How do you know?" asked Crooks.

"June 16," said Mac. "It's my birthday."

CHAPTER 29

27 Avenue Montaigne
Paris

If this was her jail cell, she should have engineered her capture long ago.

Ava Attal stood at the window of her room on the fifth floor of Tariq al-Sabah's grand townhome. The windows were locked. She was certain the glass was bulletproof. Even if she could get out, it was a long way down. She didn't bother about the door. Locked, of course.

The room was the size of her old apartment in Tel Aviv. Walls cardinal red. Gilded moldings. A bed big enough for a family of four. The furniture was traditional French—she didn't know which king—one of the Louis's. Chairs, sofas, inlaid tables. The floor was parquet, with Oriental throw rugs positioned here and there. More paintings on the walls than in the Louvre and the Musée d'Orsay combined. There was a domed camera in the ceiling, and probably others she couldn't see. She didn't know if she was the first "guest" or if others had been imprisoned here as well.

Ava did her best to act as if she were at home on a Saturday morning. If, that is, she didn't have her phone or laptop and couldn't call her parents or Mac. Or if she couldn't go outside for a run in the forest or take Katya into town for a *pain au chocolat* and some stale bread to feed the ducks. Or if, more immediately, her hands weren't bound by flex-cuffs tightly enough to cut into her flesh if she moved too quickly.

The Tourists

Ava was not someone who could do nothing. Even with her constraints, she managed to browse several magazines on the dresser. TNT had been so nice as to make sure the *Gulf Architectural Digest* featuring this very property sat on top of the stack. She thumbed through it and laughed when she saw that her private prison was featured. "The VIP Guest Room," it was called. "Perfect for even the most demanding visitor." Ava didn't agree. Most visitors preferred doors to be unlocked and to come and go as they pleased.

A knock on the door. The turn of a key. A heavy tumbler retreated.

Ava turned. Ah, breakfast. One man brought the tray to the table, the other stayed at the door. She waited until they'd left. Croissants, butter, and jam. Orange juice. A rasher of bacon. Urns of hot chocolate and coffee. A teapot with a choice of Earl Grey, Lapsang souchong, or English breakfast. All served on crockery from the Hôtel Plaza Athénée next door and with a note to call extension 211 to schedule a pickup when finished. There was room service and then there was *room service*.

It all looked marvelous. She picked up a croissant. The thought of eating, however, made her gag. It was the ketamine they'd pumped into her neck. A nibble. No, she couldn't.

A minute later the door opened. No knock this time. A flutter of black and white and there he was. Tariq al-Sabah. "Greetings, Colonel Attal, or should I say, 'Shalom'?"

"How about 'I'm sorry for kidnapping you and holding you against your will'?"

Tariq stared at her, not one to be told what to do.

"Well?" said Ava.

Seven months had passed since she'd seen him in St. Moritz, her midnight visit to the Chesa Grischuna, his postmodern chalet in the Alps. He'd changed. He looked older, fatigued, a little wary. Not like his old self at all. His beard had come back. He wore it like his father—a thick, well-manicured goatee. No suit today. Back to jeans, a black turtleneck, and a blazer. This was Paris TNT.

"You," he said, his smile charming. "My wicked girl."

"Not wicked," said Ava. "Not a girl. And not yours."

"For one night you were all those."

"You were a mark," said Ava. "Don't fool yourself."

"I had my suspicions," said Tariq. "One win for you. And now, a win for me. I think we will find that I came out on top."

"You killed them," said Ava.

"I'd rather think it was you," said Tariq. "Getting involved where you don't belong. How did you expect us to react? Or did you think we wouldn't find out? You and that old warhorse. How old is he? Eighty? Ninety? Some people should really know when to hang it up."

"You can't make the world go back," said Ava. "Not you. Not Ben-Gold."

"Who's talking about the world?" said Tariq. "I'm concerned about my country. Nothing else."

"You're concerned about yourself," said Ava.

"That too," said Tariq. He looked over the breakfast tray, picked up a croissant, and took a bite. "What? No likee? On a diet?" He dropped the uneaten bit onto the plate. "I'm curious. What exactly did you think you could do?"

Stop you, thought Ava. That was the glib answer—perhaps one she should have thought through before embarking on her course of action. Save innocent lives. Help your brother succeed. They all sounded naive, given how things had turned out. Anyway, it no longer mattered what she'd believed she could do. What mattered was what she could do. Concretely. Now. And so, here she was. A prisoner.

"Jabr will be disappointed," said Tariq. "He really was close to pulling it off. His grand plan. They're all here, you know. Over at the Élysée Palace with the president. All the great families under one roof. The Maktoums, the Sauds, the Al-Sabahs. Your coreligionists are there too. What does one call a gathering of Zionists? A "drove"? Oh, I'm sorry. That's the word for a sty full of swine. Same difference, I suppose."

"What scares you so much?" asked Ava.

The Tourists

"You tell me," said TNT, arms spread open. The rising influencer eager to take his role on a bigger stage.

"Insignificance," said Ava.

"Hardly as simple as that," said Tariq. "But not altogether wrong. I like to think it's more self-realization. You know. Be all that you can be."

"We can still change things," said Ava. "Call off the match. Shake hands and go home."

"And the upside?" asked TNT. "For me? For my country?"

"It won't work," said Ava. "Others know."

"What others?" asked TNT. "I don't see anyone coming to your rescue. Your own people have given you up. Your warnings have fallen on deaf ears, or rather, *dead ears*. You're persona non grata. And by the way, we have him. Steinhardt. Your better half. My Saudi friends went to look for him at your hotel. He put up a fight, but he's not a young man, is he?"

Ava looked at him, at his eyes, his disposition. Looked into him. Was he lying? It was impossible to tell. People like him lied so often they gave no thought to whether their words were true or false. "I don't believe you," she said.

"You didn't really think we'd stop with you," said Tariq. "Not when we've come this far."

"Then why?"

"Leverage," said Tariq. "In case you decide not to cooperate."

Ava walked to the window. She'd tried to leave word for Mac to leave, but since when was he someone to take advice? She thought of Katya and for a moment was overwhelmed. No, she didn't believe it. Tariq was lying. She'd sent a message this morning to let Mac know that she was alive. Bad tradecraft, but still.

"I'll never cooperate," said Ava.

"Famous last words," said Tariq. "So, I must ask you. Who else have you told?"

PART II

CHAPTER 30

March—seven months earlier
Institut Alpinuum für Sport, Physiotherapie, und Zellleistung
St. Moritz, Switzerland

The Alpine Institute for Sports, Physical Therapy, and Cellular Performance occupied a modern three-story building set high on the steep hillside that was home to the village of St. Moritz, in the eastern Swiss canton of Grisons. From its windows, clients had a breathtaking view over the village and the entire Engadin Valley. They saw the famous wainscoted tower of Badrutt's Palace Hotel and next door, Confiserie Hanselmann; the sweeping lake on the valley floor; and the polo fields bordering it. But most of all they saw the mountains. The Piz Nair and the Piz Corvatsch and the Corviglia, towering sentinels gathered all around, slopes blanketed by newly fallen snow.

It was a bluebird day, in the parlance of the ski bums and tourists who flocked to St. Moritz during the winter. Not a cloud in the sky, the sun impossibly bright, the sky vividly blue. But Ava Attal, her T-shirt drenched with sweat, lungs fighting for breath, couldn't give a fig for the view. She was in pain. And she wanted it to stop.

"One more rep," commanded her trainer. "You're almost there."

"You've been saying that for an hour," said Ava, as she raised the fifteen-pound dumbbells to shoulder height.

"Hold it," said the trainer. "Three-two-one. There!"

Ava lowered the weights to her side. "Another?"

The trainer shook her head. "You're done," she said, taking the weights. "You killed it."

"I think you killed me." Ava sat on a bench and toweled the sweat from her eyes. Week twelve completed. Not bad, young lady. She raised her right arm. For the first time since her surgery, there was no strain, no discomfort. She shouted with joy. Everyone in the gym looked her way. She waved to them unabashedly. "I'm getting better!"

A few clapped. Others rolled their eyes. Ava didn't mind. Five months earlier she'd been given up for dead. Anything was an improvement.

The trainer returned and told her Dr. Lutz wanted to see her in his office. "Right away, Frau Attal."

Ava threw the towel around her neck and took the elevator to the first floor. The door to Dr. Gerhard Lutz's office stood open. A tall, rangy man with shaggy gray hair and furious black eyebrows ushered her inside.

"We need to talk," said Lutz.

"Is something wrong?" asked Ava. "Has there been a setback?"

"No, no, nothing like that," said Lutz. "You're doing just fine. Your shoulder is healing faster than expected. I didn't mean to frighten you."

Ava regarded her doctor. He was a serious man, seventy years old, fit as an athlete in his prime. He wore a white lab coat over a plaid button-down shirt, as well as jeans and climbing boots. Gerhard Lutz was a renowned orthopedic surgeon and pioneer in the use of stem cells to aid recovery. Five months earlier he had operated on Ava's shoulder and upper arm, reattaching the pectoralis muscle to the humerus.

She had not injured herself playing a sport or taking a nasty fall on the ski slopes. Her injuries were inflicted by a bullet, a 5.56 mm full-metal-jacket round fired from a Heckler & Koch machine gun. The bullet had entered her upper-right torso two inches below the collarbone and exited her back four inches lower, shattering a rib and shredding muscle and flesh. The exit wound was the circumference of a baseball. Miraculously, the bullet had missed all major organs.

Lutz closed the door and locked it.

"Are you all right?" she asked.

"Concerned," said Lutz. "Please take a seat."

A week had passed since Ava graduated from her shoulder brace. She sat facing Lutz's desk, right arm crossed over her chest, left hand cradling her elbow.

"I'm not by nature a nosy man," said Lutz, settling into his chair. "Between my patients, running the clinic, and listening to my wife, I have more than enough to keep me occupied."

"I imagine so," said Ava.

"But now and again, I may hear something that requires my attention. Or in this case, requires your attention. The attention of the people you work for."

"We appreciate it," said Ava.

"I do what I can," said Lutz. "God has smiled on me." He was referring to a separate calling, a responsibility besides that of caregiver.

Gerhard Lutz was born Schmuel Luznicki in Poland ten years after the Second World War. As a child he had immigrated to Switzerland. His parents changed the family name. To be a Jew was to be a pariah. Luznicki became Lutz. He, himself, chose the name Gerhard, after the prolific German striker playing for Bayern Munich, Gerhard "Gerd" Müller.

On Friday evenings, the Lutz family once again became the Luznickis. They closed the curtains and locked the doors before lighting the candles and saying kiddush. An Israeli aid agency paid for his university education and, later, trips to Jerusalem and the Holy Land. He never forgot his debt or his heritage. Today, he called himself a Sayanim, a friend of Israel.

And so, as a Sayanim, Gerhard Lutz knew all about Ava and her work for Mossad, Israel's foreign intelligence agency. Shortly after the shooting, someone had whispered in his ear that a longtime operative had been wounded performing a duty that reflected admirably on the State of Israel. Sadly, the operative possessed nowhere near the resources necessary to pay for his services. Surgery. A private clinic. Rehabilitation. The bill would be astronomical. Might he consider offering the operative his services gratis? The answer was yes. Gerhard Lutz never turned down a request to help his country.

"Do you know the Al-Sabahs?" he asked.

"Everyone knows of the Al-Sabahs," said Ava. "Very few people actually know them."

Lutz met her gaze. A look passed between them. A shared distaste. The Al-Sabahs. Ruling family of Qatar. Funders of Al Jazeera, the pan-Arab news agency. Vocal proponents of Palestinian rights. Less vocally, the Al-Sabah family was financier of all causes anti-Zionist. After the Republic of Iran, it was the largest source of funding for Hamas, Hezbollah, ISIS, and every other flag-waving faction whose singular intent was the destruction not only of Israel but of every last Jew in the Holy Land and, to be honest, everywhere else on God's green earth.

Yes, Ava knew of the Al-Sabahs. But she didn't know them.

"Last month I operated on one of them," said Lutz. "Tariq bin Nayan bin Tariq. One of the emir's sons. Torn meniscus. An accident on the Cresta Run."

The Cresta Run. Ava knew it vaguely. Some kind of treacherous course undertaken on a toboggan.

"Nice young man," Lutz continued. "Handsome, engaging. Strong handshake, not the dead fish most of them give you. Speaks French beautifully. Even a little Swiss German."

Ava nodded. Purposely, she kept silent. It was Lutz's decision to tell her as much as he felt comfortable sharing. She did not want him to feel coerced, not for a moment. Sources were inevitably more forthcoming when giving information freely.

"As I was saying," Lutz continued, "the door to the examining room was ajar, just a crack. I was finishing with his chart. He was on the phone, and I noticed that he was speaking Arabic. It was hardly unusual. Of course, I speak Arabic as well. My wife is Egyptian. It was his tone that drew my attention. He was agitated. He wasn't yelling; quite the opposite. He was speaking quietly but having great difficulty doing so. Do you understand?"

"Yes," said Ava, not wanting to break his momentum.

"He was imploring someone to visit him," Lutz went on. "He said he must come to examine some kind of device. I didn't quite hear what, but he said he needed this man, I believe his name was Abbasi, Dr. Abbasi, to help construct something he called a viable transmitter."

"A transmitter?" Ava repeated. She was officially interested.

Lutz nodded, drawing his bushy eyebrows together. "Tariq asked him repeatedly if he needed to be worried about being in proximity to this device. He said the word 'radiation' three times, or maybe it was 'radioactive.' I'm not sure now. Oh, yes, and he said, 'It doesn't matter where I got it. I have it.'"

"And whatever 'it' is," said Ava, "requires a viable transmitter and may or may not be radioactive."

Again Lutz nodded. "You see, I convinced myself he was talking about a bomb," he added, almost shyly. "He never said the word, but he sounded deadly serious. He even had a name for it."

"A name?" said Ava.

"For the device, whatever it was that required this transmitter. It will come to me."

"When was this?" asked Ava.

"Two weeks ago," said Lutz. "Just after your last visit."

"Two weeks?" It required all Ava's control to remain calm, outwardly unperturbed. *And you waited this long to tell me?*

"I know it's all very vague," said Lutz. "But again, it was how he was talking. He was worked up; as I said, agitated. It was so unlike him. He's a smooth customer. Very charming. In control of himself."

Ava laughed softly to lessen the tension. "I'm sure there's a harmless explanation. Lots of products contain radioactive ingredients.

Fluorescent lights, for example. Or watch dials . . . the tritium on the hour markers. Or medical imaging equipment."

"Possibly," said Lutz, half-heartedly. "He did make a joke about it."

"What was that?" asked Ava.

"Something about keeping it away from his testicles—'his nuts,' he said—because he didn't want to go sterile before he had children."

Ava was looking at her phone. By now, she'd brought Tariq al-Sabah up on social media. "A bomb? I doubt it. He appears to be the opposite of a jihadi . . . unless they've begun tooling around Manhattan in exotic sports cars. Did bin Laden ever try the Cresta Run?"

"You're discounting what I told you," retorted Lutz. "Don't lessen it."

"I didn't mean to," said Ava.

"Please believe me, Frau Attal. There was nothing in the least whimsical about his tone. He was deadly serious."

"I believe you," said Ava.

"Now I remember," said Lutz. "The device's name. What he called it."

"Go on," said Ava.

"You see, I didn't get it at first. I thought he was referencing the Bible, some type of scripture maybe. I mean, everyone knows it."

"Tell me," said Ava.

"Samson."

For a moment, Ava felt nothing. She looked out the window, remarking on the scenic view. From Lutz's office, she could see down the hillside to the St. Moritzersee, its surface dotted by whitecaps. Despite the cold, a few windsurfers were taking advantage of the strong winds.

Samson.

A coincidence, she argued. It couldn't be her Samson. Not a chance. How could Tariq al-Sabah know what they'd called it? Besides, it had been so long. Everyone had given up the device for lost. After a time, it had been decided that its theft was hardly the disaster it had at first seemed. The device was inoperable without a transmitter. Even then, and most crucially, one needed a code to detonate the weapon. All codes were held and controlled with religious zeal. One man held the key. The Israeli minister of defense.

But Ava didn't believe in coincidences. Not in her line of work. If Tariq bin Nayan bin Tariq al-Sabah was speaking to an Iranian named Abbasi about building a transmitter for a radioactive device he called "Samson," she had no business but to believe it was her Samson. A one-kiloton tactical nuclear weapon that she'd lost on a freezing night on the Golan Heights over a decade ago.

After all, she mused, there was nothing like a little uranium-235 to fry a man's nuts and guarantee he would never have children.

All this passed through Ava's mind in a heartbeat. Well, maybe two. She returned her attention to Lutz. "Are you seeing him again soon?" she asked.

"Next week," said Lutz. "Stem cell infusion. Thursday at eleven."

"It might be smart for me to come back then," said Ava. "A follow-up."

"Oh no, Frau Attal," said Lutz. "That's not necessary. It can wait a month."

"Next week," said Ava, grimacing, touching her shoulder. "I have a feeling something isn't knitting properly. Why don't we schedule an infusion for me? Let's say Thursday at eleven."

Lutz needed a moment. "Oh, yes, an infusion. A little soon, but we can make an exception. Thursday. Eleven o'clock. That works."

He escorted her to the door.

"What will you do?" he asked, his voice a whisper. "You and the people you work for?"

Ava placed her good hand on his shoulder. She stared at him a moment, then shook her head, ever so slightly. It meant: *"Don't ask. Never ask."*

CHAPTER 31

Confiserie Hanselmann
St. Moritz

Codename: Samson.

Eleven tactical nuclear weapons, each with a strength of one kiloton, deployed across a twenty-six mile stretch of the Israeli–Syrian border in the Golan Heights, approximately two miles between each. It was 1984 or 1985. Israel had invaded Lebanon a few years before. The horrors of Sabra and Shatila had enflamed the region. Al-Assad the Lion threatened war. Hussein in Jordan echoed the call.

On King Saul Boulevard in Tel Aviv, the prime minister and his cabinet deemed it the pinnacle of reason to create a modern-day Siegfried line to forestall any attack from the north. One kiloton equaled one thousand tons of TNT. Hiroshima was thirteen kilotons. Everyone in the cabinet agreed that they were being judicious; timid, even. After all, just think what they might have done? If an attack did come—and the aggressors tried to cross the Green Line, God help them—it would be the last ever attempted by Israel's neighbors.

Since then, the devices—"mines" they were officially called, so as not to scare anyone—lay dormant, one encrypted signal away from detonation. With time, threats of an invasion lessened. Prime ministers came and went. Even Ariel Sharon grew less bellicose, some said conciliatory. The new cabinet had second thoughts. Perhaps "judicious" wasn't the right word. "Reckless," "inflammatory," even "outrageous" were more appropriate. Over time, public opinion shifted. The world no longer viewed Israel as a victim. It had become the dominant force in the region. Right or wrong, more and more countries called Israel an "oppressor."

The outbreak of civil war in Syria forced a new perspective. The border region—once maintained by the United Nations Disengagement Observer Force—devolved into a fractious combat zone. Syrian government troops fought antigovernment rebels. The rebels fought ISIS-backed militias. The militias fought among themselves. In short, chaos.

Samson was no longer a viable military option. It was a liability.

And so, with the utmost secrecy, Ava and her team had been sent to remove the spines from the dragon's back. They retrieved ten and delivered each to a bunker deep in the ground beneath Tel Nof Airbase, where they were to be kept with their much larger, more powerful brethren.

It was the eleventh where things went wrong. Terribly wrong.

Pondering these events, Ava sat alone at a table in the far corner of Confiserie Hanselmann. It was her habit to reward herself with a hot chocolate and a piece of linzer torte after surviving the grueling sessions of physical therapy. She sipped the hot chocolate, ate a bite of the raspberry-flavored torte.

Ava knew what she should do. She should call the office. She should tell them everything she'd heard and be done with it. She was on medical leave. Her last posting was with the diplomatic service. Before that, she'd worked as an analyst handling liaisons with US and British intelligence shops. She hadn't been a *katsa*, a covert foreign agent, in twelve years.

So, of course, she did the opposite. Act now. Explain later. Her North Star.

It didn't matter that she was still recovering from a near-fatal wound and could barely pick up a coffee cup, or that she had no official remit from her government to act on its behalf. In her mind, she was back at the job. She had uncovered the information. Gerd Lutz was her joe. It was her case to work. Besides, she told herself (in case she needed further justification for her actions), time was a factor. Who knew how long it would be before the boys back home acted, or, more importantly, whether they would act at all? They didn't know Lutz. They hadn't heard the fear in his voice.

Things couldn't be clearer. She had no choice but to act on her own. Decision made.

Ava got to work. She did the usual. Google. Social media. There were enough pictures to fill an encyclopedia. An article from a local paper caught her attention. "St. Moritz Chalet Sells for Record Price." It was called the Chesa Grischuna, and two years earlier, TNT, "the jet-setting Qatari prince," had paid 150 million Swiss francs for "the jewel of the Engadin."

A quick check showed the Chesa Grischuna to be only a short walk.

Ava peered out the window. It was the height of ski season. Men and women walked past the window, dressed chicly, paragons of fashion. Ava stuck out by contrast. Put simply, she was dressed too plainly. No one looks closely at a tourist. They might look closely at a tall, athletic woman with vaguely ethnic features dressed as if she were about to embark on night reconnaissance.

Directly across the street, no more than ten steps away, stood the Bogner boutique. There was a mannequin wearing a red parka with a fur-lined hood she would never be caught dead in, a fur *shapka* and fawn ski pants tighter than anything she'd worn since she was eighteen. It was a start.

Forty minutes later, she found herself hiking up the *Alpenstraße* in the direction of the Suvretta House, on the western outskirts of town, and dressed like Ursula Andress or Brigitte Bardot. It had been a long time since she'd walked any distance. St. Moritz Dorf sat at an altitude of

1,869 meters, or nearly six thousand feet. Hardly the top of Everest, but she was winded all the same.

She rounded a bend. The tall pine trees lining the road fell away. To her right, a broad snow-covered hillside came into view. And built on that hillside, towering high over the road, all glass and steel, the Chesa Grischuna, TNT's alpine residence. "Chesa" meant "chalet" in Romansh, the ancient dialect spoken in the eastern corner of Switzerland, but the Chesa Grischuna looked less like a chalet than anything she'd ever seen. Not a balcony or window box or geranium to be seen. No eaved roof. No wood or plaster anywhere. It was sleek, modern, and aesthetically beautiful, as it should be, thought Ava, for the 150 million francs TNT had paid for it several years earlier. Three stories above ground, four stories below, according to the article in the *St. Moritz Zeitung*. Swimming pool, bowling alley, cinema, ten-car garage, and, not to be missed, a *Fonduestube mit Kachelofen*, or cheese room. Everything a Middle Eastern prince could desire.

Ava continued walking, taking no pains to hide her interest in the chalet. It would be more conspicuous had she not stared. What, she asked herself, does a thirty-three-year-old prince—an heir to the largest fortune on earth, a collector of exotic automobiles, a connoisseur of fine cuisine—want with a nuclear weapon?

The answer was frightening, if vague. Nothing good.

She came to a wooden bench on the side of the road. A heart was cut out of the top and an inscription read "Rolando Wyss, friend of the mountains." She sat down, grateful for some rest. Her shoulder ached, and so did her legs. She took a bite of a truffle, another of Hanselmann's divine creations. When in doubt, eat chocolate.

It was just past three, an hour later in Tel Aviv. It was, she decided later, the moment that she returned to active duty. It was important to remember, if only so she could put in for full pay and benefits.

"Zvi, that you?" she asked, phone to her ear. Zvi Gelber, deputy director of Tzomet—the division of Mossad in charge of foreign intelligence collection, including the recruitment and running of agents—was a legend in the service. He had to be eighty, if a day, though for all Ava knew, he could be older. He'd been at Mossad since the days of Golda Meir and Moshe Dayan, the days when the continued existence of the Israeli State was still in question. They called him "the old man."

"Who's this? My phone says Ava Attal, but that can't be. Rumor is she's married a Swiss gnome and is living in a vault, counting gold coins and nibbling on cheese."

"Very funny," said Ava. "Not married and, sadly, no gold coins. But I am in Switzerland, and I do have a gnome—a garden gnome."

"One out of three ain't bad," said Gelber. "I know you're calling to see how I'm doing. Seventy-seven, nearly deaf, and missing my favorite *katsa*."

"Zvi, stop it."

"But honestly, how are you?" asked Gelber. "How's my favorite *katsa* . . . other than very, very lucky?"

"Alive," said Ava. "Getting better. And yes, damned lucky."

"One day you'll tell me everything."

"One day. I promise."

"Let's get to it," said Gelber, all business. "What gives?"

"Tariq bin Nayan bin Tariq al-Sabah. And don't ask me to repeat it. I'm sitting in front of his chalet in St. Moritz, and he might hear me."

"The playboy prince," said Gelber. "You probably know the A-side. You're calling for the B-side."

"If there is one."

"This is the Middle East," said Gelber. "There's always a B-side. He's quite the schemer. Son number two from wife number one. One brother ahead of him, two behind, from wife three, but they're eight and ten years old. He's not the playboy everyone thinks. Tariq made a name for himself last year during the talks between Israel and Hamas. Both sides listened to him. A voice of reason. Next-gen Gulf leader. Until . . ."

"Until," said Ava.

The Tourists

"The oldest brother, Jabr, got sick of him. He didn't want anyone stealing his spotlight. There could be only one Al-Sabah at the table. His father, the emir, has aged out. Jabr saw his brother as a threat. He banished him from the talks. Good idea, if you ask me. Jabr didn't want a replay of Saudi Arabia circa 2017. He didn't want to find himself locked up in the Ritz-Carlton signing away his life and his power. He bought TNT a Bugatti as a payoff. Four million out the door, but it was a bargain, all things considered."

Gelber was referring to the coup in Saudi Arabia staged by Mohammed bin Salman, or MBS, once a wayward prince and today the country's de facto ruler. Over the course of several months starting in 2017, MBS, having secured the loyalty of the secret police, arrested and imprisoned over three hundred family members in the Riyadh Ritz-Carlton hotel. There, he kept them prisoner until each signed over their assets to him and pledged their loyalty. To refuse meant a long prison sentence, the arrest of their loved ones, or worse.

"Did Jabr have reason to worry?" asked Ava.

"Do you mean, was TNT planning a coup? Hard to say. We saw no outward indication that he was trying to turn the security services against his brother. Given that TNT spends so much time out of the country, I'd say doubtful. But there was something about him. I had a bad feeling. I think Jabr acted out of an abundance of caution. Better safe than sorry. No one's heard a peep from TNT since. Until you asked about him, I'd put him out of my mind. Now I'm wondering if I was lazy and complacent. Why the interest?"

"Chatter," said Ava. "Probably nothing."

"And yet there you are, seated in front of his chalet."

"Do me a favor," said Ava. "Ask around. See if you can find out what he's been doing lately. Any friends he shouldn't have. Keeping bad company."

"You mean, did he take his firing sitting down?"

"You tell me," said Ava. "Oh, and see if the name Abbasi means anything. I'm guessing Iranian. Dr. Abbasi."

"It doesn't ring a bell right off the bat, but I'll give it a check."

"And Zvi, step on some toes if you have to," said Ava. "We might have a situation."

"You can't keep this to yourself," said Gelber. "What's got you so worried?"

"I don't want to be a Cassandra," said Ava. "Could be a big nothingburger."

"What do you care? You're retired."

"On medical leave."

Gelber laughed knowingly. "Ava, Ava, Ava. I'm not as deaf as all that."

"All what?"

"That I can't hear the sharp, polished edge of ambition in your voice. You're coming back. I'll alert King Saul Boulevard."

"Don't you dare," said Ava. "This is between us. Now move your tuchus."

CHAPTER 32

***Institut Alpinuum für Sport, Physiotherapie, und Zellleistung
St. Moritz***

Ava arrived late for her appointment.

It was ten past eleven, according to her new "preowned" Rolex. A men's 18-karat President. White dial with Roman numeral appliqué. Diamond bezel. In St. Moritz you were what you wore. She was dolled up in Bogner's latest. Après-ski pants, sports sweater, belt—all black, all tighter than anything she'd worn since high school. Her hair was pulled back into a French chignon. She drew the line at makeup. A little mascara, a little lipstick, and that was it. The getup went against every tenet of her training. *Never disguise yourself. Be yourself, but more.* A covert operative's cardinal rule.

But rules were for another day. And as for cardinals . . . well, Ava was Jewish. In the end, she'd decided on another dictum.

When in Rome . . .

A nurse led her to a padded chair with armrests. She offered her a glass of orange juice, and Ava made a joke about preferring champagne. If she sounded as awkward to others' ears as she did to her own, she was in big trouble. She only half listened as the nurse outlined the procedure for her stem cell infusion. She kept one eye on the handsome younger man seated a few chairs to her right. Dr. Lutz, it seemed, had managed for them to be the only two patients that morning. What a coincidence.

TNT was a few minutes ahead of her. He sat comfortably with tubes running into both arms, earbuds in, reading a pink newspaper. The *Financial Times*. How endearingly old school. For someone constantly on the move, he looked remarkably well rested.

Zvi Gelber had moved his tuchus, indeed. He did not disappoint.

"He's singlehandedly doing more for global warming than a Chinese coal-fired plant," Gelber told her the day before, during her train ride from Zinal. "The Office tracks him 24/7. In the last three months, TNT and his private jet have touched down in Damascus and Tehran four times. Paris five times. We're talking round trip from Doha, Qatar. Los Angeles, New York, Zurich, and some place called Samedan, wherever that is."

Samedan was the airstrip Ava could see with her own eyes, whose lone runway either began or ended a stone's throw from the St. Moritzersee. There was no sign of TNT's jet, but that was probably because he kept it in a hangar.

"But what concerns me more," continued Gelber, "are the trips to Jerusalem. Four times in the past sixty days."

"What's he doing visiting Jerusalem so often?" asked Ava. "Converting?"

"That's the thing, my dear. He never actually set foot in Jerusalem. Not in the city, anyway. He stayed at the airport. David Ben-Gurion International. Immigration has no record of his naturalization. I checked. TNT never left the plane."

"Refueling?"

"Refueling doesn't take three hours. Besides, fuel costs in Israel are five times higher than in Qatar. He flies a Gulfstream G700. The plane has a range of seven thousand nautical miles. He didn't land there to refuel."

"He landed to speak with someone," said Ava.

"Agreed," said Gelber. "Someone who couldn't risk being seen in public with a Qatari royal."

"Someone who couldn't risk talking to him on the phone either," said Ava. "Government."

"Ah, Ava, always one step ahead."

But, of course, it was Zvi Gelber who was one step ahead. "You checked?" Ava asked.

"Some toes even I can't step on," said Gelber.

"Zvi, be serious. What happened?"

"Your boy has friends in high places," said Gelber. "Eyes, ears, who knows what else."

"In the Office?" she asked, meaning inside Mossad.

"Just a little friction," said Gelber. "Queries not answered quickly enough or at all. Funny glances. People suddenly interested in what I have going. You know, 'friction.' Remember, sweetheart, we're not the only ones with spies in every capital."

"And Abbasi?"

"Nothing off the bat. Common name. About five thousand of them in Tehran alone. Don't worry, I haven't given up. Let's just say I'm being a little more careful about my inquiries than usual. What's the old saying? 'Just because you are paranoid doesn't mean they're not watching you.'"

"Be careful," said Ava.

"Always," said Gelber.

That was yesterday.

Ava opened her purse—an ice-blue Fendi Peekaboo, another acquisition that had nearly drained her retirement account—and took out a tablet. She'd spent an hour on the train queuing up her reading material. *Tatler*, *OK!*, *Vogue*. She was aware of the newspaper coming down, being carefully folded. A look her way. A polite cough. She was too busy reading her gossip rags to notice.

"You," the voice was soft, urgent, and somehow conspiratorial.

Ava pretended not to hear.

"You," Tariq repeated. She glanced in his direction. "What did you hurt?"

"Shoulder," said Ava, needing a moment to size him up and decide if he were worth the effort. She returned her attention to the tablet. David Beckham had thrown an outlandish surprise party for Victoria at Covent Garden. The guest list was impressive. Elton John and David Furnish, Jennifer Lawrence. Music by Brandi Carlile.

"Knee," said Tariq.

"You're going to live forever," said Ava, eyes glued to her tablet. "You and your knee."

"As long as I make it to fifty," said Tariq.

"Fifty? You'll be ancient."

"Practically fermenting." A laugh. Much too warm. Much too friendly. "My name's Tariq."

American English without a trace of an accent. All those years in California had paid off. Ava lowered the tablet and for the first time gave him her full attention. "I know who you are. I saw the car outside." She inclined the tablet so he could see it. "You're not in this week's issue."

"I've been busy," said Tariq. "Travel."

"Anywhere exciting?" she asked, holding his gaze. Who did you meet in Israel? All those stops at David Ben-Gurion Airport. And what about Damascus? Tehran? Not a playboy's usual itinerary.

"Here and there," said Tariq. "Mostly business."

"I expected Rome or Ibiza."

"Much closer to home, I'm afraid."

Ava feigned a pout. "No time for pleasure? I'm disappointed."

"Maybe a little," he said, eyes flashing. "But shhh . . . don't tell anyone."

"Your secret is safe with me." Ava knew better than to press him on the subject. Another day. "By the way, I prefer the Ferrari."

"It was a gift, the Bugatti. From my brother."

Jabr al-Sabah. Age thirty-nine. Heir to the throne. Impediment to his brother's ambition. And from the look in Tariq's eyes: enemy. "Generous of him," said Ava.

"Not exactly," said Tariq. "But I took it all the same."

"You're not close?"

"Who said that?" asked Tariq.

"You wanted something else," said Ava. "That's it. A Porsche, maybe."

"Maybe," said Tariq, staring at her a little too hard.

"This your first time?" asked Ava, pleasantly, deflecting the hard gaze. "Stem cells, I mean."

"I had surgery a month ago," said Tariq. "Ripped my meniscus to shreds. Silly accident. Bobsledding . . ." No, Ava wasn't interested. "Anyway, Dr. Lutz suggested the stem cells to speed up the recovery. And you?"

Ava touched her shoulder. "My second infusion. Soon I'll be as young as you."

"Shame," said Tariq, leaning over the arm of his chair. "Pity to waste all that experience."

"Be careful," said Ava. "I'm practically fermenting."

"I don't believe it," said Tariq.

"Believe it," said Ava.

"Well, then so much the better."

"You're a cheeky one."

"I appreciate the finer things."

"Like the Bugatti?" said Ava.

"Not just automobiles," said Tariq, eyes not leaving her. "I know quality when I see it."

"Anything that is fast and flashy," said Ava, refusing to take him seriously.

"Flashy is overrated."

"Says the man in the Vuitton sweatsuit and Patek Philippe Nautilus—diamond encrusted, of course."

Tariq sighed, defeated for the moment. He sat back in his chair. "To be honest, I've gotten myself into a bit of a trap," he said, ruminatively. "All these posts and pictures. The fans are insatiable. They want three, four, five interactions a day or they'll find someone else."

"Let them," said Ava. "Why should you care?"

"It's who I am," said Tariq. "TNT. I have a reputation to live up to. Do you want to know a secret? It's a mask. The whole thing. I have other ambitions. Politics. Service. It's complicated."

"The gift from your brother?"

Again, Tariq grew testy at the mention of his brother. "How did you know?"

"I'm a woman," said Ava. "I know a thing or two about jealousy. I'm guessing he bought you the car to buy you off. He knows you're smarter, more popular . . . better looking. He's scared."

"He should be," said Tariq. "Bloody bastard can't just—" He bit his tongue as the nurse came into the room. She checked their drip bags, then removed the needle from Ava's arm. After swabbing the puncture, she then applied a bandage and instructed her not to remove it for several hours. "Dr. Lutz will see you when you're ready."

Ava stood and took a moment to slide the tablet into her purse and gather her belongings. "Goodbye, then," she said. "Don't keep your mask on too long. You look rather nice without it."

Tariq rose from his chair, guiding his IV bag alongside him. "You will have dinner with me this evening," he said. "Chesa Veglia. Palace Hotel. Eight o'clock."

Ava slid her purse onto her arm. For a few minutes, she'd forgotten that he was a real prince of a real country. A man accustomed to getting his way and having the money to pay for it. A man who rarely heard the word "no." "You don't even know my name."

"What is your name?"

Ava studied him for long enough to make him squirm. "Ava Mercier."

"Madame Mercier," said Tariq, with a bow of the head. "I am Tariq bin Nayan bin Tariq al-Sabah."

"Your Excellency," she replied, her eyes skirting the floor. "Dinner in two weeks, when I return to see Dr. Lutz. I prefer the Grand Hotel Kronenhof in Pontresina. You will wear a proper suit and proper shoes. I know quality too."

"As you wish."

She touched his sleeve. "Who knows? By then, the stem cells may kick in."

"Yours or mine?" he asked.

Ava lowered her face to his, her lips nearly brushing his ear. "Both of ours."

Afterward, she sat with Gerhard Lutz in his office.

"How often do you send out bills?" she asked.

"Monthly."

"By email?"

"And hard copy letter," said Lutz.

"This month, you will send me his invoice first. Only after I return it to you will you send it to Tariq al-Sabah."

"What will you do?"

"Please, Gerd. We never had this discussion."

CHAPTER 33

Grand Hotel Kronenhof
Pontresina, Switzerland

He was, Ava had to admit, a handsome man.

As requested, he had dressed in a suit. Navy blue with the faintest pinstripe. White shirt with a spread collar. Solid navy tie. He'd cut his hair short, parted on the side, shiny with pomade. And the beard—the ever-present two-day stubble, the badge of hipness of every male under forty—it was gone. He was clean shaven. His face was tan from a day's skiing. The color in his cheeks served to better contrast his eyes. They were not the obsidian black of a descendant of the Gulf, but a sparkling whiskey brown, nearly hazel. The transformation was startling. Gone was the cocksure Qatari prince. Enter the suave Italian gentleman.

"Be careful," Zvi Gelber had implored her during a last, furious conversation earlier that day. "He knows someone's watching."

She'd taken precautions from the start. Pontresina was eight kilometers away from St. Moritz, a postage-stamp-sized hamlet in its own valley. Neutral ground, in Ava's mind. She'd insisted on meeting him there. No ride necessary, thank you very much.

Tariq al-Sabah stood by the entrance to the hotel. "You came," he said, holding the door as she swept into the lobby.

"You dressed," said Ava.

"It gave me the chance to pick up a new suit."

"Very smart," she said, stepping closer to him, violating his private sphere, and running a finger along the lapel. "Shoes too."

"These?" said Tariq. "John Lobbs. Had them made years ago." He smelled of sandalwood and something herbaceous, an alluring combination.

Ava turned her back and allowed him to remove her camel overcoat. Beneath it she wore a black dress with spaghetti straps, tight in the waist, the hem much too high for a woman her age. It was winter, so she wore black hose and black heels that added three inches to her height. God save her, she felt as if she were walking on a high wire. One gust would topple her. Not much jewelry—just around her neck a silver chain that plunged into her décolletage. *You may look, but be discreet.* Her hair alone had taken an hour, straightening and combing and smoothing, until it was as sleek and shiny as a raven's wing. And makeup, far too much makeup. Scheherazade in the sultan's harem.

Ava Attal would not be caught dead wearing any of it; not the dress, the heels, the necklace, or the makeup. But tonight she wasn't Ava Attal. Tonight she was Ava Marie Mercier, a covert operative working on behalf of the State of Israel. Her mission (and it was entirely of her own making) was to seduce Tariq al-Sabah of Qatar—minister of the interior, noted influencer, car enthusiast, stinted politician, and nascent terrorist—with the express goal of stealing sophisticated engineering plans he had taken possession of two days earlier from Dr. Reza Abbasi.

"Have you been here before?" she asked.

"First time," said Tariq. "A little old fashioned for my taste."

"I like old fashioned," said Ava.

The Kronenhof was one of Switzerland's oldest grand hotels. A nineteenth-century wedding cake with turrets and spires and, inside, trompe l'oeil paintings on the ceiling. Even the new furniture looked as if it were from a bygone era.

She led the way downstairs to the Kronenstübli. Tariq opened the door to the restaurant. The room was empty save a single table at its center—white tablecloth, sparkling glassware, a sterling ice bucket by its side, a bottle of champagne peeking from beneath a towel. "I hope you don't mind," said Tariq, as the captain helped them to their chairs. "I don't like crowds."

"Not at all," said Ava. "Now we can talk about anything we like."

"And I won't take a picture of my dish," said Tariq.

"Torture, I know."

He smiled, and she smiled back. There was something between them. He knew it. She knew it. They'd felt it at the clinic, and they hadn't been mistaken. She hated it when it was like this: when there was chemistry. Later, it might make things easier, but now she felt vulnerable and exposed. It was easier to pretend with a man you despised.

To steel herself, she replayed her conversation with Zvi Gelber from the day before. The one where her entire plan nearly crashed down upon her.

"You've been a naughty girl," said Zvi Gelber.

"You're in," said Ava, feeling a rush of excitement.

She was on the train to St. Moritz, a six-hour ride. They rode comfortably alongside the Rhine, hardly more than a turbulent stream. Beyond it, the magnificent Grand Resort Bad Ragaz.

"Don't thank me," said Gelber. "Thank Zeus."

"Zeus?" said Ava. "I thought you used Pegasus."

"It's an upgrade," said Gelber. "Who needs a flying horse when you can have the god of gods?"

Zeus (formerly Pegasus) was the name of the spyware attached to the invoice Dr. Lutz had emailed to TNT. Once downloaded—*Click on the link*—Zeus took over a device's operating system and gave Zvi Gelber and his team of computer geniuses the ability to steal text messages, emails, key logs, and every bit of information from every app on his phone, as well as any other device linked to it. At the same time, Zeus allowed Gelber to take over the device's camera and microphone. He could film videos, snap pictures, and eavesdrop in real time.

The Tourists

"We found Abbasi," said Gelber. "Don't ask how."

Abbasi. The man with whom, according to Gerhard Lutz, TNT had been so urgently speaking.

"You can run, but you can't hide," continued Gelber. "He's been scrubbed. All mention of him removed from the net. Reza Abbasi. Professor emeritus of nuclear physics at Tehran University. Ranking member of Al-Quds Brigade of the Revolutionary Guard, and most recently, and the reason for his public disappearance, reactor group chief at Natanz Nuclear Facility."

Natanz Nuclear Facility, where the Iranians were busy enriching uranium with hopes of one day building a nuclear weapon. The most secret facility in all the Middle East. "I had no idea," said Ava. "I didn't want to alarm you unnecessarily."

"Consider me necessarily alarmed," said Gelber. "Now tell me everything. Spill."

Ava relayed all Lutz had told her about TNT's conversation with Abbasi. When she finished, Gelber was silent. "Zvi? You there?"

"Lutz heard him say the name 'Samson,'" said Gelber, as if he were questioning her on the stand. "You're sure?"

"Now you know why I called."

"Good girl," said Gelber. "It was smart to come to me."

"Of course I did," said Ava. "You're my rabbi." "Rabbi" meant the person she trusted above all others. "Did you find anything?"

"First the good news," said Gelber. "We confirmed the call from Tariq al-Sabah to Reza Abbasi. Thirty-two minutes in length. Date matches what Lutz said. Substantial email correspondence between them followed. Both men were cagey. They know enough not to write anything incriminating. There was no mention of any kind of bomb or device. Abbasi met with Tariq al-Sabah in Doha a week ago and agreed to a fee of one million US to provide plans for a transmitter designed for the one-kiloton device we liked to call 'Samson.'"

Ava felt her breath catch. Not good news at all. The worst possible news.

"Abbasi traveled to the Samedan airport three days ago," said Gelber. "TNT insisted he deliver the plans by hand."

"Why did he insist on hand delivery?"

"Now the bad news," said Gelber. "Because he's scared."

"Of what?"

"He's concerned he's being watched."

"He's always being watched," said Ava. "It's what he does. He wants the whole world to look at him."

"Not like this," said Gelber. "We believe that Al-Sabah's phone is hardened. He has software installed to detect spyware."

"I thought Zeus was undetectable," said Ava.

"It is," said Zvi. "Unless you have the software that tells you you've been hacked and then solves the problem."

"How did he get that?"

"He bought it."

"Aren't Zeus and Pegasus made at home? In Israel. By our people. Why are they giving it to him?"

"Money," said Gelber. "Zeus is made and sold by a private corporation. The NSO Group in Herzliya. They don't know Al-Sabah's a bad guy. He's just a client happy to pay their fees."

"So he knows he's been hacked?"

"Operational security demands we assume so."

"Shit."

"It'll take him some time to find out by whom," said Gelber. "If he even checks."

He'll check, thought Ava. I would. "How long?"

"A few days," said Gelber. "Maybe sooner."

"And then he'll be able to see that Zeus was attached to an invoice issued by Lutz's office."

"If he looks closely enough," said Gelber.

"We're blown."

"Not necessarily," said Gelber. "But, Ava, listen to me. I don't want you to hang around to find out."

Ava closed her eyes, her neck stiffening. She knew the feeling. Forward or back. Time to decide. "Abbasi delivered the plans," she said. "You're sure."

"There's a photograph taken in TNT's office in his chalet. A selfie of the prince with Abbasi. There's a blueprint tube on his desk that has initials from the Natanz Facility. We think the plans are inside it."

Decision made. "Good to know, Zvi. No worries. I can look after myself."

"One more thing," said Gelber. "Did you talk to anyone else about this? Anyone but me?"

"No."

"It's okay if you did. I just need to know."

"No, Zvi, I didn't. Why? More friction?"

"I might have found who visited TNT on the tarmac at Ben Gurion," said Gelber. "Yehudi Rosenfeld."

"Who's that?"

"Bad egg," said Gelber. "Working for an even worse egg. Itmar Ben-Gold."

Itmar Ben-Gold. Former leader of the Kach Party before it was declared illegal. Hardest of the hardliners. And by some inexplicable disaster, the current minister of defense. "Ben-Gold? What is he doing talking to Tariq al-Sabah?"

"Keep an eye out when you're looking for the plans," said Gelber. "We'd love to know."

Dinner was a Swiss feast. *Eierschwämmli*, or spring mushrooms, sautéed in butter. A leaf salad with her favorite French dressing. Veal steak with *morilles*. And, of course, *rösti*. All of it washed down by a series of exquisite wines. TNT took a sip of each. "To taste, not to drink," he said. He did, however, drink the champagne. Lots of it.

"It's ours," said Tariq, holding his glass high. "Domaine du Roi. We purchased the estate last year. What do you think?"

Ava said she thought it was wonderful.

She asked about him, his childhood, his education, his love of winter sports. She knew the answers already. She'd spent the past fourteen days digging up everything she could on him. Eventually, their conversation turned to his brother, Crown Prince Jabr, the man who'd given him the Bugatti. And by the look in TNT's eyes, his archrival.

"You seem so calm," said Ava. "Blissfully detached from it all."

TNT flushed. "Do I? I suppose I must. Dissent is not tolerated."

"You sound like a Russian afraid of being thrown in the gulag."

"Not so different," said Tariq. "It is just hotter where I live."

"So?" asked Ava, as she finished her veal. "Dissent, how?"

"They cannot be allowed to win," said TNT.

"Who?"

"They. Zionists. The Jews. Israel."

"I thought that was the common view," said Ava. "Hardly dissent."

"You would think so," said TNT. "After the wars, the annexation; after the intifadas and October seventh and the genocide in Gaza. But no. There are those who think differently. Appeasers."

"Disgusting," said Ava, with a shake of her head. "After so much suffering and mistreatment."

"It is not your battle."

"No, it is not," said Ava. "But I have eyes. I have ears. I have a heart."

"So you agree?" TNT reached across the table to take her hand.

"We share the same philosophy," said Ava.

"My brother . . ." TNT sighed, his eyes narrowing, looking past her, looking at something he disliked.

"What has he done?"

"He does not share the same philosophy," said TNT. "He is an appeaser. He says the battle is done. The war is over. It's time to make peace. The Jews won."

"You're kidding! Your brother, Jabr . . . the one you mentioned."

"Our next emir," said Tariq. "If that can be believed."

"What will he do?"

The Tourists

"A treaty. He calls it the 'Greater Gulf Co-Prosperity Sphere.' The Saudis, the Emiratis, even King Hussein of Jordan is going along with it. A treaty with the Jews. A partnership with Israel. Peace across the region."

"And you, Qatar?" asked Ava.

"We are insignificant," said Tariq. "We have natural gas, lots of it, but nothing else. We are negotiators without a mandate of our own. Middlemen. Influencers." A laugh aimed at himself. "And soon, not even that."

"What will you do?" asked Ava, playing the affronted, not willing to accept things the way they were.

TNT looked at her, as if weighing her impassioned plea. Real or an act? He suddenly looked older, mature, capable, and, most of all, cunning. For the first time, she felt as if she were looking at the real man. The man behind the mask.

"You will do something," Ava went on unabashedly. She was ordering him to act, if not for himself, then for her. For all who shared their philosophy.

"Oh yes," said Tariq. "I will do something. Jabr cannot buy me off . . . buy our country off . . . with an automobile. There are others who think like me. Those with more power. Others who will not tolerate being pushed to one side." He stopped abruptly. He stared at her openly. She was unable to gauge his feelings. Suspicion? Anger? Worse. *He knew that she was the enemy.* As quickly, his features softened. He laughed quietly, then wagged a finger at her. "You," he said.

"What?" asked Ava.

"You are wicked, aren't you?"

To hear him, it sounded like a compliment. Yet what did he know? He hadn't even asked her a question about herself yet. That would come.

Ava smiled. "Dessert?"

"At my home."

CHAPTER 34

Chesa Grischuna
St. Moritz

They drove home in the Bugatti.

The road back to St. Moritz was narrow, two lanes, and at this time of night deserted. No music to get her in the mood—just the throaty rumble of the engine to accompany them. For his part, Tariq didn't spend time telling her what a magnificent automobile it was. This horsepower, that many valves, this kind of steering. She didn't ask. To her, it was a car like any other. To his credit, Tariq resisted the opportunity to show off. Or so she thought. The car drove so smoothly; how fast could they be going? Then she looked at the speedometer and saw he'd been doing two hundred kilometers all along. The road began a series of twists and turns. Now she felt it, the rapid acceleration and deceleration, gravity forcing her derriere to get to know every inch of her bucket seat, then propelling her against her shoulder belt. She could sense him smiling, enjoying her unease, daring her to ask him, "Slower, please." Ava kept her eyes straight ahead and made sure she smiled herself. She'd spent too much time in far more uncomfortable vehicles in far more dangerous environs. Tariq, go ahead. Drive as fast as you desire.

They arrived at the chalet at the stroke of midnight. The garage door was open. First, they descended a driveway so steep it reminded

The Tourists

her of a ride at an amusement park. The lights were on. She counted four cars parked in their stalls. Tariq stopped the car on a dime. If there was a dignified way of climbing out of a sports car six inches off the ground, Ava didn't know it. Tariq, ever the gentleman, dashed to her side and offered a hand to help her out.

"Welcome to the Chesa Grischuna," he said.

A man stood at the elevator, holding the door. Not a Swiss; security flown in from the Gulf. Tariq didn't address him. He merely extended an arm for Ava to go first. They rode to the top floor. Seven floors, just like the newspaper had reported. It was a room from a dream. Twenty-foot ceilings. Exposed rafters. A floor-to-ceiling window facing south and inviting the mountains inside to join them.

Tariq motioned for her to sit on a sofa of tanned leather. Another man brought dessert. Peach Melba, he announced, placing the bowls on a marble coffee table. A juvenile choice, thought Ava. She took a bite. Heaven.

"I've been terribly rude," said Tariq, studiously ignoring the dessert. "Only talking about me and my family and politics. Excuse me. I know nothing of you."

"Not my favorite subject," said Ava.

A laugh. "You are the first woman in history to say that."

"I'm private."

"Family? Husband? Children? Dogs? Cats?"

And so the interrogation begins, thought Ava. She was surprised he'd waited this long. She was beginning to realize that he was not like other Arab men. He rejected the chauvinism and inbred egotism prevalent in the men of his culture: *You are a male. You must act this way.* But if his manners were more refined, they didn't camouflage his unquestioned superiority or unapologetic entitlement: *I am a prince.*

"Never married," said Ava. "No children. Parents in Dijon. Papa is a chef. He runs a restaurant. The Lion d'Or. Not the one in Geneva. Quite good. Traditional cuisine, obviously. And yes, a dog. A Bernese mountain dog. Fritz."

"Where's home?" he asked.

"Zinal," she said. "Do you know it?"

"Someplace high in the mountains. Population a hundred fifty and a few goats."

"Ah, you've been."

"Live there all alone, do you?"

"No," said Ava, forthrightly. There. Care to know more? Ask.

"Long way to come for physical therapy."

"I like Dr. Lutz," said Ava. "Three days every other week. I think of it as a short vacation."

"Did you know he's a Jew?" he asked, as if a "Jew" were some kind of curiosity.

"Why should I care?"

"Wise to know something about those you spend time with," said Tariq.

"Dr. Lutz is treating me," said Ava. "I spend time with people I care about."

"You didn't answer the question," said Tariq.

"No, I didn't know," said Ava, unbothered. If he was trying to bait her, he had failed.

"And you?" he asked, his voice harder. She noticed that his posture had stiffened. The real interrogation had begun.

"Yes?" said Ava, meeting his gaze. Me what?

"Are you a Jew?" European history's most important question.

"Catholic," she answered. "Ava Marie Mercier. Named after the prayer."

He studied her, running a finger along her inner arm. "Practicing?"

"Now you are getting personal," she said, scooting closer to him. "You are allowed one more question."

"What would you like for breakfast?"

Ava gave him a moment to savor his wit. "I don't do this kind of thing," she said.

"And yet here you are."

"Perhaps I got carried away," she said. "I was so happy to see a grown man not wearing tennis shoes."

"At least you know I won't fall in love with you," said Tariq.

"Is that a compliment?"

"What I meant was that I won't disturb your relationship with Herr Steinhardt."

"He allows me to do as I please," said Ava, not missing a beat.

"I wouldn't."

Tariq ran a finger across the nape of her neck, teasing her hair.

"Tell me, Prince Tariq, what else do you know about me?"

"Don't call me that," he said. "Not you."

"Why not?" said Ava. "You're looking into me as if I were one of your subjects."

"A man in my position can't afford to be ignorant," he said.

"Do you think I want something from you?" asked Ava.

"Everyone wants something from a prince," said Tariq. "Believe me, it's tiresome."

"I'm sure you're right," said Ava. She slid her arm from his. "But there must be some price for being given everything in the world." She picked up her purse. "Maybe we'll see each other again at the clinic."

"You're angry," said Tariq.

"Not at all," said Ava. "I'm experienced. Remember?"

"Tell me you are who you say," said Tariq. "Ava Marie Mercier, living far from the world in Zinal. Give me your word, and I will believe you."

"Who else would I be?" said Ava.

"I apologize," said Tariq.

She stared at him for a long moment. The moon had come out from the clouds. It hung high above the mountains and cast a faint light into the room. She stepped forward and kissed him. "Coffee and toast," she said. "For breakfast."

"Here," said Tariq, sliding his hand around Ava's waist, pulling her close, kissing her.

"Here?" Ava peered over his shoulder. No sign of the man who'd brought dessert. "What about . . ."

"Jerry," said Tariq. "He knows better."

"I think you do like people watching you all the time," said Ava.

Tariq bit her lower lip. "Beds are so boring."

"You prefer?"

"Anywhere else." He kissed her deeply, and she reacted as any other woman might. She allowed her private passions to run wild. She pressed her loins against his. She ran a hand up his back, then lower, cupping his buttocks. He'd made his intentions clear. He had no intention of falling in love with her. He wanted her once. A princely conquest. It was her job to fan his desires, not satisfy them, not entirely. She must persuade him that experience was something to be savored, not once, but time and again. Zvi Gelber's warning, not only about TNT and his sinister dealings with Dr. Abbasi but also that others at home in Israel might be party to his machinations, served to heighten her performance, if, indeed, it was that. Somewhere in her mind, a voice commanded her not to fail.

Did she think of Mac? Yes, but only in passing. Did her actions compromise her love for him? No. Did they betray the trust between them? No, she refused to believe so. She didn't write the rules of the game. Sometimes she believed there weren't any. There were just ends. Objectives.

A man, an agent like her, might beat someone with his bare fists to get what he needed. Another might lie. Another kill. Sex, violence, deceit, bribery, extortion: all were the agent's tools. When she swore an oath to her country and accepted her commission, it was with full knowledge that one day she might be called upon to use them, one and all. Over the years, she had. She'd screwed, bribed, extorted, and killed for her country. What was a spy but an expert in the exploitation of weakness? Human, political, technological. Tonight, here, at this minute, TNT's lust was such a weakness. And Ava would exploit it as best she could without reservation or remorse.

The Tourists

Gently, she pushed him away. She stepped back so that her figure might be silhouetted against the midnight sky, so that the moon's beams would dance upon her skin. She unzipped her dress and eased it over her hips, allowing it to drop to the floor. Beneath it she wore lace undergarments, *porte-jarretelles* to hold her stockings.

Tariq unbuttoned his shirt with care and pulled his arms from his sleeves. His chest was hairless, well-muscled, his shoulders rounded, his stomach rigid. It was impossible not to feel something.

"Touch yourself," he said, and waited until she did, studying her hungrily.

He removed his shoes and his pants, eyes never leaving her. He slid his briefs over his feet. He stepped closer to her and stroked himself, preening, watching Ava as she watched him. She moaned and moved a hand toward him. He shook his head. "Just watch."

"I want you," she whispered.

"Watch," he said.

"But—"

"Take off your brassiere," he said.

Ava unclasped her bra and slowly pulled it off. She followed his eyes and heard him sigh. She dropped the bra at his feet and caressed herself, feeling her nipples grow taut.

Tariq intensified his efforts. His breaths grew ragged. "Take me," he commanded.

Ava fell to her knees and put him inside her mouth. He came violently. His back arched. He cried out. Ava continued to pleasure him, pressing her face into his nether regions, holding it there until his spasms ended.

"Please," he said.

She held him in her mouth a moment longer. He stumbled backward, a hand on the couch to steady himself.

"You," he said after a moment.

"You're right," said Ava. "I am wicked."

CHAPTER 35

Chesa Grischuna
St. Moritz

Two a.m.

Ava slid her arm from beneath his pillow. Cautiously, she pulled back the duvet. She sat up and listened. Tariq breathed slowly, his face turned away from her. Next to him on his nightstand stood a bottle of mineral water. This was a special bottle, however, one that Ava had stealthily and surreptitiously supplemented with a draft of Valium and Xanax run up by the local compounding pharmacy at the request of Dr. Lutz. Nothing too strong, just a little something to nudge him into deep REM sleep. With luck, he'd awake feeling better and more refreshed than ever.

Ava slid off the bed and stood. The bedroom was cool, a humidifier running in one corner and an air purifier in another. She waited for Tariq to stir. She discerned no movement nor change in breathing. The drugs had done their work. She padded to the bathroom, where she took her phone from her clutch. She had no bathrobe or T-shirt to protect her modesty. She considered wrapping a towel around herself but decided it would be more trouble than it was worth. She returned to the bedroom and walked directly to the door. No more worrying about waking Tariq. She was operational. The handle turned silently. She drew a breath, ordering her heart to calm down, and meanwhile rehearsed the path to Tariq's office. Downstairs, turn left, continue to the end of the hallway, last room on the left. She'd found a sales prospectus for the Chesa Grischuna on the net, with a detailed floor plan and pictures of every room. Clients interested in purchasing a 150-million-franc property preferred to learn as much about it as possible before visiting.

A last breath and go. She opened the door and peeked into the hall. One step and she froze. There, not ten feet away, sat Jerry, asleep in a high-backed chair, chin resting on his chest. She walked past him, heel to toe, on the plush carpeting. If he woke, she'd ask where the kitchen was. Look at her, she was famished. He'd know better than to ask why.

She found the stairs and descended two flights to the fifth floor, or the second above ground. Left down the hall. Last door. Her fingers closed around the handle. Please, let it be unlocked. She was so lousy with a pick. She turned the handle. Open.

Ava closed the door behind her. She pulled up the photo of TNT and Abbasi in her mind. The desk was against the far wall, beneath a window looking onto the hillside behind the chalet. There were two chairs in front of it and a low table carved from a tree trunk. It was dark. No matter how well her eyes adjusted, she needed light to see. She turned on her phone's flashlight and took a step forward. Sconces on the walls came to life, illuminating the room. She gasped, turning toward the door behind her, expecting to find someone. The door remained closed. A motion sensor, she realized. There was a picture window to her right. For anyone looking in, she was as well lit as an actress on a Broadway stage. A mad search for a dimmer, but to no avail.

She crossed the room to Tariq's desk. The furniture was spare and sleek, what she thought of as Scandinavian design. She needed less than a minute to find what she'd come for. The blueprint tube sat on the credenza behind the desk. Stenciled on it in bold, black lettering were the initials "NNF," for Natanz Nuclear Facility.

Ava popped the endcap. Inside were twenty sheets of drawings, all standard engineering scale, thirty-four by twenty-two inches. One by one, she laid them flat on the desk and photographed them. Until now, everything she'd told Zvi Gelber was conjecture and hearsay. The word of an interested observer. He said that. He said this. As for the meetings between TNT and Abbasi, first in Doha, then here yesterday in St. Moritz, there was no proof as to the subject of their discussions.

Until now.

The drawings meant nothing to her. She couldn't tell a circuit from a resistor. She could, however, read the names of the engineers who'd drawn up the plans—written in that perfect blocky script in blue ink on the bottom right of each page—and the header identifying the subject: *Binomial Transmitter*.

The name provoked a shiver.

All those years ago, sometime in the weeks before Ava had been sent to retrieve the first weapon from the Golan Heights, she was called into a meeting with a general attached to the nuclear command. Once he'd been a professor of nuclear physics at a university in Germany. She remembered the general's stony face and his flat, matter-of-fact voice as he'd described in horrific, skin-crawling detail what would happen when Samson detonated:

"We are talking about a one-kiloton device, maybe a little less. A chunk of enriched uranium the size of a golf ball. These things work in three ways. First, there is the blast; then, there is the heat; and finally, the radiation. One KT, that's a thousand tons of dynamite. Two million pounds. Enough to fill a hundred dump trucks.

"So, you press the button. Boom. First thing is the blast. In a second, far less actually, shock waves travel two hundred meters in every direction, with a pressure of twenty pounds per square inch greater than normal atmospheric pressure—'over pressure,' it is called—flattening everything it comes in contact with. Wood, cement, steel: everything. At the same time, the plutonium ignites into a fireball with temperatures as high as the center of the sun. Anyone close by—one hundred meters, two hundred—is vaporized. Think about turning on the lights. On. Off. On. Off. There is nothing left. Not even ashes.

"Then there is the radiation. At the moment of detonation, the device releases an extraordinary burst of gamma and neutron radiation lethal to anyone directly exposed to it. Even if you survive the blast, you'll be dead in an hour, your bones literally dissolving inside your body.

"In the blink of an eye, a city block is leveled. Maybe a few stronger buildings remain, maybe not. Ninety-nine out of one hundred people dead. The others wish they were. The blast wave continues to expand. The wall of fire and heat ignites materials far away. There's flying glass, debris, fallout. The electromagnetic pulse wipes out all computers, phones, anything with electrical insides. Gas lines explode. In short, devastation.

"These devices are designed to be detonated at ground level. Think of a crater one hundred feet deep, ten times as wide. All that dirt or concrete and anything nearby is shot into the sky, coated with radioactive atoms, coming back to earth who knows where."

"Stop," said Ava.

"And of course the secondary effects—"

"Stop, I said!"

"I'm sorry," said the general. "I get carried away. But you get the picture."

Yes, Ava had gotten the picture. It was not one she would ever forget.

No one seeing the plans for the transmitter could mistake them for anything other than what they were. Nor could they deny who had produced them and on whose orders. Every photograph carried a GPS location. The plans were in Tariq al-Sabah's residence in St. Moritz. Emails between TNT and Abbasi confirmed a million-dollar payment for work done. The drawings, combined with Ava's firsthand testimony of Tariq's enmity toward his brother and his fury about a rapprochement between the major Gulf countries and Israel, painted a damning picture. The "where" and "when" of a coming attack might be unknown, but the "who" and the "why" were firmly established.

Tariq al-Sabah intended to use Samson, an Israeli-manufactured one-kiloton nuclear device, to end all hopes of a Greater Gulf Co-Prosperity Sphere.

Then in a flash of insight, Ava understood why TNT had secretly met with Yehudi Rosenfeld—or perhaps, Itmar Ben-Gold himself.

Ben-Gold and his Kach Party despised the idea of rapprochement as much as Tariq did. Once Israel allied itself with progressive Arab interests, it became, by definition, progressive itself. If a spirit of "All for one and one for all" was to prevail, Ben-Gold and his Kach Party, who preached isolation and colonialism, would not have a seat at the table. Like the tiny but rich state of Qatar, Ben-Gold and Kach would be bypassed—not middlemen, not influencers, but outsiders. Israel had spoken, and it had decided on the path of peace, prosperity, and inclusivity. It went without saying that a fanatic like Ben-Gold would do everything within his power to prevent any such thing from coming to pass.

Ava recalled Zvi Gelber's remarks about TNT's involvement in the peace negotiations between Hamas and Israel. It must have been there that he'd met Ben-Gold. The two bonded over their mutual dislike of Crown Prince of Qatar Jabr al-Sabah's plan for the Greater Gulf Co-Prosperity Sphere. She would never know who approached whom first. It was probably an offhand comment. "Can you believe this nonsense?" or "This is ridiculous." A look of shared dislike, mutual hatred even. Nothing more was needed to plant the seeds of an alliance. The enemy of my enemy is my friend.

The final iteration in her cascade of insights proved the most chilling. TNT possessed Samson. TNT also possessed plans to build the transmitter necessary to detonate it. Only one thing was missing. The code needed to detonate the warhead. In fact, there were two. One code to deactivate the safety. The second to blow the thing up. Who had the codes? The Israeli minister of defense. Itmar Ben-Gold. It was too perfect.

Ava returned the plans to the blueprint tube and placed it where she'd found it, the initials "NNF" facing up. It was the dead of night. She had a bottle of wine sloshing through her veins, and she felt as amped as if she were under live fire. She knew too much while the rest of the world knew nothing. It was a terrible responsibility.

With haste, Ava emailed the pictures of the engineering plans to Zvi Gelber. She had no time to wait for a confirmation of receipt. At any moment, TNT or Jerry or another unseen member of his security team might throw open the door and discover her trespassing. She could no longer say she was searching for the kitchen. A naked woman with a cell phone in her hand painted an incriminating picture. She could feel the executioner's blade brushing her neck. One after the other, she deleted the photographs. All the while, she rehearsed new explanations for why she might be prowling through the house at 2:27 in the morning. None held a tablespoon of water. When she'd finished erasing the pictures, she crept to the door and peeked out. Look and listen. She neither saw nor heard a soul. The house was asleep.

Ava scurried from the office and dashed up the stairs two at a time, halting at the seventh-floor landing. The chair was empty. Jerry was no longer at his post. She didn't bother looking for him. Sometimes the best defense is offense. Eyes to the fore, she crossed the landing and reentered the bedroom. The curtains were open. By the moon's half light, she could see that TNT hadn't moved. Keeping up her unapologetic, forthright bearing, she went to the bathroom and left the door ajar. She turned on the lights. She used the facilities and flushed afterward. She washed her hands. She coughed. Sometimes noise was quieter than silence. When she returned to bed, she drew herself up next to Tariq and held him. He shifted, mumbling a few words, and was still.

Ava lay awake for an hour.

Finally, she slept.

She woke with a start. A bright morning. Blue sky. Sun in her eyes. Tariq was not in bed. She rolled over. A man stood in the doorway; someone she had not seen before.

"Good morning, Madame," he said. "I am to inform you that the prince has left the premises."

Ava pulled the sheet to her neck. "Pardon me," she said. "Tariq is gone?"

"Yes, Madame."

"Where to?"

"Home."

"Which home?"

"Qatar, Madame," replied the man. "We have prepared coffee and toast for you, as requested. When you are ready. There is clothing for you in the dressing room."

"Where is the dressing room?"

The man gestured to his right, and Ava saw an open door adjacent to the bathroom.

"Thank you," she said. "I'll be down in a few minutes for breakfast."

She waited until the man left and shut the door behind himself, then rose. How, she wondered, had TNT slipped out of bed without her knowing? She was not by nature a heavy sleeper.

She walked to the dressing room, in fact a walk-in closet as big as the bedroom. Racks ran the perimeter. A pale-blue ottoman sat in its center. Not clothing, but an entire wardrobe. Blouses and blazers and parkas. Blue, white, red, green. Until then she'd refused to be impressed. But this . . . this was too much. Her hand touched fur, and she stopped. A mink coat. Not mink, sable. Only the finest for Tariq's conquests.

Ava settled on blue slacks and a white turtleneck and black ski jacket. There were shoes too. Twenty pairs? Twenty-five? She picked a pair of zip-up après-ski boots.

Everything fit perfectly.

There were five men in the kitchen, seated around a large dining table. None said a word to her. Ava ate standing. If they were relaxed now that the boss was gone, so was she.

"I'd like to call him," she said, after finishing her toast.

No one answered. They stared at her without malice and without interest or even acknowledgment. Finally, one of the men stood. He could have been TNT's double. "Back to the hotel," he said.

"I'll walk."

CHAPTER 36

Sport Hotel Corviglia
St. Moritz

Ava called Zvi the moment she was back in her hotel room.

"Did you get them?"

"Beautiful," said Gelber. "I congratulate you."

"I figured it out, Zvi," she said, forcing herself to calm down. "The whole thing. What TNT is planning. We've got to take this to the chief."

"Slow down, there," said Gelber. "First we need to authenticate the plans."

"You saw them," said Ava. "The blueprint tube has the lab's name stenciled on it. You confirmed payment was made. This is happening."

"You done good," said Gelber. "Now you need to give us some time on our side."

Time? The one thing they did not have was time. Ava cocked her head. Was she mistaken or did she hear equivocation in his voice? "I want to come home," she said. "We can take it to the chief together."

"That's premature," said Gelber.

"He has Samson," said Ava.

"We don't know that."

"He gave Abbasi the device's serial number," said Ava.

"Listen, kiddo," said Gelber. "You're worked up. I know how you feel. I was in the field, too, once, a million years ago. I can hear it in your voice. You think you've found something, and now the whole world has to know."

"The whole world does have to know," said Ava.

"But you need to stand down and let us do our thing now."

"Are you listening to me?" Ava shouted.

"You're not the only one on the line here," said Gelber.

"What is it, Zvi?" she asked. "More friction?"

"You need to step back," said Gelber. "We have everything we need at the moment."

"I haven't told you what I figured out," she retorted. "It's about his brother, Jabr. He was right to be worried. TNT is planning some kind of coup. He's not going to just stick everyone in a fancy hotel. He's going to blow them up."

"Ava . . . that's enough."

"That's not all, Zvi," she went on, unbothered. "I think we're helping him."

"Ava."

"Ben-Gold. Kach. They're all in it."

"Not another word."

Ava drew a breath. She'd known Zvi Gelber twenty years. Never once had he yelled at her. Her first inclination was to blame herself. She was way out of line. She had no right to bark instructions at the chief of Tzomet, a man with a lifetime of service to the Office and to the country. She wasn't, she reminded herself, even an active agent. She'd spent the past seven years in Zurich as consul general, a member of the diplomatic corps. She gazed out the window at the snow-covered peaks. From her room, she had a clear view up the hillside to the Institut Alpinuum. A wave of anger surged through her chest, flushing her neck, so strong as to make her shudder. No, dammit, she wasn't out of line. She'd risked her life to get the engineering plans. Was it naive to believe that a man who possessed a nuclear device would kill to protect it? And what about Gerhard Lutz? He'd stuck his neck out to eavesdrop on a client. He'd put Israel before self. How would TNT feel about that if he found out?

"Zvi," she said testily, brimming with vitriol. And then it came to her. She shut her mouth. Gelber was protecting her. He didn't want her to get into any more trouble than she was already in. But what kind of trouble? From whom? Oh, Ava, a voice inside her remonstrated. You were right. We are helping TNT. *Not we, but him. Them.* Ben-Gold and Yehudi Rosenfeld and the Kach party. She wasn't the one at risk. It was Zvi Gelber himself.

Mossad reported to the minister of defense. Word had trickled up the chain that Gelber was looking into TNT. He was the one following up on Ava's leads. It was Gelber who had looked into TNT's travels; Gelber who had dug around to see who'd snuck into Ben Gurion Airport and boarded TNT's jet. It was Gelber who tracked down Dr. Abbasi, and now Gelber who'd received the blueprints of the firing mechanism. Gelber was the immediate threat.

"You're right," said Ava, apologetically. "I went too far. I'm sorry. I'll step back. Take your time, Zvi. Now that I thought things over, I see that the whole thing might be a trap. Some kind of disinformation."

"Smart thinking," said Gelber. "Too much, too fast. I don't like it when things come so easy."

"What was I thinking?" said Ava.

"Just doing your job," said Zvi. "Time for a rest. Let those wounds heal."

"Thanks, Zvi. I appreciate it."

"Stay tuned," he said. "We'll reach out when we've got something. If you don't hear from us, enjoy your convalescence."

"Zvi?"

"Bye, kiddo."

CHAPTER 37

Zinal

A month went by.

Ava didn't know time could pass so slowly. She was reminded of Einstein's adage about relativity: "Put your hand on a hot stove for a minute, and it feels like an hour. Sit with a pretty girl for an hour, and it seems like a minute." Where, she wondered, does waiting thirty days for a call about a pending terrorist attack fit on the spectrum?

Worse, it was the time of year in the mountains when each day brought a new season. Rain, sun, snow, but most often rain. It was hard to believe that April could be colder than January. Stem cells or no, the cold and damp ravaged her shoulder. She returned to St. Moritz and the Institut Alpinuum once. It was not TNT's day for treatment. She did not visit the Chesa Grischuna. Dr. Lutz was likewise absent. She had a strong suspicion that he'd been told to avoid contact with her.

In Zinal it was off-peak season. The town was so quiet as to appear deserted. A two-lane road ran through the village, flanked by commercial stores: sporting goods, boutiques, a pharmacy, and a tearoom. Half were shuttered for vacation. She could stroll from one end of town to the other and not see a soul.

Each morning she'd walk with Katya to the tearoom and get a *pain au chocolat* and a coffee. Often, they sat alone. The tearoom played canned music on a loop—music that dated to her parents' era. If she heard "Moon River" one more time, she swore she'd take a gun from Mac's locker and blow the place apart.

And so, Mac . . .

Of all her missions, jobs, assignments, and ops, none was harder than hiding her investigation into TNT from Mackenzie Dekker. She went to bed thinking about Samson and TNT and what he was planning with Itmar Ben-Gold, and she woke up with the same terrifying thoughts, though no further along in her deliberations. No one had forbidden her from speaking to Mac. It was her own doing. She just assumed she mustn't. It was experience gleaned from twenty years on the job. Keep your mouth shut.

Nearly two months earlier, after Lutz had initially told her about TNT, she'd returned home abuzz with her newly adopted mission. Practically a zealot. Lutz's revelations had a life of their own and threatened to dance off the tip of her tongue ten times a day. Mac attributed her bright mood to the gains made in physical therapy and her accelerating recovery. He had started homeschooling Katya at the new year. He was too busy deciding which books to read and what history lessons to impart to read too much into her changed behavior. Independence was a trait he cherished. Respect for the other's space a cornerstone of their relationship. But after stopping herself once, then twice, the urge to share her new mission lessened. A kind of shell formed around her interest in TNT. Instead of sharing it, she zealously kept it hidden. It had become her secret addiction.

It was Katya who knew something was different with her. Often Ava would catch her staring at her in the open, unashamed manner that children reserve for their loved ones. Ava would see the look and smile.

"My mommy used to smile at me like that too," Katya would say.

"Like what?"

"When she had a secret she couldn't tell me."

"But I don't have a secret," said Ava.

"She said that too."

Late at night, Ava would shut herself up in Mac's man cave beneath the house, officially the *Luftschutzraum*, and scour the net for news about TNT. Mostly, this involved studying TNT's posts on social media to see where his travels had taken him. Paris. St.-Tropez. Beverly Hills. Nothing nefarious there, unless the Bvlgari boutique on Rodeo Drive had of late become a hotbed of terrorist intrigue. The sales assistant, a lithe brunette modeling a ruby-and-diamond necklace, did not appear to be a member of ISIS.

One picture posted on the Qatari royal website bothered her. It showed TNT shaking hands with several Swiss bankers in front of a factory in Zug. The caption read *Vital investments in cutting-edge technology*. The name of the factory was partially obscured, but with a little digging, Ava discovered it to be the Künzli Maschinen und Technikfabrik. The company name was innocuous enough. Its primary product was not: high-speed centrifuges used in the enrichment of uranium. Such a company would have little problem fabricating a transmitter.

She considered sending the picture to Zvi. She refrained. He had to have seen the picture already and drawn the same conclusion. So, why hadn't he called? He knew how to evade surveillance. He was not one to let a brush with authority interfere with his labors. He had not made it to such a lofty position without breaking a few rules, offending the powers that be.

Gelber's silence summoned her worst fears. She thought of TNT and Ben-Gold together. Together they were already powerful. What if they had recruited others to their cabal? What about the Saudis who'd been forced to pledge allegiance to Prince Mohammed bin Salman, MBS? Surely, a good many of them would be only too eager to join the cause. Backward, not forward. The past was the future. One Middle East divided under God forever.

Ava also took pains to find any mention of Jabr al-Sabah. She poured over Al Jazeera, the Gulf newspapers, and Qatari television. There could be little doubt that Jabr was the new face of Qatar. He was in Abu Dhabi, in Ankara, in Riyadh. Often the visits were unofficial, with no mention made of meeting this or that government official. But Ava knew better. Jabr was shaking hands, building support, and changing minds.

Several times, Mac nearly caught her. She found herself so engrossed in her research she failed to hear him come down the stairs. When she at last spotted him, she rushed to close the browser and grew flustered.

"I think you're looking at something naughty," said Mac.

"That's me," Ava agreed, pasting on a smile. "The porn queen."

"Come on, let me see," said Mac. "What is it?"

"Too late," she said, showing him the home screen. "You have to be faster than that."

But beneath the banter, her heart was threatening to break free of her blouse. Why did she feel so guilty when she was just doing her job?

June arrived, and with it the sun. Temperatures soared. All over the mountainside, flowers blossomed. Streams overflowed their banks as the snow rapidly melted. The fine weather brought laughter and smiles. Ava, however, was not a party to the Chalet Ponderosa's festive mood. Each day that passed without hearing from Zvi Gelber heightened her anxiety. She knew that he was every bit as concerned as she about TNT's intentions. Yet after seven weeks, she still had not heard back from him. How long did it take to authenticate engineering schemas? Behind her impatience lay a scarier, more insidious worry. Someone or something was stymieing Gelber's queries.

She could no longer wait.

Someone had to act.

CHAPTER 38

Zinal

A lazy Saturday.

After a week of stubborn rain, the sun appeared. Early June, but it felt like August. Not a breath of wind, the air buzzing with the scents and sounds of the Alps. The tinkle of cowbells drifted down the hillside.

Mac had left after breakfast and taken Katya for a walk to the dairy a few kilometers up the mountain to visit Martin, Mac's Eritrean friend, and his children. There would be a picnic, a swim in the lake, time to pick flowers and chase dragonflies. Ava was alone in the chalet, left to her own devices.

Her willpower crumbled like an earthen dam. Slowly, then very, very fast.

She found the burners in the bottom drawer of Mac's desk. She counted a half dozen in their factory packaging. She pulled off the plastic wrap and plugged in one to charge. She apologized to Zvi in advance for calling. It was for his own good, she told him. She had a feeling something was wrong. Besides, she'd make sure no one would know it was her.

It had been the picture of TNT in Zug that did it. If Ben-Gold was suspicious of being found out by Zvi Gelber, he would surely have shared those concerns with TNT. He would have warned him not to be so public with his movements. He would have told him to stick to

The Tourists

posting photographs of fancy cars, jewelry, and women with big boobs. "Do not post a picture in front of the factory that may or may not be manufacturing the transmitter for a nuclear device in your possession. People are watching. Zvi Gelber is watching."

But no, TNT had posted it all the same. The picture indicated that TNT believed he no longer had to worry. No one was on their trail. The dogs had been called off.

But no one, she knew, called off Zvi Gelber. He was the OG attack dog.

Ava unplugged the phone and composed Gelber's number. The call took a moment to go through. When it connected, it went directly to voicemail. No rings. Phone off.

Ava didn't like that. Zvi never turned his phone off. Tzomet was in charge of running agents. It was his job to be available 24/7. Lives were at stake. The greeting began, and Ava's heart sank further. "The party is not available at this time. Please leave—"

She ended the call. Where was Zvi's personal greeting? Where was his trademark sandpaper growl . . . the voice that had smoked ten thousand cigarettes and cursed out as many agents? *"It's Zvi. Say something and keep it short."*

She consulted her own phone for the general number of Tzomet at the Mossad headquarters. She asked the operator for Gelber.

"A moment please."

So far, so good, thought Ava. At least they didn't hang up on me.

"Hello."

Ava answered in French-accented English. "Mr. Gelber please. Marie Klen. *Le Monde.*" Mossad wasn't the CIA. Everyone knew what everyone did.

"I'm sorry, but Mr. Gelber isn't available."

Ava remembered the phones in his office. Push-button landlines common in a corporate office thirty years ago. No readout of the incoming number. "When will he be in? He promised us an interview about the recent developments in Lebanon."

"May I take a number?"

"Is Mr. Gelber ill? We haven't heard from him."

"Mr. Gelber can't be reached at the moment. If you'll give me your name and number, I'll have someone contact you shortly."

Ava hung up. She was in no mood to be put off. Not without a fight. Suddenly, there was nothing more important than talking to Zvi. She dialed the main number once more. "Colonel Ava Attal for Zvi Gelber."

She was put through. The same anodyne voice said, "Yes?"

Ava gave her name and rank. "I need to speak with Zvi. It's urgent."

"One moment, Colonel Attal. I'll connect you."

Ava let go a gasp of relief. So, Zvi was still there, after all. Why was he playing hard to get? If he'd changed his number, why hadn't he told her? Her worry about his welfare quickly turned into anger at his mistreatment of her. He had no right to keep her in the dark.

"Hello, Colonel Attal?"

"Zvi?" It was not his voice. Silk instead of sandpaper. Hebrew with a trace of a French accent.

"This is Yehudi Rosenfeld. I'm glad we have a chance to talk."

Rosenfeld. Ben-Gold's deputy and official attack dog.

"I'd like to speak with Zvi," said Ava.

"That won't be possible."

"Where is he?"

"You're meddling in matters far beyond your grasp," said Rosenfeld.

"Where's Zvi?"

"I wouldn't worry about Zvi Gelber, Colonel. I'd be far more worried about myself, if I were you."

"Is that a threat?"

"For now, it's a piece of advice," said Rosenfeld. "Freely and sincerely given. Your inquiries are not welcome. In fact, you should assume they are regarded as hostile and with intent to harm the State of Israel."

"What have you done with him?" asked Ava.

"Zvi got what he deserved. Be sure that you will, too, if you continue in your unfounded pursuits. I hear Zinal, Switzerland, is a lovely place. Stay there. Goodbye, Colonel."

The call came in the middle of the night.

"Please don't talk. Just listen. I'm a friend of Zvi's. I worked as his assistant for the past three years. Zvi is dead. He was kidnapped from his home a week ago. His body was found a few days later in Gaza. He'd been tortured then shot in the head. They blame Hamas. It wasn't. About five of us who worked closely with Zvi were let go the same day. No explanation, but we knew. The others are scared. Two have already left the country. I won't leave. I want to help. My name is Dahlia Shugar."

PART III

CHAPTER 39

Present day
Épernay, France

They had left Paris an hour ago.

It was a speed run on the A4 through Montreuil-aux-Lions and Château-Thierry, following the eastward course of the river Marne. TNT kept his foot on the pedal, passing at every opportunity. Two hundred twenty kilometers per hour and not a tick less. He'd triggered four traffic cams that he knew. At this speed, that was €1,500 a pop. Once more, he caught a flash of light in his rearview. Make that five. Speeding tickets were not his concern. Not today.

"We don't grow all the grapes ourselves," said TNT. "We only have a few hundred hectares under cultivation. Hardly enough to make fifty thousand bottles of champagne each year. We buy from all the vineyards in the area."

"Couldn't you have asked for the champagne to be delivered?" said Dahlia Shugar. "It's nice of you to go yourself."

"We have other business," said TNT.

"What kind of business?" she asked.

"I could have just had the champagne delivered, you know."

Dahlia turned toward him, eyes narrowing as she took in the meaning of his words. She was wearing a tan trench coat and a scarf in her hair, with dark sunglasses. She looked very French, very mature. So beautiful. But there was something more there. He didn't know what, and it bothered him. She was smarter than he'd first thought. Not so innocent as she made out to be. There was something behind her eyes. She watched too closely. She listened too intently. Half of him wanted to tell her everything. The other half wanted to send her back to Los Angeles on the first plane. It was too late for that now.

"So, it's time?" asked Dahlia.

TNT nodded. "Are you ready?"

"I think so."

They left the superhighway. The road narrowed to two lanes. They were in the old France, the France of deep, impenetrable forests and rolling meadows and fertile farmland. They passed through the town of Châtillon-sur-Marne and into the province of Champagne. Vineyards stretched as far as the eye could see. The vendage was two weeks past. The vines were barren, their gnarled and twisted branches lonely and at rest.

TNT turned his head and met her eye. Suddenly, he was less certain than he'd been. Not just about her. About everything. Until now, he'd forgotten that he could still turn back. He was a prince. He was beholden to no one. Then he thought of all that he'd done, the lives already taken, the other people relying on him. Others with as much power, perhaps more will. No, he decided, there was no turning back. Not for Dahlia. And not for him.

"I need your help," Tariq had said to her one month before.

A trip to LA. Dinner at Mr. Chow. Some fun in his suite at the Beverly Wilshire. That feeling again that she was special.

"For what?" Dahlia sat up in bed, the sheets gathered at her waist, so proud of her body. So unlike women from his country.

"Intrigue," he said. "Politics. Maybe a coup."

"I know what the first two mean," she said. "But a coup? You mean like a takeover."

"You make it sound like a bad thing," said TNT.

"I work at Bvlgari," said Dahlia. "Do you want us to make you a crown?"

"Not a bad idea," he said. "But not yet."

"You're serious?" Her tone said it all. Not mocking. Not disbelief. An honest desire to learn more.

He nodded. He knew then why he could talk to her so freely. She didn't question him. She didn't laugh. She treated him as he deserved to be treated. With absolute respect.

He felt as if she knew the real him. "Is it too much to want to lead my people?"

"No," said Dahlia. "You're a prince. You should lead them."

"My brother is in the way. He's firstborn. He's the heir—"

"And you're the spare," said Dahlia, taking his hand. "How can we change that?"

He loved her for the question. His own Lady Macbeth and they weren't even married. He regarded her closely. Until now, he'd told no one about his plans. He hadn't realized the burden he was carrying. He had a sudden, undeniable urge to tell her. Why not? The fact that he barely knew her made her that much more trustworthy. No secret alliances to worry about. No ties to his homeland. No unsavory agendas. She was who she said. Most importantly, she loved him.

"I have an idea," said Tariq.

And so he told her. About Jabr. About his brother's plans with Israel. About how Jabr would damn Qatar to a meaningless future. He told her about the upcoming conference in Paris. Israel, Saudi Arabia, the Emirates. An unholy alliance. The death of Arabia as he knew it.

"Someone has to stop him," he said.

"You," said Dahlia, as if giving him an order.

"Yes, me." And saying it to her, he believed it. "There will be blood."

"A coup," said Dahlia. "Isn't there always?"

"I'm offering you a different life," said Tariq. "Maybe a better one."

"Is that a promise?" she asked.

"A pledge."

Dahlia looked at him. "I want a better life; definitely a different life."

"Do you?" Tariq was caught off guard by her earnestness. He was used to flattery and duplicity and, well, anything but honesty. Her plainspoken appeal frightened him. "Tell me why."

She stood, taking the sheet with her, wrapping it around herself. She crossed the room and sat in a chair by the fireplace. "Look at you. You're rich. You're handsome. You're smart. You have manners. You are a prince of one of the wealthiest countries in the world. I ask myself, what interest could this man possibly have in me? I know why, of course. Well, one reason at least. But all along I've wanted to show you that I'm more than this." She gestured at the bed, the bottle of champagne upended in the ice bucket, the tin of caviar nearby. "I don't know why I care, but I do. I think it's because I know you're not just a guy that cares about putting pictures of himself all over social media. You can't hide behind your cars and your watches and your vintage kicks forever. There's more to you. I know it. Multitudes. And yes, I want to be there when you discover it too. That's the better life I want. A better life for you."

It was not the answer Tariq expected. He had expected talk of money and travel and material desires. Pay me this. Give me that. Instead, it was she who offered him something. Confidence. Belief. Destiny.

A different life.

A better life.

A life as emir.

Rain began to fall. A sudden squall, battering the windscreen, essentially blinding them. Tariq almost missed the turnoff to Épernay. He spun the wheel to the right, losing the back end for a moment. He heard Dahlia gasp. He accelerated out of the slide, fast enough that the safety belts locked up. A wheel slipped off the road, but just for an instant. The car jolted violently.

"Don't worry," he said, gaining control of the vehicle, slowing dramatically.

She exhaled and gave him a look. Was that a tear in her eye?

"I'm sorry," he said. "I didn't mean to frighten you."

"I'm not as brave as I appear," said Dahlia.

"Braver, I think," said Tariq.

The rain ceased as suddenly as it had begun. One moment the sky was brooding and black, the next they'd left the clouds behind. They passed a sign reading **Champagne**.

"I need to know something," said Dahlia.

A dangerous question at any time. "Please," said Tariq.

"You never told me who the woman was. In the restaurant."

"Someone who was in the way," said Tariq.

"The enemy," said Dahlia. "You already told me that."

It was the explanation he'd given her before the Jules Verne. "Exactly."

"I need to know her name."

"Which one?" said Tariq. "She's a spy. An Israeli. She has many names, most of them false. 'The enemy.' Isn't that enough?"

Dahlia kept her eyes straight ahead. "How do you know her?"

"Bad luck," said Tariq. "Our paths crossed a few months ago. I thought she was a friend."

Dahlia shifted in her seat. "Did you sleep with her?"

"Why do you ask?"

"I saw how she looked at you."

Tariq knew better than to answer. She could read him like a book. "She stole something from me," he said, sternly. "Something important. I discovered she'd gone to her old boss and told him."

"Mossad?"

"How do you know about Mossad?"

"An 'Israeli spy,'" said Dahlia. "Of course I know about Mossad. I read books. I watched *Fauda*."

"Who did you root for?" said Tariq. "The good guys or the bad guys?"

"How did you find out?" asked Dahlia, ignoring his hint to change the subject.

"What?"

"About her going to her bosses."

Tariq smiled tightly. He'd known it would come to this. He couldn't begrudge her wanting to know. "We're not doing this alone, you and I," said Tariq. "There are others hoping for the same outcome."

"Israelis," said Dahlia.

"They'd better be," said Tariq, with a laugh. Then seriously: "Yes, Israelis. Members of their government. Men who'd prefer that I rule Qatar, not my brother."

Dahlia nodded, and he could see that the answer pleased her. "What did she want? I mean, why was it so important to meet her at the restaurant?"

"To blackmail me," said Tariq.

"To sell you back what she'd stolen," said Dahlia.

"More to convince me not to go ahead," said Tariq. "Stop or else."

"So she knew," said Dahlia. "About what we plan to do."

"She thought she knew," said Tariq. "Mostly, she was trying to save herself."

"Are you worried?" said Dahlia. "You know . . . that she told others?"

"No difference if she did," said Tariq. "I made sure no one would believe her. We made sure. My friends and I."

"Did you kill her?" she asked.

"Does it matter?"

"I'd like to know."

"No, I didn't," said Tariq. "Not yet."

"But you will?"

"We will need someone to blame for my brother's death," said Tariq. "It can't be an Arab killing an Arab. And it certainly can't be me. She's a Jew. She will do nicely. Her name is Ava. Ava Marie Mercier Attal."

"Thank you," said Dahlia.

"You were right to ask," said Tariq. "You should know."

Dahlia put her hand in his and squeezed. "There will be blood," she said.

"It's a coup," said Tariq. "There's always blood."

CHAPTER 40

27 Avenue Montaigne
Paris

Ava was free.

The flex-cuffs that had bound her hands lay on the floor, severed by a retractable X-Acto knife. The knife sat on the windowsill, next to a flash drive and a miniature cell phone—a BM70: three inches long, an inch wide, as thin as the latest iPhone. A text on the thumbnail-sized screen read **TNT has Samson. Driving to Epernay, his vineyard. Maids cleaning rooms. Posse watching TV. Be careful.**

Ava slid the phone and flash drive into her pocket, picked up the X-Acto, and crossed the room to the door. She pressed down on the handle. Locked. A girl could hope, couldn't she? Entry was governed by a biometric scanner on the other side of the door. There was no corresponding panel inside the bedroom, which meant that once unlocked, the door remained open until an authorized party relocked it upon leaving. Whether the door was alarmed, she didn't know.

It was no mystery how Ava had smuggled in the necessary tools. On arriving yesterday afternoon, she'd been searched; her phone, billfold, and cosmetics were taken from her. It was an amateurish search—polite, even. Nothing like what a prisoner got when checking into a place like Shikma, the maximum-security facility in southern Israel housing

Hezbollah and Hamas fighters. The intake procedure there was neither amateurish nor polite. No need to elaborate.

Ava had long experience crossing hostile borders, living behind enemy lines, living with the enemy himself. Damascus, Amman, Beirut, other places she was prohibited from discussing. She knew what to take with her and how to transport it to avoid detection. No one ever said spying was glamorous.

Ava dug the X-Acto knife into the wood above the escutcheon and methodically hollowed out a space until the wiring connecting the lock to the scanner was visible. With care, she drew the bundle of wires out of the door. There were two ways to do this. Cut them all and cross her fingers. Or mimic the signal transmitted when the scanner generated a positive match. To do this, she had to send an electric current to the lock mechanism itself. Today, however, Ava didn't have a choice. Pinching the wires together, she severed them with the razor-sharp blade. Fingers crossed and a silent prayer.

Ava turned the handle. The bolt slid home. A smile, but only for a second. She cracked the door, listening for activity. Nothing. She opened it a little more and peered outside. She neither heard nor saw anyone.

Whispering a prayer, she stepped into the hallway. Just as she had memorized the layout of the Chesa Grischuna, TNT's chalet in St. Moritz, she had committed to memory the layout of 27 Avenue Montaigne, his home in Paris. It was easy enough. She'd found several articles in architectural and design magazines, both current and from years past, showcasing the building's various incarnations. Tariq wasn't the first public figure who'd owned the house. Before him was a British rock star, and before the rock star, a flamboyant Italian industrialist. Each in turn had redecorated the home, top to bottom, and each had invited magazines to chronicle their impeccable taste. Ava had studied numerous photographs of the primary bedroom, the kitchen, the living areas. In addition, she had benefited from a private resource, if one of her own devising. Dahlia Shugar.

It was Dahlia who had drawn up the exact floor plan of the *maison particulier*.

It was Dahlia who'd told her that TNT's security was cloistered on the first floor, most likely watching a soccer match on the billion-inch screen their master had provided for their entertainment. Tariq had a rule: no security personnel allowed in living quarters, which meant floors two through six.

It was Dahlia who'd told Ava that there were no cameras inside the residence. TNT liked his privacy. It was his custom to have sex in unorthodox places. The floor of his office was one of his favorites, followed by the bathroom, where he liked to watch himself in the mirror.

And it was Dahlia who'd texted her that she and Tariq had left the premises and were en route to his vineyard, the Domaine du Roi. But why? Ava wanted to know the purpose of the visit. Had he taken Samson with them, or was the weapon here someplace where she might find it? She didn't dare text Dahlia to ask.

From the beginning they'd known it would be a honey trap. They'd studied TNT's posts, searching for the right place to engineer a meeting. Dahlia held both US and Israeli passports. Going back over the years, they noted that TNT had close ties to Southern California, Beverly Hills in particular. It ended up being a choice between the Soho House, a private-membership social club in West Hollywood, and the Bvlgari boutique on Rodeo Drive. They chose Bvlgari.

TNT never failed to visit the store on each trip. Sources confirmed he spent hours in the boutique deciding among the offerings, often dropping a million dollars or more. The intimate atmosphere combined with the likelihood of an extended encounter gave Dahlia the opportunity to use her every feminine wile to win him over.

By comparison, the Soho House was simply too busy, too filled with distraction. Hundreds of men and women wandered in and out every day. Worse still, it was what Dahlia, who had served two years in the Israeli Air Force, termed a "target-rich environment." She would hardly be the only attractive woman present.

Bvlgari it was.

The right choice, as it turned out.

Ava walked down the hall to the paneled doors that led to the primary bedroom—and that Dahlia had promised were always open. Ava pressed the lever. *Et voilà.* A woman true to her word.

The bedroom was smaller than she'd imagined, but more opulent. A king-size bed suited for the Sun King himself. Gold-and-ivory bedspread, frilly pillows, a canopy and four posts gilded in eighteen-karat gold.

The door to TNT's closet stood ajar. A peek inside revealed it to be as large as the bedroom itself. Enough clothing for a Baltic army. Boxes and boxes of shoes stacked floor to ceiling. Fifty? One hundred?

"Look at the ceiling," Dahlia had commanded a week before. Ava lifted her eyes. A magnificent reimagining of Michelangelo's Sistine Chapel, the most famous panel—*The Creation of Adam*, God reaching out to Adam. In this case, however, Adam was Tariq al-Sabah in all his glory. Top marks for accuracy from a woman who'd been there.

Ava made her way to the guest closet on the opposite side of the room. Dahlia's things hung on the rack, hardly enough to notice . . . not that she'd needed to bring her entire wardrobe. The floor was cluttered with a slew of boxes and bags, fruits of their daily assaults on Paris's finest boutiques. Chanel. Fendi. Prada. Handbags. Belts. Scarves. And shoes, nearly all of them with fire-engine red soles. Just saying the designers' names made her feel overworked and underpaid.

But Ava hadn't come to gawk.

She located the orange chamois bag she'd come for, high on the top shelf. She loosened its strings and removed a brown crocodile handbag with a gold buckle in the shape of an "H." She unsnapped the bag and rooted around inside of it. She found what she was looking for tucked into the side pocket. A compact Glock 25 the size of her palm. Only six shots, but if she did her job properly, she'd have four left over. The term was "double tap." Saying it made her feel glad to be overworked and underpaid.

There was something else in the bag. Slim, rectangular, a bit bigger than a cigarette lighter. A magnetic lockpick that Dahlia had stolen from the Office her last day on the job.

Ava heard the door to the bedroom open. Voices. The maids. She shut the closet door and slid around the tower of bags and boxes, squatting behind them so as not to be seen. A second later, someone opened the door. A hand turned on the light. Ava kept her head down, face buried in her thighs. She heard clothing being hung on the racks. Soft whistling. The smell of fresh-milled soap. She sensed a presence withdraw. One woman called for fresh towels. Another laughed about the sheets being disheveled.

Minutes passed. The closet door remained open, the light above her head illuminated. Ava's thighs began to ache. Her knees begged to stand. She didn't dare move. With growing anger, she listened as the maids cleaned the bathroom just feet away, chatting among themselves, clearly in no haste. Ava lifted herself a few inches and raised her head. A maid walked past, and Ava ducked, resuming her squat. Her muscles caught fire. She couldn't stay this way much longer. Count to ten, she told herself. Anyone can make it to ten. And when she had, she counted to ten once more. Tears came to her eyes. Her legs began to shake. Please, she pleaded with them fervently. Go. Finish and go.

And then, just like that, the light above her went off. The closet door was shut. She heard the door to the bedroom close. Blessed silence.

Ava rose slowly. For a moment, the pain worsened as blood flowed back into her muscles. Then, relief. Ava stood tall. She gasped. Nothing had ever felt so good.

She waited a minute before opening the door and venturing into the bathroom, then back into the bedroom. With patience, she opened the door and peered into the hall.

The coast was clear.

Time to go to work.

CHAPTER 41

Épernay

The headquarters and historic home of the Domaine du Roi were located on the Avenue de Champagne in the town of Épernay. "Domaine du Roi" meant "the king's domain," and the main building suited the name nicely. Not quite a palace, but not far from one. A tall, rectangular stone tower flanked by two long wings, the buildings newly painted a pale mint green, maroon shutters at every window and wrought iron Juliet balconies.

TNT passed through imposing gates into a cobblestone courtyard and stopped the car. A slim, energetic woman dressed in tight jeans and a khaki twill jacket bounded down the stairs of the main administration building. Tariq recognized her as the cellar master but for the life of him could not remember her name.

"The champagne you requested is inside," said the woman. Was it Claire? "Cuvée 1968. One case."

"And the methuselah," said Tariq.

"And the methuselah," said Claire, referring to the name given a six-liter bottle of champagne. "In the cavern. As you requested."

"I'll be giving Mademoiselle Shugar a tour," said Tariq.

"Allow me," said the woman, affronted. "It would be a pleasure."

"Thank you, but no," said Tariq. "I can manage."

Tariq took his backpack from the rear seat. "Follow me."

The Tourists

He circled the main building, snaking between stacks of empty picking crates twenty feet high, and opened the door to an old stone outbuilding. Dahlia followed close behind. He led the way down a flight of stairs, deeper and deeper underground. With each step the air grew damper, more chill, more redolent of earth and stone. They arrived at a domed cavern hewn from limestone. Tunnels stemmed in all four directions.

"Fifteen miles of these things under the town," said Tariq. "Been there for hundreds of years. Who knows where they all lead?"

The cavern was dim and musty, with torch lights bolted to the walls. He turned left and headed down a narrow tunnel, passing room after room filled floor to ceiling with racks of champagne. Thousands of bottles.

After a few minutes, they came to an intersection of sorts. A man waited for them, dressed in work clothes, a cloth cap tilted rakishly on his head. "Everything you requested is inside," he said.

Tariq palmed him €1,000, the notes rolled tightly and bound by a rubber band. "*Merci*, Charles."

"I am happy to help," said Charles. "Whatever you need."

"That won't be necessary," said Tariq.

He opened the door to a large, high-ceilinged room lit by fluorescent lights. To the right was an old, worn wooden table with some tools on it. Tariq shut the door and locked it. He placed his backpack on the table and removed the package. "This is Samson."

Dahlia looked at it, then back at Tariq. "It has a name."

"It does," said Tariq. "But not from me."

"And so?" asked Dahlia, approaching the table with caution. "What is Samson . . . exactly?"

Tariq had thought long and hard about what to tell Dahlia. The truth was out of the question. A half truth would do nicely. "An explosive," he said.

"It doesn't look very big."

"Just big enough," said Tariq. "Plastic. Enough to destroy a room. Maybe two."

"Your brother will be in the room," said Dahlia.

"I hope so," said Tariq. "Otherwise, we're wasting our time." He saw the worry in her eyes. Suddenly, everything they'd talked about was real. Her new and better life. The meaning of the word "coup."

"When will this happen? Where?"

"Soon," said Tariq. "Maybe tomorrow. I will tell you when I know."

"I think you know already," said Dahlia.

Tariq stared at her, offering her a deceptive smile, nothing more. "We have work to do."

The methuselah sat on a table. It was a giant bottle of champagne, six liters to be exact, or eight normal bottles, and packed in a coffin of sorts: a pale wooden crate shaped more like a triangle than a box, broad at the bottom, slim at the top, not quite tapering to a point.

Tariq removed the bottle and stood it on the table. It was heavy, nearly twenty pounds. Charles had not only provided the champagne but also the large professional bottle cutter TNT needed for his work. Using the tools, TNT removed the bottom of the bottle and drained the champagne. He set aside the bottle and turned his attention to Samson. He opened its protective casing and, with exquisite attention, freed it. Naked, the nuclear device resembled a stainless steel ingot, a little longer than a shoebox, half as wide and deep, with several pin lights on the top.

"Is it on?" asked Dahlia.

"It's on," said Tariq.

Nearby sat a block of black polyethylene foam: four feet long, three feet wide, and ten inches in depth. After setting Samson in the center of the block, he drew an outline of the device and with an X-Acto knife carved out a depression into which Samson might snugly fit. Next, he reshaped the foam block until it matched the dimensions of the bottle. He was no Michelangelo, but with care, he achieved the desired specifications.

"Hold it still," he said, laying the bottle on its side.

The Tourists

Dahlia held the neck of the bottle as Tariq slid the foam creation inside of it. It wasn't a perfect fit, but it would do. He slid a few pieces of foam here and there until it was immobile. Using both hands, he picked up the bottle and shook it. Satisfied it was in place, he applied a coat of industrial glue and reattached the bottom, pressing the two pieces together as hard as he could for as long as he could.

He waited a few minutes, then set it upright. He examined the bottle from all sides, shining the light from his phone at it. No matter how he tried, he could not see inside the dark, opaque glass.

"I think we did it," he said, admiring his achievement. "Can you see anything?"

Dahlia looked at the bottle from several angles. "It looks like a bottle of champagne."

"An f-ing big one," said Tariq, and they laughed. He kissed her, then slid a hand beneath her blouse, cupping her breast. "Proud of me?"

"Immensely," said Dahlia, pressing herself against him.

He kissed her again. All this manual labor had him feeling like a working man. He took her hand and put it on him.

"Not here," said Dahlia, recognizing at once his intentions.

"Yes here. It's my vineyard. I can act how I please."

He lifted her and set her on the table, spreading her legs. He unbuckled his pants and pulled them to his knees.

"Be quick," said Dahlia, slipping off her panties.

He lifted himself on his tiptoes and touched her. Dahlia gasped.

At that moment, his phone rang. It was a ringtone reserved for one person. He looked at the screen. Not now. He gave Dahlia a look. Be quiet.

"Yes, Father."

"Where is the champagne?" demanded the emir.

"What do you mean, 'Where is the champagne?' It's here. At the vineyard."

"We need it. Now."

"I'm in Épernay," said Tariq. "I'm picking it up myself."

Dahlia slid herself onto him, both hands behind his back. If he wouldn't thrust, she would do her best.

"When can you be back?"

"Two hours," said Tariq.

"Pardon me," said the emir. "I didn't get that."

"Two hours," repeated Tariq, as Dahlia bit his ear. "Stop it."

"What's that?"

"No, I mean, why are you so concerned? We do not need it until tomorrow."

"Your brother just phoned," said the emir. "They are to make the announcement tonight."

"What? Tonight?" The news hit Tariq like a blow to the stomach. He withdrew and turned away. "What happened to all the talking?"

"Everything has been agreed," said the emir. "The French president wishes to address the country. He wants to make sure no one can change their mind."

Tariq struggled to pull up his pants with one hand. "You're sure?"

"Yes, I'm sure. Just bring the champagne."

"Of course, Father. I'm on my way. One thing: Did Jabr tell you where the announcement is to be made?"

"Where do you think?" said the emir. "The Palace of Versailles."

CHAPTER 42

Passy, sixteenth arrondissement
Paris

"Think it'll work?" asked Mac.

"My part or your part?" said Harry Crooks.

"I thought it's one plan," said Mac. "Both parts together."

"I'm not the one breaking into a prince's mansion," said Crooks. "All I can promise is that you'll have a chance to get in. A chance, nothing more. After that, you're on your own."

"You're a real confidence builder," said Mac.

"Confidence is one door down," said Crooks. "Next to bullshit and vanity. I'm selling the truth. It was confidence that put me in this chair."

They'd spent an hour discussing how to get into Tariq al-Sabah's *maison particulier*. The problem wasn't how to break in so much as how to lessen the chance of discovery once he was inside. A six-story home. Twenty-two rooms. An unknown number of occupants, including armed security. The odds were overwhelmingly against Mac discovering Ava before he himself was discovered. The solution was plain to see. It was also impossible. Somehow Mac must convince TNT and everyone else in the house to get out.

If Mac couldn't do it, he had to find someone who could.

The time had gotten to 1:00 p.m. The clouds had parted. A weak autumn sun shone through a pale sky. Mac flipped through photographs of TNT's Paris residence. His problem was that the magazines showcased the same rooms each time: the living room, the primary bedroom, the study, the kitchen. While he was able to glean a little bit of handy information about each room, he was left with little or no idea where in the six-story building they were located. All he knew was that Tariq would not keep Ava in any of them. She was locked up somewhere else.

Most helpful was a photo essay about the home's expansive rooftop garden. Mac wasn't interested in what flowers Tariq al-Sabah was growing or the bougainvillea hanging from the trellises. He was drawn to several photographs showing the door leading to the rooftop garden. To look at, it was a hundred years old, weather beaten, in need of paint, and guarded by a simple Schlage lock. It was, Mac decided, the only thing in the entire building TNT hadn't renovated.

He had his way in.

But, as they'd already concluded, getting in wasn't the problem. It was what happened afterward.

Crooks handed Mac a cell phone. "It's all set up. When you're ready, call 112. The number that will appear on their call screens belongs to TNT, if that was him that kidnapped Ava."

"It was him," said Mac.

Crooks called it "spoofing," using software to disguise a caller's number by substituting another for it. Most often, it was used by telemarketers to fool people into answering what otherwise might appear on their phone's register as *Spam* or an unwanted solicitation. "You can't just call and ask for help," Crooks had said. "Before they send anyone out, they have to confirm who exactly it is calling."

"How long before they show?" asked Mac.

"To TNT's place?" Crooks spun in his chair. "A Qatari prince on the Avenue Montaigne? Fifteen minutes tops."

Mac liked fifteen minutes. He didn't want to be hanging around TNT's rooftop garden longer than that.

"Did you finish writing the speech?" asked Crooks.

"More like three lines," said Mac. "What do you think?"

The Tourists

Crooks read Mac's words. "How did you get through school with penmanship like that? At college in Ghana, they would have beat my knuckles bloody."

"Palmer Method went out with my mother," said Mac.

"Easier to decipher cuneiform," said Crooks.

"Just read it," said Mac.

"Yeah," said Crooks assuredly as he read the text. "I'd buy it. Especially if it came from Tariq's mouth." He returned his attention to his monitor. "Look at this. I found something that nicely suits our purposes. Not too long. Impeccable audio quality."

Crooks hit play. The video clip showed TNT, attired in his native garb, addressing a gathering of business owners at a store opening in Doha. "It will be our government's policy," said TNT, in his American-accented English, "to support all business owners and entrepreneurs with an initial interest-free loan of seventy-five thousand US dollars. Repayment is not required for a period of ten years. If, in that time, the business employs more than twenty persons, the loan will be forgiven in its entirety."

Crooks hit Stop.

"Is that all you need?" asked Mac.

"More than an adequate sample size," said Crooks. "First let me upload the audio sample. Next, I type in your little speech. Done." He turned to face Mac. "It may take a minute to generate. These new AI chips are fast. All the same, it takes billions and billions of iterations to generate an accurate aural copy."

The computer pinged. Crooks gave Mac a look. "Here we go." He hit Play. Mac listened as the computer read aloud the lines Mac had written. It was him. It was TNT speaking.

"The program's called Parrot," said Crooks. "It used the speech we uploaded of TNT talking to the businessmen in Doha to clone his voice. Then it turned around and used the cloned voice to read the lines you'd written."

"That's scary as hell," said Mac. "No way you can tell the clone from the real thing."

"The future is now," said Crooks. "We are who we choose to be... or who we want others to think we are."

"So once I've got the cops on the line," said Mac, "I access the program and hit Play."

"One more thing," said Crooks.

"What's that?"

"Pray."

Crooks rolled his wheelchair across the room to an antique wooden dresser. He opened the bottom drawer and withdrew a compact item wrapped tightly in a blue-and-white cloth. "Last used May the twenty-eighth, the year of our Lord 1982. Goose Green Airfield. Las Malvinas Islands. 'The Falklands' for you and me." He unfolded the cloth and handed Mac a pistol.

"What is this?"

"My old service weapon. Browning nine millimeter." Crooks unfurled the cloth, and Mac saw that it was an Argentine flag. "Took this down myself from enemy HQ. Thought it was all over. Remember what I said about confidence. I'd forgotten to double-check that we'd cleared the building. One guy was left. Course, it had to be the Argentine Army's version of Rambo. Shot him twice in the chest before I ran out of ammo. Before the SOB went down, he lobbed his last grenade at us... me and my squad. Eight men. Not one of us wounded in three days of battle. I had no choice but to jump on it."

Mac looked at the flag. There was blood on one corner. "You did the right thing."

"Course I did," said Crooks. "Else we'd all have been dead." He tapped the arms of his chair. "For queen and country. Oh, and don't worry about the gun. I take it out every so often, clean it, have a trip down memory lane. I swear that when I hold it, I can hear the gunfire, smell the smoke. Do you miss it, Mac? You know, the battlefield?"

The Tourists

"No," said Mac. "I've had my share. But I miss the mission. It told me who I am."

"Now you have a new one," said Crooks.

"We have one," said Mac.

Crooks smiled at the thought. "Mind, you can't shoot anyone," he said. "Murder. Mission or not."

"What about self-defense?" asked Mac.

"You're the one breaking and entering," said Crooks.

"Guess we'll have to play it by ear," said Mac.

Crooks unwrapped a silk handkerchief and dumped nine bullets into Mac's palm. "If you need any more, you're screwed."

Mac fed them into the magazine. It was harder than he remembered.

"By the way," said Crooks. "What do you call this . . . what we're doing?"

"'Swatting,'" said Mac. "Sending a Special Weapons and Tactics team to a house to respond to a threat."

"No SWAT here," said Crooks. "In France, we have RAID. Search, assistance, intervention, and deterrence."

"Call it 'raiding' then," said Mac. "Same difference."

CHAPTER 43

Le Marais
Paris

Eliza Porter Elkins and Don Baker stood at the entry to Gerard Rosenfeld's building on the Rue des Rosiers. It was cool and dreary, but Eliza was sweating. She could feel the beads of perspiration on her forehead and on the back of her neck. There was no reason to be nervous. She was visiting a French citizen to ask him a few questions. She could walk away anytime. There was no one scouring the city for her. There was no red flag next to her name and work ID. All the same, she was sweating. Now, at this advanced stage of her career, she finally knew how it felt to be an agent. She didn't like it.

They found Rosenfeld's name on the directory beside the front door.

"Don't ring," said Baker, grabbing her arm as she put her finger to the buzzer.

"Sorry," said Eliza, ruffled. "I'm new to this. But what if he won't let us in?"

"Leave that to me," said Baker.

Just then, a resident exited the building. Baker led Eliza into the foyer before the door could close. They took the lift to the third floor. There were two apartments, one to either side of the landing. Neither door had a nameplate or a number.

"Do we just knock?" asked Eliza.

The Tourists

Baker shook his head. He was looking at something, and whatever it was, he didn't like it. He took a few deliberate steps toward the door to their right. "Oh boy," he whispered.

Eliza followed at his shoulder. "What is it?"

Baker crouched and pointed to a dark, gelatinous puddle on the tiled flooring. He tested the gob with a finger, rubbing it as if assaying its composition. "Blood." He stood. "I'm guessing this is Rosenfeld's place."

Baker turned the doorknob. Unlocked. Not a good sign. He shot her a glance, then eased the door open. They listened for a moment. Not a sound. The silence was too much. Eliza couldn't abide the notion of trespassing. You didn't just walk into someone's home unannounced.

"Bonj—"

"Shh!" Baker made a sign to shut up. "Wait here," he said.

Eliza nodded. She was happy to let Baker go by himself. She put her hand on the doorframe, not that she needed to steady herself.

Baker advanced down the hall, opening a door to his left, another to his right, peering inside each room. She didn't know someone could move so quietly, especially someone like Don Baker. It came to her that she didn't know him at all. He glanced back at her and shook his head. No one was there.

Somewhere inside the building, a door slammed. A voice called out a name. A dog barked ferociously, then quieted. Eliza stepped inside the apartment and closed the door.

"Don," she called, wondering if he was mad at her, if he was keeping quiet to spook her, payback for not having read him in to the situation earlier.

On the drive over, she'd finally given him the details of the conference underway since Wednesday at the Élysée Palace. A gathering of potentates from across the Gulf, with a view to formally enact a diplomatic and mercantile alliance between the Kingdom of Saudi Arabia, the United Arab Emirates, Jordan, and Israel, with Bahrain and Qatar signing a separate nonbinding codicil. (Though Qatar was sponsoring the talks, all parties agreed it had been too close to nearly all the regional terrorist entities—Hamas, Hezbollah, ISIS, and the Iranian Revolutionary Guards—to be awarded full member status.) The agreement called for the establishment of permanent embassies in all signatory countries, along with the exchange of ambassadors, the relaxing of tariffs across a broad swath of products, and the opening of channels of communication between military commands.

It was a triumph of oil and technology over history and religion. Arab oil and Israeli technology. The Holy Bible and the Quran had yielded to the modern scriptures of *Forbes* and *Fortune*. This was the twenty-first century. There was no future in enmity. It was time to put aside past grievances and embrace one another, warts and all.

As with all milestones in the region, it was hailed as a victory by some and as blasphemy by others. Eliza was concerned about the latter group. Over the past months, the Agency had picked up significant chatter about the coming conference. Some was couched in language of those seeking to prevent an act of violence. Far more, however, hinted at efforts to prevent an agreement from being signed and urging action to be taken. Violent action.

The president was adamant in his support of an agreement. It was the best chance to bring lasting peace to the region since the establishment of the Israeli state in 1948. Nothing could be permitted to derail the historic efforts.

For "nothing," Eliza substituted Mac Dekker, and now, Ava Attal.

"Don?" she called out again.

"Eliza," he answered in a quavering voice. "Get in here."

Even so, she proceeded slowly. She was in no hurry to learn what had prompted Baker's anxiety. Bracing herself, she entered the living room. It was the smell that told her something was wrong. A sharp ferrous scent that prized at her nostrils and threatened to turn her stomach. She was reminded of her youth and of bitter cold mornings hunting in the Smoky Mountains. When field dressing a deer, the first action is to empty the carcass of internal organs. She had been taught to insert the knife below the throat and cut all the way to the groin. The pressure with which the intestines and stomach and liver burst from the ruptured cavity had amazed her. Accompanying the exposed organs was the sharp ferrous scent of blood and offal and all the nasty things living creatures kept inside of them.

Eliza smelled that now. She noted the look of horror on Baker's face. She told herself to be ready. This was bad. But nothing could have prepared her for the sight of the two individuals, man and woman—Rosenfeld and his wife?—seated on the couch. Both were bound hand and foot and gagged. Both had been shot in the head, the woman through the left eye, the man in the forehead; both shots had left powder burns. The man's belly had been cut open and his intestines—oily, gray, and coiled—had spread onto his arms and lap.

Eliza swung her head away, gagging. When she opened her eyes and somehow focused them, she was looking at a polished wooden table crowded with framed photographs. She immediately recognized one of the men. It was Itmar Ben-Gold, Israeli minister of defense, whom she'd met numerous times while at the State Department. Shaking Ben-Gold's hand was a slight, pleasant-looking man with a halo of frizzy gray hair. It was the same frizzy gray hair that belonged to the dead man seated just feet from her.

"This wasn't Mac," said Baker.

"Then who?" It was difficult for Eliza to speak, let alone think. "Who, Don? We know he was here. We know he believed Rosenfeld could help him find Ava Attal. Who else would do this?"

Baker didn't respond.

"Look at the pictures," said Eliza, pointing the table. "Rosenfeld was tied into the Israeli government. There's the prime minister. There's Rabin. There's Sharon. This is about this weekend. Put two and two together. Ava Attal on the run. The dead Saudis. Now this. There's a reason Mac came to Paris this weekend. He's going to disrupt the conference. Don't tell me it's coincidence."

"What does Mac care about the peace conference?" asked Baker. "It has to be her."

"Ava Attal did this?" demanded Eliza. "Tied them up. Tortured them. Police didn't see her running from the apartment at four a.m. They spotted Mac Dekker."

"Eliza, no."

"Tell me if I'm wrong, Don, but isn't this what he did in Iraq? Hunt down the bad guys, interrogate them, kill them. That was his job, right? Know what he said to me once? 'Sooner or later, we always get 'em.'"

"You said you didn't know him," Baker retorted angrily.

"I lied," said Eliza. "So sue me."

"What the hell? When? Where?"

"Iraq. A million years ago. It's none of your business. What does it matter, anyway?"

"If it didn't matter, you would have told me in the first place," said Baker. "Is that why you jumped on the red flag?"

"Of course not," said Eliza. "There was no other choice, not this weekend. Not with what's at stake."

"You never gave him a chance."

"The person at my desk doesn't have that luxury."

"Maybe," said Baker. "Maybe not. I just wonder what else there is you're not telling me."

"You know all you need to," said Eliza. "You'll have to take my word for it."

Baker looked away, lips pursed, shaking his head. "What if she's doing the same thing we are?" he asked. "Ava Attal."

"What's that?" asked Eliza. "Trying to stop a bad guy from ruining the conference?"

"Yes, exactly that," said Baker.

"Doesn't play," said Eliza. "If she knew something was up, all she had to do was go to her own people. Why keep silent? You've got it ass backwards, Don. She's the one we're after. Her and Mac."

Baker gave her a look that let her know how he felt. Any other day, she'd have canned him for it. He shrugged violently. "You want to call the police?"

"No," said Eliza, regaining her senses. "We can't be tied up here all day answering questions. Like McGee said, best not to involve ourselves in police matters."

But Baker wasn't listening. Something had caught his attention. "Don?"

"Check this out." He kneeled to pick up a cell phone lying next to the sofa leg.

"So?" said Eliza. "We don't have time to hack it. Maybe McGee can get some of his team on it."

"Step back," said Baker. "You don't have to look if you don't want to."

Baker circled the sofa to Gerard Rosenfeld's side. Taking care to avoid the entrails, he took hold of Rosenfeld's right arm. Using his free hand, Baker selected Rosenfeld's pointer finger and placed the tip in his mouth. He kept it there for fifteen seconds, then removed it and dried it with his jacket. Next, he took the phone he'd just found, activated the home screen, and pressed Rosenfeld's now warm finger to the On button.

"Never," said Eliza, looking on with disgust.

"Sometimes," said Baker, showing her the phone, "you need a little luck."

"It worked?" asked Eliza.

"We're in," said Baker.

"Son of a bitch," said Eliza. Then: "Pardon my French."

They moved into the kitchen and sat at the table, examining the phone's apps. The call register showed two calls to Yehudi Rosenfeld— Israeli country code, Jerusalem city code. The first, made at 4:16 a.m., was an outgoing call that lasted ninety seconds. The second, at 4:21, was an incoming call that lasted fifteen minutes. A text message to Yehudi Rosenfeld, read by the recipient at 4:14, said simply, **They know you are working with Tariq al-Nayan-al Sabah.**

"He goes by TNT," said Baker.

"I know who he is," said Eliza. "I've met him on several occasions. He's as smooth as they come."

"If he's working with Rosenfeld, that means he's working with Itmar Ben-Gold."

"Give me a minute to process this."

"Gerard Rosenfeld texted his brother," said Baker, "then called him when he didn't hear back right away. Probably left a message on his machine. Yehudi wakes up, sees the text and the call, and promptly freaks out. He calls Gerard to get the full download. They're the ones we should be after."

"All the chatter was right."

"It usually is," said Baker. "Now we know what exactly it was all about."

Eliza picked up the photograph of Itmar Ben-Gold. "He's minister of defense. That means he has say over Mossad, Shin Bet, all their security apparatus."

"What if Ava Attal did go to him?" said Baker.

"And he shut her down," said Eliza. "He'd have to if he's working with Tariq al-Sabah."

"So she took matters into her own hands."

"But why, Don? Tell me why."

"To do the right thing?" said Baker. "Wouldn't you?"

Eliza Porter Elkins didn't have an answer. She hated herself for it. "So what do we do now?"

"We do what Mac's going to do," said Baker. "Find TNT."

CHAPTER 44

27 Avenue Montaigne
Paris

The door to TNT's private office was locked. Ava couldn't have been happier. A locked box held secrets. This was doubly true, given TNT's devil-may-care personality. Security was the other guy's problem. But not today. Today, even Prince Tariq al-Sabah was sure to take every precaution to safeguard his plans.

A biometric security system governed entry. Ava ignored it. She pressed the lockpick against the door. A powerful electromagnetic pulse overrode the system and unlocked the door. It was the same device that she had used in Dubai fifteen years earlier when she'd infiltrated the glitzy Gulf city as part of a team to assassinate Mahmoud Al-Mabhouh, the criminal mastermind who had overseen Hamas's finances. Not a pleasant memory. The lockpick was practically the only thing that had gone right.

Ava slid inside the office. It was a large room, nearly half the size of the fourth floor. Three dormer windows overlooked the Avenue Montaigne. The decor was spare, all earth tones, with Italian furniture and modern art on every wall. Haring, Basquiat, Lichtenstein. The desk was a slab of red Carrara marble the size of an aircraft carrier.

She found the laptop where she'd been told it would be: dead center in front of TNT's chair. Ava sat and opened the computer. One thing Dahlia hadn't provided was the six-digit passcode.

She inserted the thumb drive she'd smuggled in. The malware was two years old, practically obsolete, but it was all she had. Odds were that TNT had hardened the laptop the same as he had his phone. There was no more relying on Zvi Gelber or Unit 8200. No phishing or other clever ploys involved. It was a blunt-force attack. A head-on assault on the laptop's operating system.

A folder labeled "Tools" appeared on the screen. She double-clicked it, and it asked if she wanted to install a program labeled **Break-in.exe**. It sounded like a good idea. She checked **Yes, I agree** and double-clicked again. A rectangular box appeared, to measure the installation progress. It took ten minutes to advance from 2 percent to 6 percent. And there it stalled. A minute passed. Then another.

The malware had two functions. First, it mirrored the laptop's hard drive, making a copy of every program and the program's contents. Every email, text, photograph, document, spreadsheet, and file. All of it. At the same time, once installed, the malware allowed Ava herself to operate the laptop as if it were her own. She didn't need a password to access any of the programs. The malware would have retrieved them for her from the operating system. All she had to do was say "Open Sesame" and hit the Return key. If that wasn't magic, she didn't know what was.

Ava shifted impatiently in the chair. She slipped the pistol from her waistband and set it on the table. Nice and close in case of surprises. Her gaze wandered the office, admiring the artwork, the furniture. How, she asked herself, had it come to this? From the Golan Heights to the Avenue Montaigne? She held out her hand, palm up, turning it so that the scar tissue shimmered beneath the light. Boiling water, she'd told Mac. A kitchen accident before they'd met. She rubbed her thumb across the hard pink skin. A memory of her grasping the superheated metal door provoked a stab of pain. She flinched. If only she'd held onto the handle a little longer, if only she'd pulled a little harder.

The Tourists

Nothing would bring back Jonny or Benny. She couldn't blame herself for their deaths. It was an operation in enemy territory. These things happened. Men and women died. Ava was a professional. She knew that. But not a night passed when she didn't for a moment, however fleeting, see their faces and ask herself what she might have done differently—*what she should have done differently*.

But Samson . . .

Samson was on her. You didn't let the bad guys get their hands on something like Samson. You didn't cut and run and let a bunch of Islamic fundamentalist hotheads take possession of a nuclear device. It didn't matter if there were fifty of them or a hundred. You stood your ground and killed as many as you could with your thirty-year-old Uzi submachine gun that jammed every tenth bullet and your two magazines of nine-millimeter bullets.

At least, that's what Ava had done in her dreams. She'd stood defiantly before the burning pickup truck and guarded Samson with her life. In her dreams, the Uzi never jammed and her magazines were endless and not one bullet from one jihadist gun struck her. In her dreams, she'd won; she'd beaten them back, all of them; she'd sent them home to their squalid camps with their tails between their legs.

Waking, her bedclothes drenched in sweat, eyes wide with terror and victory, she'd known that her dreams were a lie. A vainglorious deception. In fact, she'd done none of those things. And as the days and months and years passed, her decision to run, to abandon Samson, tormented her that much more.

The day that Dr. Gerhard Lutz had pulled her into his office and urgently relayed the details of the conversation he'd overheard, she'd known her years of running were over. The bill for her failure had come due. The day of reckoning had arrived. Time to pay.

At length, the rectangular box began to fill. Twenty percent. Now thirty. In her mind, she had an image of a high-powered drill penetrating a vault. She had nothing to do but wait.

"Come on, Dahlia. Report in. You're messing up my operational security. Where are you? Do you have Samson? When are you coming back?"

Seventy percent.

And then, as if she'd snapped her fingers to order it to finish up, the progress bar read 100 percent and glowed a cheerful bright green.

Ava was in.

CHAPTER 45

Hôtel Plaza Athénée
Paris

At two o'clock on this autumn Saturday afternoon, the lobby of the Hôtel Plaza Athénée, one of the oldest and most revered hotels in all Paris, was a symphony of elegant chaos. A party of a dozen Saudis—a sheikh, his wives, their children—milled around the reception desk as keys were handed out and the children morosely argued about who would sleep in what room. Elsewhere, two older European women dressed in matching black dresses walked their matching white poodles across the marble floor and toward the gallery. A look between them made clear they did not care for the Saudi contingent. In a far corner, the concierge was going over the evening's offerings at the opera. Mac caught the words "misanthrope" and "Molière." A bellman dressed in the same uniform one might have seen a hundred years earlier guided a trolley piled high with Louis Vuitton steamer trunks toward the elevators. The strains from a string quartet playing Vivaldi's *Four Seasons* drifted from the Gallerie.

In the splendid, perfumed confusion, no one paid Mac Dekker and Harry Crooks the least attention as they crossed the marble floor. A hotelier waved Mac and Crooks to the reception desk. "Welcome," he said. "Will you be checking in?"

Mac wheeled Harry closer. Crooks gave his name. "I believe it's a suite."

"Just the one night?"

"Just the one," said Crooks.

"Passports and credit card," said the hotelier.

"My assistant won't be staying," said Crooks.

Mac looked on stone faced as the hotelier took Crooks's passport and credit card. Mac had ditched his suit and borrowed from Crook's closet. The black cable-knit sweater fit perfectly. The trousers, also black, were two inches short, but who was looking? For his part, Crooks was dressed in a blazer and slacks with a silver silk ascot to make sure everyone knew he was the boss.

The hotelier gave them a suite on the fifth floor, with a view onto the rear courtyard. There were better rooms, and one from which Mac might have climbed onto the roof, but they were too expensive, and besides, Mac couldn't risk being seen from the street.

Once in the room, Mac opened his travel bag. Inside was a coil of climbing rope and Harry's Browning pistol. Mac threw the rope over a shoulder, then palmed the pistol. He chambered a round and slid it into his waistband.

"If it misfires," he said, "you're in trouble."

"Actually, the opposite," said Crooks. They shared a laugh. "But Mac. Trust me. I've never sent a man into a battle with a dodgy firearm. I'm not going to start today."

The room grew quiet. It was that moment before the green light. The moment when the atmosphere hardened and it became difficult to smile or really to say anything at all. It was time for a prayer and for Mac to remind himself why he was there. To recall all that had led to this moment; to take a breath and commit.

I'm here to do a job.

I am here to save the woman who is my life.

Mac withdrew one of the phones and a slim executive tape recorder. "Give it to me again."

The Tourists

"Play the message once and hang up," said Crooks. "It's more effective that way. It leaves them uneasy. They won't want to take a chance. They record everything anyway. If they want to listen again, they can."

"Fifteen minutes," said Mac.

"Give or take," said Crooks. "Don't go in until they arrive. Believe me, you're going to know when they get there. More importantly, everyone in that house will know it. Police here don't mess about. They come in heavy."

Mac didn't need reminding. Jo Goldenberg. *Charlie Hebdo.* The Bataclan. Too much blood had been spilled in the city.

"See you for dinner," he said.

"Bring Ava," said Crooks. "Can't wait to meet her."

"Deal."

Mac left the room. He took the elevator to the top floor. He couldn't spend too much time patrolling the hallways. There were cameras everywhere. Someone would see him, either staff or security. On cue, a bellman emerged from an unmarked door, pushing a luggage trolley. Mac stopped in his tracks and pressed his back against the wall. The bellman never gave him a look. Mac stuck his foot against the doorjamb in the nick of time. He peered inside. A service elevator. The bellman rounded a corner. Mac slid inside the room and pressed the Call button. The elevator doors opened immediately. There was only one button higher than six. "R" for "roof." His destination. The car jerked and briefly climbed. When the doors opened, Mac was in a different world. No carpeted hallways, no flowered wallpaper. Instead, concrete, chipped paint, and a stuttering fluorescent light. He opened a door that gave onto a long hallway. The ceiling was low, made lower by exposed pipes. Ducking his head, he walked to the end of the corridor and spotted a sign marked ACCÈS AU TOIT. "Access to the roof." The door was locked. He had no pick. He tried the doorknob again, and it rattled loosely, its screws barely holding. He retraced his steps. There was a fire extinguisher in a recessed case built into the wall. He took it out.

Decent weight. Solid. He returned to the rooftop door. A look over his shoulder. No one in sight. He brought the bottom of the extinguisher down onto the doorknob. Wood splintered. The brass knob clattered onto the floor. He pushed the door open.

A short flight of stairs led to a second door with a push bar. He depressed it, and the door swung open. A blast of fresh air, a drop of rain on his cheek. The door closed behind him. The roof was flat and barren, covered with old, beat-up tar paper. A dozen satellite dishes of varying sizes huddled in one corner. No missing the Eiffel Tower about a half a mile away. He proceeded to the roof's western boundary. A steep slate mansard roof fell to the adjacent building. From there, a drop of ten feet to the rooftop garden he had looked at in so many magazines. The red door hadn't changed a bit.

Mac jogged to the northern corner of the roof. Standing on his tiptoes, he enjoyed an unobstructed view into the courtyard of TNT's mansion. A half dozen men stood near a pair of black SUVs. A few of the men were dressed in traditional Arab clothing, a few in business suits, all milling about. No sign of the Bugatti or any of the cars the prince was famous for.

It was then that he heard it. The magnificent whine. The rugged, mellifluous song of a perfectly tuned internal combustion engine. He hurried to the southern side of the roof and gazed down on the Avenue Montaigne. He wasn't mistaken. It was him. It was TNT in his Bugatti Chiron.

Mac followed the car into the courtyard. A woman got out of the passenger side, then TNT. They joined the others. Something was transferred from the Bugatti into an SUV. He couldn't see what exactly, except that it was a large rectangular box.

It was time.

Mac called 112. The answer was immediate. *"Service d'urgence."*

Mac placed the tape recorder next to the phone and pressed Play. "Hello, police. I need your help, please. Right away. My name is Prince Tariq bin Nayan bin Tariq al-Sabah. There are armed men in my house. They have guns, rifles, machine guns. Terrorists. They have already killed one of my bodyguards. They are shooting again. Can you hear? It is the woman they want. I know it. Please. I am at 27 Avenue Montaigne. I can't talk anymore. I can hear them coming." And here, in a flash of inspiration, Harry Crooks had instructed the AI clone to speak in Tariq's native Arabic and say, "Please Lord, come quickly. My life depends on it. Inshallah."

Mac lowered the recorder. The operator said in a calm voice, "Stay on the line. Do you know how many men are inside? Sir, are you there? Are you there? *Sir?*"

Mac ended the call. He looked at his watch.

Fifteen minutes.

CHAPTER 46

Centre sapeurs et pompiers service d'urgence
Paris

Sophie d'Avent should not have taken the call. It was past 2:00 p.m. Technically, her shift had ended twelve minutes earlier. She was only at work in the first place as a favor to her boyfriend, Jules, who had had too much to drink the night before while out carousing with his old high school buddies.

"Sir, are you there? Are you there? *Sir?*" said Sophie, in the cool, dispassionate voice she'd been taught. They're already scared enough, her teachers had lectured, referring to callers of the 112 number, the national emergency number—staffed and supervised by the *sapeurs-pompiers*, the Paris Fire Brigade, which was part of the French Army. They don't need you to frighten them more. *"Du calme, Sophie. Toujours du calme."*

No one responded. Her monitor showed that the call had ended, terminated on the caller's side. Her monitor also indicated the caller's number, call duration, and the location of the nearest cellular transmission towers to the handset.

Sophie was still officially a probationer. She'd joined the *sapeurs-pompiers* after completing basic training several months earlier. This was France. Until someone was promoted or a position emptied out, a probationer in the *sapeurs-pompiers* she would remain. All the same, she was ambitious and conscientious. She knew panic when she heard it. And she knew to take the word "terrorist" seriously.

Barely a second had passed before Sophie patched in her superior, Sergeant Diallo. "I have a code one. Paris. Eighth arrondissement."

Code one was the Emergency Response Grading System's highest level of alert. It required credible mention of a violent act, past, present, or future.

Sophie replayed the call.

"Run a trace," said Sergeant Diallo.

"The handset is registered to the Embassy of Qatar. 1 Rue de Tilsitt."

"Triangulate location," said Diallo.

"27 Avenue Montaigne. The residence is owned by Tariq bin Nayan bin Tariq al-Sabah."

"Corroboration with the caller established," said Diallo. "Call the number back. Try and reestablish communication."

"No answer," said Sophie.

"I'll take it from here," said Sergeant Diallo. "Good work."

The call from Sergeant Diallo reached RAID headquarters in Bièvres, Essonne—twelve miles southwest of Paris—at 2:14. "RAID" stood for "search, assistance, intervention, and deterrence," and it was the elite tactical unit of the French National Police. RAID's primary responsibilities included hostage recovery, protection of VIPs, and counterterrorism.

"Possible attack in progress," said Diallo, upon reaching the incident commander. He replayed the message, simultaneously transferring it and all accompanying data.

The incident commander listened to the message, ended the call, and immediately punched a button on his console marked *BRI—PAR*. Security and Intervention Brigade / Paris Prefecture. He verbally relayed the contents of the call, along with the address and the instructions "Go in hard. We can't risk anything. Not this weekend."

Two minutes later, a tactical attack squad rolled out of a complex of buildings in Neuilly. The squad numbered sixteen officers and six vehicles. The officers were armed to the teeth, each carrying a machine gun, a pistol, grenades, and sufficient ammunition to last hours.

"Time to location: twelve minutes."

CHAPTER 47

Avenue Montaigne
Paris

Sooner or later, Dekker had to show.

Cyrille de Montcalm resumed her trajet of the Avenue Montaigne. She'd been on her feet seven hours. Back and forth. Back and forth. Maybe two hundred meters in each direction, two city blocks. She was on the parade ground all over again. *"Attention, les soldats! Marchez!"* Past Dior. Past Gucci. Past the law offices of Yvan Merlotti. Past the medical clinic of Dr. Henri Bernard. To distract herself from her aching feet, she'd memorized them all.

Sooner or later, Dekker had to show.

Cyrille felt her phone buzz in her pocket. She didn't bother checking. Another message from the lieutenant. "I don't care how ill you are, get in here." "This is your tenth sick day this year. Unacceptable." Or "If you're not here by three, don't bother coming in tomorrow either!"

Go ahead, she retorted silently, jabbing her finger into his imaginary chest. Fire me. Just go and try.

The benefits of being good at the job. The ability to tell your boss to jump in the lake. But only so often.

It was then she noted the splotch of blood on her boot, just there on the toe cap. Gerard Rosenfeld's blood. She bent and rubbed it off with a fingernail. How could she have been so careless? A cop with the DNA of her victim on her shoe.

Rosenfeld had told her more than she'd wanted to know. It was her policy not to get mixed up in her client's affairs. She didn't need to understand the whys and wherefores. It only made the job more difficult. Why would she want to know anything about Israel or Mossad? Her thinking changed once Rosenfeld mentioned that it was a Middle Eastern prince who had kidnapped Dekker's woman. At that instant, she decided she needed to know as much as possible. She was pleased with her decision. It was amazing what someone would tell you if you provided the proper motivation. She had no doubt that Tariq al-Sabah would be eminently grateful for her efforts to rid him of Mac Dekker. It was worth missing a day of work.

Behind Cyrille came the noise of a loud, high-pitched engine downshifting—third to second—then the squeal of brakes. She spun. What kind of car was that? She couldn't take her eyes off the vehicle as it slowed and turned sharply into the carriageway of 27 Avenue Montaigne.

She stepped forward, craning her neck for a closer look. It was him. It was the man Rosenfeld called TNT. The prince. No mistaking him, though Cyrille's eyes were drawn to the woman in the passenger seat. Now that . . . that was something.

The car swung into the courtyard and disappeared from view.

Cyrille looked up and down the sidewalk. Her instincts told her that Dekker was somewhere nearby. If she'd seen the prince come home, so had he. But no, she didn't spot him. She'd had her bit of luck, and she'd blown it.

Cyrille resumed her trajet. Back and forth.

Sooner or later, Dekker would show.

CHAPTER 48

27 Avenue Montaigne
Paris

Ava stared transfixed as the laptop came to life.

First the wallpaper. A picture of the Bugatti, what else? A blink and the screen filled with folders and files and jpgs and pdfs. Half were labeled in Arabic, half in English.

Ava guided the cursor to the dock running vertically on the left-hand side of the screen and opened the launchpad, showing TNT's applications. She made a beeline for Mail and tapped the track pad twice. TNT's mailbox filled the screen. She ran down the list of correspondents. She didn't recognize any names. Her eye jumped to the subject lines. All appeared innocuous. Appointments with government officials, lunches with friends, comments on proposed spending, a new art exhibit, confirmation of a speaking engagement at Georgetown University's Ar-Rayyan campus.

Nowhere did she see the names Rosenfeld, Ben-Gold, or Abbasi.

For once, TNT was showing some operational security. The securest method to communicate sensitive material was through a message app tied to his phone—like Telegram or Signal. She returned to the launchpad and browsed the icons TNT visited regularly. Nothing.

Then she saw it. The last app, or most infrequently visited. Phone Mirroring.

Ava double-clicked the icon. A window appeared, demanding the passcode to unlock TNT's phone. There was no way she could guess a six-digit code. She didn't intend to try. Another dead end.

Or was it? She still had her magic box.

Ava dragged the icon labeled Phone Mirroring from the launchpad and placed it inside her malware's toolbox. Let it do the heavy lifting.

She tapped her finger. If TNT was using his phone, there was no way to access it with or without the code. Only one user at a time was granted control of its operating system. Sometimes you needed to be lucky.

The screen blinked once, twice, then went dark.

"No," said Ava. This was not the luck she was hoping for.

She hit Return.

"Do not let me down. Not now."

The screen came back to life. Dead center was a picture of the home page of TNT's phone. Six rows of four icons, and at the bottom the standard Phone, Mail, Music, and browser. There at the top right was a familiar navy blue icon. Signal.

Ava double-clicked it. "And God said, 'Let there be light.'"

TNT's inbox appeared. Chats, video calls, messages. She skimmed the inbox, registering the name of his correspondents and the subject lines. The most recent chat was with "Rosenfeld, Y."

Hallelujah.

She typed the name into the search bar, and a history of their correspondence appeared.

The first exchange dated to February of this year, eight months earlier: **Confirm meeting. Room 714. Four Seasons Doha.** A week later, TNT to Rosenfeld: **Arrive DBR tomorrow at 11.** "DBR" for David Ben-Gurion Airport outside Jerusalem. And then a response from Rosenfeld: **The Minister will attend.**

Ava continued reading. Plenty of back and forth. More meets, dates, and times. In Israel. In Qatar. No need for phone calls when you can meet on TNT's private jet.

Then this. TNT to Rosenfeld: Tech Specifications / Samson. Below in the text field: a twelve-digit serial number and a formal request for engineering blueprints. Ava noted the date. Exactly three weeks before Dr. Lutz had called her into his office and expressed his concern over the phone call he'd overheard.

Then, a week later: Rosenfeld to TNT. Tech Specs with an attachment and a note to contact Dr. Abbasi, Natanz Research Facility, Islamic Republic of Iran. Ava could presume that TNT had been speaking with Abbasi on that day in Dr. Lutz's office. Here was the mother lode. Ava opened the attachment. Pages and pages of engineering schemas. She had it. Proof that Yehudi Rosenfeld—and by extension, his master, Defense Minister Itmar Ben-Gold—had provided Tariq al-Sabah the top secret plans for the tactical nuclear weapon code-named "Samson."

A flurry of messages followed. More meetings. More queries. And then, the day after she spent the night at the Chesa Grischuna—the night she'd crept into Tariq al-Sabah's office and photographed page after page of the engineering blueprints for manufacturing a nuclear trigger, provided by Dr. Abbasi—an abrupt change of tone.

Rosenfeld to TNT: Security Breach. With a note to check all locked down on your end. And the next day: Leak? Mossad asking questions. *Mossad* meaning Zvi Gelber.

Ava recalled their troubling conversation, Zvi doing his best to warn her off. By then, he must have learned that Ben-Gold was involved. Ben-Gold, his nominal master. She had heard the fear in his voice. Zvi Gelber was nobody's fool. He knew what was coming.

I'm sorry, Zvi. I had no one else to go to.

A day later, a reply from TNT to Rosenfeld: Run check on Ava Marie Mercier. Swiss resident, French national. Dangerous?

The response from Israel was a week in coming: Refrain from all further contact. Mercier real name: Attal, Ava. Colonel (Retired). Mossad.

A succinct reply followed. TNT to Rosenfeld: Shit.

And then radio silence. No further communication between the two. Ava would wager that Rosenfeld had done his best to delete all record of their digital epistolary relationship. TNT, however, was of a more lax mindset.

Ava returned to the main mailbox. There was more. Hundreds of messages between TNT and various government officials from nearly every country in the region. Too many to read. One, however, caught her eye.

Jabr al-Sabah to TNT: **Paris Peace Conference. Location and Times.**

Ava had no choice but to read it.

Location: The Élysée Palace, Rue du Faubourg St.-Honoré. Time: Wednesday through Sunday. Ten a.m. A list of participants from Saudi Arabia, the UAE, Jordan, Israel, France, and of course, Qatar. Several notable names were missing. Itmar Ben-Gold, Israel's minister of defense; Yehudi Rosenfeld, his deputy; and Tariq al-Sabah, Qatar's minister of the interior. A brotherly note followed: **Your presence is not required or requested. Stay the hell away.**

Ava shook her head. The history of the Middle East writ small. Brother vs. brother. Tribe vs. tribe. People vs. people.

Just then, the miniature phone rattled. Incoming message from Dahlia Shugar. **Home. TNT talking to father. Be safe.**

Ava slid the phone back into her pocket. She returned her attention to the laptop.

Be safe.

Not just yet.

CHAPTER 49

27 Avenue Montaigne
Paris

"Father, I came as quickly as I could."

Tariq al-Sabah kissed his father on both cheeks.

"Always the car," said the emir. "You should have ordered the champagne delivered. Instead, you are spending time speeding here and there in the company of a woman—an infidel, I see—no doubt showing off. When will you grow up and be more like your brother?"

They stood in the courtyard of his *maison particulier*. A slew of attendants milled nearby. Tariq took Dahlia by the arm. "Go inside," he whispered in her ear. "I'll be right up."

"Of course, darling." Dahlia kissed him on the cheek. "Don't be long."

Tariq nodded, knowing she was making a show of herself, before returning his attention to his father.

The emir was dressed in his finest ceremonial robes. Tariq noted that he was wearing a girdle to disguise his waistline and that he'd applied some eyeliner to make his gaze fiercer than it already was. The Real Housewives would approve.

"I have the champagne as Jabr requested," said Tariq. "Also a present for the French president."

He barked a few commands to his father's retainers. One man retrieved the case of champagne. Another hefted the crate containing the methuselah of Domaine du Roi.

"What's this?" said the emir, throwing his arms in the air.

"Something uniquely French," said Tariq. "I doubt the president has seen anything quite like it."

For a moment the emir studied the crate. "You're sure?" There was no mistaking the interest in his father's eye.

"Never," said Tariq. "Something to commemorate his role in securing the agreement. It's a treasure. He will never forget it."

The emir squinted to read the stenciling on the crate. His mouth twisted. His eyes narrowed. He nodded. Decision made. "Even I haven't seen a bottle this large. Agreed. We will open it to celebrate the signing of the accord."

"Do you think?" said Tariq, a little excitement in his voice, but not too much.

"I'll insist," said the emir enthusiastically. It was his idea now. Let anyone suggest otherwise! "It will be televised, of course. There will be an audience. I'll make sure Jabr helps him to open it. My son, the future emir, alongside the French president to usher in a new era of peace and prosperity in the Middle East. The name of our country will be synonymous with the cause of diplomacy and progress. Yes, I'll give it to the president."

"I'll be there," said Tariq.

"I'll make sure there is a place saved for you in the audience," said the emir.

"Has the exact location been announced?"

"The Salon de la Paix, next to the Hall of Mirrors. I'm told many treaties have been signed there. A historic location for a historic event. Your name will be on the list. Just yours."

Tariq shrugged, sighed painfully. "Father, please. I cannot leave her behind. She is visiting from America. It is good for our image.

The Tourists

Remember old King Hussein and Queen Noor of Jordan. She was American too."

"A rich American," said the emir. "A blue blood. And your woman?"

"An example of the new generation," said Tariq. "She is hardworking, intelligent, and independent."

"Spare me, my son," said the emir, eye to eye with Tariq. "Anyone can see why you keep company with her."

Tariq bowed his head. A father was always correct, was he not? "And so?"

The emir smiled. He patted Tariq's shoulder, one man to another. The Al-Sabahs knew a thing or two about desire. "Fine. But she must dress like a princess."

"You have my word, Father."

"So then," said the emir, raising a hand, signaling for his SUV door to be opened. "We must be off. First we must visit your brother at the conference. Shake hands with all our friends, old and new. Profess our goodwill."

"Give Jabr my congratulations," said Tariq.

"You will give them to him yourself, as is your duty," said his father.

Tariq bowed once more, his jaw clenched. It would be the last time, God help him. "I will see you at Versailles," he said, kissing his father, then helping him into the vehicle. He stepped back and took a few pictures as the champagne was loaded into the rear bay. The doors slammed. Engines came to life. The armada drove out of the carriageway.

Tariq remained in the courtyard until all the cars had departed, hand high, a smile on his face. A great event, indeed!

The moment they disappeared, the hand fell, the smile vanished. He ran up the stairs and into the house and ducked into the alcove. He closed the door behind him and placed a call. "It's on its way," he said.

"We were beginning to get worried," said Yehudi Rosenfeld.

"I'm sending you a picture."

"So it worked," said Rosenfeld, a few seconds later.

"Did you have any doubts?"

"A wise man always has doubts," said Rosenfeld. "And Colonel Attal?"

"You'll hear back from me shortly."

"If you're not up to the task, we can find someone who is."

"I don't foresee any problems," said Tariq. "If you happen to see my father at the Élysée Palace, feel free to mention to him and my brother what a fine idea it is to toast the agreement with their very own champagne."

"I'll be sure to," said Rosenfeld.

"And the codes? You do have them."

"The minister has them," said Rosenfeld. "He is anxious to give them to you as planned. Just take care of Ava Attal. You know what they say about loose ends. We can't have any."

"Our meeting stands, then," said Tariq.

"Five forty-five," said Yehudi Rosenfeld. "Vespers. Chapel of St. Genevieve. On the right, halfway to the altar."

"I'll be there," said Tariq.

CHAPTER 50

27 Avenue Montaigne
Fourth floor
Paris

A single knock at the door. Ava ran to open it. Dahlia rushed past her, cheeks flushed, a tear running down her cheek.

"Where is he?" asked Ava.

"Talking to his father," said Dahlia. "They're all gathered in the courtyard. The emir, his minions. Everyone in their finest *thobes*. It's really happening. Tonight, I think. Tariq's upset because they've moved everything up. It's in the champagne. Samson is . . . in the bottle I mean."

Ava took Dahlia's hand and guided her to the sofa. "Slow down. Start over."

Dahlia wiped at her cheek. "Samson is inside a bottle of champagne. A giant bottle. A 'methuselah,' he called it." She spread her hands from her knee to her head to indicate its size. "He packed it in foam. I saw it. It's working. There are pin lights on top, and they're all on. Red. He has a transmitter he carries in his backpack. My God, Ava, it's happening."

"Of course it's happening," said Ava, voice cold and hard as steel. She was every bit as agitated as Dahlia, but this was not the time for emotion. It was a time for resolve. "And we're going to make sure he doesn't succeed. You and I. That's why we came here."

"There will be blood," Dahlia whispered.

"What?"

"It's what he always says. If there is a coup, there will be blood."

"Samson's in the champagne," said Ava. Why not? If they could fit it inside a backpack, why not into a large bottle? "And what will they do with it?"

Dahlia drew a breath and swallowed. Her eyes cleared, and she sat up straighter. "Tariq suggested to his father that he give the champagne to the French president to commemorate the signing of the agreement. A symbol of France and Qatar's commitment to peace, or something like that."

"Where is it taking place?" asked Ava. "The signing. I imagine there will be an announcement."

"Versailles," said Dahlia. "I don't know where."

"Tonight?" said Ava. "Too soon."

"Tariq had to rush home to bring his brother a case of champagne and the methuselah."

"Does he have the codes?"

Dahlia shook her head. "I haven't heard anything about codes. He told me that Samson was just a big bomb. Enough to kill everyone in the room so that he would become emir. They want to blame it on you."

"Nice of them," said Ava. "But that ship has sailed." She turned her head, then jumped to her feet and dashed to the window. "Hear that?"

Dahlia stood. "What is it?"

"Sirens," said Ava. "The police."

CHAPTER 51

27 Avenue Montaigne
Paris

And so, Ava Attal, mused Tariq as he exited the lift on the sixth floor, walking slower than he might. Retired colonel of Mossad. She'd fooled him once. He would admit it. He didn't blame himself. An attractive woman. Maybe more than that. Available. Clearly attracted to him, but old enough to know better. How could he resist? He remembered their first meeting at the clinic, their dinner in Pontresina, her admirable skills. Hindsight confirmed his every action. There was no way he could have acted differently.

Yehudi Rosenfeld was insistent he learn how much she knew about his and his master's involvement. Who besides Zvi Gelber had she told? The Americans? The Brits? The French? Or had she kept everything to herself? It was up to TNT to find out. Interrogation and all that went with it was not something that came naturally. He was a persuader, a cajoler, a dealmaker: "You give me this, I'll give you that."

And if she refused?

Simple enough. He'd threaten to kill Steinhardt, her Swiss lover. She had no choice but to believe he'd been captured. It was just a question of how much she cared for him. Steinhardt or Samson? A dubious proposition. What was in it for her? After all, Ava knew about

Gelber and Lutz. She was not a person to delude herself. She knew what awaited her.

No loose ends.

And then? He'd do what was required of him.

Tariq entered his bedroom, a slightly sour feeling in his stomach. From his nightstand he retrieved his service weapon. An officer in the Qatari Armed Forces carried a Beretta M9 similar to his counterpart in the US Army. He chambered a round, set the safety, and slid it into his waistband. It had been a while since he'd fired his pistol. He hoped his skills hadn't deserted him. A bullet to the heart. Quick, painless, and, fingers crossed, not too bloody. The carpets in that room had cost a fortune.

Tariq arrived at the guest room. He placed his eye to the biometric lock. The pin light turned from red to green.

"Hello, again," he said, entering the room with élan, the genial host. He looked around. One more step, a pit growing in his stomach. The room was empty. "Ava?"

He rushed to the bathroom, opened the closets, then dropped to his knees and checked under the bed. Infantile, he knew, but what else was he to do? He got to his feet, his heart hammering his ribs. Another look around the room to confirm his worst nightmare.

Ava Attal was not there.

Before he could ask how or when, or what now, Tariq heard a siren wailing from the street below. Two notes. High, low. Then a second siren, and a third. He rushed to the window. A line of police cars approached from the direction of the Champs-Élysées. Not just police cars—military vehicles too. Jeeps, a truck, some kind of armored car. The last in line stopped to block off traffic. Troops spilled from the back of the truck. Dark uniforms, helmets, machine guns. He recognized them. The counterterrorism brigade.

Tariq watched, wondering what might have happened in his neighborhood. Had there been a shooting he hadn't heard about? Some kind of attack?

Barricades were erected. Soldiers closed off the street. Similar efforts were made on the west side of the Avenue Montaigne. He followed the lead police car, light bar flashing, as it pulled up directly in front of his carriageway. He watched with growing interest as the officer climbed out and looked up at his house.

Tariq forgot about Ava Attal.

The counterterrorism brigade had come for him.

They knew.

It was over before it had even begun. Ava had told them about Samson. Tariq could think of no other reason for their heated presence.

For a few moments, he was unable to move. He had difficulty breathing. A voice in his head rang out: This isn't possible. This cannot be happening.

Only the buzzing of his phone interrupted his wild panic. "Yes," he managed, after answering.

"The police want to see you." It was his houseman, Mohammed, and he sounded rattled.

"What is it about?"

"Someone phoned them and reported that we are under attack."

"What?"

"A terrorist attack," said Mohammed. "Here in the house. They claimed one person was dead and that there was shooting inside."

"What? An attack? Nonsense." The message was so bizarre, so unexpected, that for a moment it didn't register.

"And something about a female hostage," said Mohammed. "They wish to search the house."

Finally, the words sank in. It was all a mistake. Some kind of crank call. Tariq had an overwhelming desire to laugh. It wasn't about Samson at all. "But why? Tell them no one's in the house, just us. It's a prank."

"I tried, but they insist. You see, they say it was you who called."

"Me? How can that be?"

"The call came from your number."

The urge to laugh left Tariq as quickly as it had come. He had no time to consider how such a call could have been made. That was for later. Right now, he had another priority. He couldn't allow the police to find Ava Attal. She was inside somewhere, hiding who knew where, doing who knew what. He'd exchanged one danger for another.

A new voice came over the line. "This is Captain Chardin, RAID. Is this Tariq al-Sabah? You have two minutes to come to the door. We are initiating a search of your home. Any action taken against us will be considered hostile."

"Wait . . . there's been a misunderstanding."

"Two minutes." The call ended.

Tariq took the pistol from his waistband. It felt different from just a minute ago. It was no longer an instrument to threaten. Something alien, something he did not want to use. He clutched the grip welcomingly. *You and I are friends, and we're going to do what we should have done a long time ago.*

Tariq ran out of the room and down the hallway. Which way had she gone? Upstairs or downstairs? Down. There was no way out from the top floor unless you considered the roof. And where would she go from there? Jump?

No. Ava Attal was inside, and he would find her.

CHAPTER 52

27 Avenue Montaigne
Rooftop
Paris

Mac turned his head into the wind. A siren; then, a second. He checked his watch. Fourteen minutes. God bless you, Harry. He caught sight of a police car tearing around the corner a few blocks away. A fleet of law enforcement vehicles followed. Pulling up the rear was an armored personal carrier with a battering ram attached and giant tires that belonged on a tractor.

"*You're going to know when they get there,*" Crooks had promised. "*They come in heavy.*"

Mac walked to the parapet and put one foot over the top. It was a short slide down the steep mansard roof, and from there, a ten-foot drop onto the roof of TNT's home. There was a narrow band of empty roof directly below him, and just past that, a broad glass skylight. Beware. Farther along, the flower beds, all covered by tarps. Mac made sure the pistol fit snugly in his waistband. He tested the mansard roof with the toe of his shoe. It was as slick as a chalkboard.

Mac looped the rope around an old chimney, nearly as tall as himself, and tied a bowline to secure it. He returned to the parapet and tossed the rope over. Any other time he'd fashion a saddle and clip in. Today it was old-fashioned hand-over-hand climbing.

A deep breath. He threw his left foot onto the roof, grabbed the rope with both hands, and began to descend. He made it three steps before slipping, landing hard on his hip. He caught himself and found his footing. Another few steps and he touched the gutter. Up and over. The rest of the way was a redbrick wall. Easy enough. He dropped the last few feet and landed softly.

Mac hurried to the rooftop door. He was relieved to discover that the lock had not been changed: an old-fashioned single-key Schlage. He studied the door's perimeter for contacts indicating the presence of an alarm system. He found none. He gave the doorknob a twist. Locked. Can't win 'em all.

The sirens stopped. From the street below rose the brutish hollow thuds of doors slamming, then orders being shouted. Mac stepped to the front of the building. A careful look over the side. The RAID team had pulled up across the street. A dozen officers—all clad in dark battle dress—gathered near the command vehicle. At either end of the block, barricades were put in place. Mac went to the far side of the roof and checked the courtyard. TNT's car was still there.

He returned to the rooftop door. There was no time to bother with a pick, even if he had one. He freed Crooks's pistol from his waistband, turned it around to hold by the muzzle, and brought the butt down on the doorknob. The knob held fast. It was stronger than it looked. Mac struck it once more, to the same effect. He stepped away, scouring the roof for something to pry open the door. He spotted a garden hoe half buried in a dormant bed. Maybe, he thought.

He yanked the hoe out of the dirt and wiped the blade on his trousers, cleaning away the moist soil. Lifting the hoe so that it was parallel to the doorknob, he jimmied the blade into the doorjamb. He placed his left hand at the top of the pole and gave a quick, violent wrench. Wood splintered. The door flung open, banging against the wall. Another anxious moment waiting for an alarm to sound. Nothing.

Mac dropped the hoe and entered TNT's house.

The Tourists

Six floors below, Cyrille de Montcalm heard the sirens and knew at once that it was him. This was Mac Dekker's doing.

The RAID vehicles sped along the Avenue Montaigne, the command car coming to a halt across the street from the entrance to the prince's home. A tall, black-haired man got out. No helmet. No weapon. A Kevlar vest over his uniform. A profile to rival de Gaulle's. She knew him. Luc Chardin, deputy commander of the RAID battalion stationed at Neuilly.

Cyrille hung back, biding her time. She allowed the other vehicles to arrive and the men to take up position. The first job, she knew, was to clear the sidewalks, get all bystanders out of harm's way. Only then would they go in.

A young officer barely old enough to have his first shave approached her, waving his arms and shouting for her to scram.

"What's going on?" said Cyrille, showing him her badge, holding it at eye level so he'd be sure to read her identification.

"Leave it to us," said the soldier.

"I'm not going to ask you again, junior."

The soldier calmed down. "You know who lives there?"

"Tell me."

"Some Middle Eastern prince. He called in saying that there was an active shooter in his residence. Terrorists, even. One person dead. A female hostage."

"Sounds dangerous."

"It's what we do," said the soldier. "Just stay clear."

Cyrille nodded and backed off.

There was no shooter in the house. She'd been walking past the place for hours and hadn't heard a thing, nor had she seen a group of so-called terrorists storm the place. It was a ploy. Dekker had to get in there to find his woman. He couldn't ring the doorbell and traipse in through the front door. He needed another way in.

Like that, Cyrille's eyes flew to the roof of the residence. The police report filed after the Saudis were killed at the Hotel Bristol had stated that the suspect, Steinhardt, had escaped by climbing out the fourth floor window. She was certain that these private residences had rooftop gardens, places to take some sun, have a few cocktails on a sunny day, enjoy the high life.

Oh, you clever bastard, thought Cyrille with true appreciation. Last night Dekker had talked his way into the Jules Verne, then convinced Gerard Rosenfeld to open his door to a stranger at two in the morning. And today? Maybe a hotel room at the Plaza Athénée? A visit to the hotel roof? She could see that the buildings shared a common wall. It was a decent drop from one to the other, but he could do it. A man desperate to rescue his woman could do just about anything.

He was there, Cyrille convinced herself. Mac Dekker was already inside.

It was up to her to find him before the police.

CHAPTER 53

27 Avenue Montaigne
Paris

Mac ran to the end of the hallway and opened a pair of double doors. "Ava?"

He entered without waiting for an answer. It was TNT's bedroom. He recognized it from a photo essay in one magazine or another. He crossed the room and poked his head into the bathroom. More gold and marble than a Roman mausoleum. Who lived here? The Emperor Nero? Not by a long shot. The Roman Empire had nothing on the Gulf states.

Mac retraced his steps and hurried down the hall to the opposite side of the house. There was an elevator and, next to it, stairs leading to the floor below. He took the stairs two at a time, stopping on the intermediate landing. He peered over the balustrade, from which one could see to the ground floor. A flurry of voices drifted up from far below. The pounding of boots on the stairs. Men coming or going. He didn't know which. The police would not take kindly to finding an armed intruder. Mac had searched too many homes, buildings, and hideouts to count. The rule was "shoot first, ask questions later." He had, in effect, called the cops on himself.

Mac continued down to the fifth floor. "Ava," he called out again. He moved briskly along the corridor and pulled up next to a door with a biometric lock. Not something one usually saw in a private residence. He banged once. "Ava."

He tried the door. It opened at once. He entered a cavernous guest room that might have belonged to Madame de Pompadour. In the center of the room was a trolley set with a white tablecloth and offering a bountiful breakfast. The coffee was cold, the croissants already hardening. Cloth napkins remained folded and were embroidered with the name of the hotel next door, the Plaza Athénée. Tucked beneath one was a card with a number to call for pick up. *Pick up?* Evidently, there was a passage between the two buildings, either TNT's doing or a remnant from the past.

A sound from the hall. Mac spun. No one was there. Just his imagination playing tricks on him. He moved toward the bed. The sheets were unbothered, but it was apparent that someone had lain atop the duvet. The pillow was out of place and terribly wrinkled. He put his nose to the sheets. His heart soared. It was Ava's perfume.

The sweet, floral scent stopped Mac cold. It was strong, unmistakable, and most important, fresh. Ava was here. He touched the duvet and imagined he could feel her lingering warmth. He spotted a long dark hair. He knew then that she was alive. He'd never assumed otherwise, at least not aloud. All the same, somewhere deep inside of him—a place hollowed by repeated disappointments, roughened by the deaths of too many close friends—he'd made the first preparations for the unthinkable. Those awful and cowardly doubts vanished in a heartbeat.

Ava was alive.

Mac stepped away from the bed. Experience tempered his ebullience. If anything, he needed to move faster, more purposefully, and, now more than ever, without mercy. Kidnapping merited punishment. *Shoot first, ask questions later.*

He ducked a head into the bathroom. "Ava," he whispered to the wilderness of marble and mirror. His mute, wide-eyed reflection ordered him to find her and quickly.

Mac hurried across the guest room, the toe of his shoe kicking a length of black plastic across the parquet floor. Not plastic. Something else. Something strangely familiar. He stooped to pick it up. A flex-cuff. A second cuff lay partially hidden beneath the curtains. He noted that the plastic had been neatly severed. Ava's jailer had not freed her. For that, one needed a key, not a razor.

Ava, or someone else, had cut off the cuffs.

Cyrille de Montcalm watched the line of men exit the front door of 27 Avenue Montaigne and file past Luc Chardin onto the sidewalk, where they were escorted a safe distance away. A few wore traditional Arab dress; others were in jeans and T-shirts. Every last one had a beard of some type. The prince's posse.

And the prince, the handsome one they called TNT? Cyrille didn't see him.

Luc Chardin raised an arm, then lowered it. Signal to go. A squad of soldiers entered the residence, machine guns at the ready. Another squad jogged into the courtyard to enter through the side door. Two stragglers brought up the rear. Cyrille hung her badge around her neck and ran across the street to join them, drawing her weapon.

"Go," she said to the last man in line. "Keep moving."

The man looked at her badge, her gun, mostly her face. He saw what he needed to convince him. "Stay close," he said.

And just like that, she was in.

CHAPTER 54

27 Avenue Montaigne
Paris

Tariq bounded down the stairs as if he were a teenager all over again. He threw open the door to the study, arm outstretched, the pistol carving an arc from bookshelves to the globe to the couch where he'd sat with Paul Sassoon in the first hours of this morning. The room was dim and gloomy, shades drawn, silent. He knew at once she was not here. The air was too still, like a storage room that had been padlocked for years.

He crossed the hall. A peek into the guest water closet. Empty. Next to it, a linen closet. Nowhere to hide, but he opened it all the same, threatening the five-hundred-thread-count Frette sheets with a wave of his pistol. He slammed the door and continued down the corridor. His office to the right; the light on the biometric lock burned red. He tried the door anyway. Locked. At least one place he didn't need to look. He ran to the end of the hall. Burnished oak doors led to the media room. Above the doors was an old-fashioned cinema marquee advertising *Casablanca, starring Humphrey Bogart and Ingrid Bergman*. He nudged the door with his shoulder. The room was pitch dark. He hit the light switch while calling out Ava's name. He trained the gun on the rows of recliners, the projection booth—of course, there wasn't a real projector; everything was digital—then swung it to the screen. He checked every row to make sure she wasn't lying flat.

Tariq paused and drew a breath. Where might she hide on the fourth floor? he asked himself. Or had he been mistaken? Had she, in fact, gone to a higher floor? Might she be searching for something in his bedroom? Who knew what she might think he was hiding there? Another set of plans from Dr. Abbasi? He grunted with dissatisfaction. And in that instant, he heard a voice. Muffled, distant, escaping from behind a wall, but there was no doubting it. Tariq retraced his steps to his office. The pin light burned red. The door was locked. Only the retina from his left eye could open it. He put his ear to the door and heard a thump, as if a book had dropped to the floor. Apparently not.

He laid his hand on the door lever. If Ava Attal could cut off her flex-cuffs and escape a locked room, who knew what else she was capable of, what tools she might possess, or who might be helping her? A terrible thought entered his mind. For a moment he wasn't sure what troubled him more: that until this instant he'd never entertained it or that deep down in the core of his being he knew that it was true. It was Dahlia. Dahlia Shugar was abetting Ava Attal. Dahlia, whose love and adoration he had accepted as his due, like one more thumbs-up on IG or a heart on TikTok. Of course Dahlia loved him. Didn't everyone?

A rage took hold of him, an anger he had never in his thirty-three years known: an all-consuming will to do harm no matter the cost. Tariq put his eye to the retinal scanner. The pin light turned green. He raised his gun to his cheek, his finger brushing the trigger, trembling with anticipation. And like that he was in action. He threw open the door and burst into the room. One giant step. Ava sat at his desk, folding his laptop closed. Dahlia stood beside her.

"No," cried Dahlia, lifting her hand, gesturing for him to stop.

Tariq shot her before he knew what he was doing. Then he shot her again because the trigger was so light, and a third time. She fell without uttering a sound, but there was a splat of gore on the wall behind her: bright red and looking remarkably like a hand, its fingers splayed.

Ears ringing, he turned the pistol on Ava. She had a gun herself, and in the instant before she fired, he saw that it was very small, almost like a toy. He didn't feel the bullet; at least not as he'd imagined. There was a moment of intense heat in his side. A sharp, brief pinprick above his hip. He fired at her and missed, though barely ten feet separated them. The bullet hit the laptop, sending it spinning off the desk. Ava toppled out of the chair and onto the floor. A pall of cordite filled the room. To his ear, the weapons' reports continued undiminished, growing louder even, unbearably painful.

Tariq's feet had developed a mind of their own. Before he could take charge of his actions, he was in the corridor, head spinning, vision blurry, and yes, he had definitely been shot, because something just didn't feel right.

"Al-Sabah!"

Tariq turned toward the strident male voice, firing repeatedly, wildly. He glimpsed a tall, broad-shouldered man, graying black hair—not a policeman, at least not one of those he'd seen on the street, dressed in their assault uniforms. No, it was Steinhardt, the man dining with Ava Attal yesterday at the Jules Verne. One moment Steinhardt was there, the next he was gone, taking cover behind the corner.

Tariq retreated, firing again and again, the bullets blasting gobs of plaster out of the walls, shattering a sconce. A last look. No sign of Steinhardt. Tariq ran down the hall, turned a corner, ran some more. He opened a narrow door painted the same ecru as the walls, its outline barely visible. A back staircase for the help. He flipped the light switch and slowed for a moment. He touched his side. His fingers came away moist. A little blood, but not a lot. Amazingly, there was no pain. Not even a twinge. Even so, the sight made him queasy.

He ran down the spiral staircase, one hand on the railing just in case. He reached the basement and bent double, gasping for breath. Above his head, he heard the martial *tom-tom-tom* of boots pounding into the entryway.

Tariq crossed the cement floor, threading his way around unwanted furniture, steamer trunks, a bicycle, until he came to a door painted bright white with gold trim and the words *Plaza Athénée* inscribed in swirling script. He stopped to gather himself. He checked his clothing, tucking in his shirt. A small stain on his sweater, dark on dark, hardly noticeable. He ran his fingers through his hair and blew a blast of wind through his lips. He felt light headed, giddy with the rush of having made a narrow escape . . . or, perhaps, of having cheated death.

Tariq tilted his head, catching from afar the strains of classical music. The violin quartet in the Gallerie. He opened the door, and the music was clearer. Vivaldi. One of the seasons; no idea which. It was high tea. Not today, thought Tariq, but soon. Maybe next week.

Right now, he had an appointment to keep.

Vespers. Five forty-five. The St. Genevieve chapel.

CHAPTER 55

27 Avenue Montaigne
Paris

Mac peeked around the corner.

The corridor was empty. TNT was gone.

Mac rose from a crouch and advanced down the hallway. He stopped a few inches from the doorway.

"Ava," he called. "Are you in there?"

"Mac?"

"Yeah, it's me." He peeked inside, keeping his pistol trained on the doors at the end of the hallway.

Ava stood from behind a desk of red marble, furiously pushing her hair out of her face. Her eyes were wide, "adrenaline eyes," and she was wearing the dress from the day before, but otherwise she appeared unharmed. "Did you get him?" she asked, half out of breath.

"You mean TNT?"

"Go," she shouted, waving a pistol at him. "Find him. Kill him."

Mac ran to the end of the hall, looking both ways, not seeing anyone. Any emotion he'd had upon finding her alive and seemingly unhurt came and went before it registered. Her mission had become his. Kill TNT. Aye, aye, sir. Good to see you too.

Mac entered the media room, then rushed down the adjacent hallway. There was no sign of TNT and no time to search for him, no matter the urgency in Ava's voice. She might want him dead, but the police were in the house. It was a matter of minutes, less even, until they reached the fourth floor.

Mac retraced his steps to the office. "He ran away."

"Shit," said Ava. She was kneeling beside a woman who lay on the floor just behind the desk. The woman's head was canted unnaturally, her eyes open. It was a position he'd seen too often.

"A friend?"

"Something like that," said Ava. "Her name was Dahlia. She worked with Zvi."

Mac nodded. Zvi was Zvi Gelber. They'd met once or twice back in the day. No time for questions, no matter how badly he wanted to know. Knowing that Zvi Gelber was involved was enough. "We have to leave."

"So it was you," said Ava, pointing to the window.

"I needed a distraction," said Mac. "Get everyone out of the house."

"To find me."

"Yes."

"She said you wouldn't listen," whispered Ava.

"Pardon me?"

"The message in the hotel. 'Get out.' Guess it didn't sink in."

"I only saw it after two guys tried to kill me," said Mac. "I wasn't in the mood to take advice from anyone."

"I didn't know," said Ava.

"You wanted him to kidnap you," said Mac.

Ava nodded, and a piece of the puzzle fell into place.

"Did you get what you came for?" asked Mac.

"Think so." Ava picked up the laptop off the floor, then came closer and kissed him. "Good to see you."

"Sure?"

"I'm sure," said Ava. "I had him, you know."

"Yeah, you did," said Mac.

"Thanks anyway," said Ava. "Maybe I didn't have him."

291

"We can't take her," said Mac, gesturing to the woman. Dahlia.

"No," said Ava. "It's all right."

"I'm sorry."

"It's not over," said Ava. "There's a bomb. He means to use it."

"I saw the tablets in your medicine bag," said Mac. "The ones from Israel. It took me a little, but I figured it out. For radiation sickness. That kind of bomb?"

"The bad kind," said Ava.

The sound of activity on the floors below them grew louder, more frantic. Doors opening and slamming. Raised voices.

"We're going up and out," said Mac. "Roof, then hotel next door."

"You have it all set," said Ava.

"Don't go in if you don't know how to get out."

Mac led the way upstairs, moving quietly and resolutely. No time for talk. A glance into the stairwell; two floors below he caught a rustle of blue. The police officers' voices carried through the building as they called to one another, going room to room, checking for gunmen or terrorists or anyone killed or wounded, as TNT (or at least his voice) had claimed in his call to the emergency services. They reached the top floor. "Where to?" she asked.

Mac pointed to a door at the end of the hall. "Stairs to the roof."

"What are we waiting for?"

Mac hurried to the door and held it open, allowing Ava to pass. He closed the door behind him, checking if there was a lock. There wasn't. Up a short flight of stairs. The door to the roof was open, and as he walked through it, he recalled with crystalline clarity that he had closed it behind him. It was a rule to conceal your activity. Leave things as they were. *Or had he?*

He jogged past the skylight to the brick wall and took hold of the rope. "When's the last time you walked the wall?"

"Never," said Ava. "That was your training."

"Always a first time," said Mac.

He pulled the rope tight and handed the end to her. "Give me your shoes. Make it to the top of the wall, then onto the roof of the hotel. It's a little slick. If you need to, take off your stockings; it will be easier with bare feet."

Ava removed her shoes and handed them to Mac. "What then?"

"I have a room at the hotel. Regroup. Figure out how to find this guy."

"Versailles," said Ava. "There was an important international conference in town this weekend, and they are going to sign a treaty there."

"Let me guess," said Mac. "Israel, Saudi Arabia, and Qatar are involved."

"Ten points," said Ava.

"First thing: We tell the cops," said Mac. "Better yet, we call your people in Paris."

"They won't listen," said Ava. "That's why I'm here. And forget the police. By now, I'm on some sort of watch list. Believe me, these guys are thorough."

"Then the Agency."

"You?" Ava stepped closer to Mac. "Don't you get it? This is on us." She took the rope in both hands and pulled it taut, giving Mac a side-eye. "If you say 'You got this,' I'll kill you."

"One step, then another. Walk the wall."

Ava placed her left foot on the wall and hauled herself upward. Right foot. Left foot. Suddenly, she was halfway to the top. "Harder than it looks," she said, between clenched teeth. She glanced over her shoulder. "Mac! Down!"

Mac threw himself onto the ground. He knew an order when he heard it. As he fell, he looked behind him. A slight woman in dark clothing fired a gun at him. The bullet struck the wall, a few inches below Ava. Ava let go of the rope and fell to the rooftop. Mac rolled to his left, reaching for his pistol. A bullet grazed his shoulder, paralyzing his arm. No matter how he tried, it refused to move.

The shooter approached him, pistol held with both hands, aimed squarely at him. Mac lay helpless. He remembered the shadow stalking him early that morning, an elfin figure wearing a beret. And Jane's warning about the red flag on his name.

The woman stopped a few feet away and took dead aim.

Mac stared her in the eye.

Like that, her head jerked backward. A spray of blood and brain erupted from the back of her skull, a red vapor, here then gone. She collapsed, falling to one side and landing on the skylight. Glass fractured, then gave way. The woman crashed into the room below.

Ava had already replaced her pistol and taken hold of the rope. "Later," she said. "We have a lot of catching up to do."

With redoubled effort, she climbed the wall. Mac stood below her, still dazed, unable to think of anything to say. It had begun to rain, the sky growing darker by the minute, a cold snapping wind out of the north.

Ava reached the top of the brick wall. She put a foot on the slate roof, tested it, then pulled off her stockings one at a time. "Almost there," she said. "Go ahead. Come up."

"I'm outta here," said Mac. "Finally."

Before the words had left his mouth, police stormed onto the roof. A half dozen counterterrorism troops formed a semicircle around him, assault rifles at their shoulders.

"You. Don't move," shouted a female officer. "Both of you. You are under arrest."

CHAPTER 56

Hôtel Plaza Athénée
Lobby
Paris

It was Vivaldi. *The Four Seasons*. "Autumn," which was appropriate given the month and the weather. The French had a word for it, *"variable,"* which Harry deciphered as "rainy until it isn't." He sat at a small two-top adjacent to the Gallerie and as far from the string quartet as possible. He kept his eyes on the entry, through which he glimpsed a police car, blue strobes, a jeep, and a procession of uniformed soldiers coming and going. Harry checked his phone. Mac had promised to text the moment he found Ava. In the meantime, Harry was to act as lookout.

A waiter arrived, carrying espresso and pastry. He set down the plate and cutlery. As he stood to ask if he might bring Monsieur anything else, another man bumped into him. It was enough contact to make the waiter stagger and drop his serving tray. The tray landed noisily. Heads turned. The man stopped to help the waiter regain his balance and, in doing so, nudged Harry. Harry wouldn't have looked twice except for the man's smell. So close, Harry could not help but be overwhelmed by it. The man, whoever he was, gave off a sour, rank odor. It was not the smell of sweat from exertion. It was the other kind. A sweat born of fear and anxiety and flight. He carried another scent with him: smoke.

More specifically, gunpowder. The combination took Harry back forty years. It was a smell soldiers knew from the battlefield.

The man touched Harry's shoulder. "I'm sorry, sir. Accept my apologies."

"It was nothing," said Harry, smiling, even as the man's reek stung his nostrils.

The man continued toward the front doors. Harry watched him. He noted his attire: dark trousers, dark sweater, dazzlingly white tennis shoes, and a leather backpack more likely to be seen on a woman. For a moment the man turned and looked over his shoulder. Harry saw his face full on. He was ashamed he had not recognized him earlier. It was the man from the video clip talking to businessmen in Doha. It was Mac's prince. Tariq al-Sabah.

Harry put down his espresso and followed him across the lobby. He regarded the man's progress, noting a slight limp, right leg, and saw that he kept his hand pressed to his right hip, as if cramping.

A crowd had gathered by the entry. Doormen stood on the sidewalk outside, shoulder to shoulder, arms outstretched, forming a kind of human barrier. Tariq al-Sabah forded his way through the crowd to the front doors, then onto the sidewalk. No chance Harry could follow. He could only watch. It was evident the doormen knew the prince. A conversation ensued, Al-Sabah no doubt requesting permission to leave the premises. The doormen shook their heads resolutely. Tariq stepped closer and appeared to whisper something. In a snap, the doormen's attitudes changed. Money. What else? Both dropped their arms and guided Al-Sabah between them and onto the street. A second later, he had disappeared.

"Dammit," said Harry loud enough to draw several stares.

And then a miracle. Before Harry could return to his table, Al-Sabah was back, forcibly escorted into the hotel at the hands of two policemen and given a shove so he knew to stay there. Harry smiled.

Al-Sabah retraced his steps across the lobby. His limp had grown more noticeable, no doubt as a result of the policemen's friendly treatment. He paused near the reception desk, checked his watch, then set off down the corridor adjacent to the Gallerie. Harry followed, conscious of how he stuck out. You didn't see a Black man in a wheelchair rolling around a hotel like this one every day. Al-Sabah, however, never looked back, not once. He turned down a hall lined with boutiques of one sort or another—nothing Harry would desire in a million years—and, seconds later, exited the hotel through a side door onto the Rue du Boccador.

Harry reached the door in time to see Al-Sabah hailing a taxi. He was grimacing, and Harry knew that he was hurt. It was only natural to assume that Mac was responsible. The thought galvanized him. Al-Sabah was on the run, the bloody kidnapping bastard. There was no sign of Mac; no message whatsoever from him. He refused to assume the worst. It fell to Harry, then, to give chase.

Harry made his way through the exit and onto the sidewalk. Traffic was backed up in both directions due to the road closure, more or less at a standstill. He caught Al-Sabah's profile in a taxi across the street. Another cab was parked nearby. Harry saw his opportunity. He rapped on the window. The driver helped him into the back seat, folded his chair, and placed it into the trunk.

"See that taxi?" said Harry, pointing at the Renault several cars in front of them. "Please follow it."

"Any idea where he is going?" asked the driver.

"Just follow it, please," said Harry. "It's a family emergency."

The taxi driver turned on the meter. "Whatever you like," he said. "But I don't think we will be going anywhere for a good long while."

CHAPTER 57

Élysée Palace
Paris

The limousine bearing the emir of Qatar, His Excellency Nayan bin Tariq al-Sabah, and his son, Prince Jabr, departed the Élysée Palace at 4:00 p.m. under a steady rain. Father and son sat side by side in the back seat. Neither spoke. The emir maintained a fractious relationship with his oldest son and heir to the throne. Whereas he could be light and frivolous with Tariq, he was always the taciturn martinet to Jabr. Perhaps it was because he expected different things from them. Jabr had been groomed his entire life to one day rule the country. He required more discipline, less humor; more scolding, less forgiveness. A head of state had few friends. Cultivating an outgoing, gregarious personality was a liability. Let Tariq be the smiling, handsome face of Qatar. Jabr must be its strong, stoic face.

The emir's choices had paid off. Jabr had excelled his entire life. Top boy at Eton. A gifted athlete. Instrumental in securing the 2022 FIFA World Cup. In a sense, he'd always been a visionary.

It was Jabr who had come up with the idea of a Greater Gulf Co-Prosperity Sphere. And Jabr who had convinced the countries of the Gulf to sign the treaty. It was Jabr who had faced down the Jews and the Saudis—both intractable, unreasonable, and contentious to the bone—and forced concessions from each. It was Jabr who had persuaded the

French president to serve as host to the conference. The UK was out of the question, as was the United States; their histories in the region had left too many scars. When all was said and done, the treaty was Jabr's and Jabr's alone.

The limousine made slow, fitful progress across the city. Evening traffic was as snarled as ever. Thank God they'd left when they did, as they needed a full hour to reach Versailles on the western outskirts of the city.

It was his first time visiting the magnificent palace, and he couldn't help but lean forward to take in its immense grandeur. It wasn't especially tall or especially showy, but he was awed by its sheer size, its weight, and its elegance. This, then, was civilization. This was majesty.

The limousine passed through a cordon of security and stopped at the grand entry.

"It looks like the entire French Army is here," said the emir, half in admiration.

"Good," said Jabr. "There are many people who would like to stop our progress. Haters."

As they left the car, a dozen soldiers surrounded them, forming a protective phalanx and guiding them inside. They had taken only ten steps when Jabr suddenly stopped. He turned to his deputy. "Go get the champagne," he commanded. "The big bottle. The methuselah."

The deputy returned to the limousine and fetched the large crate. Jabr took it from him. He turned to his father. "Wouldn't do to forget this," he said. "It's the only good idea Tariq has ever had."

CHAPTER 58

Prefecture de Police
Paris

"So," said one of the policemen. "Just tell us who you really are. We know anyway. No need to continue lying."

There were two officials from French law enforcement: a man and a woman. The man was Mac's age; tall, barrel chested, with a halo of gray hair and a dapper mustache. He wore a nice suit, charcoal gray, and a dark necktie with the tie clip identifying him as a former legionnaire, a member of the French Foreign Legion. He was the fed, probably from the DGSE, the spy service. The woman was short and skinny, maybe forty, with jeans, a leather jacket, brown hair cut in an unfashionable bob. A heavy smoker, by the lines crimping her mouth and the pall that came off her every time she leaned across the table. She was a local, Mac figured—Paris police, one of the shooter's former colleagues. Neither gave a name.

Mac sat on one side of the desk. They sat on the other. Ava was in another room, most probably suffering the same treatment. The clock on the wall read 5:20 p.m. Mac's arm was in a sling, thanks to a paramedic. The bullet had creased the ball of his shoulder, digging a shallow canal out of soft tissue and muscle. Initial treatment was an antiseptic, a shot for the pain, and a bandage. A doctor had been summoned, but he could wait.

The Tourists

"My name is Robert Steinhardt," said Mac. "I am a Swiss citizen. I reside in Zinal, Switzerland. The Chalet Ponderosa." Not exactly name, rank, and serial number, but close enough.

"And this?" said the woman, pounding a finger on a photograph of a much younger Mac Dekker, staring at them from what might be called a modern-day version of a "Wanted" poster. A sheet with name, alias, physical description, and a disconcertingly accurate summary of his career at the CIA and before. Neither official said how they'd come upon it, but Mac knew all the same. The woman Ava had killed on the roof of TNT's house was a contract assassin. She had taken the red flag on Mac. She was the same person, he was convinced, who'd shot at him earlier that morning as he fled Gerard Rosenfeld's apartment. Twice she'd missed, the second time, just. Mac could consider himself lucky, if not blessed. Or maybe not so much. The problem was that the shooter was also a police officer. Her name was Sergeant Cyrille de Montcalm of the DGSI and, he'd been told, a possessor of a spotless record, a longtime veteran of the force held in the highest esteem by her colleagues.

"I'm sorry," said Mac, barely glancing at the picture. "That's not me. I'm Robert Steinhardt."

"Yes, we know," said the man. "From Zinal. I must say you're not bad. I almost believe. Almost."

Mac showed neither joy nor sorrow at the compliment. In truth, he was more accustomed to being on the opposite side of the table. His years in Iraq and Afghanistan had involved more talking than killing. Over time, he had become an expert in eliciting information from the most hostile of adversaries and less of one in the vagaries of human behavior.

"Tell us again what you are doing in Paris," said the woman. It was the third time through. Standard interrogation policy. Play. Rewind. Play again. Trip 'em up on the small stuff, and eventually they cop to the big stuff. Human behavior 101.

Mac started at the top. A romantic weekend in Paris. A proposal of marriage. When Ava disappeared from the restaurant, he made it his mission to find her. As any man would, he added, appealing to the Gallic male's sense of chivalry. He loved her. He could do no less.

"And the men in the Hotel Bristol?"

Mac had never seen them before. He had no idea why Saudi diplomats wished to kill him. He fought back. What choice did he have? Of course he ran. Otherwise, he never would have found Ava. Mac wasn't lying. Not really. He was telling the truth, as seen by a retired CIA operative sworn to never reveal his identity. In other words, the truth according to Robert Steinhardt.

Yes, he had gone to the restaurant Jules Verne late last night to view its security cameras. Yes, he had visited Gerard Rosenfeld's apartment. Yes, he had broken into Tariq al-Sabah's home. Why shouldn't he have done? He had seen Al-Sabah's image on the security cameras. Gerard Rosenfeld had confirmed his identity, as well as admitted to having acted himself as a coconspirator. It was Tariq al-Sabah who had kidnapped Ava from the restaurant—and, Mac added forcefully, who had killed Dahlia Shugar.

"He's the man you should be questioning," Mac added, with righteous indignation.

As for Sergeant Montcalm, it was self-defense. Kill or be killed.

"Remind us why a prince from Qatar would do these things?" said the male officer, stroking his dapper mustache. "Kidnapping, murder. Come now, isn't that a bit far fetched?"

And so, the decision to tell or not to tell. To Mac's mind, he had to give them all the information he possessed, whether they chose to believe him or not.

"Ava believed that he was behind some kind of plot to disrupt a conference taking place here in Paris this weekend," said Mac. "I imagine he found out that she knew about his plans and took steps to silence her."

"And you, Mr. Steinhardt—you knew nothing about this?"

"I did not," said Mac.

"You live with this woman," the male official continued. "You know her past."

"She served as Israel's consul general in Zurich."

"Her other past."

"She worked in some capacity for the Israeli government," said Mac. "At home and overseas."

"And what capacity might that be?"

"In the diplomatic service," said Mac. "It wasn't something we talked about. It was long ago."

"The diplomatic service?" asked the male official, not bothering to conceal his disbelief.

"Yes."

"And how did this simple diplomatic worker uncover this heinous plot? A plan to disrupt a major international conference, no less?"

"To bomb it," said Mac.

"Yes, as you said before. To bomb it."

"I don't know," said Mac. For once, he was telling the truth. Ava had mentioned Zvi Gelber, but apart from that, he was in the dark.

The man dropped into a chair, looking at the ceiling and loosing a breath.

"And you are Robert Steinhardt, retired trader, import/export, blah, blah, blah," said the woman. "Stop serving us warmed up dog shit. You think I don't know what this is?" She picked up the "Wanted" paper. "It's a hit sheet. Someone wants you dead. You, Mackenzie David Dekker. Not Robert Steinhardt. You. Mac Dekker, KIA Lebanon nine years ago. You think we don't have our own sources?"

"I'm Robert Steinhardt," responded Mac.

"Maybe it's you who wants to bomb this conference," suggested the woman, throwing herself in his face. "What do you think of that?"

"I'd like to see Ava, please," said Mac, softly.

"You mean Colonel Attal of Mossad?"

"Just Ava."

"And I'd like to sleep with David Beckham," shouted the woman. "Neither of us has a snowball's chance in hell of getting what we want." She threw up her arms in a gesture of surrender and left the room, slamming the door behind her.

It was an act, Mac knew, as a former practitioner of the craft. Now he could expect the other part: She's pissed, but her partner . . . maybe he and Mac could work something out. Man to man.

The dapper cop looked at Mac. "You want a coffee?"

Mac said no, thank you.

"Sure? No trouble."

Mac shook his head. The last thing he'd managed to do before being arrested was to swallow his last go pill. Well, his last two, if he was being honest. Despite the fact he'd slept three hours in the last thirty-six, been moving nonstop all that time, and taken a bullet, he felt okay. Better than that. Battle bright. His mind was agile and alert, working all the angles, even if deep down, he knew there weren't any. He and Ava were locked away and would be for days, no matter what they said. There was no bail in France. No habeas corpus, at least not right away. No one would put stock in anything either of them said. Not if he refused to admit to his real name. Not if Ava was on the outs with her former bosses and a suspect in her own right. A police officer was dead, and they had killed her. Another woman lay dead inside the house. That is where the investigation began and ended.

"I was over there too," said the cop. "Beirut. They used to call it 'the Paris of the Levant.' Beautiful city. The women."

"Yes," said Mac. "I heard it was beautiful once."

"I guess we never crossed paths," the man went on. "Too bad. My name is Vincent, by the way. My real name."

"I'm Robert. Call me Robbie."

"You were with Special Activities," said Vincent. "I heard this. Talented with a rifle. You had a partner, Russian name, who went over to them. It was big news for a day or two. So Zinal? That's where a man goes to die. I'll have to remember that. The Chalet Ponderosa. Sounds nice."

"It is," said Mac.

They regarded one another, Mac sensing that maybe, just maybe, Vincent might grant his words credence. The French authorities knew who he was. The picture on the hit sheet was twenty years old, but there was no mistaking that it was Mac. How long must he continue the charade?

"I wasn't lying about the bomb," said Mac. "It's happening."

"And the rest? Your name? Hers? Her past?"

Mac looked at Vincent. His silence was enough. The rest was true, but he'd never say it.

Heated voices drifted in from another room. He saw shadows moving on the other side of the opaque glass. Some kind of argument. Then in English: "Goddamn it, he's ours. We're taking him now."

Vincent peered over his shoulder, then back at Mac. "You have friends here?"

"Not that I know," said Mac.

"Maybe they came from Zinal," said Vincent, with an unhappy chuckle. "I guess it was only a matter of time. This place is a sieve."

"Versailles," whispered Mac, placing a hand on Vincent's forearm. "Something's happening there tonight. Am I right? A treaty signing, something like that? If I were you, I'd have a look."

"Versailles?"

"Yeah," said Mac, looking Vincent hard in the eye. "I heard it from a guy named Dekker and a retired operative from Mossad."

The door flew open. The female cop stormed in, followed by three people Mac knew from days past and present. Don Baker; a tall, attractive blond woman who looked much too familiar; and his daughter, Jane.

"We told you to get the hell out of town," she said. "Don't you ever listen?"

CHAPTER 59

Île de la Cité
Paris

"Here we are," said the cab driver.

The taxi braked forcefully, veering to the left. Tariq's eyes opened. He lifted his chin from his chest. "What?" he muttered, unaware he'd been dozing.

Tires brushed the curb as the vehicle came to a halt. Tariq stared out the window at a large building, a monolith bathed in light. Despite the short rest, he felt worse than he had before, as queasy as if he were on the deck of a rocking boat. Spots danced at the perimeter of his vision. He touched his side and winced.

"Twenty-eight euros," said the driver.

Tariq fished a wad of bills from his pocket and handed the driver a €100 note. "Keep it."

The driver accepted the bill with a concerned look, his eyes on a spot of blood decorating one corner.

Tariq opened the door and hauled himself from the car. He took a step, and his knees buckled. He stumbled, barely catching himself before he fell to the pavement. He gathered himself, squaring his shoulders, drawing a breath. He could do this. A stiff breeze lashed his face. He tasted rain on his lips. The cold, damp air and the bracing scent of the Seine revived him. The nausea left him. His vision cleared. He remembered why he was here.

Vespers. Five forty-five. The codes.

Tariq gazed wide eyed at the structure towering before him. He raised his head to appreciate its enormity. For all his time in Paris, he had never visited. Why should he? The last time he was in a church of any kind was back at Eton Chapel a million years ago. But this was not a church, this was a cathedral. Perhaps the most famous cathedral in the world. Notre-Dame de Paris.

Tariq checked his watch. The time was 5:42.

After all this, right on schedule.

Go ahead, he told himself. Say it. *It was fated.* And yes, Tariq believed it.

The broad plaza in front of the cathedral was nearly deserted. Police officers stood near the tall ornate doors to the cathedral. "Portals," he recalled. He dropped his pistol into a waste bin, then ran a hand through his hair and mopped his forehead with his sleeve.

A guard at the center portal looked inside his backpack. No need to hide the transmitter. For all intents and purposes, it was a cell phone. The transmitter, however, could only call one number. Once connected, Tariq must enter two sixteen-digit codes: the first to remove the weapon's safety, essentially unlocking it; the second to detonate it.

Tariq entered the cathedral. He allowed his eyes to adjust to the dim interior and to take in the chandeliers hanging everywhere, the Gothic flying buttresses high above, the ribbed vaults, the stained-glass windows. He refused to be awed. It was not his god.

He turned to his left and walked behind the back row of chairs, half filled, and turned right down the aisle running down the left side of the nave. Memories from a theology class rose from a foggy past. The interior of a cathedral was built in the shape of a Latin cross. The nave ran down its center. The transept crossed the T, so to speak, and the altar sat at the far end. As it was, so shall it ever be.

Every few steps, a small chapel was set back into the wall, almost a grotto. He stopped at the sixth in line, where there was a statue of a woman holding a small child. A bronze nameplate identified her as St. Genevieve.

"She saved Paris from Attila the Hun," said a voice behind him. "Don't ask me how."

Tariq turned. "Hello, Yehudi. Interesting spot to meet."

"I couldn't think of a safer place," said Yehudi Rosenfeld.

"An Arab and a Jew conversing inside a cathedral," said Tariq. "Nothing to see here, officer."

"Not an Arab and a Jew," said Rosenfeld. "Look around you. What do you see?"

Tariq's eye wandered the interior of the cathedral. Even at this hour, it was crowded with men and women ambling slowly here and there, heads upturned, reading guidebooks, listening to audio tours. "Tourists," he said.

"Exactly what we are," said Yehudi Rosenfeld. "Tourists."

CHAPTER 60

Île de la Cité
Paris

Harry Crooks dialed Mac's number again. Again, the call rolled to voicemail.

"Goddamn you, Dekker," he said, staring out the window at the imposing facade of the cathedral. "Call me back. I've got him. I've got your bloody prince. He just walked into bloody Notre-Dame."

Harry hung up. He wasn't sure what to do. He couldn't just stay here. Mac was an old friend—more than that. They'd worked together, fought a common foe. He was a brother. But Harry was sixty-seven years old and a cripple. These days they called him "handicapped" or "physically challenged," but no matter how you softened the words, the facts remained the same. He was stuck in this damned chair. It had been a long time since he'd felt sorry for himself, and the sentiment took him by surprise. He was Harry friggin' Crooks, the scourge of the Special Air Service, winner of the Victoria Cross. As long as his heart kept beating, he would be a warrior. To hell with the chair; he'd do his best.

"Let me out," he said to the driver. "What do I owe you?"

Two minutes later, Harry Crooks was charging across the Place Jean-Paul II toward the cathedral of Notre-Dame. He was done feeling sorry for himself. Three words rolled off his tongue, filling him with the fire of his youth. He hadn't said them aloud since the day he'd taken off his uniform for the last time.

Who Dares Wins.

The motto of the British SAS.

CHAPTER 61

Préfecture de Police, Île de la Cité
Paris

Mac Dekker stood shivering beneath the portico at the entrance to the Préfecture de Police, encircled by Don Baker, Eliza Porter Elkins, and his daughter, Jane McCall. He looked from face to face, rubbing his shoulder, rocking on his feet, whiplashed by his dramatic reversal of fortune.

Ten minutes earlier he'd been facing an unknown spell in prison—a week, a month, the rest of his life. He'd been separated once more from the woman he loved. More importantly, he'd lost any chance to stop what was coming: the detonation of a nuclear device at the Palace of Versailles. Now, in the blink of an eye, all that was behind him. He was a free man. All charges against him had been dropped (provisionally, at least). He'd been told that Ava was to be freed as well. But he felt no closer to doing what had to be done.

"Can I have a word?" asked Mac, pulling Jane aside before anyone could say no.

"Sure. What is it?"

Jane was nearly as tall as him, blond, blue eyed, and nearly as fit. She'd dropped twenty pounds since he'd last seen her. Her cheeks had hollowed, her gaze lost its warmth. Dressed in a tailored black suit, crisp blouse, she looked every bit the agent on the rise. He knew her future, and he didn't like it. "Spill," he said. "What are you doing here? I want it all. *Please.*"

Jane stepped closer, eyeing him warily, as if measuring what to tell him. "Ava contacted me in August."

"August," said Mac. "That's two months ago."

"It goes back farther than that," said Jane.

"How far?"

"March, I believe."

"Ava's known about this since March?" said Mac.

Jane nodded. "Not all of it, but the beginnings."

Mac winced. He couldn't help it. March? His breath left him, and he experienced a wave of dizziness. He wasn't sure what surprised him more: how terribly hurt he felt or how he could have missed it. "She never said anything."

"She couldn't," said Jane. "She knew you."

"That I'd want to help," said Mac.

"That you'd jeopardize everything you have together. Your new life. Your freedom. Katya. She thought you'd gotten off light the last time. Odds were against that happening again."

Mac set aside his feelings—his anger, his humiliation, the damage to his fragile male ego—to consider this. More true than false, he decided. He had gotten off light. *Even so . . .* "You said 'the beginnings.' Give me the rest."

Jane laid out the story, stating the facts as she knew them. Her words. She told him about Dr. Gerhard Lutz, about Ava's meeting TNT at the clinic in St. Moritz, and about her subsequent theft of the blueprints for a new transmitter designed by Dr. Abbasi of the Natanz Research Facility.

"She stole them from his house?" asked Mac, interested in clarification.

"Yes."

Mac felt his stomach clutch. He knew better than to ask how.

"Did you know about Samson?" asked Jane.

Mac shook his head and listened intently as Jane recounted how Ava had lost possession of the tactical nuclear weapon.

"It nearly broke her," said Jane. "The weight of it, losing something like that. She held herself responsible. And then, after so many years, the chance to retrieve it falls into her lap. What choice did she have?"

Jane continued her narrative, stating that Ava only came to her after her contacts at Mossad had been killed—not just Zvi Gelber, but Dr. Lutz too. And after a man named Rosenfeld, a deputy of Itmar Ben-Gold, the Israeli minister of defense, warned her to back off.

"Yehudi Rosenfeld," said Mac. "I've heard the name."

Jane said that she had submitted Ava's information, including the blueprints from Iran, to her superiors at the Agency, in this case colleagues working in the Directorate of Analysis. The response took longer than such an urgent matter demanded. A week passed. Then another. Something was up. She could feel it.

Finally, an answer came: The plans were deemed bogus, though how and why, no one specified. Further, there was nothing in the files about Israel having ever lost a nuclear weapon, one named "Samson" or anything else. It was Jane's turn to receive a slap on the hand. Langley ordered her not to pursue the matter. Ava Attal, they stated, was considered by Mossad to be compromised. No other explanation was given, excepting one caveat. Continued contact with Ava was forbidden and would jeopardize Jane's current posting, her career, and maybe—one sinister email confided— more than that. Mossad had a way of dealing with enemies.

"But you didn't let it go," said Mac.

Jane pulled a face. *As if.* Mac felt a surge of pride. Yes, she was still his daughter. "I called Ava the same day to tell her what happened," she said. "Ava wasn't compromised; it was Ben-Gold and, evidently, Langley as well that were compromised. I told her I'd do whatever I could to help."

"You knew about the Jules Verne?" he said.

"Sure."

"And that she wanted to get kidnapped?"

"That was part of it."

"Only part?"

"The plan was for Ava to neutralize TNT. First, she needed to obtain proof of his ties to Ben-Gold. It's what she's trained to do."

"Steal documents?"

"No, Dad, the other thing," said Jane.

"The other thing?" Mac wasn't trying to be purposefully obtuse. He knew what Jane meant; he just couldn't get himself to believe it.

"Wet work," said Jane.

"Ava?"

Jane nodded.

"I see," said Mac, though he didn't really. He'd always thought that lies were what you told your enemies.

Wet work. Neutralize. Liquidate. Assassinate. The agency had a hundred words for it except one: *kill*. Something else Mac hadn't known about her. He could see that there were going to be a lot of long nights when they got back to the Chalet Ponderosa. *"Lucy, you got some splaining to do."*

Black humor, maybe, but, hey, sometimes that was all there was.

"Who told you about the red flag?" asked Mac.

Jane pursed her lips.

"Who?" Mac repeated, looking at the others.

"That would be me," said Baker, immediately appealing to Elkins. "He's a friend. I had to."

"Later, Don," said Elkins. "And don't worry, I won't forget."

"Not that it helped," said Mac to his old friend. "I hope it made your conscience feel better."

"Screw you, Mac."

"Back at ya, buddy." Mac returned his attention to his daughter. He nodded and drew her toward him. "Thank you," he said. "For everything."

"I did the best I could."

"I know that," said Mac. He kissed her on the cheek, then turned to face the others. "So now? Don't tell me we can't do a damn thing about it."

"We've taken every measure possible," said Elkins.

"Then why are we here and not hauling ass to Versailles?" asked Mac.

"Excuse me," said Elkins. "Remind me when you started working for the French authorities? We've given them everything we have; that means all the information your Ava copied from Tariq al-Sabah's laptop. Vincent Dalin is the deputy chief of the DGSE. I trust him to use it expeditiously."

"There's too much for him to process," said Jane. "This is a live op. He needs to act on the intel real time."

"Listen to her," said Mac. "She knows."

"It's not our country," said Elkins.

"How many times are you going to say that?" demanded Mac.

"As many times as necessary," said Elkins.

"Mac, please," added Baker. "Chill."

Mac ran a hand over his mouth. "Chill?" he said. "Are you kidding me? Do you realize what is about to go down? If that device goes off, you can forget about the couple thousand it will kill right away. That's the tip of the iceberg. They're going to have to evacuate the entire city. Ten million people or more. And by yesterday." Mac raised his left hand above his head, gauging the wind. "Feel that? Breeze coming out of the west at ten to fifteen miles per hour. I know. It was our job to reckon wind velocity before taking a shot. Versailles is over that way. Due west. All the fallout from that bomb is going to come straight into the center of the city. There will be no getting away, not in time. You're talking tens of thousands of innocent people dead and tens of thousands more who'll die from cancer. Paris will be an exclusion zone for twenty years."

"Please," said Jane. "Talk to Vincent again. Convince him."

"As far as Deputy Director Dalin is concerned," said Elkins, "Mac is en route to the airport to catch a flight to the States. How do you think we got you out?"

"Maybe you had your daddy call," said Mac. "The senator."

"You SOB," said Elkins.

"I knew I was in trouble when I heard you'd joined the Agency," said Mac. "You never forgot about that crazy old man in Iraq. That was a bomb, too, wasn't it?"

"And I thought I had a long memory," said Elkins. "Pot meet kettle. On the contrary. You should thank me."

"For what? Red-flagging me?"

"For believing you. For realizing that I was wrong about you. For getting to the Al-Sabahs' mansion in time to see you being dragged out in cuffs. The reason you're a free man at this instant is because I swore an affidavit that you are a current employee in good standing of the Central Intelligence Agency. Why else do you think they let you go? Your charm and good looks? Sorry, Mac, your ass is mine, and you'll do what I tell you."

"You didn't," said Mac.

"Dad, she did," said Jane. "Cut her some slack."

"That'll be the day," said Mac. He pointed an accusing finger at her. "Did you know she wanted me to leave the Agency and go to work for her father, the senator? Now, she kindly gives me my job back. Make up your mind, Lizzie."

"That's enough, Dekker," said Baker, coming between them. "Put a sock in it."

A uniformed policeman opened the door to the prefecture. Behind him, Vincent Dalin led Ava Attal outside. Someone had provided her a navy peacoat, to cover her dress, and a pair of well-used sneakers. Dalin extended a hand to Elkins. "This concludes matters," he said.

"Thank you, Vincent," said Elkins in her most syrupy voice. "If there's ever anything I can do."

"Happy to help," said Dalin, practically bowing and kissing her hand. The French. Blond hair, big boobs, and they melt every time.

"Did you read the files, Vincent?" asked Mac, testily.

Dalin cleared his throat. "Interesting material. Madame Attal made a persuasive case."

"That means you're shutting it down," said Mac. "The conference. You're evacuating Versailles. You're going after TNT."

"I've given the dossier to my superiors," said Dalin.

"And?"

"I believe Madame Attal is telling the truth. I've offered my recommendation that we act immediately."

"Thank God," said Mac. "Good news." He looked at Ava, expecting her to share his relief. She kept her eyes cast down, saying nothing. "What is it? What's wrong?"

"I can't be trusted," said Ava. "I'm a foreign agent acting without permission on French soil. The fruits of my investigation are tainted a priori. I should be lucky I'm not locked away for ten years, isn't that right?"

"You're kidding?" said Mac.

"That is not my personal opinion," said Dalin. "However, my superiors must look to the larger question. Qatar is a close ally of France and the principal supplier of our natural gas. They are also, alongside the French president, the sponsor of a historic conference, which against all odds has reached a successful conclusion. The idea that Tariq, himself a Qatari, the minister of the interior, no less, would try and sabotage the conference is unimaginable."

"But you have the proof," said Mac. "Ava risked her life to get it. What are you waiting for?"

"Consider your freedom a token of my good faith," said Vincent Dalin, with an edge. "Questions remain to be answered about the slaying of two Saudi diplomats yesterday afternoon at the Hotel Bristol, as well as the shooting of Mademoiselle Shugar and Sergeant Montcalm. Blood has been spilled. It is our practice to hold the suspects until evidence is found to exonerate them . . . *or not.*"

"I'm grateful," said Mac. *"Merci."*

"De rien." Dalin held out a hand. Mac shook it. A look passed between them. They were professionals. Dalin would do what he could. But don't expect anything.

"Hurry," said Mac. "Please."

Dalin nodded gravely, said good evening, and reentered the prefecture.

A black Mercedes sedan entered the parking lot and pulled up to the stairs. A tall, bearded man got out of the driver's seat. "Ready to roll?" he said. "They're gassing up the plane."

"This is Sam McGee, our Paris resident," said Elkins. "He'll be driving you to the airport."

"I don't think we should leave until this plays out," said Mac.

"Mac, please," said Ava.

"You need to leave," said Baker, a hand on his shoulder.

"Get off me," said Mac.

"Let's go," said Ava. "It is out of our hands. We tried."

Mac looked at Elkins. No matter how hard he tried, he couldn't find a way to thank her. "Yeah," he said to Ava. "We tried."

Together they descended the stairs. McGee held the passenger door open. *Tried.* Was there any uglier word? Mac wanted to cry.

As he ducked his head, he felt his phone rattle. He pulled it from his pocket. Voicemail from Harry Crooks. He hit Play.

"Goddamn you, Dekker. Call me back. I've got him. I've got your bloody prince. He just walked into bloody Notre-Dame."

Mac handed the phone to Ava and replayed the message. Her eyes met his. "A friend?" she whispered.

"A good friend."

"Well, then," said Ava.

Mac gazed across the parking lot, through the open gates, and across a broad public square. Two hundred meters away, bathed in white spotlights, stood a massive medieval cathedral whose construction had begun in the year 1163 and was completed in the year 1345. It was a straight shot from the prefecture steps to the front doors of Notre-Dame de Paris.

He grabbed Ava's hand. "Shall we, my love?"

They ran.

CHAPTER 62

Salon of Peace
Palace of Versailles
Versailles, France

The Salon of Peace, located at the southern end of the Hall of Mirrors in the Palace of Versailles, hummed with expectation. Ten rows of chairs bisected by a center aisle seated two hundred guests, including the delegations from the United Arab Emirates, Saudi Arabia, Israel, Qatar, Bahrain, and Jordan. Additionally, sixteen members of the French foreign office, twelve Germans, ten Brits, and two Americans. Paintings of Greek gods, of victories and defeats stared at them from every wall. Flags lined the perimeter of the ornate room. The green, black, and red colors of Islamic states. The blue and white of Israel. The *bleu, blanc, et rouge* of France. Television cameras flanked a lectern, behind which stood the president of France.

It was not the first treaty ever signed in the room. In 1783, the Treaty of Paris concluded hostilities between Great Britain and the nascent United States of America. The year 1871 saw the signing of a treaty ending the Franco-Prussian War; in this case, France the ignominious loser. The Treaty of Versailles was signed in 1919 to formally end the First World War, known at the time as the "Great War." The signatories were too numerous to list but included the United Kingdom, France, Germany, and the United States.

Tonight, another treaty would be signed, not to end a conflict or officially terminate armed hostilities but to create a new alliance that would prevent any such calamity from occurring again. In a region as scarred by turmoil as any in history, the treaty would ensure peace, commerce, and the peaceful exchange of cultures. It was, in short, a miracle.

At 5:40 p.m., the president of France, Jean-Pierre Renaud—a short, vain man with hair dyed shoe-polish black and a bulbous nose that betrayed his lifelong love of wine—took his place behind the lectern.

"Ladies and gentlemen, please."

All discussion ceased. The room grew quiet.

"On behalf of the French Republic, it is my honor to welcome you here tonight to bear witness to an event of historic significance, an event that will reshape the modern Middle East and, in so doing, reshape the entire world."

The president paused, bathing in the warmth of the audience's applause, basking in the international community's respect. He glanced at his remarks, printed in large letters, for he detested wearing reading glasses. A look to his right and left acknowledging the negotiators from the signatory countries. His eyes continued to the far side of the room, where a long table had been erected and covered by a white damask tablecloth. Standing at the center of the table was a bottle of champagne like no other. A methuselah, no less. A monument to one of France's greatest creations.

The president continued with his remarks. If he spoke a bit too quickly, he was to be excused. He was counting the minutes until he uncorked the bottle and filled his glass. He was, after all, a connoisseur.

Everyone knew that the Domaine du Roi '68 was one of the finest vintages in history.

CHAPTER 63

Notre-Dame de Paris

"Follow me," said Yehudi Rosenfeld. "There's someone who'd like to say hello."

"I hope it isn't far," said Tariq.

"Not far at all," said Rosenfeld. "Just one question."

"Oh?"

"You're not scared of heights?"

Tariq couldn't tell if Rosenfeld was joking or not. He was in no mood to jump through hoops. This was hardly the time. He followed Rosenfeld down the aisle and back toward the entry. Instead of turning left, however, Rosenfelt turned sharply to the right, walking past a table of votive candles. Beyond a stout pillar was a narrow door guarded by a large bearded man wearing a dark blazer two sizes too small. Seeing Rosenfeld, he swiftly opened the door.

"I hope you don't mind a few steps," said Rosenfeld. "The minister thought you'd like to share the view."

"The view," said Tariq, only then registering the white stone staircase behind the door. "Of what?"

"Versailles, of course," said Rosenfeld. "If it's not too cloudy, we should have a front-row seat."

Tariq didn't relish the idea of climbing two steps, let alone over two hundred. "I don't think that is a good idea," he said. "It may be safer inside."

"We're thirteen miles away," said Rosenfeld. "The blast will peter out less than a mile from the palace. The shock wave shouldn't get farther than three or four. This is a baby bomb. We're not barbarians."

"And after that?" asked Tariq.

"I give us thirty minutes before any fallout reaches us," said Rosenfeld. "We have our plans in place."

Rosenfeld started up the stairs. Tariq followed, reluctantly at first, shy of mind and body. The narrow staircase was barely wide enough for one person and spiraled steeply upward. Round and round. To gaze at the steps above him was to risk vertigo. Tariq stopped counting at eighty. By then, he was holding his side, grimacing with every exertion.

Then a strange thing occurred. Instead of weakening his resolve, the pain and fatigue strengthened it. He must continue, he told himself, not for himself, but for his people. The concept of sacrifice was novel, if not alien, and he seized upon it enthusiastically. It was not a matter of fulfilling his own destiny but of giving his all to fulfill his country's. Jabr was a traitor. He, Tariq, was its savior. What better proof than his willingness to suffer on its behalf? His breathing labored, sweat crowning his brow, Tariq climbed faster and faster, fueled by a messianic fervor.

And then, they were there.

Rosenfeld stepped through an open door and onto a narrow walkway bordered by a chest-high parapet. Below lay the glittering lights of the city of Paris. There was the Eiffel Tower, flashing blue, white, and red in celebration of the city's role in this latest diplomatic triumph. To the north, shining like a golden bulb, was the dome of Sacré-Cœur. It was windy, a drizzle falling, clouds blanketing the city. Beneath the clouds, visibility was unlimited in every direction.

"Over here." A short, corpulent man shouted, his English heavily accented. He wore a dark overcoat and open-collared white shirt, a kippah visible on his head. "I had to call in a favor to let us up here."

The Tourists

"Itmar, hello," said Tariq, catching his breath.

"My colleagues banned me from the announcement," said Itmar Ben-Gold. "I told them, fine. What do I care? I won't go. I think I got the better deal." He handed Tariq his phone. "Live feed from Versailles. It's there. You did it."

Tariq regarded the screen, wiping perspiration from his brow. The camera was trained on the French president, standing behind a lectern while addressing a large audience. Tariq recognized his father and brother seated in the front row, as well as other officials from his own and neighboring countries. On any other day, he might have called them "colleagues"—"friends," even.

"See it?" said Itmar Ben-Gold. "There. To the right. On the table. You can't miss it." He laughed with malice. "In front of their very own eyes."

Tariq brought the phone closer. The methuselah of champagne stood prominently on a side table, a few dozen crystal flutes neatly lined up to either side. He noted the bottles of apple cider, as well, for those who refused to raise a glass filled with an alcoholic beverage. His father would not be one of them. A hundred euros to one, the emir would sneak a sip.

"Ready when you are," said Ben-Gold.

Tariq took off his backpack. "Let me get it." He unzipped a pouch and removed the transmitter.

"That's it?" said Rosenfeld skeptically.

"What did you expect?" said Tariq.

Ben-Gold pointed to his phone. "Your brother is speaking."

Tariq peered at Jabr, despising him. How the tables had turned. "I'm ready."

"Twelve . . . ten." Ben-Gold slowly recited the sixteen-digit code that deactivated Samson's safety. "Three . . . seven."

Tariq entered the numbers dutifully.

". . . and one."

Tariq hit send. A moment passed. He kept his eyes on the screen.

"Well?" said Ben-Gold.

A light glowed green on the transmitter's screen. "Samson is primed," said Tariq. His hand was shaking. Not nerves. Fatigue. He was just tired. He looked to his left at the profile of the Chimera, the gargoyle-like statue perched on the ledge as it looked over the city, casting away evil spirits. It seemed to be looking at him too. Mocking him.

"The second code," said Tariq.

"Wait," said Ben-Gold. "I want to see them all together, shaking hands and smiling like Sadat and Begin. Filthy bastards." He looked up from his phone and stared hatefully at Tariq. "We will never be friends with your kind."

"The detonation code, please," said Tariq.

"Wait, I said."

"Itmar, now."

But Ben-Gold didn't take orders from anyone, especially an Arab. "What? Are you nervous? No one knows we are here. Is it the man downstairs? He works here. He was doing me a favor. A question of interfaith kindness." Ben-Gold approached him. "Is there something I should know?"

"This isn't the time to gloat," said Tariq. "Let us do what we came for."

"You look unwell," said Ben-Gold. "What is it? Something's wrong. I can tell. Look, you're bleeding."

Tariq felt something warm at the corner of his mouth, tasted salt and iron. He was bleeding internally. He wiped it with the back of his hand. "The code, minister," he said, banishing his pain, towering over the smaller man. "Now, Itmar."

Ben-Gold stared at him a moment longer. "Four . . . seven . . . nineteen . . ."

Mac found Harry Crooks just inside the cathedral, positioned by the nearest pillar. "You missed him," said Harry. "He was here. He met another man. They spoke for a minute, then left through another exit."

"What did the man look like?" asked Ava.

Harry glanced at Mac, who nodded. *Yes, that's Ava. Go ahead. You can tell us.* "Red hair," said Harry. "Beard, three-piece suit."

"Rosenfeld," said Ava.

"They went through that door over there," said Harry, rolling his chair past the central portal, then pointing to a door cut into the far corner of the cathedral. "And Mac, he's hurt. He isn't walking correctly."

"You hit him," said Mac, remembering Jane's words about Ava's training. Wet work. Of course she hit him.

Ava frowned. "Maybe."

"Quick now," said Crooks. "Don't waste your time talking to me."

Mac put a hand on Crooks's shoulder. "Thank you."

He hurried across the church, past the table of votive candles, winding his way through the mill of visitors. He found the door Crooks had mentioned. "North stairs," read a sign on the wall next to it. He tried the handle. Locked.

"Sir, please, the tower is closed." A tall, burly man in a docent's blazer rushed toward them. "No entry is permitted."

"I need to speak with the men who just went upstairs," said Mac.

"That's not possible," said the man. "Their visit was by private arrangement."

"May I have a word," said Ava, offering an intimate smile, a hand on his arm. "We're close friends of Mr. Rosenfeld and Prince Al-Sabah."

"A prince? He told me he was from Israel. Mr. Ben-Gold. He is an important man."

"We work with Mr. Ben-Gold," said Ava. "The three of them are expecting us. I'm sure we won't be long."

The guard studied them. An older couple—she, an attractive woman in a lovely dress; he, a respectable man with a steady gaze. He pulled a key from his belt and unlocked the door. "A quarter of an hour at most," he said. "Shalom."

Ava took off up the narrow, pale steps, running as fast as she could. Mac did his best to keep up, one hand brushing the interior wall to keep his balance. Round and round. They passed several small windows cut high into the stone wall, the view affording them a peek over the square below, each time higher and higher.

A torrent of cold air flooded the staircase from above. Ava stopped dead and bent close to the steps above her. Mac followed her lead. A doorway several steps above her opened onto a walkway. He could just make out the silhouettes of the gargoyles perched on the parapet.

"I see them," said Ava. "Ben-Gold is there."

"Just the three?" asked Mac.

"As far as I can tell."

"You don't happen to have a gun," he said.

"I'd prefer a grenade," said Ava. "But I suppose we'd damage the building."

"Forgot mine back at the hotel," said Mac. "Or was it in your suitcase next to your pistol?"

"Get the transmitter," said Ava. "My guess is that TNT has it. He has to enter a code to set off the bomb."

"Samson?" said Mac.

"Jane told you."

Mac nodded. "How big?"

"One kiloton," said Ava.

Mac swore.

"You go first," said Ava. "And Mac . . . no mercy."

"No mercy," said Mac.

He scooted past her. He peeked around the doorway, saw the men bathed in shadow. A short, fat man was closest, back to him. Behind him, a tall, thin, bearded man; and next to him, TNT, looking his way, holding something in his left hand and tapping on its screen. The transmitter.

Mac drew a breath and rushed through the doorway. No mercy.

"Fifteen," pronounced the short man as Mac slugged him in the solar plexus, then clutched his overcoat and threw him to the ground. It was Itmar Ben-Gold. Mac jumped over the prostrate body, taking

Yehudi Rosenfeld by the lapels and slamming him into the tower wall. Rosenfeld's head struck the stone with a sickening thud. Mac took his face in his hand and bashed his head into the wall again. Instead of dropping, however, Rosenfeld grabbed onto Mac's shoulders, fingers digging into him like an eagle's talons.

"Twelve," gasped Ben-Gold, rolling onto his side. "Twelve! The last one."

As Mac struggled with Rosenfeld, Tariq al-Sabah spun and ran in the opposite direction down the walkway, rounding a corner.

"Move." Ava pushed her way past Mac in pursuit of TNT. Her toe caught an uneven stone. She stumbled. Her knee scraped the ground. "Shit."

TNT had disappeared into a doorway at the top of several steps. There was only one staircase up and down. Ava ran after him, mounting the stairs and reentering the tower. She saw him immediately, maybe ten steps farther along. He moved with a stutter step, two or three steps quickly, then a step off balance. She caught up to him, throwing out a hand to grab an ankle. Her fingers latched onto his calf. He fell and cried out, dropping the transmitter. Ava climbed a step, reaching for the device. Tariq kicked her viciously, the blow glancing off Ava's jaw, stunning her. He was up again, transmitter in hand, and climbing. Ava took a step. Her foot came out of the sneaker, and she fell.

"Dammit." She tore off the other shoe and ran up the stairs, her breath ragged, as winded as she could recall ever being. Round and round. Up and up. The staircase growing narrower, if that was possible. Then she caught sight of him, first a foot, then another, then the entire man.

"Tariq," she called. "Stop. Don't!"

TNT glanced at her over his shoulder. He looked different than she recalled, even from this afternoon. His eyes burned with a zeal, a mania, evident even in the dimly lit stairwell. No, he would not stop.

Ava redoubled her efforts, reaching out to trip him, just missing again and again. Like that they reached the top. Tariq lurched through an open doorway onto a broad wood-plank floor. The ceiling stood open high above them, a latticework of exposed rafters. From the rafters hung numerous bells, some new, some old, some small, some enormous. They had reached a belfry of Notre-Dame.

Tariq stood facing her, the transmitter in his hand. His eyes flitted from the screen to Ava.

"Twelve," he panted. He raised a hand, and she could see his fingers trembling, he more fatigued than she, unable to govern his limbs.

"Please," she shouted. "Don't."

Tariq brought his index finger to the screen. "Too late."

The bells of Notre Dame began to toll. First the bourdon, the largest bell and lowest in tone, then another and another, five in all, in slow succession, the concuss of copper on copper deafening, pounding their ears unlike any sound they'd known, reverberating throughout their entire bodies.

Tariq dropped the transmitter and covered his ears. Ava dove across the floor, and her fingers closed around the transmitter. She had it. She rolled onto her back, bringing the device to her eyes, seeing the number twelve on the screen. Tariq kicked her in the ribs, and she drew herself into a ball to protect the transmitter. He kicked her again. "Give it to me," he shouted. "It's mine."

The kicking stopped.

Amid the cacophonous tolling bells, Ava heard a cry, a scream, and a thud below her. She uncoiled herself and saw Mac standing above her.

"Are you okay?" asked Mac.

Ava could only read his lips. She nodded. He extended a hand and pulled her to her feet.

Ava looked around her. There was no sign of TNT. She showed Mac the transmitter and shrugged. Had they stopped it?

Mac pointed to the west. Toward Versailles. The skyline was clear, a tapestry of glittering lights.

A minute later, the bells ceased.

"Where is he?" asked Ava.

"No mercy." Mac looked over the railing. Ava followed his gaze and found Tariq al-Sabah a hundred feet below, his body caught in the woodwork, his torso impaled on an exposed rod of steel rebar.

Ava looked at the transmitter. "What do I do with this?"

"Don't touch it," said Mac.

EPILOGUE

Pontresina, Switzerland

It was a picture-postcard day. Bluebird sky, a warm sun, fresh snow from the night before. Mac and Ava walked hand in hand along a manicured footpath through the forest. Katya ran ahead, offering acorns to the black squirrels darting here and there. The squirrels were cheeky enough to scamper up her pant leg and take them from her fingers, eliciting screams of delight.

"Never been here," said Mac. "Beautiful hotel."

"One of the oldest in the country," said Ava. "I've always meant to come."

"Does this mean you want to stay in Switzerland?"

Ava offered him her sphinx's smile, a flash of her dark eyes.

The last months had passed at a dizzying pace. It was a period of uncertainty. Of triumph and joy; of doubt and recrimination; of questioning . . . well, *everything*. There was no chance of Mac Dekker simply disappearing once again, of resuming life as Robbie Steinhardt as he had after his brief adventure over a year before. The cat was out of the bag. Everyone knew that Mac Dekker was alive. There was nothing the CIA could do about it. Not that they wanted to. Mac was a hero, a credit to the Agency. He had stopped an attack more heinous than any known to the Western world in recent times. Ava's role, though far more crucial—it was she who discovered the plot in the first place and conducted all the legwork in defiance of her own government, at considerable risk to life and limb—was kept quiet. If the world might be happy to accept TNT as its evil successor to bin Laden or 'Arafat or Carlos the Jackal, it could not be allowed to put Itmar Ben-Gold in the same basket. In the end Samson had belonged to Israel, and it was upon Israel that ultimate responsibility lay. A decision was quickly made by France, Israel, Qatar, and the United States to deny the entire incident. Samson had never been lost. Tariq al-Sabah had not purchased it from Hamas. Itmar Ben-Gold had not supplied him with the detonation codes. No nuclear device had been smuggled into the Palace of Versailles inside a champagne bottle or anything else. None of these things had happened.

And to make sure none of these nonevents ever happened again, Mac and Ava were subjected to countless debriefings from the intelligence services of all countries involved, and a few that weren't, as a gesture of goodwill.

Personally, it was a season of détente. Talk of the future was put on hold. There were no discussions about whether Provence or Porto might prove the nicer place to settle down. Ava, for her part, was in Tel Aviv so often that she had no opportunity to find Zinal dull. Mac's debriefings took place mostly on Zoom, though Vincent Dalin visited once "looking for a retirement home" and had proved to be excellent company, even if he made a large dent in Mac's wine cellar.

There had been a memorable day in November when Jabr al-Sabah had paid a visit to award Mac Qatar's highest honor, the Pendant of Independence. The medal came with a cash gift of $10 million, honorary Qatari citizenship, and a residence of his choosing in Doha. Nothing exceeds like excess.

In fact, both Mac and Ava were so busy that they never seemed to find the right time for their "big talk." Mac's sense of betrayal and distrust—hers of him and his of her—faded as the weeks went by. He was still angry that she hadn't whispered a word of her "mission" to him. Jane's explanation that Ava hadn't wanted to jeopardize all that they had built—especially Mac's relationship to Katya—rankled him less and less. The flip side was that Mac began to blame himself more and more for having failed to spot anything anomalous about Ava's behavior. (Just how in the hell had she managed it without him suspecting for even one second?) It seemed to be the tenor of the era in which they lived that fault must be spread evenly. Gray was the Pantone color of the year. Deep down, Mac knew it was malarky, but to say so risked upsetting his world as much as Ava feared. He had to accept that maybe he would never really know her. Mystery had always been a trait he'd found most attractive in her. Philosophically speaking, he thought, how much do any of us know about the ones we love? Especially the ones we love most dearly? In the end, we see what we want to see.

And Mac saw a smart, formidable, overwhelmingly attractive woman with whom he wanted to spend the rest of his life. Nothing, he realized, could change that.

Katya disappeared around a corner, and Mac called for her to slow down.

"Let her play," said Ava. "You can't protect her from everything."

"But I'll never stop trying."

"No," said Ava. "I know you won't."

The forest fell away. The path emerged in the sunlight and offered a panoramic view of the valley, stretching as far as the eye could see. If ever there was a right place to do it, this was it.

Mac felt in his pocket for the jewelry box. Check. He dropped Ava's hand and turned to face her. "Well," he said. "Should we try this again?"

"Are you sure?"

"I am."

"Go ahead, Mr. Dekker. I'm listening."

"I'm paraphrasing."

"Just go!"

"It's been a tough year," he began. "The operation. All the work to get better. Both of us taking care of a little girl. A daughter. On top of that, wondering if and when they were going to come after us . . . well, me, at least. I think we managed pretty well."

"Very well," said Ava.

"What I mean to say is that I enjoy being with you."

"I enjoy being with you," said Ava.

"We make a good team," said Mac.

"We do."

"And we both agree we have to find a new place to live," he said.

"I'm glad we do," said Ava.

"What I want to say is that I love you very much."

"I love you too."

Mac's hand tightened on the box. *Here goes nothing.* "So, I wanted to ask you . . ."

Just then, Mac's phone rang. "I wanted to ask you . . ."

The phone rang again. "Go ahead," said Ava. "It might be important."

"Sorry." Mac looked at the screen. US country code. Virginia area code. A prefix he'd never forget. "Hello."

"Hello Mac, this is Deputy Director Eliza Porter Elkins."

"Um, I'm busy right now. Can I call you back?"

"A plane is landing at Samedan airport near St. Moritz in thirty minutes. You are going to be there when it arrives."

"I'm sorry, you must want a different Mac Dekker."

"I wasn't lying when I told the French police you were an employee of the Central Intelligence Agency. I checked the records. Mac Dekker was never officially declared dead. Your ass still belongs to your country."

"Where am I going?" asked Mac.

"I'll tell you when I see you," said Elkins. "Don't be late."

The call ended.

"Mac? Mac? What is it? I don't like the look in your eyes."

"Retirement is over," said Mac. "I'm back."

AUTHOR'S NOTE

The Tourists is a work of fiction. Certain liberties were taken regarding the location and placement of some buildings and addresses within the city of Paris.

In case you find yourself visiting the City of Light, please do not look for the prince's "hôtel de ville" next to the Hôtel Plaza Athénée. The current occupants might be very surprised.

ACKNOWLEDGMENTS

Thank you to Richard and Gideon Pine and my team at Inkwell Management. Nearly thirty years together and still going strong. The Gold Standard.

At Thomas and Mercer, thanks to Liz Pearsons and Grace Doyle, and all the talented professionals that shepherded the book to publication.

A warm mention to Megan Beattie at MB Communications, a gifted publicist and champion of an author's work.

Finally, a shout-out to my old friend Christopher Lambert, who joined me at the restaurant Jules Verne to enjoy a wonderful meal and talk about our projects, past and present.

ABOUT THE AUTHOR

Photo © Katja Reich

Christopher Reich is the *New York Times* bestselling author of *Matterhorn*, *The Take*, *Numbered Account*, *Rules of Deception*, and many other thrillers. His novel *The Patriots Club* won the International Thriller Writers award for Best Novel in 2006. He lives in Newport Beach, California.